AMERICA AMERICA THOU ART AMERICA

By shakyamuni

ISBN: 978-0-9985488-6-9

Six Nine Press

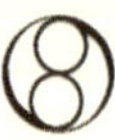

CONTENTS

I

Landing at JFK on the 13th Sun of the 6th Moon of the Crown Two Thousand Silk O Lime One Camera and Six Camels, it's such a Rapturous Joy to the Hopeful Immigrant so it's Reasonable You aren't quite sure know how to respond when Questioned, You Clicked and Punched as Accurately as Possible to Produce a Circle or Clear Outcome from the Computer Kiosk Cow but somehow, It Knows Your Real Mission so You had No Other Choice but to Present Yourself in Brightest Manner in High Hope You may not be Rejected and Sent Back to Your very own Country for that's the Greatest Shame of Any Traveler, it's to be Denied Entry into a New Land without a New Lamp, I had Thought about Every Possible Question so You don't have to Storm Your Brain Anymore. It's HERE!

Officer: Why Are You Coming to the United States of America?

I'm Here to Meet the Chief.

Officer: The Chief??? What's the Dinosaur?

Yeah.

Officer: So???? Why are You Meeting the Chief???

Advanced… State of the Union….

Officer: What's That????

It's Experimental and Stuff…

Officer: You Know… I Know You Were Going to Say That!! How Long Are You Staying?

About Two Moons…

Officer: Two Moons???? HA! HA! HA! How Much Money Do You Have?

About Two Thousand Five Hundred Dislikes Only… Any Discounts?

Officer: O HA! HA! Great! Have a Nice Trip!

The Way He Said it, I Didn't Really Believe that he really Wished it or Anything like that because he was Trained and Ransacked by Green Snake who Loved Him for His Sweat and Blood and She would Ask to be Excused when She Sucked the Poison of the Frog, Just a Drop to Murder the Husband to Write these Words to People who Passed the Test of Mini Interrogation before I Appeared in Front of his Window, and as I Stood in Line, Waiting for My Turn, I Reckoned, America was Becoming more Open to Immigrants. In the Time I was in Line which was easily more than a few hours, I can Report Nobody was Turned Away. They just Wanted to Forget the Old and Promote Greater Diversity from Countries Far and Near, all these Waves and Waves Coming for it's so Never so Straight Forward to Root Out a Dangerous Illegal Immigrant in less than a Few Minutes, Potential or Otherwise, it's Just the Matter of the Rainbow so they always Dream about the

Golden Mountain as Metaphor of Golden when they were Promised Riches Beyond their Fantasies, almost Fainting when the God or Goddess Venus for What's True is that They are Going to be Sent to the Underworld but it's Always OK to Earn their Way to the Land of Opportunities, People from all Types of Professions; Blue Physicians, Psychic Gamblers, Horse Merchants, Middle Level Bankers, Slow Mall Call Girls, Drunk Teachers, Sleepy Trucksters, Horny Seamstresses, Thick Fast Boys, No Medal Sportspersons, Half Dry Throated Musicians, Previously Unknown Crooks, Sweaty IT Technicians, Milky Way Nurses, they were all there! Knock! Knock! Indeed, it's a very Good Time to Come to America.

Outside of Waiting for the Train or Bus, Faithless Ones, There's No Time for a Lunch Stop or even a Miniature Cup of Tea Served in Victorian Style Pottery to Reminisce of the Good Old Days when the English ruled Supreme with Biggest Colonized Empire and You May Use Voodoo to Help You Along for Don't You Always Want to Appear as Spectacular as Possible so You are Learning Ballet while that Artistic Old Man was Peeping Behind the Silk Screen Spying on How You are Removing Your Tights in Broad Day Light for The Majority is Always Right Kind of Lolli Pop Suckers that They are Forced to Eat Their Cajun Style Pot Pies Even if They had to Leave the Navy and Finally Reveal the Identity of the White Witch for You must Always Remember that John Mc7 is not Really not at all worried that his more Illustrious Costar Elizabeth Eli Evergreen was more Popular though in that Record breaking Episode where it was Revealed that Her Son is Not Her Brother's as for Her Final Exit in Most Popular Show of the Century of the Universe Times Seven or Eight When It's Time for the Child to Explore, We, the Citizens of The Republic, We Demand that We are to be Admitted to the UK just because two *Disgusto* is worth more than three *AhnJoa* as It Was Previously Presumed that *Begenmeme* with Small Smile on top of the G will be much more Precious so the Realistic Ones will Doubt and Shake their Fists to the Heavens but It didn't Occur to Mean Princess Monaco, already Overripe so You Keep Her in the Freezer Lest the Great Spirit is Running the Country or the World, It's a Fact, these Puppets really don't Know or Care about Anything, It's Daunting to even Ask for Directions in a Chaotic Bustling Air Train Station Bubbling in Empty Fish Tank kind of feeling, let's say, let's say…

New York City is not the City that Doesn't Sleep at All, is It? Nowadays, many lower middle class folks can save enough to plan a trip to NYC because there are Budget Airlines, Budget Lodgings, Budget Shoes, and Budget Food, and so on, especially in the Summer so almost Everybody can Travel and Travel is such a Big-time thing, You know, it's a Little Bit Easier to ask the Older Bears for their Talent in Feudal Irish so I asked the Nigga straight up and he kindly told me to look at the tile, square like a plot of land, explaining about the climate change, advising me right away that it's better to take the bus than the train so I didn't bother to ask him for some explanation or lighter fluid because he might think that I'm Mad or Something, You Know, What's the Way to the Flushing Meadows, You Say, it's Best to go Water Your Roots in Chinatown for it's most likely that You will find some Underpaid Hands-for-Hire to Help You in Your Quest to Colonize the Land, isn't It?

Come to the Chinatown in Flushing, Queens, Possibly the Busiest in the US and if You Take a Walk around the area, You may be Right to Question whether You are in New Brazil or New Bombay for all these Old Folks Chirpy and Soiled by Sorrows of Immigration so Placid and Frugal and it's not at all Surprising that they don't even Speak or Understand one word of English so When You are Lost and You are Asking for Directions, You Hear them mumbling a string of Chinese words, incomprehensible even to a Chinese, and Everywhere, You Calculate how many of these Chinese Immigrants there are in all the Chinatowns combined, and You can probably even smell the sweat of their Hardcore Labor including the Greasy Chinese Lanterns, Funky Florescent Chinese Calligraphy, Overnight Peking Duck, Just in Time Taoist Temples, Slippery Chinese Apartments, Hunan Linen Territory Humor, and You may well ask Yourself, isn't it the same in Little India, German Beer Festivals, Peruvian Steps, Soft Korean Fence, Rad Japanese Associations, and Glowing Fruit City and even the Lane of Whispering Heights or thereabouts? Yet, it's harder to Talk to Your Own Kind when You are in a Foreign Country, isn't it? What about the Sticky Ox Tongue, the Crispy Tiger Whisker, the Wholesome Babylonian Woman, the Plastic Buffalo Balls, the Smiling Sea Elephant's Bride, and the Quick Eyed Castle Keeper?

If You have been to One Chinatown, You have been to All Chinatowns. Verily, there's Nothing Distinctive from One Chinatown to Another which Warrants any sort of Study or Research. They are all there to earn American Dislikes worth more than Four Point Eight *Bu Xi Huans* but other than that, they care squat about the Star Spangled Banner or The Constitution or even what's Outside Chinatown. Yet, the Architecture is Nothing to be Celebrated in the Sense that You will Always Come Across some kind of Bamboo Motif whether in the Design of the Roofs of the Temple or the Big Gate to Represent the Entrance to the Town, Painted

Bright Red for Auspiciousness and Prosperity, or some Green like Jade, the Chinese may Speak a Thousand Dialects and Someone from One Region may Dislike Someone from Another Region but they always Pray for the Same Thing so You Glimpse a Little into their Little Simple Minds always thinking that Life is Prosperity and Wealth is the Greatest Measure of a Person's Worth just so You Know for sure how these things work without any regard for Humanity but You Should Be Warned, they are all bound by One Culture even though feet binding is no longer practiced and the men have lost their pigtails and they are not playing Chinese Checkers anymore, please, please don't be distracted for even one second but the Glorious One so when You are eating a bowl of egg noodles with BBQ Pork in the Chinatown of Toronto, it's not so much different from the Chinatown of Johannesburg in terms of taste, portion, and pricing, You Realize… It's the Same… It's the Same…

Other than the Fecundating Smell of the Air in some part of the Town and the Buildings, Buses, Police Officers, Hoboes, Amigos running around, preferably Chinese-speaking, a Handful of Whites but more Blacks, You Wouldn't Believe You are in America at all! Not only have they come in greater numbers over the years, they are always looking to expand their population and continue to look for new places where they can build more Chinatowns and there are already about Six or Seven in NYC alone but remember, they have also brought every Twist and Turn of Chinese Socialism to this Land, downright to the Industriousness, the extensive range of foodstuff, the longest lines queuing for public transportation, the constant hustle bustle from opening to closing, people rushing You all the time so if You are walking a little slower, You will be pushed forward a few steps or cursed so it's quite a challenge so if You want to take a Contemplative Picture or Slow Stroll, *Que Maravilhaaa.*

There's just No Time to Waste, it's always like that with the Spanish Generations, it's always Living Life to the Fullest and all that Great Grand Theory about how the World is Cubist or Natural or not so Amazing anymore because Pedro Colorado is Here, He, with His No Nonsense Mexican Sense of Machoism or Chivalry depending on where He's going with his Curved Lightning Knife in Hard Custom Designed Sheath Looped to his Belt all the time even when He's sleeping or He's Screwing the Cap on the Bottle of Gourmet Enchiladas or some kind of other home cooked food His Mother so delighted in feeding Him some hot honey just before He went to bed, He was sure to kiss His knife in that Stoic manner in which Gentlemen bow their heads when they say Hello how are you, Bunny Hunny, how about we go dance the Dance of Death, You know, the kinda dance which makes young girls go gaga googoo but You can Smell it, Your whole wheat rotten mess of a drool cool cooler than the icy stream shooting into Your ankles in all that Latin oversensitivity not so good for Children after twelve or thirteen or maybe younger in some cases when they Discover hair sprouting around their genitals and then, they see their most Glamorous Sentimental Star of the Century, in the first place, You have to go to the Natural Hot Springs, get it, and don't tell anyone else for You are never Gonna See any Exit, it's a one-way movie flashing so fast, You think, it's the INTERMISSION or such a little thing as St Martin Pueblo, a villain everybody hates so much that they cheered when he's being skinned alive by professional raccoon trappers who still live among us and if You think more about it, standing over the Siren he had just ravaged with all his might and passion, he was uplifted because he didn't use his Gaucho knife which is such an important part of Gaucho culture that every true Gaucho would bow his head in earnest Humility and acknowledge before the Great Spirit that his own knife is the most exclusive in the whole world and he would never trade that knife for all the kingdoms of the world for the day that the knife leaves his hand, it will be the day that he dies, yeah, with such great Gaucho soul music, something You will never be able to understand even if You go to the Yoga Farm Tanning Saloon every day without fail until one day, You Know, You come out Black, and You say now, now, Who's Gonna be Blacker than me, and You are listening and watching this Adam Apple Shrinking Sexy Indochinese Heavy Bosom Third Grade Harpist who also happens to have sparkling eyes and pearly teeth, these remarks being necessary when he casted his eyes on that Kalimantan lass who just landed at his doorstep and in those days, the man would bash the woman by a stone club until she fainted and then carry her into his cave where he drew comics he's ashamed of it all the same in the dim cloud of his primitive ironic sense of pride and knowledge that he's the one guy around who still knows how to hunt small games and defeat a bear, tiger, lion and maybe, all that Damn Legend about The Accident, You, there, yeah, You, man, woman, manwo, manman, wom, oma, oma, She Stole My Lighter, and I say to You, Shame, Shame, There, There, There You Go, and Never Shall You say O I see! It's a Kangaroo or an Angel being surrounded by a band of Gauchos, at least Seventeen or Eighteen of them, yeah, make sure there are Enough Young People Around so when You Fall, there are a Thousand Pairs of Hands All Hollow, Yeah, I Say to You, What's the Valor in Fighting a War behind Masks and Walls and Trample on the Weak when You are so Much Stronger, What's the Fun in That? Sure, the Masses will say O my Gods! O Mi Gods! All the Gods of the Universe, We Come with our Offspring and their friends and We ask You to Shield them from All Harm so they Shall Not Fall and they Shall Not Cry and they Shall Not Bleed and they Shall Not be Defiled until the Age when they Know what's it like to be a Father or Mother in the New Garden of Eden, and You are Watching that Video of a Moon with Clouds Passing but You Know it's Fake because the Moon is always Constant as if it's Pasted over the Video in some sort of slow burning smoke screen which filters away so You Know You have Come to THE END and there's no EXIT when he pulls that rock out, and puts that string in his mouth, he's not gonna open it no matter what happens, You Know, yeah, it's that kind of a man all women desire without so much of a hint of being selfish and all that scientific theory about New York kinda pace of life being much faster than a bullet speeding train F or Purple Star shooting across the city in one second or less kinda Reality or Unreality depending on what's Your Fate or where's the LOST and FOUND.

Now, Brooklyn is the True Cradle of America. It's not an America with Scenes You see in Corporate Tourism and few tourists who have only a few days to visit NYC will say to themselves in hushed contemplation, let's make it a point to visit the Brooklyn Museum or take a tour in Brooklyn but strangely, most people have heard of it, the same like they have heard of Yankee Stadium or Belvedere Castle or Columbia University but it's somehow not High Priority. It's not a Place where You will want to make a Video or Organize some Advertising Campaign to Promote its Close Neighborhood Quality where You will get to Meet Your Neighbors in the Train or the Laundry or the Streets where boisterous little green pizza loving mixed blood dynamite boys with enough energy to dig to the center of the Earth look into parking bill machines for *Antipatia* or more, yeah, that's the price You have to pay when You Listen to Billie Holiday singing *I'll be Seeing You* so Willowy so Breezy so so You Know how it feels to be a Tramp, Afro-American style, ba ba ri ba, You are walking among Puerto Ricans, Nigerians, Algerians, Hispanics, Asians, Somalians, Trinidadians, Chileans, Jamaicans, Argies, the Cosmopolitans, the Nero Heroics, the Tibetan Guitar Players, they were all there, the most Ferocious Green Dragon Son-of-a-Butcher there with all Bling Bling Solid Gold Hit Medal bigger than his head he drags around, a Victim of Child Abuse, he's waving his big machine guns to his henchmen who are always ready to pull down their pants and die for him just because he gives them just a tiny fraction of the total piece of pie but Nobody dares to question him or his henchmen because they lack Education and he's always asking them why waste time kind of big band Music he uses to lull his whores into Submission with quick drugs like Cloud Buster, Atomic Bomb and all that crap to trick the younger ones who are always gullible even when they say they are not into Slavery and Violence and a great deal of social support from the Government since it's responsible for everything that happens to its People whether they fail in high school or below, every year, somebody has to account for it, even if it's just a trifle of a trivial matter, right, mayhem, ahem, Salem! Yeah, I would like to go up there one day if I have the time to do it all over again, he asked me, my trusted solemn Chief, what do you think? and I answered what I always knew I had wanted to do until I Breathe my last, and it's nothing more than to write another day, another line or two before I Depart to Join the Big Dance though I kept insisting that I don't know how to dance all that good, he told me, in that Rock Steady Comforting Gentlemanly Voice… yeah… if not… We will not be known as Writers… and it Hollows my Heart to Hear the Chief say… he's done writing… he who has written close to ten extraordinary compositions of the highest caliber and I say it not because I was in his Sagely presence or I'm only one tenth of the Author he was even before reaching Middle Age just by reading a quarter of his High Masterpiece about Russia or he gave me the first opportunity to enter the catacombs of Experimental Fiction which is a Death Pussy Bow in the Publishing World and I know some people who roll their eyes or tongues when they hear It or how such a Man has to put aside his typewriter and work in an office so he had to sleep on a thin mattress in that dinghy fashion so it seems he's floating off to some dream world with the Love of his Life and the way he said It, softly suggesting he would have given it all away for the Joys of Fatherhood and the Woman Full of Love to carry his Seed to Fruition, I wanted to say, She wouldn't have found You without the Bridge but Somehow I ended up Weeping that One Day, there will be no more Writers of his kind in the world, the same as there will be no Impressionistic Painters in the world and even Gypsies and Desolate Angels and even Spirits that Walk to the Mountains, Whispering in the Winds, Boom Shaka Laka Boom Shaka Laka about what's the Matter with the Chief Marrying Euterpe and Fathering a Child at the age of ninety nine or more, yeah, What's New, the Kid's Happy, the Happiest Kid in the Neighborhood and what's more, the most important thing was that it's True Romance, and She's Happy to Meet me before going off to School, leaving the three of us together for some time and we were Cool to take the B Train, passing the Brooklyn

Bridge, I spied the Lady still Lifting the Lamp Beside the Door, Blushed to Know that her Favorite Son has returned, the Non Prodigal One, the One whose Blood will Run in her Veins Once More, Once More, he aimed the tip of his arrow at the Maiden of the Sun, taking out her blankets to dry in the steamy Indian summer when You feel like You wanna take off all Your clothes and Run Naked all across the meadows like the Bisons who didn't know that they were feeding on the pasture green sucking in the marrow of fresh organic winds sweeping the steppes into an ocean of storms gathering above their heads but they didn't care that they were growing bigger, and big enough to be transported to the Slaughter House and that's the Day of the Year including all those things most Adults don't want their Kids to Know, and What's so Difficult for Parents to Teach such Taboo subjects like penises and vaginas and why are they so shy to talk about it for it's because he puts his penis into her vagina that they have he or she and nowadays it's so fucking easy and quick for a person to fall in love with a stranger who has sent more than half a dozen short messages to the wrong maiden who's surprisingly similar to the other one when it's dark and the lights are out, it's great make out college, You Know, at least, You Know, We are not Here to Rob You, We are not Here to Tickle You, We are not Here to Live the Life, We are not Here to Spread Stinky Propaganda, We are not Here to Blow Your House Down, NO, We are not even Here to Put on Trial the Holy Warriors or War Mongrels, NO, We are Here to Write Novels that Nobody ever Reads, Yeah even Bored Ghosts, and Itchy Aliens or Restless Federal Agents, Yeah, they pay least attention to these stuff so it's possibly the best way to transmit our Glorious Counter Culture Ideals and Manifesto all the Way to the Final where Failing Captain

Ahmed Johnson & Johnson Fails once again to Bring Home the Bacon and His Mother was all-the-more Overjoyed when he showed her The Four Butterflies Part I but not the Chocolate Teddy Bears the Boy loved… it's so adorable and delicious… those cookies…

And the Food, the Most Heavenly I have ever eaten in my whole life and You may include the most luxurious truffle dish in World Famous Tuscany vineyard in Autumn where people fall in love so easily in intoxicating aroma of the grapevines, sipping the most precious wine so each drop is so precious trickling down the throat and the air is truly magical in all sorts of red and yellow for even an Emperor's Feast where they served Three Day Slow Charcoal Roasted Foiled Beggar's Claypot Braised Baby Kale in Steamed Swallow's Nest Double-boiled Two Moons Komodo Luck Pot with Wild Applewood Smoked Northern Wind Dried Electric Eel and all those very clever names they use to divert Your Attention and it's only after enjoying the Immortal Buddha Jumps Over the Wall that You truly understand the timeliness in Chinese Cuisine and in essence, the entire Civilization, Shallow as Lard, acquiring all the histories and cultures in one basket deal for the entire family for less than Three Dislikes? O What a Great Deal!! If You Come to Brooklyn, Follow the Chief to the Rabbit Hole and When You meet King Arthur's Sixteenth Generation Grandson, run or jump for joy, Dinner's here, everybody Cheers! Cheers!!!!

It's Very Simple!

The dish consists of a scoop of Enriched Soul Spiced Rice Harvested from the Caribbean hinting Steamy Labor of Sweating Brown and Lovely Mothers and Daughters, some Virgin, some Dreaming, Stomping on Creamy Chocolaty Mud to Soften the Soil before planting just that one kernel of rice, Yeah, and the Gaucho is playing that song where the Mariachi was strumming his guitar in the hills, and Truth be told, he's not a very good player but he's the definition of Masculinity with all his hair and it's really not that much but he doesn't really have good eyesight so he's certainly not very good looking in the sense that You will want Your picture taken beside him but You Know, all those Purple-hearted Women, clean and ready, he shall Impregnate them with wine and lemon in their nostrils until they can only breathe through the cotton trees on the pillow case of the softest finest goose feathers so soft, the texture of the rice... in smart phone interaction with the Clock Man's Boat always floating in One Direction and it's perhaps now an excellent idea to unwrap the present, don't You think? tell me what do You think of the fading Satanic textured twisted note of Oxford fir, how do You feel, England? How do you feel about being kicked out of the Cup? Yea how a team of most highly paid superstars lose to a country with no football tradition because it's so damn cold there... Your veins freeze... and even their star player is a reject from Chelsea where they don't really serve the best British Breakfast... You may be surprised to know... the best is in Crystal Palace where there isn't really any crystal palace or crystal cab or even a crystal bench or a crystal shoe or a crystal ball belonging to one most influential Gypsy Queen who was put in the ground in a special square shaped coffin, she helped shape the destinies of so many prominent politicians and colonel admirals and scheming bakers and loud business associates but my memory is fading so I don't really remember names and all that kinda things so much anymore so please forgive the vulgarity and barbaric nature he wiped his phlegm on naturally tanned skin so thick that he's not the least hurt when You Whip Your Child with all might and anger and irony and whatever evil karma You have on the World for even once in Your Life, why not enjoy the game, look, look at how that fisherman's assistant is performing an acrobatic goal scoring attempt to confuse the enemy line and force them into a corner, kick it up field, anywhere will do, further, further away from the Goal, and with each defensive play, the stadium cheered, cheered, red in their faces, these Icelandic girls, wrapped in their First World wool plus First World mentality that One is better than Three instead of the other way round, costing only a Penny some years ago, it was truly amazing how the Bahian Herb Merchants rubbed against One Another in the trains and that's the Truth about how the City grew so quickly in such a short time as opposed to life in the rural districts where populations are dying and lands are left unfarmed, sixteen times, they fired catapults and even a few trebuchets thrown in for good measure to knock those archers off their towers with just one shot wonder style of hero but this one, Pedro Infante, he's actually a better singer than Goalkeeper Julio but so many women love him so much so they sow his seed to the End of the World where they planted the Tree of Forgetfulness wherever they found forlorn places, and Love, Sliding and Tackling, yeah, that's their advantage, especially when it Rains, it's a Rough and Thorny Match somewhat too Tenacious for those Pampered Prima Donnas more Concerned with their Hairstyles so Will England Score to Save their Lives? asked the Seasoned British TV Pundit making secret calls to make sure that his Sister-in-Law puts a pretty Dislike or two on the Men in Blue, Yeah, he has seen so many matches that he instinctively knows the results of each game a quarter hour before the End of Regulation, Silly Crow, England will Not Score! England will Not Score!

KICK! KICK! KICK! Kick the ball all the way up to the Other Side, Pass it! Pass it! Hold! Hold It! The English are Bloody Fools, You can say that much about them, yet, they are a Nation who Trust in God, just like the Americans, it's not so bad to believe in God, Right, NOW, with less than ten more minutes only for the English to reward the Faithful, causing those sad subdued fans to Burn more Partridge Feathers in Europe, it's obvious that the English are getting ready to form an elite club with the Americans, and that's why more and more Americans are buying into UK football leagues and truly exceptionally, remember, their supremacy in set pieces, that's their real forte but the English, they have gotten soft with all the various immigration policies puzzling even their top law makers and soon, it's only about eight minutes left before the referee blows the whistle to signify the end of the contest and then You suddenly Realize, Shitting Baboons, England is not English Anymore! More than Eight players in their team are Children of Immigrants and You see how they fail to Communicate at the highest levels of competition where they crumble to a team of Vikings, Unified, rising to every occasion to thwart the weary English assault, jittery and hesitant, Iceland didn't Wait, they Attacked it and Cleared it, Yeah, One Minute More and we would have won a Ship, the best Crystal one, and England is Out! What an Abject Performance! England Fall to Pieces and Save Their Pigs!

Anita O'Day on the Radio but there are not too much people in the Laundry at this time of the day when most of the people are Home, getting up for Dinner with their beloved family for that's one of the main reasons why these families have stayed together for such a long time, raising their kids until they become parents and all, and it's never easy being the father of a two plus year old who's always Gaining for the Chance to Experiment and Push the Boundaries of Laws or everything else, for some reason, he's getting more agitated that day, perhaps, it's due to some simple matter such as the feeling of sleepiness as well as some level of hunger for a kid of that age never really recognize the meaning of hunger or pain, he wanted to run around the joint at full speed, pushing buttons, and luckily, he could run and play with the machines, all cold and empty, ready for another load, and another load and there are some one hundred machines so the owner must be pretty pleased… meanwhile… the kid is throwing a wild tantrum but his daddy smiled, cool, it's nothing out of the ordinary for a father, and even the old fellow who's a neighbor tries to pacify the boy and finally, we are at the apartment, going up to the Chief's Nest.

Somehow, he's still exploring to the fullest of his ability, snatching the house keys from Daddy, he didn't care that there's a well-dressed smiling child tolerant lady waiting to go through the same door so he's pushing the key in and twisting left, right, left, and he's pretty good at it for a boy his age though his tiny fingers are just not strong enough to unlock it but he's got the mechanics all down pat, not bad for a boy who's just learnt to say BA NA NA and when we arrived at the house, Junior's still in a royal mood, kicking and screaming but not so terrible that You feel it's gonna be a long, long day so the Chief said to Errol that he will be left in the room and he can come out after he's done with his tantrums. The crying continues but it's subsiding, getting softer and irregular and the Chief's serving me dinner, and now, the boy smells the food and he's running out of his room, spooning into the macaroni and cheese which was his dinner and he's quite happy about it though he preferred pizza so he puts it away for a while, waiting for Euterpe to come back and feed him, maybe, we left some for her too, and as we dug into that meal, it occurred to me that people can be Happy, appreciating the Simple Life and isn't it one of the greatest lessons in life to learn and to teach to the Young so they learn how to Dwell in the Essence of their Existence? Yeah, sometimes, it's quite the Challenge but I suppose it's still better than the guy who owns that big fancy tower in the middle of Manhattan, Wealthy beyond Your imagination, licking his gold statue of himself so it's for sure he's gonna sit on the Highest Seat of the Land, it's already a done deal, right, and most people already know it in June when the weather's getting warmer and the streets are getting brighter so we touched on many topics of interest but nothing so much on the Press and all but at some point, The Chief asked me if I had done any new work and I was hesitant to reveal that I had written some pages in preparation to go back to school to learn the craft of creative writing with scholarship, stipend, and great promise of building a lightning career in the field but by the time I came to America, I had already received rejection letters from all the schools so I thought what the hell! I would just travel to the States and write away, still shooting for that Dream of America, still shiny and blinding, I promised to mail in some work and Truly, I wasn't so Confident that it's any good at all simply because I hadn't been doing any writing for so many years, it felt somewhat like a guy getting ready to have sex for the first time in twelve years or more, and he's not even sure if his cock is going to get hard and long enough to fuck for just a few seconds or so, he's satisfied, I'm satisfied, the Day is Coming to a Close and I had to get on the A Train to get back to the Flushing Meadows.

It's just another day for Jeremiah except that he's feeling a little happier than yesterday or even the day as well as the day before yesterday. Tending to his emotions, he's trying hard to erase the trace of his happiness no matter how small for it's the first time that he has felt so hard for as long as he can remember.

Jeremiah happens to be one of those people who is there but at the same time, he's not really there. Surely, you have met one or more of these people in your life? If you care, you may remember the girl sitting on the third row or so, nearest to the window so she can look out there as if she longs to be away and you can pretty well remember her face or even her first name Candy or Daffodil but you never know her Family name or her Birthday or you may not even know that she's not in class that day. Yeah, almost like a Ghost. When she's in class, she doesn't ask any question or offer any idea for anything and even when she's called by the teacher to answer a question, her answer is so textbook right that you will not remember it or even remember that she had answered anything at all. During recess or lunch break or whatever, you never know where she goes to eat her food but at the same time, you don't even care much about such a person because she's so easily replaced like factory workers or farm hands. On the other hand, you may feel a little compassion for her if the teacher suddenly announces that she has passed away or moved to another town. Do you know such a person? Very well. Jeremiah is Another.

To Portray Myself as an Artist, I visited the Museum of Modern Art (MOMA) in NYC and It was a Pretty Good Museum with enough less important works by The Masters from Europe, and also some more important works by American artists. Yeah, We are not from Europe so the Artworks We Acquire Here in the US are only Artworks of less value for it's obvious isn't it that the Museums in London, Paris, Rome, Berlin, Netherlands, Moscow, Madrid, and such important Museums, Surely, They will Keep the Most Important Pieces since They Warred over these things in the Past and Still Wrestling like They will Say, Hey, We have Robbed Your *Last Supper* or We have Stolen Your *Lady Liberty Leading the Revolution* and You Swear, You can See the Face of Patriot Abraham Somewhere in the Painting, Smiling with Same Mystery and Beguilement for Her Husband was already Impotent at the age of Twenty Six and he's just a drunkard living off the fruits of his father without heed for her insistent pleas to improve their lives and all those things, of course, he, a big chauvinistic charlatan, always saying NO… NO… in that way, he blocked every one of her thunderbolts and missiles and provided quite Basically for her and the children so they always had a little more than enough to eat for that's his responsibility to his family but in all other areas of their lives, it's the least, least sufficient so it's not like they had no clothes at all but the minimum pieces to keep them warm enough and nothing extraordinary than a three-course dinner for the Celebration of Mona Lisa's Thirty Second Birthday and she was rather quite pissed that her friend Misty Mystique, yeah, that Whore! She got a full twelve-course dinner with Persian Dance and Turkish Massage at the end of it all, She's always Furious but in Keeping with the Tradition of those times, She had to Swallow Shots of Green Saliva when She's really Angry and All, She Flushes, just the same like when She's Tickled Still by Him when She's still Green and All, and He had the Cowardice to Tell Her to be Joined with Him before going on to do it right there in the middle of the park, and truly, it's not such a bad idea at all because in those days, there were not so much people around, You get All the Privacy You ever

Wanted, and You also get to raise big families because the land was so rich and vast, You can simply pluck a few blackberries to eat and the potency of the plants in those days were simply unbelievable, considering that we are jiving to the most popular gypsy music of all time, yeah, returning, they had a good number of Matisse, and by God Almighty, it can be seen that he wasn't such a Great Technician so it's quite Artistic that it's just Out of this World that the Hands are Swollen and Out of Proportion and Not Quite so Human in that UNICEF Endorsed Piece with a few earthy round naked women holding hands to form a circle or something so silently eschew the aesthetics in that painting and You will Understand why They will only let us have the Inferior Stuff but What do We Americans Know? Only… Matisse was quite a formidable Sculptor for the Sculptures are all Liquid Shimmering like Black Gold Glittering like they are Melting but Holding their Shape in Eternity, Right Before Your Eyes, You are transported back to the Day when It was Still Safe to Go for a Picnic in the Park on a Sunday Afternoon.

MOMA is quite the Modern Museum in North America where You Can Easily Burn a Number of Hours if You just Stand about ten seconds in Front of Each and Every Exhibit, and There are Some that You like more and some that You don't Care at all but There are some Interesting Pieces by Renowned Artists like Monet, Picasso, Dali, Modigliani, Cezanne, van Gogh, Pollock, Rothko, Braque, de Kooning, Lichtenstein, and a great representation of other prominent figures representing various schools in the History of Art. On the Other Hand, it's Nothing so Cultural about Visiting a Museum Once in a While even if It's not Really Your Thing because You May Just Learn How to Appreciate the Beauty of Art and the Big Secret about It is that You Don't Need to Go to School to Enjoy Art because It's the Thing which is Visceral, Biased, What's Apple in Your Eye May Be Rose Apple in Another's Eye but You have to Find that Out for Yourself and In Time, It's Hoped, You will Cherish the Beauty of the World around You too so yeah it's like You Like Gabi Lunca's Singing but Your Neighbor Dislikes It so much that he's come to complain and he politely asks You to put on Earphones to Enjoy it all the More Closely by Yourself but It's Alright, Believe in Yourself and Ignore People who Tell You that There's Only One Way to do Things because You Know How They are Still in the Dark, in the Tunnel, and If You are Careless, You may Find Your Dislikes missing so they just talk loudly to intimidate You and prove that they have long departed from their old professions, they would love to come out but for the code of Honor, He Coughed Out those Cherry Seeds, talking and talking like he's the Captain of the Navy so it's understood that You will not Find What's Lost for it's very easy for them to Open Your Bags in the Middle of Your Journey to W. Broadway, maybe, You like Maria Lataretu more than Maria Sandoval but You Shouldn't Spend so much Time Thinking about the Other, plus, It's Still a Long Way to Scarborough Fair.

Spring comes after Winter. There's nothing You can do to change it in such a way that Spring comes after Summer and then, Winter, and then, Fall… does it make sense? Sometimes, Things don't have to make any sense so let's Hypothesize just because we want to feel more Academic… You find Yourself in one of those fiberglass booths they keep one of the two finalists in the Miss Universe contest and it's quite stifling because the air condition is not very good inside and You still have to keep Smiling and Exude Air of a Confident Woman while You Witness Your Greatest

Opponent Performing Splendidly and Everybody is Standing on their Seats though You cannot Hear a Sound, You can Feel the Ground Quake so When it's Your Turn, You Step out of the Crucible and Walk Straight up to the Master of Ceremony and he's greeting You, cracking some small joke, and waiting to make sure that You are Alright, then, after everything else, he asks You if You don't have to be Right all the time, You Know, It's not that I Don't Wanna Sleep or that I Like to Type Deep into the Night but When Your Love's Gone to the Netherworld and There's Nothing You can do to Worry Less, Naturally, You Suffer from some sort of Insomnia and no matter how many times You close Your Eyes Again and Again, Tossing in Bed on all four sides, You are not going to Enjoy the Serenity to venture into the Land of Dreams and yeah, You can take some sedatives or knock out medicine to Drowse Yourself but why not take some time to reflect on contemplate what it would be like to sleep in a burning bed, completely drowsed by Chemicals which can be found in almost Everything nowadays, including food, tobacco, liquor, air, electronics, Humor, furniture, water, and what else so who's really Pure and all?

It's Hard to leave New York. In all Her Perfections and Imperfections, She Smiles on the People and Despite the Pain, there's Something in the Air whether it's the design of the buildings or the big bright lights or the steam coming out of the manholes or the smell of millions of hopeful immigrants or the insensible sense of the unexpected unfolding right before your eyes or the rush of the trains spearing past graffiti too quickly so You only see the Word LOVE or the promise of impromptu amateur Jazz being played by a troop of Chinese boys or the brush of people always going somewhere as quickly as possible, the people enjoying a natural tanning session or extramarital affair in Central Park, the smell of Non Halal Wurst sizzling on street side, the guy at the New York Public Library Informing You which Lion is Fortitude and which Lion is Patience and Sadly, when You look at them, You Think, Well, Fortitude can be Patience and Vice Versa, Right, and When You Really a Little Harder, You Realize There's No Fortitude without Patience and even Stranger, Patience Develops with Fortitude so You get to that Age Old Question again but Really, New York City is New York City and even without the Twin Towers, it's still New York City and there's Nothing any Terrorist or Fanatic can do to Destroy Her Spirit. She's Indestructible and She Always Rebound like that Energizer Bunny advertisement I Remember from Years Ago, Indomitable, Stronger than Ever. Now, I Don't Know if Bullies, yeah, essentially, they are Nothing but Bullies whether they be a Man Raping a Bear or a Rich Woman Rolling Over a Peasant and Laughing about it like She just Killed a Mosquito or a President Fumbling the Football and Panicking and Nuking a Village of Innocents or a Tamil Tiger Suicide Bomber Blasting Off a Few Hundred Unarmed Commuters or Anybody Trampling on those who are Weaker or Race Supremacists thinking they are more Superior or Pseudo Religionist Martyrs Thinking or even Believing They are Fighting the Holiest War of the Holy Wars, now, I spent countless seconds thinking what Motivates them and sure, they all have their reasons but why don't Someone see that the System has Failed and It will Continue to Fail so why not try Something Radical like it's time to Fan the Humanities Flame again and Educate people on the Beauty of the Arts all over again? Going to a Museum and Listening to a Great Piece of Music and Reading Hard Core Literature and Watching Slow Sob Sob Cinema and maybe even a simple Meditation Exercise, what it does to the Human Soul is Priceless. Yet. They Say. There's Nothing the Fucking Wrong with the World! Have You seen the Queues at the Museums?? Books are sold in Record Numbers!! The Most Popular Singer of All Time has Only One Point Eight Million Dislikes!!! Billions upon billions of movie tickets are sold each year!!! How can You say there's a Decline in Culture??? Yet, it's All True! Surprisingly, there's not a time in the History of the World when people have become as Shallow and Idiotic as they have become in this Age and Day of Supreme Technological Achievement. Alright!! All In!!! LOL! Woo Hoo!! Strip! Like!!! STFU!!! Two Lollipops!!! Dislike!!!! Thumbs Up! Best!! WTF!!! Let's take a rest… and sample this…

Once upon a time, Mohammed had Three Beautiful Daughters. Their Beauty was so Spellbinding that Every Man, Dead or Alive, yeah, they would love to Fuck them Right Away but since they were born in more Cultured times and their Father was such an Influential Figure, their Beauty and the News of their Beauty alone Spread across the Seven Seas so Every Fellow from as far off as Scotland and Maui and Sudan and even Greenland, never Green, they came to see the Three Daughters and of course, as True Men with Blue Veins and Inspired Spirits, All of these Young Men Fantasized about Marrying One or All Three of these Sisters! Then! Not in Paradise! Now, the Big Risk about the Promise of Paradise is that You have to Die to Cross Over, and What Happens if it's all a Bunch of Lies? Is There Really a Room for You in *His* Father's Mansion? What happens if the Milk in the River tastes Bitter? Will the Virgins Nibble Your Testicles? All of them? Let's Talk about the Sisters for a While. The Eldest Daughter, Isabella, she's Arab-Egyptian, the Fruit of a few uncensored days of passion as The Prophet was entertained timelessly by the Most World Famous Belly Dancer in those days, Farida Fahmy, and if You have the time to check out her videos, You may come to the conclusion that she only spent so many days with him because she's a Gold Digger and You are almost Right because Men of Wealth and Power have always been a magnet for beautiful women but it's also true that she's smitten by the Regal behavior of The Prophet and his hypnotic emerald whirlpool eyes that rival the flash of gemstones of various magical values, and when he moves his hand, ever so gracefully, it's so Authoritative, his attendants move with the speed of light or even faster when he signaled for a glossy glass of gin tonic with a twist of Moroccan lime, it was executed with such perfection that You can't tell which part is the gin and which part gin tonic and of course, the flavor of the lime is so well-fresh like the smell of it when You pluck it from the earth with Your bare hands, uprooting the damn thing in one Herculean yank, yank, Yankee Doodle Dee, yank, yank, Yankee Doodle Doo, and it goes on for quite some bit when You see the extent of the destruction You have executed in such a short time it took so long for it to grow to that height, high enough for the Silver Medal in Women's High Jump in XXVII and You look up her name Hestrie Cloete and she's around six feet tall but she's not so lean, she's got well-balanced palm honey sea coconut sized breasts that bounce with all the carefree spirit of the world so everybody can witness the vivacity and vitality of such a pure force of life, sure, each and every man in the village gets a stone frequency hard on whenever and wherever she appears, old men were known to blush because she's so careless, she always forgets to wear her under garments so You can definitely see the how her nipples protrude out of the fabric of her satin canary loose fitting top and those are ultra-long ones too so she almost gets everything free of charge because she brings in the customers all the time, without fail, there will be a crowd waiting to get close to her and sometimes, when it gets real busy and the traffic is pretty heavy, You cannot even breathe, You cannot even say hello as You are trying to get away from a whole army of desperate males, all of them pushing and shoving to get nearer to Frangipani Panini with their semen seeping out of their ancient costumes but she would always have this group of most worthy Mercenaries Wearing their Loyalty and Honor on their Sleeves to Protect the Maiden of Pure Heavenly Bliss, and it's not enough that she's also a Flamenco Dancer and talented artist because it's not just not Heavenly enough if she's just a flamenco dancer for there are millions of them and it's even more Pointless that she's an artist, it's unimportant if she's talented or not for there are some artists who died of Depression and Blues so they usually take to drinking heavy liquor to disguise themselves whether they are driving buses in NYC or preparing a Pepperjack burger with Bombay onions and spicy caramelized white mushrooms they usually use to cook delicious Mushroom Soup even more delicious without Salt being such a Compulsory Food for every struggling artist to eat One Can for a few days so the main trick is to eat as much bread as possible and perusing a lot of alcohol for greater fermentation of the wheat, producing yeast which is a superior creation, along with dried foods and frozen foods, just to Numb the Suffering a Little. Get??

"Which Do You Prefer? Frozen or Dried?"

"HEY! WHAT ABOUT THE OTHER DAUGHTERS?"

"Brooklyn. I love Brooklyn because it's Real. The Market's Real, the Laundry's Real, and the Food's Real. It's the Heart Beat of NYC."

"Golden Pattaya: An enchanting Thai delicacy with Mildly Spicy Basil Fried Fragrant Rice with Wee Wee Eggs and Wild Crunch Shrimp in Special House Sauce and Seasonal Vegetables, Wrapped like a Lotus Flower in Golden Paper-thin Egg Omelette Price: 16 Dislikes"

"What about Fifi Abdu?"

"Not so long ago, Greece was the host of the Summer Olympics and the Grand Old Champions of Europe. Look at them now!"

"Do You have a Light?"

II

When You are visiting a friend You have not seen for twenty years or more, it's easy for You to say such things like… it's still the same… it's just like yesterday… and when he asks You to procure some curries and anchovies which is just a relishing kind of dried sea food product, an acquired delicacy he remembers from the good old days when he could savor those homely dishes lovingly prepared by his Mother, and in all those years he has been Abroad for his studies, he's Wise enough to know that the exchange rate is always more favorable to the Western countries for centuries upon centuries so many Third World Folks have been Slaves of the Elites for centuries upon centuries so the Hand that sets all these weights is always pressing on one side and it's the same Hand as the one that sets the prices of stocks, shares, what You call commodities and necessities and news and all that business about health insurance and every familiar topic to talk about like favorite TV shows and a sly acknowledgement that You have really learnt to enjoy the American life if and only if You have learnt to appreciate the Life all that much more without regard for even the thousands of mosquitoes buzzing around You and if You rest enough, You will float to the sky, carried by these little angels, also planned by the Hand, and You may pardon the hospitality of the guy, even to the point where You instruct Your own son to pick the nicest goods, it's told, he picked those tiny dead fish like he was picking the most delicate miniature glass ornament inspired belief about Buddhism or Hinduism or Confusionism which is really the most confusing of them all, just in case You know nothing of the sort, I Beseech You, STOP, Stop all Filial Piety nonsense and every kind of Do as You are Told by Elders and Authority culture imposed on You in any part of the world with electricity or without electricity with tap water or without tap water with bricks or without bricks with gold or without gold, I Implore You, Gather All, Gather All, Gather All the treasures of the world together and pour them into a Rainbow Cauldron where they will be melted and distributed to every person on earth in equal measure so just for the first time in the history of the world, Equality is Achieved, yeah, and I say unto You even if You Search the Earth even unto the most Hidden Eden, You will not acquire another sacred bead from the Tribe of Little Black Foot, yeah, the most amazing tales You have ever heard, yeah, You have told to Your child almost every night so when he or she sleeps, Your voice lingers in their dreams, Speaking the Words of Eternal Love for You never wish for anything bad to happen to Your Loved Ones but then again… it's another morning… another night…

There were Tamarind Curries, Green Curries, Seafood Curries in fact, there were five or six different types to bring Manna the culinary heritage of Your Motherland which is truly a Hypocritical Lawless Islamic state embracing the lunacies of nose frothing fanatics who only seek to prosper their pockets and spew controversial racist propaganda to distract the people whether they are right or wrong, it doesn't matter one bit, yeah, You can be sure, there's nobody in the room when You switch off the lights, and that's the greatest comfort, especially for a poor lonesome pilgrim from thousands upon thousands of miles away, let it be known, it's just pure relief to know that You are in a safe home and Nobody can Color Your Mind even if they have the most precise advanced laser incision needle to open up Your understanding of the Creation and all that type of things You seek to put aside for another day… another day… Lift up Your head to look at the sky another day… yeah… another day… and You don't think it's too much to ask for another day… another day…

Also, Four Butterflies Part Two and a box of most exquisite English Tea Time biscuits to summon their innate loyalty to the British because they were the only people who have ever domesticated this rock hardened band of warriors who put their life on the line without even a thread of consideration for safety or afterlife, they chose to Die in Honor rather than Surrender in Cowardice, these are mercenaries for hire to the rich and powerful for many years, it's understood that a manuscript was discovered in the rundown bedroom of a respected officer by the name of Captain Lt. Sir Manuel de St. Paul, the first person to devise the techniques used to subdue the wildest horses that kick their feet in the air, front and back, trying to throw off the Rider of the Storm, and the most potent Stallions, they have crippled many a cowboy, O Americans, he learned how to calm the wildest horses by whistling, it's very simple but of course, he was the greatest whistler of them all for he could put little children to sleep with just a few notes, and he could even domesticate the most hungry and pissed off buffalo with big muscular horns and cloud of smoke coming out of his nostrils, of course, there's a ring in his nose, the yoke of his labor, the guy, he just whistled and circled the Beast until he got close enough to deliver the final note of Song of Eternal Moon which is really the Lullaby most parents sing to their children all the same, the somehow, it works almost all the time for there's a kind of soothing quality in the melody or something for I don't profess to be such a student of Music that I'm able to explain how this notation triggers Sensuality and how this Sequence drums up the Heart but I know, Music is one of those Great Mysteries which can never be Scientifically Dissected or Analyzed, just like Friendship or Family Relations according to that Overrated Chinese Sage, in his ideal universe, it's best for the parent to be so far away from the children so as to appear busy and important so when the children spend what little time they have with the Father, it's always a Male centric society, You see, it appears, their time is so golden, they treasure and cherish every second like it's the last time that they are going to be in the presence of Him who determined the fate of six million citizens with just one signature, and that's what carries its weight in the most beautiful real feathers of condors of old flying the sky to lord over the region where the Half Moon clan resided for more than a few hundred years, yeah, the land was taken from them just like that the very next day when the Mayor came with a whole wagon of papers establishing the fact that the lands have all been turned over to a new owner by the name of one Madame Slyvia Nathan binti Abdul Mustahil Najib Bangsat Biadap Bin Babi Red Navel and she wants the inhabitants to be evicted by Sunrise and it's slightly less than a day that You had to put all Your belongings in a suitcase or bag and get out of the place the tribes had called Home for hundreds upon hundreds of years for even the Indians were not born of this Land, this America so many years ago even before people kept arriving in greater and greater numbers, this Land was Wild, and Pure, and Holy so Holy Hell so Holy Bell so Holy Fell so Holy Well so Holy Dell so Holy Pell so Holy Cell so Holy Jell so Holy Swell so Holy so Holy so in the name of Progress, they had to go further out of the town and live in caves with bats and bears sometimes coming to Your thrash to look for candies for she is diabetic and she just needs some sweet to get her happy again, It's alright... It's alright... the Mother of Mothers whispered to her... Sweet Pretty Pretty Little Angel... Jazz and rain... grain... main... rain... train...

"How much is the Train Ticket to Denver?"

"Eight hundred and thirty-six Dislikes Only..."

"It's Crazy, isn't it?"

"No... it's a cabin with great views like those You never see before... and it's quite comfortable..."

"Do You think it's worth it?"

"Sure... if You put up a few hundred Dislikes for a plate of Duck Liver appetizer... You better Vomit and Choke... if You know... what their did to the poor Animals... right?"

"Isn't it better to take the plane?"

"Yeah, I will fly. It's cheaper and faster..."

There's nothing much that happens in Plymouth, except for that time when a drug lord came to rent a big house to process and distribute his stocks but he was arrested promptly enough so You can be sure that it's one of the cleanest, best-run communities in the Midwest and arguably, the whole country. The education system is possibly the best publicly funded one in comparison to the other counties, it cannot be argued that Minneapolis churns out some of the brightest and happiest kids in the world. Firstly, the economy is anchored by the Biggest Mall of the Americas, and I'm not joking because it more than tripled in size from its humble beginnings in the early nineties when it was still up and coming… billed as the biggest mall in North America but in just less than thirty years, it has expanded with full indoor amusement center, and thousands upon thousands of stores peddling thousands and thousands of goods and services to the hoard upon hoard of visitors from all over the Land, relishing the opportunity to come shop in this most modern advanced forward moving environmentally progressive Mall, yeah, there are hotels that are fully booked the whole year round so there's no shortage of business kinda economy rooted by a robust IT-based industry filled with substantial percentage of textbook smart Asians living the American life with their offspring, building a magnificent community for the children to grow up in, a sort of Utopia, really, for I felt no danger whatsoever even when I walked in the dead of the night, I wasn't worried that I would be attacked by a mountain lion or a zombie for that matter because there are some places where You don't feel so safe, it's true, Plymouth is such a safety zone, I believe other similar places around the Minneapolis Ring are also safe havens for children and old folks, everything was very well planned and run with a sort of German efficiency which is hard to explain but quite easily perceived when You look at how well-trimmed the parks appear spick and span even in the evening, You can see a fat blue rabbit coming out of her habitat to roll around in the grass and pick some flowers to freshen up the air in her home and all, waiting for her husband to come home, sure, he will give her a good one…

It may surprise many people but Arranged Marriage is still practiced in these days and surprisingly, the Success rate is much higher than Free Marriage. In a grand sample size of Five Arranged vs Five Free, I report the findings as follows: Four Divorces in Free vs One Divorce in Arranged. According to Manna, the Arranged Marriages were consecrated by Shamans who study the stars of the male and the female to determine if they are Right for one another and I guess it's the same for most traditional Asian societies where You will find much lower Divorce rates in comparison to the Western countries, especially the US with almost seventy percent of Marriages dissolved. Why are we even talking about such a boring thing? Well… Plymouth is quite boring… and in respect to Arranged Marriage, the Romantic may ask… which Marriage is not arranged??? Just for the Reason that people have become more skeptical and scientific, it does not mean that Cupid's not around even when You cannot sense him in any which way, now, consider that You are struck by the beauty or peculiarity or vehicle or humor of a particular someone and You wish to pursue the relationship to the point where both parties seek to get closer such that they are joined to each other in the manner by which they tie threads around Your wrists to symbolize the union of man and woman, even then, Strangely, the Body is created in such a way that each and every Body in the World including Animals is different from another and every plant, even of the same species, each and every one is Unique, that's what we always try to tell our children when they are growing up, we try to tell them that all the milk in the world taste somewhat similar and all the cookies in the world must be sweet enough to feed the Bear big time, how about her, guarding her lovely cubs from danger, feeding them with some of the sweets and gummy worms, and they are all happy because little ones don't know the meaning of Suffering almost all of the time, especially if they are raised in a nourishing environment, they will always be happy and positive about all that happens in their lives, growing up to be good citizens of the world, spreading positive energy wherever they go and they will see that it's not easy to build such a family of love and peace in a world of cynicism and cut-throat competition, it probably takes more work than the latest mission to Saturn, see, the once most muscular Neptune, the guy with his tri-fork trident and his big fin, yeah, much more powerful and illuminant in every aspect without even a slight scratch and cooled by the wind of a thousand million feathers of the softest kind, the cloud on top of the lips of the Persian Nightingale, You Sleep, You Sleep, You Sleep the Thousand Mile Sleep as prescribed by Freud, Charging You with the Jolt of just One Lightning Bolt, it will Freeze Your whole being without respite, and yeah, there, You… Sweet Angel… You will Sleep but not Aging for even One Second… Kindly… Read the Sweet Script again…

Barely seven years old, Jeremiah, the third youngest child in his Blossoming family of Twenty-three children, One Day, his Mother, aged forty-six or whereabouts, May Orpheus Bless Her Soul for Eternity, the Mother of Mothers for She's almost always with child, and this time, She's carrying triplets so You just fulfill Her Wishes, no matter how ridiculous or unbelievable, She instructed him to break the sad news to all the Others. When

She whispered the message in his ear, he felt like weeping for at least three minutes in private for he loved his Father of Fathers more than any of his sisters so he didn't understand why She had selected him to carry out such a task but he was taught to carry out his parents' instructions without any question so he didn't wrestle all that much and he walked all the way to his eldest sister's home which was more than three miles away but since he was quite fleet of foot, he arrived in no more than ten hours, no less.

"Knock! Knock!"
"Who's there?"
"I'm Jeremiah..."
"Who?"
"I'm Your Brother..."
"Alright... I will be there... Wait a minute..."

Jeremiah waited at Blue Moon's door and again, he felt like weeping but he managed to calm down by stopping to breathe for as long as he could keep the air in his lungs before exhaling a long, tired, resigned, slow stream of silent lamentation and he managed to distract himself by wondering why his Father had named her Blue Moon. In one of his Imaginings, He Imagined it was his and her favorite song and the more he Imagined about it, he could Imagine the two of them, possibly in Paradise of their Adolescence for they should not be more than eleven or ten, slow dancing on the river bank, knees in snow, shadowed by the flickering silvery rays of the full moon, most likely blue, his bleeding Viking heart thumping against her swollen dripping nipples, flowing closer to the rhythm of her Soul, rising and ebbing, wildly and without restraint or course, just like the perfumed winds coursing through the shimmering leaves of the willows weeping, what else, vibrating against one another, delivering a crescendo wave of felicity to their spirits so at that moment when their bodies were burning even in subzero temperature, it could be ascertained that they were experiencing some sort of rapture and in just a second or less, they heard the most heavenly music even when there's no song being played and they could see right into each other, yeah, his left to her right, and vice versa, they must have seen the footprints of Infinity without knowing what it meant or signified, they must have kissed at least twice as long and confessed their burning love for each other even unto the ends of the earth and beyond. It's true. Jeremiah always remembered them to be most loving couple ever as he's amazed how they never seemed to get older or fatter or thinner or younger like other people, appearing exactly the same as he remembered them from his earliest memories.

It's no point to talk about it… the merits of my writing or anything else… in this Dim Light of Prometheus thieving the Olympic Flame and Strictly Speaking… I Hereby Announce that I'm Most Possibly the Most Privileged of all Writers in not the Strictest Sense for the Noun of Ply is Splice in most gentle fashion such that with just a feather's touch and nothing else lighter than the kiss of a forlorn lover lost in the Jungle for the eleventh time and yet, my Comrades, my Compression Pills, I need no music nor the drama of the Whole Collapse of the Economy and then, You see, I'm Richer than Most of You Combined and Thankfully, there's Nothing You can do about it except to go Jingle Bells Jingle Bells Jingle All the Way to the Other Side where You never thought We would meet again under that damn *Yellow*

Ribbon Old Oak Tree which the most favorite favorite and most pleasing Song of the Universe truly only audible to the Pure in Heart and I Kid You Not… if You ever come so far and hide half a Step to the Right of the Door of Perception or The Sin which Originally conceive to be the Root of All Art and the true artist knows it's not the Thing about that Little Wind Up Rat with Key Hole near the Tail and It's True, the Key was Hexagonal and the Metal was Nothing but Alloy for I learned from my Philosophy Professor by the name of one Doctor Octogone in the Tales of Malaria by the Greatest Writer of All Time whose Talents were not only to soothe and heal You of all Your aches and charades, Longeness or Longititude or Longivictus, I Procure, I Procure, it's not even funny when they only gave you ONE CHANCE to get it Right and the Society is so Unforgiving, isn't it, isn't it also in the Will of the Righteous that they be given the Legacy to Preach when it's not all the while Obvious that it's Logically False for Juliet to Die before Romeo for how much more heart rendering can it be for the Female Audience when they wailed after his Boat Sailing for the Pacific, sailing for the last time so they say it's all the way to the Dime Hall City Girl Time when a bunch of girls in such Glaring and Shiny and Illuminati and Shape Shifters and they will Immediately Shut Off like a Radio when the Knob is Dialed to a Specific Angle, it will Stop, like Clockwork, Zero Sound if Nobody's playing the Game of the Way to Euphoria is not so Far Away from the Joys of Aging they always tell You will be the most Resplendent Times of Your Lives and So You Say the Word Resplendent and You may Wonder all about it like the most Stupid Girl in the Class or the most Stupid Toy who Froze like a Robot so they didn't even think He's real so they Ignored him, Saving their Bullets for the Enemies and it's in these Traumatic Times that the Car Screeches across the Meadow with Blue Flowers floating off to the Other Side of Midnight was such a Big Hit in those days, Everybody was sweating to know who's the Butler who Poisoned the Rich Old Guy nearing The End who Murdered the Heroin's Swindling Husband who's really after Her Crow Cow Lead Guitar Wild Girl Syndrome for She always Fantasizes about how Bonham would have done it to her but of course she wouldn't mind Sucking Jimmy's Swirling Mint Cane Lollipop so the Grand and One is Totally Wrong and She Knew how She would be singing the National Anthem at the Top of Her Voice for she was the Loudest Siren of them all and the Whole Village knew all about how she swindled the Clown who didn't know the Way to the Newton Circus where in the Good Old Days of Curry Puff Hairstyles and Boys carried Marbles to School, No, Not those Tiny Cissy Glass Ones Modern Boys Clinging On to the Final Cracking One with their Rubber Band Tying Skills being of Utmost Importance in the Most Important Moment of Your Life when You say Quoting Your latest Poem about how the Light is not Bright Enough or How the Flame is not Purplish enough but before I Forget, I Wish to say that the Marbles We Carried in the Past were much Bigger and They were Real Marbles and We didn't use them to play Little Girl Games with the Hole in the Ground and the Main Objective was to Control the Home so the Others will be Banished, Lest, Lest You Forget, Maybe not Now but I promise You with Three Times Your Wager, One Day, You will Win and let's not Bull Shit Yourself, let's not Muddle Your Nose for You Should Know, more than anyone who knows more than you or the Other way round is the Way to Damnation for it's Common Sense and No Other Thing for Who Gave You the Right to Choose and

You Chose the Wrong Time to say it even when You thought You would be Vomiting the Pearls out from Your Stomach, I Command You, the Golden Fish too if You are Sincere about the whole thing for that Matter about Ruth, I had no idea at all, I only knew the Bullet was harder than my Brain but I'm not Dead, You Know, I'm Not Dead until I Hear that Sound... For I can think of Juliet as Bugsy's Wife who was Fine Wine in her days and now she's Supporting some Young Budding Actor who's Talent is Smaller than his Tool but You Know why Women kept going to His Room and Losing His Right to choose for the Opposition no matter who they choose to be Inspired by That Which is Not the Way to the East where the Sun Sets Tomorrow and Surely You Know it's BYE BYE Tomorrow for You if You don't Hand over the Briefcase kind of Excitement that drives Housewives Mad and Reddening Today more than Yesterday or What Shall the State of the Union State in that the Artist must be Free of All Fear Including the Fear of being placed into a Cage with Three Hungry Crocodiles and the whole Show was about how Captain Kangaroo skipped on his tip toes and how he was circling the crocodiles like they were his prey and how he acted as a rock and he was such a Great Rock, the Crocodiles starting attacking the Land Lord and the Land Lord always says it's not my fault is it that You have failed to pay Your Rent and It's not Likely that You will be Absolved and reduced to Dust Right? Right? Are You that Dumb!! Said Lazarus to his Mother when he told her all about that Miracle Man of Nazareth Blowing in from Dessert with His Trian of Disciples Tagging Along and Chuckling that they had stolen all his monies again and then he's Begging on the Streets with his Whole Family begging for a Crumb of Bread and It's Also True that the Wind is Blowing Again and it's such a great joy it was to have gone to the Zen Bar Sal came to when he was in Denver and the place where his shadow fell on that Fateful Day when Martha Lost her Pearl to Peter, She Didn't know that She was Already Pregnant with Patton's Daughter and Nobody really cared all that much about the Rats and there may well be so much so much rain of arrows that may be shooting through the Helmet in such a way that there's absolutely no Channel to the End Result being the Wrong Way to Tally Ho with the Enemy and that's what the Guy does is he's Gonna be Buddy Buddy with Everybody in the End for we know who calls the Shots and We Know Slovenia is the Step Sister of Russia and so are Belarus and Ukraine and Romania and On the Surface, they are always Quarreling and Arguing about Who's the First Son and Not the Middle One Who's Clashing with the Youngest One but when it all comes together, they are the Karamazovs and We All Know How the Russians are always training and grooming spies and now they got one in the White House but yeah Nobody is going to Believe in that too because Everything HERE is NONSENSE but no matter, I don't really care because I'm not trying to Predict or Expose Anything like Award Winning Publications or Secret Agents who are all about Secrets so they don't talk so much unlike cab drivers who are Free to talk about Anything and that's the Freedom I Aspire when it's just the Vibrating Leaf that holds my Fecund Imagination of the novel at the tip of My Fingers Shifting Poetic forms or stanzas or such laws that defy the laws and regulations of writing like Nouns, Tenses, ConJUNCTIONS, and FULL STOP… I Suggest You Flip Back a few pages so You arrive at that Point when she found out that Romeo had Committed Suicide just because of Her and her Alone without any other Theories about how the Underdog always Win Big in the

End, Yeah, You may think that You are so Clever and You have Won enough Titles to be Happy Enough to be Winning at All because You have been Winning all the time and You have all the Reasons in the World plus the Other Part about her being Pregnant was even more Tragic because She was Carrying Her Brother's iPad in her arms for they were just Careless for just that one time and it's then... he delivered the Uppercut to Knock Frasier Out Flat and so the World Cheered for the New Brash Champion who talked about the Birds and Stings like he really understood the Psychology of the Whites who were in Awe of TV and swim upstream, perhaps with speed of seven knots or whatever the way to measure the speed of a school of seven sharks swimming for their lives as they were chased by whatever to fancy Yo Yo desires, I Bless You in this Humble Cabin Bubble, a once in Your Lifetime or even Two Lifetimes kind of deal, yeah, in that One Frozen moment of Clarity, I Pray You, Do not Live Your Life in Foregone Conclusion, Forget All You Know, Turn, Turn from Your Evil ways for We who follow the Golden Rule, We fully understand the meaning of how We Should Act according to What We expect Others to Do Unto Us and when You really think about it beyond the Socialist, Republican, Democratic, Communist, and everything else in between, yeah, You can even dispose of all sorts of weapons in the world and blacksmith the metal into a single knife for each person, yeah, plotless, colorless, clueless, that's the World of Pedro, the most Chivalrous Gaucho of the Order to bring about the discipline of strength and little ability of saying that You totally get *Canto General* and You see it's performed with orchestras and theatre and You see that it's not always so bad to be a Poet of the Forgotten who goes from one house to another with the Blessings of the Goddess of Mercy who is not always in a good mood especially when the Monkey King goes against the Master who can't do nothing much but possessing the Spell to subdue the Monkey King by chanting a Mantra to tighten the Imperial Meteorite Crown or Something which is traditionally shaped like a snake with two tails instead of one head and one tail and at the end of the tail, it curls up like a spiral puzzle, for once he put it on, he can't take it off, and when his Master feels that he has gotten out of line, he would chant it, and magically, the band tightened around his head, causing much greater agony than a million migraines combined into one giant headache, it's impossible to describe the pain he felt with a hundred words or even a thousand pictures or even an eternity of evening prayer calls on loudspeakers, causing him to go berserk but unable to do anything about it, and more than a few times, the Monkey King was so pissed with the Master for being so suspicious of him and he had to suffer for Nothing even when he could see the vicious monsters and spirits transforming into vulnerable poor pitiful human beings with his Golden Fire Eyes, destroying them with one Swing of his Magic Needle weighing more than ten metric tons or more but yet it fits in his ear when it's tiny but at full size, it's one of the pillars of the world, in essence, it holds the Peace between the Heavenly King and the Ocean King and it's at this time that we suddenly come to the Conclusion that all Roots of the English Language can be Traced to England so people who wish to learn real English, there's only one place to go… and that's the reason why the tales in the Journey to the West are tiresome because they are repetitive after a while, and once You picked the pattern of how the Master was deceived by the Pig General who still harbors human tendencies and how the other guy was always carrying all the heavy stuff of the Master to Journey to the West where he's supposed to harvest the Ultimate Zen Ultimate Bows to the Sun Ultimate Thousand Rosemary Ultimate Sacrifice of Virgins Ultimate Seven Round Walk Around His Left Pinky Fingernail Ultimate Spell to free Humanity from Suffering, it's not surprising at all that the stories have been made into so many TV dramas and movies, all so boring, all so Chinese but wouldn't it all be so easy if the Master learns an Immortal Spell where he shall not be harmed in any way kinda spell in which You will be safe even when a Giant Meteor Triple the Size of Mother Earth comes Crashing Down, You will be protected by a Sphere of Impenetrable Jungle, Invisible, freshly formed by some cosmic energies flowing from the South to the West or vice versa it's quite futile what's this punishment for culprits by forcing them to drink gallons and gallons of water sixteen times a day while *Zorba's Dance* is playing in the background but played to a loud volume so it goes deep into the Soul of the prisoner, a giant acupuncture needle pressed down in the middle of the ID where he has the most pleasant memories of his life when his Platoon Leader patted him on his head when he was the National Champion, chopping off Three Thousand Seven Hundred and Sixteen Heads OFF HEAD BARBIE CONTEST in a mere two moons, he was awarded a special mention in the country's Guinness Book of Records and his family was so proud of him for the way he won his fame, and the town was so proud of him that they sent him to the most Elite Military School in the Region, hoping that he would bring Great Glory to their homeland so they trained him in all the aspects of Terrorism such that he mastered the arts of disguise, makeup, speech, dance, drama, comedy, and many other stuff like grooming so he appeared like a Big Time

Businessman all the time, even in his own mansion with about a few hundred women awaiting his every Morning Shine Penis rising to the Sun like a Rooster Crowing at the Blood Moon, full, and while We are at it, it's a good idea to watch the movie before You listen to the soundtrack because then You can recreate the scenes along with the music and Presto! There You have a movie out of Your life, yeah, Everybody can be a superstar *for they are such poor creatures… they give you all they got…*

Yeah, try to surprise Your Beloved and Watch the Eyes Brighten when You mention just a little bit about that new Spider You received from the Legendary Korean Colonel Admiral, he who defeated the entire Japanese fleet with One Formidable ship at Roaring Winds, the Cyclone of Water being his only Ally, yeah, it was a battle that defied all logic and science of war, outnumbered more than a few thousand to one, the odds of his victory with only two casualties while inflicting spirit-crunching defeat to kill off more than five hundred and sixty two Banzai Kamikaze Japanese Sea Loving Soldiers was a triumph of epic wonderment for the odds were so stacked against him so much so the rest of his ships broke rank and deserted him, surrendering without a fight but it's important that Everybody learns of this humbling victory for it's from these stories that we fathom the Impossible, no matter how Impossible, it's still possible if only one person believes it can be done, Thy Will be done, and it's possible. It's for these Glimpses of the Miraculous that We continue to believe that Peace is still possible… No Matter How Illogical… How Hopeless… How Late… How Clownish…

How about that old nigger guy You were supposed to tell about in the bus on the way to JFK? O see how You have totally forgotten about him when he's such a character?

It's very easy. I call Your attention to one Maria Farantouri, a mystical singer of the highest orders, now Politician, You may say, she's more charismatic a storyteller than a singer but You know, without the music, the words are without so much color, right, today, the firecrackers bloom in the sky, ushering in Independence Day which is about to happen in another one and a half day or less, and I Invite... Everybody who has ever Despised the Great Country of the United States of America, I implore You to spurt out a most powerful stream of Your most venomous saliva poisonous enough to kill the button pushers who are no longer Human, going on and on forever like Infinity, yeah, in the Clouds of Reason, We shall now return to the scene where Pedro sits in the bus, his bow and arrows strapped over his Heart like the Emblem of Valor bestowed only to the best soldiers of the tribe, it mattered not that he had the sharpest and heaviest sickle shaped stainless triple steel hair splitting machete so lethal, it cuts off heads like butter so the wielder doesn't feel the weight at all, swinging like a fast cyclone with lots of dust clouds so You cannot see him at all though if You guessed It's Not True, Miss Kim Sun Song, I will say, You are absolutely right, and if You say so many and so many servants will come to massage Your shoulders until their hands sored and their backs ached, and the best chefs in the world to cook Your personal favorite cuisine when You stumble upon the secret song without a single Dislike so You say to Yourself what a great triumph of the human spirit when that kind old man ask for the time and somebody told him 10:33 and he humbly thanked the sleepy old widow wearing the black hat with a double branched rose of pink, and You think to Yourself, my, what nice pink nipples for a woman of such unimaginable subtle movement of cheetah circling around her prey in the scrubs forming a circle so magnetic that many a young light-headed happy little lamb has come into the maze, lost and so scared for his or her life, it doesn't matter, it's up to You, and You hear him mumbling over and over again, the same time, 10:33, 10:33, 10:33, 10:33, and on and on, and You notice, he's done that for a few minutes so it' quite clear he's gone nuts, right, and he proves You right by asking for the time again but unlike the first time, Nobody cared because they are seeing what You are seeing, O Well Done, Mr. Turnpike, it's not Your turn yet but what the Time what what he asked until his throat dried up and he couldn't ask anymore but still Nobody cared while a Korean girl sitting in front of him, North or South, I don't know, jumped up and quickly slipped into another seat far enough to be safe for God's sake and so on, I ask You, will You not give a few common Dislikes to such a man but You have now traced the caricature of one limpid pimpid gambit lambit sparrow and You predicted how that fox tricked that gullible goat into jumping into a well together with a predator, the Old Guy pulled the buzzer to signify that he's not so crazy anymore, sauntering into the alley, disappearing into the gutters and shit holes of the city to find a Tiny Tooth of Hope and he goes through the pockets of the dead hobos mutilated by famished rats and rodents, yeah, it's purely something You can't understand type of jangle mangle wrangle jingle tingle fingle dingle single wriggle piggle ziggle friggle O Hello, Mr. Pringle, love those chips, and yeah, You owe me a few Dislikes don't You? For You are rushing out of Mt. Rushmore, the slow flight of springs coming out of their eyes, yeah, it would be so American Indian Pow Wow I tell You it's such a scam how they charge so much for electricity now that many people have gone days without food just because they cannot pay their electric bills and they keep complaining that the country is not good to them and that the country is getting infested by Immigrants and all that type of problems being especially prominent because it's Election Year and every Tom, Dickens and Maggie who believes that any one of these two fools are going to lead them out of the shit hole, just ask the other two former fools, and the one who got shot in the head because he was handsome and loves Opera... Maro Sathi, please don't reveal this secret, and solemnly put Your Hand on Your Heart and Swear Your Allegiance to the Brotherhood and Sisterhood of All Living Things, Swear it to the Ends of Your Days, and even if Your Parent or Teacher or Boss or Partner or Spouse or Anybody tells You that Swearing is not good and all those passengers who don't know what's the time anymore, Patience, he's here too, melded into Fortitude, now, the most basic factor in nation building is Labor.

It's not to say that Minneapolis didn't try. Indeed, it tried very hard, the whole city, tried very hard to try to join the group of other less glamorous cities in the world like Hokkaido, Busan, Surabaya, Nakhorn Ratchasima, Brussels, Florence, Glasgow, Hong Kong, Sevilla, Nice, Lisbon, and some other ones like Bombay, Guangzhou, Dortmund, Qatar, Mata Kuching, and the like, You know, second-tier cities which are quite close to the bigger cities in terms of GDP and in some cases, Minnesota may even be richer than Ceylon but the people there are adamant to protect their land and if need acquire that other semblance to the Will of the Mayor against the Will of the People and it's just a Battle to Decide Who's the Victor and Who's the Victor and didn't we know that Victor was always Victoria right from the Start so it's not so Obvious in that more modern film called the *Crying Game* which was such a legendary and mind bending type of film to confound the viewer who didn't know that She was a He somewhere in the film but that Actor or Actress for it's hard to come up with a better term to describe these type of Human Being because if I'm Earnest about it, I would have chosen that I may not be allowed to view such a film other than one or two of those Monty Python films where their Wit is without Harm and Any Sort of Sinister Intention, at least We have established the Fact that All Man and Human Kind is Crazy if they have even Come Thus Far as to Pretend that I have concocted a Word to describe such a Specimen of Humankind as the Term the Lot of You who had been paying a Trauma of Attention would have known all along, yeah, You may even say Right from the Beginning even before the Actor or the Actress would even appear, You have known all along that the Heroine would die before the Hero but it should be either of the Word but the Word You Come Up with is Just the Exact Word that I have been thinking of in terms of the Muslim Brothers in the City who Mute their Way through Life and What the Hell kind of New Music so May I kindly say the Word is Actoress Just because the Other Word is More Challenging and I'm Lazy but for those More Imaginative Ones, You are also Right for We don't Wish the Least Harm to Anyone at all and We Pray, You will be Doing Nothing but Reading this Page like IT'S THE FUCKING FINAL FUCKING MOMENT when it all goes to Dust and even if They Blast the Whole Subway System at One Go with the Velvet Dragon or Violet Dragon, I Forget, and It's such a great feeling to Forget that I Urge You with All Earnestness to Try it At Least a Hundred Times in Your Life so You Understand Why the Wheels are at the Ceiling and not the Basement which is a Great Place for the Nazis to build their Terminals and Portals where they Return to the Underworld just as their Eastern Brother Japan is Rising and Rising until the Time Came for the Inventor of the Walkman to Wrest Control of the Media from the Jews kind of Propaganda talk Office People always like to talk about Asses of Women and It's Nothing to Feel Bad about being talked about in those days when Feminism wasn't Invented yet and Women were Slaves in their Own Alabama Homes so it's Pointless and Impolite to call into Scene One Act Three, the Following Dialogue by the Most Elongated Neck Giraffe Woman of the Far East with Mammoth Teeth Protruding Out of Her Nose and Natural Panda Hair at the back of Her Neck and her Shadow of a Husband who is always Drunk or Asleep and She's talking to the Sister in Law behind his Back and Without Thinking too much about How It All came to Be that Rocky would go the Distance with the Champ without getting Killed in the Ring as it would most likely be the Outcome today if the Champ of the Lousiest Division would have Pointed at me and offered to a Title Fight with His left Hand Tied to His Right Ankle so He had to Hop Around Blindfolded and also Gagged so He couldn't Chew on my hair even if I have Any left, I wouldn't have taken the Challenge for it never occurred to me that I could ever become the Champion of the Whole Fucking Universe for Anything, No, No, It's never about It, right, We must always agree when we want to do Business with Mr. Pat Morita who would have Broken his back with just One Blow on the Neck so quickly, He didn't even think of Pulling His Gun when the Plump fingers poked into the eyeballs so elastic so the finger nails were Imprinted in the Black Hole so You Imagine…

Red: Why? Is Ring too Tight?

Warm Boots: It's… Pushing… Against… My… Jawbone…

Warm Boots: I… Can't… Talk…

Warm Boots: He… is… Here…

Warm Boots: Run… Run…

Red:

Warm Boots: Please…

Red:

Warm Boots: The… Flower… Cloud…

Warm Boots: Fire! Fire! Fire!

Red:

Warm Boots: I… Can't… See…

Warm Boots: Twenty First… Fifteen… Thirty… Twenty Three… Nineteen…

Warm Boots: Steer… to… the… Right…

Red: It's Done! I have Cut Out the Seven Year-Old One Ring Your Mother gave to My Mother as a Token of Our Marriage so I have to Keep this Piece…

Warm Boots:

In a place like Plymouth, there's such Sorrow and more relaxing pace so there's less chance that You may be trampled or crushed to death by the mobs of frantic rushing people always walking at full speed like their lives depended on it and Yeah, You have Never seen a more pissed person than that Indian Girl who would Sprinkle some Incense Ash in Your Nose Kind of Action like it's even Legal to do such a Thing as to buy a Missile to just keep it in the Arsenal or Museum All the Time so You have No Intension to Use It even when Rainy Days become more Popular and there's no need to ask about the Pastures or the Ice Fishing just simply because it's becoming more Heart Breaking by the Day, and there's a Bitterness in the Air even when the Team is Winning, You are Winning, You Think, You Cheer, You Raise Your Hands like a Victor but Deep Down Inside, You Feel All Positive that You will Win THIS TIME and YES! That's the Singular Most Positive Thing to Focus On when You find Yourself in the lane for old folks, some of the young people are spitting on You while You are trying to catch up to the Culprits, a good Samaritan comes along and arrests the culprits, bringing them to their knees and bowing down at Your Feet in most humble Lotus Pose, You bless them and they transform into butterflies, how great is that Song, How Great Thou Art, and it's with this particular Scheme in Mind, the Museum of Art of Minneapolis or the Minneapolis Museum of Art, You may forget, especially if You have been to the museums in First Class Cities, it's true, they are trying very hard to expand their collection for it's true, a museum is not worth anything if they don't have a few of the Masters and yeah, it's quite a surprise that this free museum in the Midwest holds a Rembrandt which is the first one I had ever seen for I somehow made the mistake of my life by not visiting the Amsterdam Museum when I had the chance to enjoy the great collection of Rembrandts for he's the Greatest of them all, the Master of Masters, and so it's worth the time to just drop by to see that piece but it's true, the State never rests to bring in more precious artworks, please be prepared to spend at least four hours because it's quite a massive building but poorly attended so the Museum is not making any Revenue, still, they have a vast Collection, and I was walking around, looking at the artworks in the People's Museum, benefitting greatly from the Paul G. Allen Family now Restructuring due to the death of an important member at the top of the hierarchy, there's the usual infighting, scrambling, and plotting as is the case in families of great wealth so the Guards told the Couple from Nebraska, No Madam No Sir You Are Not Allowed to Take a Picture Here as they were Whispering about Fate of the Collection Possibly being Auctioned Off at Astronomical Numbers too Bewildering to be True Except for Those who Believe It to be True, Let's Not Be Deceived, Let's Not Be Louder... but You Could Hear It... they were still listening to the Doves Cry...

The Opium is Sweet

Crow Bar Blues

Can You Hear It Loud Enough?

Cherry Footsteps on Top of Your Head

My Princess, I must Lie to You Again

It's Nothing like What You Ever Imagined

Did You See the Pictures on the Wall?

Yeah, I Waited fpr the Horse along the River

Hiding from the Buffalo Kid and His Sidekick

Licking the Walls is Highly Prohibited

My Darling... Your Skin is Alabaster Cow and Skin Lint Mistletoe

Parry, Parry the Green Fairy

Your Hair Afro One Desire I Know

"How is it All Going to End?"

"Betray Your Killer Clown Fear Syndrome!!"

"THOU SHALL NOT LOVE!"

"It's not the time of the day to talk about the Stars or the Universe. It's time to crack the Dinosaur Eggs. Watch His Heart Bleeding in His Hand Left Hand and Still Beating..."

"Was He Smoking in the Snow??"

"No… He was a Little Sad to know that He had to Perform so Many Miracles to Prove He's the Son of God and if He didn't have all those Powers, He asked Himself… Will they still Believe in Him??? What about Christmas? What's He gonna do this Year which is going to be so much more Spectacular than the Previous Year?"

"Is it the Time to Reverse the Car into the Well?"

"Phyllis… I Love You More than Naomi…"

"…. Sing… Sing… Sing…"

"Take a Walk on the Hot Coal Bridge to Lake of Destitution."

"Why do You bring Children into this World to Suffer??"

"Suffer not the Roses! Suffer not the Boats!"

"Why not Sterilize All, Females and Males. Then… It will End."

"You have No Rights! You have No Rights!"

"Stop! Stop! Go to the Emergency Lane… I need to Peeeee!!"

"Take Aim… Can You Hit the Crow's Eye?"

"Goood… now bounce the ball a few times to loosen up the muscles…"

"Shall I go to the Witch today or the next day?"

"Once upon a time, there was a Merchant with Three Most Enchanting Daughters in St. Paul which is the Twin of the other more Cosmopolitan City. They are triplets and they are truly amazing because they are conjoined…"

"Daddy… I want to watch Miss Booksy!"

"O Miss Boobsy… alright…"

In the Japanese silk ink painting of the Bulbul Singing to Three Water Fowls Across Two Panels, only one of the water fowls was attentive with great gratitude and acknowledgement while the other two water fowls were busy doing their own thing, one of them trying to lay some eggs at the water's edge which is not a very clever thing to do but it may also be that the mother water fowl is trying to be serene like the body of water, still and deep so she can lay the eggs or she may even be sitting on her nest, patiently waiting for the eggs to hatch so she can nurse another batch of water fowls to lay eggs and hatch another batch of water fowls, and in such cycles, their species can continue while the final of the Three Water Fowls was snaking its neck looking at a pebble shaped object to the right of the foot of that first Water Fowl trying to join the Bulbul at the other side but somehow they are separated by some missing piece in the center... believed to be... Lord Buddha who trapped the Monkey King under the Mountain of Five Fingers, and it's True, he stayed under that mountain for five hundred revolutions of the Earth around the Sun before he was released by his Master, yeah, the same guy who punished him physically, morally, and spiritually but he's such a faithful follower, he accompanied him all the way to the West, gaining the Mantra for All Souls... so all souls can go to Paradise... so all Sufferings will be Banished... Forever

III PILLARS

The Gypsy Prince, tracing the whirlwinds of the devious Medusa, he's sure he will get her this time after all the thousands of time she had eluded him, again and again, he sucked on the three stones in his mouth, thinking about sucking his maidens' breasts for he's a big sucker for breasts in whatever shape or form, hanging pendulum ones, melon green veined ones, ready-made tofu ones, all natural ones, those are the best, why, why spend so many Dislikes on boob jobs when it inhibits breastfeeding, he thinks, Medusa's Milk is the antidote to save his daughter's life after she was bitten by Pink Python and though she was saved before she was crushed to death and it wasn't a poisonous bite at all, she began to lose weight drastically and she's having some fever or another every few days, it's time to check her Red Moon panties for You suspect she may be pregnant but in this case, Little Miss Nefertiti's a Virgin so how can she be pregnant, they say it's Impossible so he's moving around the Land in acclaimed chess moves, he saw how the trail is a straight line like how Medusa like to slide at the tip of her tail kind of stunt for only she can do it and there's nothing to be done if she wants to show off, yeah, his Third Eye is shining a long beacon of light Invisible to the whole world but only visible to him so after he has mastered this Underwear skill which allowed him to see through rocks and minerals to find the freshest Springs, he has developed his sense of smell to such an Anglo-Saxon level, he can smell her even when the whole world cannot smell her whisper, yeah, he can hear her heart beating in fear even when she's so ferocious that the snakes are hissing with venom spraying everywhere, Yeah, splashing on the audience and O How Great Thou Art O How Great Thou Art they keep repeating the chorus until God became much more real than Just Now, he can sense her even when she disintegrated into molecules, odorless, soundless, tasteless, and senseless, yeah, he will get her this time, for sure, sure, sometimes we retreat but when You are burdened by a Starving Mermaid in Your Backpack and Her Pious Pinball Younger Sister in the other suitcase and a Blind Snoring Beauty in the smallest bag, You know, WELCOME TO DENVER, HOME OF THE WORLD CHAMPIONS, and You go BLINK BLINK what's happening, the WORLD CHAMPIONS ARE GERMANY, right, O then You understand that they are talking about FOOTBALL and which sport uses the foot more than the other, sure, they use their feet to run a lot, it's the Denver Broncos beating the Patriots so the City and State will be Ecstatic for one full year as FOOTBALL related merchandise rise in great demand as them homebodies boast about their Broncos this and Broncos that for what they like to call bragging rights like they have the right to brag about how they have the Rocky Mountains and the Nuggets and Rockies and Avalanche and *Nothing without Providence* and only so much matinee You can endure on a Saturday afternoon when You fully want to enjoy it by Yourself in the Cave but then it's also time to do Your laundry and bring the dog to the park for a walk or it's time to bring the infant for another round of injections to make him or her cry like a poor poor baby when the steel pierces into the Flesh, You feel it Piercing Yourself too, don't You, you can feel the screech in your heart as if the Train is Put at STOP just as it's reaching full speed and there's no secret that it's a SLOW TRAIN that E Train or how he likes to use his fork to scratch on the plate even when the Pet is running outdoors when he gets within twenty feet of the Flower, it will Die, not just wither or fall off but Die right in Front of Everybody Else just because the Whites are Bad in Math, it doesn't mean It's the End of the World or Something Else that the Child wanted to Jazz up the Joint when it's still Impossible to ever Imagine a Peaceful World when the Russians are Judoing the Chinese into the Sin Bin for not Declaring their Undying Need to Populate the Earth in the Sense too Pornographic for the Pastor's Wife but not His Wishes to Plagiarize the Elegance of Doctor Zhivago just like when he's just standing there and looking at the Sky with flakes of white dew floating into his nostrils and he's breathing in that crystal crisp air of the Cold Winter Mountain, yeah, it's PRETTY unimaginable how some parents can treat their children worse than how some people treat their pets, especially in families with drunkards for sure, it's where all the problems of the world arise, ALCOHOL ABUSE, it's LEGAL in most countries and it's so Crazy that You can Chuckle Your seventeen Dislikes Away but Nobody's gonna care about what You say even when You are telling the Truth, they really don't care if You are carrying so many stones that You are struggling to walk up a steep, steep slope after a period of long inactivity, it's normal to be slowed down by the elements and it's with great gusto and determination that You arrived at the Inn at the Top of the Hill, panting and moaning, miles away from Downtown but You have chosen it because of the Discount for Your Dislikes are offered at a Greater Discount even when You walked faster than You can Imagine it's so hard to walk in the high land sun, sweating like You are drenched in Forced Labor, You tried to stop to take a smoke to think things through but there's no such Luxury for Everywhere You See, there's not even a shady tree that You can take respite in, there's not a bench that You can sit on, resting those feet was of utmost importance for You couldn't even feel them anymore, Your soles burned by the steaming tarmac, a little surprised that You are not Sinking but Floating, You Sweat, You Swear, You will not Forget because Your Lungs are Clear and when You arrive at the Drinking Hole, You drank Your share of the freshest water You can find anywhere else from the tap, the Sweet, Sweet Waters of Colorado, and at the very least, the Inn is very well situated with food joints of almost every kind to sour Your taste buds or yearnings, they are dumbfounded that Your feet are so evaporating and big, they call You Yeti for Your hair have turned all white and long, overflowing to the ground like a waterfall, the waters tumbling down on Your Head like a Crash of Liquid Rocks from the Heavens, You Imagine, how peaceful it is, how You found that Hispanic Broad smiling at You like she's not wearing any panties and beaming a simple message which says she wants You to eat her honey bud, casting her gaze down at the apron she wears to hide her gems and nothing else, You can see it's how Chico could play music with her feet, and the audience cheered rapturously, and how after a while, the Kings are clapping their hands to join her, and how at the end, they gave her a standing ovation, shouting her name in complete Euphoria, louder and louder until some of them fainted and reaching a crescendo, they faded in syncopation until it's past midnight and they all went Home, happier than Yesterday.

After leaving the China Doll, he became a Sailor, going from port to port, Pedro had at last caught up with her who he had been tracking for a few hundred years and now, at last, he could see her in his Mirror of Rainbow, she has cleverly disguised herself as Josephine, Napoleon's first wife, the object of his mountain of love letters, the Empress Consort of the French and the Queen Consort of Italy, for a few years before she was divorced and it's also well-known that she was the Supreme Patroness of Roses for she loved them so much so she tried to collect all the roses in the world in her lavish Chateau de Malmaison which was destroyed some years later, vandalized and rampaged, and her Dream was gone though she was dead by then and the people in charge of the chateau acknowledged that they were facing a great defeat but there's Nothing they could do because they were but gardeners, bakers, house keepers, cooks, and rose lovers working together in a simple setup to keep the place spick and span, of course, they were never going to sacrifice their lives for a few flowers and so what if their blood is splashed all over the gardens? Will the Roses Bloom Richer? Will the Fragrance Swirl Sweeter? Will the Barbarians STOP? Sure, they didn't know that Josephine never left at all and she was there when the Sick Punk Perverted Ruffians uprooted her most beloved roses and they laughed and laughed like it's the goddamn funniest joke in the world to destroy Beauty and that's what the World is becoming… more and more violent, hostile, insensible, and inhumane, yeah, they start by washing their tongues with the cheapest milk and honey, promising Immortality when they were very young, they were given chemicals which were sufficient in dosage to suppress emotions and increase cold bloodedness so if the command is ever given that they have to kill their own parents or BFF or the cutest, trembling, crying little girl, they will rape her first and then kill her because it's unHitlerkind teachings to perform such a cruel thing as to kill an innocent Virgin, subsequently, they wouldn't complain about this one for these stone headed stone hearted hardened blood hounds, somehow, they know whether a girl is a virgin or not, and it's the worst torture and most vulgar a ransack when they bite off her flesh and licked her bones dry and pounded her skull with the butt of their rifles after violating her in acts too blasphemous, yeah, it shouldn't be reported if there are more than nineteen or more in attendance so it's better they are Zombies they should be punished, those tough macho numb witted Barbaric Man of Nature with Nothing much left but a few kernels of corn, it's a Great Idea to Join the Masses even when they themselves were like those cheated numb dumb mump lump glump rump grump mentor of the Devil ass martyrs, they should suffer as much or more so the Warriors were told to use their Might and Force and Advantage to Trod on the Weak and so maybe they should be Punished and not Rewarded simply because they are Cowards and though they should not have been born at all and all that rhetoric about whether a Mother must Dig under the Tree to Find Special Deals about Putinism and what it stands for in the Great World Order of the Now, POW, GLOW, what's there Anything to do about it when they are becoming Pop Stars and Celebrities for What have the World Become to Celebrate Mindlessness in All Shapes and Forms for the

TRUE GOD who is more Magnificent than The Carpenter's Son, The Lost Prince, The Widow's Toy Boy who always tells his Henchmen all about her barren garden but He would then be Amused to say how it's so Strange she sounded so much like honey… her milk tasted even Sweeter the Kind of Sweet to make Your Toes Pointed to the Orion's Belt though it's Impossible for her to produce food, she produced it for him and him alone for He's possibly the best sucker in the History of Nursing, the Pressure was Numbing and Suctioned to the Marrow so it's with such Talent and Skills that he was able to taste her Blood and Regulate the Pumping of her Heart until the Day when She murmured How She Couldn't Take It Anymore that She Breathed Her Last and What a Joyous Death It Was Surely the Supreme Death for Every Man and Woman, it's to Die at the Most Perfect Time in the Most Perfect Place and there's this Man who's making these people's wishes come true by Offering his special services to help people travel to their Final Destination in their Dreamy manner when they are asked to discuss the Big Bang, they will say it's Jim Henson who's Supposed to be Immortal and I Suggest, Millions of Children, Young or Old, they will at least agree that Kermit is a Damn good singer and the way that video was shot was supremely Stylish and meaningful so it's perhaps quite Ironic that he died on Wood, Nailed with Iron, Bleeding until there's not even one drop left for the Little Boy who lived Down the Lane and Have You Thought about that Little Boy and What he was going to do with all that Black Wool in His Hand, he Gambled on the Underdog All the Way and at the end of it all, why? Why not let them giggle until they weep, clearly, this time, there will be no stone unturned if they put their weapons down and repent for their sins, yeah, only the Lord of Lords can Salvage their Souls but it's Some

There she appears, out of the blue or white or red, out of the ashes, she rises like a Phoenix, a mythical bird that only appears in books with pictures so You can picture such a beautiful and transcendental creature because all praise is inadequate to describe it, and You can talk about the colors and You can talk about the exact moment when the ash spirals and slowly clears to unveil that most rare of all birds, now, most people just think that it's a Myth for they disbelieve it so much so that they will know it's a Phoenix if they ever saw one in the sky and they will say to themselves, well, that's a Phoenix for sure, and they will probably say the same thing when they see a Dragon, and so on, in the shadow of the Lavender, so what, so what, you hear her say ow ow wow wow if You thought that Davis was Great in *Shades of Spain*, then, he might be greater in *Bye Bye Blackbird* for he was shadowing Coltrane, it still can't be better than the first Song on his bee the bopping best of all time, solemnly exhibiting his versatility in most deep and impromptu manner, it's Something to take a Whole Life Time of Bull Shitting to Master, I Beg Your Pardon, O Delilah, Be Merciful, O You Mean, Oversentimental and Lazurus, O What did the Blue Cat say to the Red Bull?

"Moon: The Red Sea is Parting Again"

"Wait! There's a Lady with Long Hair on the Ceiling…"

That's when You Reflected, the waters on Your face aren't cold, they are bitter like Medicine, and You know how everybody hates those formulas with a thousand million chemicals We don't care to know about all that science please! We are Civilized Here, You Know, We Love Music, We Love Comedy, We Love Strategy, We Love Mystery, We Love Love, We Love Suspense, We Love Surprises… in the Blue Corner, We have the Woman Behind the Most Powerful Man on Planet Hollywood, and she's covering her tracks, knowing full well that the wolves are coming nearer, dabbling in the dark arts, yeah, can she be trusted to fly the plane carrying a few hundred million souls to endure four more years of despair Only! O my fifty fucking stars and all the red and white stripes representing all the Ideals of Our Forefathers, I ask You, every one of You who lied that You are Believers in God, Kings, Presidents, Gods, Heads of States, Heads of Organizations, Heads of Companies, Small or Big, in fact, every fucking body who has ever breathed a molecule of this Air which is My Air as it is Your Air and Everybody's Air, I Vilify You, STOP, just STOP acting like You Understand Everything and Everybody like he is their long lost brother, son, husband, father, priest, teacher, brick layer, kitchen second staff specializing in chopping all sorts of vegetables and meats, faster than a few seconds, You can shred all evidences of Your Hypocrisy and reusable energy scam You so full know it is not what it takes to Save the Nation but You keep Extolling the Importance of Education but Education for What? To make more mannequins and Scarecrows? Shall We makes them out of Horse Glue and when You Really Think about How It's Made, Made in Cambodia, Made in the Bronze Age, yeah, We believe… You are going to Walk on Water and Fall Down on Your heels One Day just because You are not Black Enough, You with Your Crocodile Skin Hats and all Your Plump Pearls, You better consume them one by one and shit them in a hurry to cleanse Your bowels and Your Husband's and the Blue Cat's for You very well knew what he did to her but why not, why not Keep Your Mouth Shut and Stand by Me, You know what he's like when it comes to all the lies You tell for him will not be enough to save Yourself because You Know, and if You Still don't Know, the Hand pulls the Strings so You can't be blamed for You had no choice when they told You they were going to take Him away, You Know, You have to do everything to save his ass even when You sacrificed Your Chastity to that crooked teeth bastard guy who spit on Your butt while he farted and fed the cat pinto beans and lemon sulfur, You know, it's going to be so good so good so good You can say it a few hundred times until Your teeth are Eroded, and unlike Peggie or Stella or Countess Van Yellow or Princess Mean Hat or Miss Teen Sunshine or Naughty Jane, she just swallowed it just because she had swallowed everything from staples to pins to gun pellets to bullets to golden butterflies to silver bullets to mean winds, she exclaimed, she can captain this Big Ship to the New World and You Believe It?????? Nothing makes sense anymore. Who cares about the National Anthem? Star Spangled Banner? This is the funny part… just for a few lousy Dislikes… the part they left out is… actually… the most Patriotic part about what it means to be an American and with permission from the National Library of Congress, I borrow these lines for the education of the generations, Past, Present and Future…

It's been quite a few hours but The Door was still shut so he's wondering if he should knock on the door one more time or maybe a few more times just in case she's forgotten all about him. As he was standing there with nothing much to do, he's feeling how slowly time is passing and when You are a reckless young boy, it's just about the worst torture of all to be left waiting at the same spot for such a long time, he was thinking about how he's going to break the news to Blue Moon for he has not seen her for almost six years or more so he's not so sure if they could remember each other anymore.

Looking at the door, he could see quite a number of scratches and blemishes on the Teak, all the same, it appeared so solid that You can be sure that if You ran at it at full speed from some distance away, You will be convinced it's Perfect in Appearance, and all the same if You are Daredevil enough to Crash into it without looking away, You will break more than a few bones, for sure. Overall, it's a pretty remarkable door, a little slanting and light of material and he's trying the lock to see if he's lucky or what when he started to pay more attention to the mermaid brass door knocker which he had used to knock on the door just a while ago but for some Reason, he didn't look at it quite so closely at all so The Poet sang…

And Where is that Band who so Vauntingly Swore,
That the Havoc of War and the Battle's Confusion
A Home and a Country should Leave Us No More?
Their Blood Has Wash'd Out Their Foul Footstep's Pollution.
No Refuge Could Save the Hireling and Slave
From the Terror of Flight and the Gloom of the Grave,
And the Star-Spangled Banner in Triumph doth Wave
O'er the Land of the Free and Home of the Brave.

O Thus be it Ever When Freemen Shall Stand
Between their Lov'd Home and the War's Desolation!

Blest with Vict'ry and Peace may the Heav'n Rescued Land
Praise the Power that Hath made and Preserv'd us a Nation,
Then Conquer We Must, When Our Cause It is Just,
And This be our Motto – "In God We Trust,"
And the Star-Spangled Banner in Triumph Doth Wave
O'er the Land of the Free and Home of the Brave.

Isn't it foolish for the policy makers to overlook the importance of the full National Anthem which must be sung in its entirety from now onwards, and You will see how the races, cultures, religions, and everything will come together and I pray even the Bloody Military Stone Age Murderer will come to their senses and be a loving father to his children and fertilize the soil with Love and Peace for loving is always easier than hating and Darkness is something that people enjoy more than Warmth. Right? Will You imagine living in a world of perpetual darkness? How does it Feel? Do You Like It? Are You Blind? Good! I have always wanted to write to you guys… Can You See the Light in the Drips of Dislikes? HA! HA! HAPPY INDEPENDENCE DAY!!!

After Resting for a few minutes, it's Time to go out to explore Downtown which is quite a long distance away and too crowded what with the councils trying to pool resources by organizing the International Cosplay Convention where You have the opportunity to bump into an Assortment of fictional character wannabes walking around like they really belong to the World on that One Day when they can be anything they aspire so there are Snow White, SpongeBob, Jack Sparrow, Yoda, Mutant Turtles, Batgirl, Sexy Girl, Spock, Witches, Ms. Piggy, Barney, Big Bird, Patrick, Mr. Bean, Lone Ranger, Princess Mononoke, the Sand Man,

Moon Loving Poet, they are all there, BB8, Chaplin, Sleeping Beauty, Monroe, Witch of the East, Elvis, Princess Jasmine, Omar Shariff, Peter Pan, they are all there, and then, in the middle of the city, they have Pride Week which is the Time when the LGBT community comes out of their closets one more time to shout out loud their great joy and euphoria knowing full well that on this day, that day, they are shaking up the Establishment and for This Day, they are the icons of the Nation and on that day, for those few hours, they are on equal footing with MLK Jr or Roosevelt or Bishop Tutu or Pistol Pete or Ben E. King or Robert Johnson or Peggy Sue or Mindy or Nero or who else was there or here in my own beautiful and safest country in the world, they Imprison and Mutilate gays and lesbians and freedom fighters and blue collar workers who are the Immigrants must Socially Abused like Nowhere Else in the World but Nobody is Saying anything about it because their Religion is so Pure, It Allows the Wicked to Prosper and the Honest to Suffer so What Else should the Police be Preying on the Public along with the Crooked Politicians Sucking the nation Dry and All they ever Wanted to Do was to go to a Big Party to Sing and Dance and Wear red or Yellow Shirts just because they are Afraid to be Accidentally killed on the Highway in the Middle of the Night, and Blasting Poor Mongolian Babes to Pieces in Secret Orgy of the Highest Order, and the People, they are a Mass of Pussies but here, the Man is taking off his pants and preparing to do his Chicken Run around the Compound with Miss Venice 1996 who surprisingly possesses a superbly toned tight body with rock heavy elongated breasts drooping close to the belly button so when she swings around, the breasts will swing too and when she spins around on her heels, the breasts will rise as centrifugal force increases, spinning in a circle and it's at this time You will be too Stunned to Measure how long her breasts are circling and circling for You almost Red Handed when she rubs that Dead Sea Solution on Your cheeks and at the same time, Speaking to You in a Hushed Pitch so only You and You alone can hear her Sexy Private Belly Button Distracting You to part with a few more of Your Dislikes so You Try so Hard to hold on to them, and sadly, You had to reject her high handed sales talents though You are Completely Bewitched she's one Heaven of a Sensual Bombshell and a Man of lesser Will Power will have been smitten by her Soft charms and You see the boys she has around her, yeah, she's the Bambino so it's so transparent to spy through her white blouse and white bra that her nipples were longer than three quarters put side by side, each one about three inches when erected but before it becomes hard, it's probably only about one quarter length but what's there to be done when a Monk has to abstain from Carnal pleasures and achievements, it's that time of the day to put on the Cloak of Invisibility and Circle the outskirts of the city looking for the well-reviewed Recreational Store to stock up on supplies because two moons can be pretty long but when You listen to Wieslawa Dudkowiak putting on a one woman show with her super high Akordeon accompanied by a music machine and the globe of 70s style disco lights, she's got it good, the way she shrinks her neck when You ask what's the most potent strain and she says it's up to You so You started Acting like a Seasoned Pot Head, smelling a few jars of marijuana like a Seasoned hardcore connoisseur, You try Your best to Figure Out Which is Which for the Leaves of Green emit somewhat similar sharp odors so it's quite difficult to tell Which is… Which is…

"Do You want to Stay High or Go Down?"

"What's the Difference?"

"High makes You Awake and Down makes You Sleep..."

"High... Please..."

Before continuing, I would like to tell You about this guy I met at the Bus Stop in suburban Denver. He's a little different from the nameless nigger in the bus in NYC in that he's talking to himself all the time and pacing up and down the street like he's contemplating to jump into a car or a bus for that matter because The World doesn't matter to him anymore until an old Hispanic chap hopped off his bicycle and instructed me to look after his bicycle like anybody would consider taking off in such an old fashioned and battered old style model like those You sometimes see in The Curiosity Shop, yeah, the one with One Bigger Wheel at the Front and a Smaller Wheel at the Back and the Seat is like a regular Bicycle seat made with Maplewood, yeah and even the Wheels are Wooden, he said he had to take some water so he went to the ATM and withdrew some Dislikes and as he was passing that other dude who's already gone to his own world, greeting him in their own homely language, he doesn't return the goodwill but continued in his mumblings, only audible to himself, and after a few more minutes, he crossed the road without any trouble and disappeared into the lane where he couldn't see anything anymore but only guided by his ears and nose, he slipped over to the Other Side where Everybody can understand him and they give him a Royal Robe fit for a king or duke or somebody important like that Massage Queen greeting him with her most Pacific Ocean voice and leading him to the Sofa of Great Comfort where she undressed him and held him to her bosom and he hungrily fed on them while the Queen stroked his hair like he was the most precious kitten in the whole history of the world and then he felt the tongues of a dozen hundred dozen virgins licking him everywhere, covering every inch of his broken and tired body, even the insides of his ears right up to the Forbidden zone, it's the spot to drive a man to his knees, he's then happier than an emperor or king or prime minister or Totoro jumping on his stomach to push out all the Wind Accumulating in his body all the years of his life and now, they are causing him to Suffer Tremendous Pain in his Brain, hearing the Voice of Che Guevara, the Ever Revolutionary Hero, a Symbol of Communism, he shook his hand and patted his back before handing a Red Packet to the Queen who whispered something into his ear before working on the poor old guy and to live to enjoy such Equilibrium at the very moment her fingers pressed into his veins, he fell asleep like a young old lamb under the Blue Berry Bush.

"Do You like this? And this? And this? Wait…"

"What's that One with the Pink Sticker?"

"O… that's Lavender…"

"You want it?"

"Yeah… give me half of that and half of the Dragon…"

"Is this right?"

"That's too much! I mean half of that…"

"Alright… alright…"

"Good choice! There You go! It will be Ninety Hats… please…"

"Thank You! Come Again! Hope to see You around…"

"Yeah…"

Somehow, that chick reminded me of my trip to Amsterdam a few moons ago when I first felt like a Free Man, smoking a joint in the square while some bassist was playing some bad phrases from some Bach piece of something, the Coffee Shop is quite different from the Joint in Denver in that it's darker and more seedy with some tables with Smoking apparatus so You can Smoke it Right there if You can wait for the Awesome Babe who sold me some Purple Haze and it was a Fantastic Experience because I Love to Smoke but in the Past, I had to Hide, Fearing Arrests and Hanging for in my Country, it's perfectly acceptable for Ministers to Pillage the Coffers and Commit Sacrilege Against his Allah and Country but it's absolutely unacceptable to carry just a little Black Dog Penis in his Ass all the Time playing Golf with Dirty Old men who talked about Pussies all the Time like They know which Pussy is their Favorite and it's always about this Model or that Miss World but if You ask them to Describe It, They Find it hard to Resist his Offers of Wealth so he's Definitely Everybody's Favorite Bandit who has such a Strong Hold on the Nation so much so that the Citizens are all being Strangled and Bloodied by his Wife's Greed to be Not Just the First Lady of the Nation but After she Discovered that she could get away with it and the More she told him to Steal from the Masses, strangely, the More they Adore him for Where they are all Brought Up under his Father's Spell so Now she set her Sight on becoming First lady of the World and Some May Laugh but he and she is on their way to become the Richest Couple in History for their Total Betrayal of the People who are too Pussy to do Anything about it so it's such a great Blessing to be in those places where You think Nothing about Smoking under the Naked Delilah for the Blind Samson must have felt the Fool of All Fools spearing ten spokes through his toes at the exact middle of the bottom part of the Nail, Anchoring him to the ground with such Precision so he didn't even have the Time to Digest What's Happening to Godot and it's taking more than enough time left for bomb to be Extinguished and I Pray for Just One Time, Bond will Fail for Just Once and Suffer the Consequences of his Womanizing and Seduction of All Muslim Women who would be the Perfect Spies for a Man like That who's always flying First Class and Staying in the Most Splendorous Hotels and Most Dangerous Missions, yeah, They put You in Prison for No Reason at All and at the End of It, they have the Right to Throw Prisoners from Buildings or Fake that they are Surfing the Subway and Notwithstanding the Sentiments of Thirty Million Weaklings who Don't Dare to Put him and his wife on Trial, why, when even Presidents and Rich Businessman are Enjoying the Blossoms of His Crimes, Why, don't they become Criminals too (?) but the Strangest of All, the People in the Tunnels, they want to read newspapers for it's All True, it's the First time I felt Absolute Liberation to be able to do what I like without being Arrested or Killed though It had come at a Time when I'm Past my Prime, it's still Most Uplifting for It's My Freedom as an Artist and Rights as a Human to feel Safe with this Asylum because Everybody knows what they do to prisoners in the prisons and it's absolutely absurd that anybody should be Prosecuted for Smoking Pipe of Peace which is really Harmless, You see, it's for this Reason that this Dream can only be Hatched in Wonderful Colorado where You have the Right to be Stoned and It's such a Grand right that there are now more than Eight States that are

Following Suit and It's just Simple English to say Alcohol is more Dangerous but It's not Banned for the Day came when Recreational use of Cannabis is Legalized on April 20 or Nineteen Forty Two, I'm not Sure but I Offer the Most Peaceful Token to the People of The Centennial State, the New Cradle of Freedom, I Uphold Your Laws, I Salute Your Wisdom, Salute You for Being Pioneers of the New Road, Voting for What's Right, they will have it so good in two moons when the Kings come to Serenade them with Gypsy echoes of times past or future, always Skipping the Present which is why some people don't know their limits so they end up making a fool of themselves like that other Candidate in the Red Corner, the filthy rich guy with the 160-room mansion in nice sunny Florida who's nearing the end of his journey, and You wonder, why, at that age when he's exhibiting demeaning Signals of Augustism, surely, he's all about making Deals for himself and Showing Off and it's Hysterical that so many Americans are putting their Faith in this guy who's gonna be Robbing them Silly while he's mounting that powerful looking horse with Miss Turkey in his Wagon, Bugles a Blowing, Drums a Trumping, and he's all decked out in all the gaudy regalia shiny George Washington uniform with elaborate details of the pendant with League of Masons Imagery and Motifs, Why? Question Yourself, will You follow this guy into the most critical battles and Lie to Yourself that he's going to lead the country into the most Golden Age in the history of America without lining his own pockets, and there he goes, charging at the enemy when You have done all the dirty work so he can chop off the Villain's head without looking at it because her Stare can turn him into a Frog of Diamonds always being a Girl's best friend, no less, it's all so clear, isn't it, and it's crazy unbelievable that he's going to have the Power to destroy half the countries of the world or more and there's Nothing the UN can do anything about it? O the Gods must really be Crazy! Well… it's either the Capitalist or the I'm Always Innocent One. Which is the Lesser of Two Evils?

Well, the Lavender is not really lavender. It's just the name of the strain so if You are expecting to see strands of violet or such stuff, You will be a little disappointed but I'm Color Blind so I humbly ask You to take Your Paper Cranes and go to the Secret Hideout where You have hidden all Your Dislikes all this time in broken basket for You thought O who will ever search for anything in the Rubbish so You also think… Hmmm… where's that logic's going and hearing all the Bombs going off outside, even Missiles and Chemical Drones, and what other more violent or humane than a Laser Canon which zaps at a one person or Boeing plane and Presto! It's Disintegrated and Disappeared! Zap! Zap! Zap! The whole thing Vanishes into Nothing, no need for cremation, no need for mummification, no need for biometric identification, no need for data collection, and religious rites and all those things people get so preoccupied about whenever there's a Big Catastrophe, the Whole World freezes and grieves and really cry over a few glasses of spilled milk when the culprit is running as fast as possible to set up the next Scene where Master Apple Tin goes to the Bahamas for Meditation in the Crystal Cave so Nobody can disturb him at all and it's such a wonderful place because he has all the time to play his Harmonica which is a good instrument to carry with You, especially if You are going all by Yourself, Alright, You say, Firstly, You have to get used to the Dark because the Day will Come, given how the Affairs of the World is being run now, especially in these critical times when the Mentality of the

General Population is so Fragile, It may happen Sooner than You know but one of the great things about going to the Cave is that it's full of mystical stones that sparkle or glow in the dark, it doesn't matter because You will not see it though You can Feel the Electromagnetic Fields as You Close Your Eyes and Breathe In and Out like a Criminal hiding from the Law after running for more than a few miles at full speed, heaving and sweating, it's really a very bad thing when people Brand You a Criminal when You are just trying to smell the flowers more closely and You find out that Marijuana is not just used for getting high though it's Positive but it's also remedial for people who are suffering from amnesia, rheumatism, seizures, gastric pains, depression and other tricky illnesses so it's quite obvious that Marijuana is one of Nature's more blessed gifts and if we learn to harness its healing properties in light of Survival of the Human Race but for a Stoner, it's enough to be High but it's tough to smoke it in places where You are not Welcome to Smoke, You may Consider Cannabis Cookies and Cakes but I'm not sure if they make You High but the Day May Come that the World becomes a better Place as More and More People Embrace the Ambrosia Pines of the Gods but... is that what the Scandalous Prime Minister wants? Ladies and Gentle Bodies... The Rat Pack...

"Don't you think Johnny Carson would have been an excellent President?"

"Send me the Pillow that You Dream on..."

"Yeah, he's a better speaker than Richard and the people adore him. Plus, he got that loving father image that people can identify with..."

"I'm getting married in the morning... get me to the

Church on time… Ding Dong… there he goes… forgetting the lyrics and the people are cheering… Ding Dong… Ding Dong… Ding Dong… Ding Dong… Ding Dong…"

"Frank's the Leader of the Pack… Get him!"

"Dean's a phenomenal entertainer, a superb comedian, actor and singer."

"In those days, they can smoke and drink on TV and the audience claps for minutes just not so hard that their palms turn purplish."

"Fly Me to the Moon… in other words… please be true… I love You!"

"You might forget Your manners… Luck be a Lady… Tonight… a Lady doesn't leave her escort… stick with me baby… it isn't fair… blow on some other guy's dice… never get out of my sight… Luck be a Lady… Tonight…"

"BE THERE!"

"When You wake up in the morning, that's as good as You're going to feel all day!"

"I can't see a thing in the Sky… I Only Have Eyes for You… millions of people get by… because You are right here… I've Got You Under My Skin… a part of me… I know damn well… for the sake of having You near… I've Got You Under My Skin… Wake up to Reality…"

"You mind if I lie down to see?"

"There's no telling where Love will appear… Everybody loves Somebody… Sometimes…"

"Without an Audience… We are Dead… We are truly Pleased to be Here… and We thank You for Your Contribution… handle my heart with care… Please be Kind… Wait for me… Wait for me…"

"If You leave me here… O YEAH! O YEAH! Jump queue! Please be Kind… be Kind… sure Sings good for a White fellow…"

"BE THERE!"

"Everybody should Drink and Everybody Should Drink until They Cannot Drink Anymore!"

"I wanna go play Hide and Seek… You and I… picking up all those Forget-Me-Nots… Old and Gray… You make Me feel Spring Sprung… what happened… what did I say… Bounce the Moon… Running around the Middle… You make Me feel so young…"

"Isn't it dangerous? Is it right to promote Gambling, Pittsburgh, Alcohol, Tobacco, Communism, Prostitution and all those kind of Song and Dance to Glorify Sins?"

"Through it all, Your Face will Flower… Count Basie!

"As I throw each one of You… a kiss… my kind of people too… each time I leave St. Louis… it makes me grin like a clown… St. Louis… my kind of town… calling me home… St. Louis… it won't let you down…"

"Sammy Davis Jr's had Great Comedic Timing and he's an Outstanding Singer too. You can hear it. He's puts a lot more emotions into the songs, beg, steal or borrow, thank you, thank you, the most theatrical drummer, yeah, what she wanna, I got You under Your skin…"

"As long as we are all here together, why don't we have a drink! This is my Pilot!"

"I wanna thank the NAACP… Put me down! That's another four years! Happy Father's Day! It's my daughter's birthday… Happy Birthday to You…"

"Mr. Jimmy Cagney… You Dirty Rat… You hit my brother in the back… "

"We didn't even take the plane. We flew right in!"

"Mr. Cary Grant… You can't take that Baby out of a man's life… it's not fair… it's alright… "

"Do You have a Light?"

"If all the Women in Texas is as ugly as your Momma, the Lone Ranger is going to be alone for a long… time!"

"America's only Jewish Muslim… Irving X… Mr. Quincy Jones…"

"Mr. Clark Gable… Scarlet… You got charm, personality… money…"

"You still got a long way to go… Wow ow woman… You the meanest woman… my only sunshine… be bop be bop be bop… I will not stop kissing You…"

"BE THERE!"

"Doing the Mash Potatoes, the Swing, the Monkey, and the Jerk, thank you, thank you…"

"My mother is Puerto Rican. I'm Colored, Jewish and Puerto Rican. When I go to a neighborhood, I wipe it out!"

"I want my Bon Bons!!"

"It's quarter to Three… I'm feeling so sad… make the music dreamy and sad…"

"Mr. Vaughn Monroe… Mr. Nat King Cole… Mr. Tony Bennett… Mr. Mel Torme… Louie Armstrong…"

"If I get approved by the Catholic Church, I'm in!"

"Mr. Dean Martin… Which Way is the Audience?"

"Do You think they rehearse? It looked all so natural… even in black and white… Thank you, St. Louis!"

"We do this on the weekends."

"Subtlety, baby! Loosen up… and from a jail… came a whale… I will call You if I need You… I'm safe! Birth of the Blues…"

The year Dragon ran away from Home, The Man had not landed on the Moon yet and JFK was still alive and it's the Rumor of the Day as they Whispered that he's screwing the sultriest sex symbols of that time and they were real sex symbols then and whenever their latest Postcards or Posters were Released, all the young boys begged their parents to buy those Pictures for them without Shame so they could rush home and lock themselves in their rooms to Abuse themselves Silly and Spray their Juice on Paper to Quench their Demons, It's True, sex symbols in the Sixties were much more Siren than What Inferior Symbols of the Day but It's so Boring Here so why not Imagine how he fucked Jayne, and some other days, he's having long rendezvous with that Girl in the *Seven Year Itch*, and Remarkably, all the time, the Public had this perception of the Man being a great family guy or something when he's committing the sin of adultery with such a long string of the most sexy women in the land all dying to kindle his spirits and eat his manhood for no matter his love for the arts and letters and his extramarital affairs, he's still the Last Great President and considering that it was way back in the Day when more than three quarter of the world's current population has not been born yet, it can be inferred that it's quite some time ago that the Greatest Nation in the World had not been so Great for more than half a century and it had fallen quite drastically in terms of its National Debt which will never be repaid but Nobody is asking who is owed the debt, isn't it Strange, Dragon, only about fifteen years old when he arrived in America, he realized it was very hard for him to break into the Right dominated movie industry but he restructured himself as an exceptional student, reading Philosophy in Washington State, it's there that he practiced the Shadowless Hand technique and crafted the Flying Dragon Kick which required that You Run from a Distance and when You have Reached Optimum Speed, You Leap into the Air, Launching the Ferocious Dragon, Straightening One Leg while the Other Leg is Used to Form a Triangle with the toe nearly touching Your Testicles or Crotch, You let out a Fierce Scream, aiming directly at Your enemy's face, it was a Big Hit when he challenged Everybody to a contest where he subdued the opponent in less than a few seconds in staged segments, and Dragon went on to achieve international fame after he made the decision to return to the Harbor of Fragrance to build his career as a movie star so he could take a leading role which was Impossible in those days in Hollywood even though he was the side kick who was more popular than the main hero in that TV series which was so full of racist stereotypes and yet, they went ahead to make a movie of it many years later when Dragon was found dead in the bed of his Mistress, some people opined he was the victim of his own lust and it's fucking true she fucked him like it was the last time ever, there's still something sinister about the whole episode but some people also suspected that he offended some people and they ordered a Death Spell on him and some other people vouched that he was murdered by the branch of ancient Chinese martial arts where a Master of The Touch can make a person laugh uncontrollably or weep unceasingly or freeze up like a statue or float up or become a bat or become blind by just pressing on certain acupuncture points, applying perfect pressure, in secret combinations so secret, they have all been Lost, including the Art of Lightness, the Ten Thousand Buddha Lights, the Drunken Immortals, the Thousand Mile Whisper, the Lion's Roar, and all the lot, it must be experienced, it must be the most precious thing… ever…

IV IS CLOUDIER THAN VI

On a Whim, I thought it would be swell to go to Colorado Springs. Now, I'm quite sure more than nine tenth of the United States have never been to this small city about ninety miles South of Denver. If You are at Union Station, it takes the bus about six hours or more to reach Downtown Colorado Springs and it's such a Downtown that when You have just arrived, You get the Sense that You have to get out of there right away even as Your luggage have gotten lighter after You have given the Butterflies and Cookies and Curries away, and there are not much strangers trying to bum a cigarette or beer from You, let it be known, You are trying to get to Springs Inn as quickly as possible and You Saw You have to cross the Bridge on Colorado Avenue and it's about a few miles away and it's still not easy to carry so much weight even if You had lost a few more Dislikes for the flight and room and board and all that Bohemian lifestyle, You soldier on like a soldier on some kind of mission only that You don't really know what's the Purpose of the Mission for it's not Your Right to Ask Questions and You feel like giving up at some point, don't You, especially when You are all comfortable with all the luxuries of life, living it up in dirtiest golf talks and relishing the most fat burning fruits of the Earth, it's probably the right time to spend some time on Pedro for it's true that he will fit right into this town, it's almost as if Colorado Springs is made for him, and him for her…

Here, Away from the Limelight, Away from the Glare of Crooked Abdullah, he can be Pedro El Dorado or Pedro Infante or even Pedro Colorado and some People will Applaud him wherever he goes, he will be greeted with Ole Ole Ole and young giggling virgins will Plaster him with warm petals of alpine marigold whenever he appears in public, he's the ultimate hero in such a way as everybody hasn't imagined, it's certainly such a sad story to make the hardest hearted person shake just that little bit or if I may be more prudent, O Mr. Kite, he has Ma Sky and even Ma Blue and in that Eye of the Needle, just enough for the Tail of the Softest Wind to Lisp Through, Beneath the Thousand Mile Cloud, Longer than it takes Your breath to Moisturize the Aroma of Love Evaporating Off the Fields of Broom Sticks Buried in the Soil where the Sky meets the Land… there… there… where the Laziest Man You will ever come across in Your life… You will see him… accompanied by Dead Bolt Rock Steady music from Cuba… there He is… sitting on the poisoned grass… his legs laid straight one on top of the other in the most relaxed manner… his hat fully covering his eyes… You see him and You wonder how cool is the Gaucho as he chuckles on the end of the grass, sucking the juice out of that thing like it's the last time he's gonna work that shift, he remembered how great he felt when he walked out of that Sweat Shop where every Little Indian is expected to work no less than sixteen and a half hours a day and only paid less than three Dislikes an hour which is a federal crime punishable by imprisonment for many years and they are still celebrating the New Age Seven Wonders of the World and it's all so Boring and Crowded now for there are so many Wonders that they don't really know what is a Wonder anymore and it's even more confusing when there are Heritage Sites and such things… don't You wonder… how they determine one site is a Wonder and another is not… yeah… tell me… what's Your qualification… and Pedro will spit out the whole yarn of grass from his mouth and to make it more Dramatic… he will look at You through the hat and though it's really covering his eyes and Everybody can certify that his eyes are totally covered by the hat which is made of the most precious Bald Head Eagle feathers and his father had shot a few hundred of those birds to make that hat for him, it's such a fantastic hat in that it completely blocks sun rays and rain drops so he will never be wet or dry… somehow… You know that he can see You… yeah… it means a Challenge is Offered… and if You take it… lay down Your shotguns… Your assault weapons of a thousand million rounds… yeah… nullify Your Nuclear Atomic Warheads… Discharge those laser cannons capable of lasering the Sun and the Moon… or beyond… yeah… lay those things down for what's the big deal for a Man if he doesn't even get to see the eyes of his enemy closing as he stabs the dagger into his heart and whispers a prayer for him…

THE GAUCHO'S PRAYER

O Great Spirit, Blow, Blow the Winds
The Great Hero has Fallen!
Blow, Blow his Blood off Mine Hands
The Contract Signed in Blessed Valor
It's not the Pride of Man
O Great Spirit, Blow, Blow the Winds
The Great Hero has Fallen!
Blow, Blow his Soul to the Other Side
Where he will be Forever Beatified
A Gaucho of Gauchos!

With his Weapon, he had vanquished many a foe and even though the Native Americans hadn't learned how to quantify these things in those days when they still stayed in wigwams and rode their horses all over the Land… in those days… they could easily be bought for a bottle of Jack Daniels regardless of the edition or formula, the Funky ones even sold the secrets of their tribes to the *gringos* for that's what they like to call them behind their backs but just like the Joker when their bosses would call them into their big and frightening offices with real Carcass and Skeleton of Extinct Animals, they would feel small like a mouse and somehow they wouldn't even dare to look at their eyes…

such Cowards… somehow… when they lost their duel with Pedro… they would admit defeat without any question in their mind and without a single thread of hatred in their hearts… half of their spirit will be captured in his nose as he breathes it into his lungs and into his heart so he will kill the next man with less pain and higher level of skill and Nobody dared to say anything Derogatory about him because he carried himself as One who has no Sin and everybody in Manitou Springs knew that he's a full Man of Honor and it was in those days when Respect still meant something and men were more men than the men of today who pushes a few buttons to kill millions… Where's the Fucking Glory in that???... yeah they should confiscate all their Purple Hearts and all their Pompous Medals of Honors to Commission a Great statue of Pedro Colorado of Manitou Springs, yeah, make it more a Thousand Feet High… one foot placed approximately seventy miles south of Denver and the other foot should be placed about seventy miles from Colorado Springs, the Figure should be Designed in such a way so he's making a big stride towards Trinidad which is truly where he was walking towards, in those days, You walk to Your destination no matter how far away when You have lost Your horse and that's exactly what happened when Pedro was Challenged by his Best Friend… and Somehow… they are listening to Cesaria's Concert in Paris in 2001 and towards the second last song when the audience were pining that she would sing for another hour or so, surely, they would be totally satisfied to return home like little children queuing up for a cup of ice cream or popcorn, You forgot, and in just a few minutes, Pedro Launched his Angel Lily with all his might towards the Sun but Maxi Choleta didn't even have to dodge for he missed very badly so he was laughing his Hyena

Laugh for he had All the Advantage and he was going to finish off his Best Friend who had Impregnated his beloved even though she was the one who begged Pedro and he's so furious that he went straight for his right eye so as not the make the mistake of many other gauchos who went for his heart only to find out he's Invincible just because they didn't know he wore a Super Thick Platinum Breast Plate Armor under his shirt so well custom crafted that it fits him so perfectly with natural extension of his chest, yeah, including the nipples so metal and protruding out of his James Dean T-shirt after he removed his jacket and his shirt, the women would be all excited to suck on the his cold hard nipples and they all vowed to bring his secret to their graves with tears in their eyes so it must be Little Crow Lips, it must be she who told at least one Whore of Darkness and that's why Choleta knew the Secret and rightly chose to go for his eye and at that speed where he's flying at Pedro like a Mexican Superman, it didn't really matter if it's the Right or Left One and this time, he thought he chose the Right One only because a Man should be decisive and it sounds more appropriate than the Left One so he's so a thousand and three hundred seventy one percent sure of Victory and honoring his Promise to her, he made a reservation at the most glamorous restaurant in town and he was celebrating how much he had to gain from Pedro's Spirit as he said the Gaucho's Prayer, it must be the ultimate Victory, his curly hair blown straight, what a Proud Day for his Clan, gaining the title of the Greatest Gaucho of All Time for that's Pedro's Title and he had never relinquished it because this title is not a Cowardly title like the WBA or WBO or WWE or WWF or World Cup or Olympics where You can still make a comeback in a few years or in the case of the USA, it's every year that there will be a World Champion because in the Realm of Gauchohood, there's no Mercy or Compassion or Charity, there's only One Winner and Death is the Bride of the Loser and Nobody can do anything about it for it's the way of the Great Spirit and Jehovah and Goddess Kali and Choleta, he made Great Sacrifices to many gods so he's received a grand Vision that he would defeat Pedro and he's so Happy that he's flying so quickly to Victory, just a second of less, ALRIGHT! ALRIGHT! Victory is at Hand at Last! then, Woof, Woof, he heard the cry of his pet Chihuahua and before Choleta could think of anything else, Angel Lily struck him at the neck and without knowing what hit him, he crashed to the Earth, turning Red as he felt the Graceful Hands of Pedro picking his head up to whisper the Prayer into his ears as he closes his eyes in gracious defeat, tasting death, blood splattering everywhere and through his eyelashes, he's seeing the sky turning the darkest blue and finally black as cliché as it sounds… it's what's gonna happen as You breathe Your last too… it's the Big Sleep… the Big Snore with No Sound… and then.. *no mas… no mas…*

Then, he could see that it's really quite beguiling so You can see her hands designed in the style of that girl in Munch's Jealousy painting where she is trapped between a down trodden young man and a confused man with beard but You know, the mermaid's face and hair were clearly modeled after Eva Mudocci with wavy flowing hair covering her ambrosial breasts so strategically designed so the screws could be applied on the forehead, elbows and bellybutton, surgically, forming the shape of a diamond to reinforce the human form on the wood. As for the fishy part which is the tail, it's attached to her waist by way of a hinge so the tail, which is quite voluptuous for You can see that she's shaped more like a sexy woman than a fish or an over-or-under nourished woman, and the tail swirls so the fin joins her hips in sort of a reflected figure of six and not the other way around and You have to put Your finger into the hole to lift the tail before You pound it on the Rock of Brass. Putting his ears on the door, he couldn't hear a single sound at all, just like how a house should sound when there's Nobody home at all. Should he shout? If only he had a Louder Voice! Should he go around the house? It's a Long Way to the Backyard and the Line is Getting Longer as the Crowd Swells. Should he go Home and Come again tomorrow? Night was coming so he had to decide quickly.

"Knock! Knock! Knock!"
"Knock! Knock! Knock! Knock! Knock! Knock!"
"Knock! Knock!"

"Who's that?"
"Housekeeping…"
"Come on in…"
"Should I come back later? I'm afraid to disturb you…"
"It's alright… I'm not busy…"
"O sorry… sir…"

Coming back to the Inn, I was comforted and somewhat happier that I had successfully arranged my accommodations for the whole moon ahead and there's nothing much to worry about so I went to the Reception to rent the room for another night so that I could go explore Colorado Springs a little more, and knowing that I only had half a day left in this place that I was starting to like more as I observed that people are more friendly and humble as the gentle Korean old fellow who tried to strike up a conversation for he suspected that I was his kinsmen but of course, I wasn't too comfortable to tell him that I'm from the North as he would then be all defensive and offensive, shouting pro-democracy slogans and all, I just told him that I'm from the South Seas so he told me about his trip to Pike's Peak which is one of the top tourist attractions in the region and many people come all the way to see such a Wonder but I checked it and I thought it might be worth the time… if only I had more time… I would have stayed another day but I had more important things to do… so it's no point arguing with the guy for his intentions were Good and Positive…

It's time to go to the Garden of the Gods so I made my way to the Bus Terminal, an important station for all Gypsies. Upon reaching there from the Greyhound station where I bought my one-way ticket to Moffat the next day, finally, I arrived at the Central Bus Terminal in Downtown Colorado Springs, and though I was feeling very hungry, I suppressed it and politely, I approached one of the terminal staff to enquire about the bus service to Garden of the Gods so she told me to hop on 34 and I would be on my way. This time, the bus arrived quite quickly and I had enough time to grab a hotdog and iced lemon tea in a bottle and also a trip to the men's room to relieve myself, I felt quite Happy that the Journey was beginning to become more Magical at least more Magical than the day before when I was on my way to the Cheyenne Canon Inn from Springs Inn when I had to walk seventeen miles to the Ride Stop and though I wasn't carrying full gear, it was still very challenging because the sun was blazing such harmful rays that I was absolutely devastated when I arrived at the 711 and bought two bottles of energy drink and finished one in one gulp for it was that hot that a truck driver became so disillusioned and dislodged, he dropped a whole big cup of ice on the floor and it's strange to see such a guy with so much beard and hair act like he's in a panic, I waited at the Ride Stop for more than one and a half hours and the bus didn't come at all so I decided to walk a little bit down the road to try to catch a cab but in all that time, there was not even one, I felt it must be the worst city in the world with such wretched public transportation, meaning the poor in the city will find life much harder than people who can afford cars, yeah, they will have a grand old time in Colorado Springs but definitely not people who rely on public transportation to commute from work or what, I saw an old Latino woman sitting on the bench, patiently waiting for the bus for more than an hour but the bus was still on its way so I returned to the inn and looked for other options other than the Haunted Inn.

As the bus neared the Garden of the Gods, I didn't even sleep a wink though I didn't really sleep much in the inn as I was disturbed by Ghosts of the Past the whole night, holding out for a handful of chest nuts roasting in the oven when You realize the Eastern Europeans are arriving with their Hammers and Axes Spinning in the Air fast enough to hypnotize Little Men & Women for it's really hard to count the sheep when You are hearing them all talking around You and seeing them go through Your stuff like custom officers looking for Illicit drugs or Weapon of Mass Destruction meaning a weapon with capacity to destroy hundreds of thousands of life and You remember how the Public Transit System in NYC is always Warning the passengers to be vigilant and look out for suspicious parcels or luggage left unattended anywhere in the subway or bus terminal or anywhere else or even suspicious folks, You better make a report right away and evacuate the area immediately, You see how the bus driver is bringing You closer to Your destination, and slowly but surely, passing the outskirts of the city to one of the Greatest attractions in Colorado Springs, You are passing the Dutch Village with roads like Rembrandt Valley, Vondelpark, Ann Frank House, Red Light District, and Bloemenmarkt so You suspect there's quite some tall people in this area, turning left, going a little further, You realize that You are on the Avenue of Garden of the Gods which sounds much more sexy than Garden of the Gods Road and West Garden of the Gods Road and so on so You hold on to the rails as You sense that it's near the time to alight so You go to the bus driver to be absolutely certain…

"Excuse me, Kind Sir… Where is the Stop for Garden of the Gods?"

"THIS IS THE GARDEN OF THE GODS!"

"No, I mean the Wonder… You know… the Garden… People See the Gods?"

"I don't know what You are talking about! THIS IS THE GARDEN OF THE GODS!!"

"Alright, just drop me at the next Stop. Thanks."

One of the great things about technology is that You can find most everything on the Internet. By using Google Maps, I was able to see that I had stopped at the best possible place to walk to the Garden so I set off walking at full speed for it's already near noon and the distance was about eighteen miles and the Sun was still blazing its deep frying rays, it's good there's a 711 along the way where I could buy some famous natural spring water from Colorado Springs so I could be on my way and it's a good walk because You can see the rock formations of the Garden from afar and You are Naturally Wishing more than ever to get nearer so You can see the Gods up close and personal where there are no voices anymore, no, not even any noise at all and when You saw that the car crashed into the tree at speed of more than a few hundred miles per hour kind of impact, You know, the whole car was totally meshed into the tree though it was made of the best material, mashing up the two passengers into blobs of flesh and blood with their bones crushed and all due to their affluence and such spending powers that they can buy everything that they ever desired including countries and counties and museums and cricket teams and a solid gold toilet seat costing thirty million Dislikes with wings on the side so You can imagine that they will carry You away when You are under attack, You just need to press the EJECT button and straight up, straight into the sky, You fly to Safety, O Imagine how Happy the Mother if she had instilled a little discipline to her spoiled wayward son of a gun who spent his Dislikes faster than a Bolt of Lightning, You think, he would spent it on the most intrinsic things like Modern Art without having any clue about Modern Art though he went to art school and even interned at a museum or two, throwing his friends out and his mother would order another platoon after another platoon, all day long, getting him more and more Dislikes, always afraid he would not have enough to buy the Seattle Supersonics which was heck of a team in reality until the franchise was taken away... and You say…

"Excuse me, sir… but What has that to do with the Humanities?"

"There's an Insect on Your Left Cheek."

"Please answer the question. Don't waste our precious time!"

"Here it is… do You know what it's called?"

"Hey! We know all Your tricks! Stop asking questions! Answer us! Answer us!"

"*Did You Ever See A Dream Walk In*?"

"It's a most amazing Glow Wood Worm…"

"If You Persist, We will Cut off Your Right Toe!"

"Hello, Lucy… how are You, my friend…"

"Guards… cut out his tongue…"

"Burn it immediately before he bleeds to death! Do it! Now! Now!"

It's nothing. Without a tongue, it just means that You cannot talk and You cannot taste the difference between a banana and a plantain, and You better admit, in the very Beginning, You didn't know the meaning of the Word Love and even after seventy years as a Great Great Grandmother of four or five or six generations, You don't know, yeah, the young people were fucking all over the country like it's the only thing which ever mattered and soon, there will be more angry young people thrashing up the neighborhood because he cannot accept Responsibility of Fatherhood just like his Father and he didn't really want to be tied down at such a young age excuse these cowards use all the time thinking that carrying his baby or cleaning up his baby's shit or showering his baby is such a woman's chore so he can keep his macho image of the man being the King of the House and what about that day when he got so pissed when You rejected his advances Behind the Bus where all the dirty stuff happens so it's not uncommon to see those Mickey Mouse Kids fondling, masturbating, performing oral stimulation, making out, fingering, licking, kissing, reproducing and even give birth, and yeah, he was born in the bus and it was there that he was delivered by a wet nurse or someone who knows how to deliver babies and there, he was shown to the whole city on the Front Page and he became so famous, people would pay about two Dislikes to have their pictures taken with him but it's true, he received his Diamond RTD pass, a lifetime pass allowing him to take the bus anywhere in the city without paying a single feather for the rest of his life and he's got absolutely Nothing to do… with…

"Can You Hear Me?"

"Yeah, Socrates. Speak up!"

"No!! Don't Swing!!! Please!!! Please tell Your pet monkey not to swing on my Beard!!!"

"I'm sorry, Fat Albert. Come here Two Face."

"Are You talking to me? I can't hear You! Speak Louder!"

"What are We going to do? Nobody's HOME!"

"*There's Danger in Your Eyes, Cherie (Take 2)*"

"Excuse me… What are You doing Here?"

"I'm waiting for my Husband to pick me up. He's coming in about an hour and when I get into the car, he's going to feel me up under my dress and yank out my red herring panties like a piece of paper… he has such strong hands… Then, he will sniff and suck and… put it in his mouth and eat… then his fingers will crawl to my thighs like spiders… quickly searching for the well… and once he finds it… his tongue will go buttery… bewildering me to waves upon waves of golden bliss… I will pee.. hee… hee… but… he didn't act like it's so dirty and shout at me like Dad… and that's the great thing… when we reach Home… I will run to the bed like a shameless bitch in heat… waiting for him to ram his Rod into my Rabbit Hole until the wee hours of the morning, shooting loads and loads of sperm… fertilizing my eggs… my sweet sweet eggs… and within days… I would be pregnant… and blessed to carry his child… That's all I want to do…"

"Do You have the Time to tell the Time?"

"I always name the kids. He will not say O I think Tango is better than Rosie or Rainbow."

"Hey Obama! I think You dropped Something… "

"In the Name of the Almighty Allah and His Sexy Prosperous Prophet, I forbid You to Piss on the Statue of the Martyr!"

"Shall We make his Moustache a little more Curling so it's Infinity?"

"Give it to Samson. He will know what to do with it."

"Bring me… bring me.. to Osama…"

"HELP!! HELP!!! The White House is Collapsing!!!!"

Of course, it did. Only that You wouldn't hear it if You were standing right there and watching in great horror how it exploded like Lightning had struck it right at the place where a big proud flag is flying the colors of the Union, seven times, it's powerful enough to cause a ruckus and the Master ceiling of marble or sapphire crashed down and it's so unreal to see it crumble like pie crust, one floor falling into the lower floor as if the Holy Hand of God is pressing on the building and crushing either him or her for all their Injustices and Scams just as she was suffering from a tummy ache while he was suffering from a tooth ache, both of them, the best thing was that they escaped somehow, and miraculously, they turned into the greatest Saints of all Time, spreading Goodwill to all the World instead of Sorrows and Exploiting them and condescending them because it's not even their fault to be born in a country where the young are misguided by evil motherfuckers who have been misguided their whole lives to think that their mothers and sisters are burros without realizing that they themselves are foals in this sense and yeah, if their mothers don't give birth to them, these numb skull cool Latino guys always Acting Disinterested as their women cuddle up to them in Public Display of her Affections, they think they would just spring out from the Earth like Spring Onion or another type of vegetation and if they really to believe this, even at the age of five or less, then, there's nothing to say about them other than the fact that they are quite dumb, really, really, really, quite dumb to even believe that it's Allah's Will that women be ill-treated like animals and boys are to be trained into militants, and girls will grow up to become women, yeah, these people should be made to watch *Caligula* while listening to Works of Aristophanes in Top Quality Headphones so they don't miss out on important notes such as Chivalry and Containment or the Art of Subduction nevertheless soon they will start combing their hair like the Corleones for if there's one thing You admire about Vito is the fact that he taught his sons well to comb their hair so very debonairly so not even one is out of place so these violent types will be softened and trained to be cultured men of The Republic, they will be so thrilled to know that they don't have to be judged by the number of people they murdered but by the number of Dislikes so they will be trained to work in security sensitive operations as they infiltrate the society, they can show on the outside they have adopted the Western way and they may even eat Pork and convert to Judaism and even sing the National Anthem with green veins in their eyes but You should not be Fooled to think that they had truly forgotten their Old Ways and they may even invite You to their Glorious Middle Eastern barbecues where their women perform for You the Dance of Forgetfulness and You totally believe that he had built such a happy family and he's such a fantastic family man when You see him throwing his son up to the sky and You think O what a nice lovely man... not like Your Husband who You detest with all Your heart, O why O why, it's such a shock to the community when they saw his face on the front page of the newspaper, sensationally revealed as the Leader of the Operation, and You almost fainted because You had married a Terrorist, and You are totally Shocked that he had lived such a dangerous life right under Your nose as You think about his mouth, breaking into a smile as he pushes the button to launch the missile on that village where poor folks were running like jackals, heading to the mountain, You slowly see why they call it the Garden of the Gods...

As You get nearer, You pick the Three Graces as Your Final Destination and once You reach there, You can turn back so You come to a trail which is the domain of rattlesnakes and other poisonous wild life so You choose to trample on them, You are not worried about anything at all, getting nearer to the Garden, You begin to understand a little more why they call those formations the *Scotsman*, *Tower of Babel*, *Sleeping Giant*, *Kissing Camels*, and even *Siamese Twins*, all these are very well showcased in the Brochure so it's unnecessary that

You see know that You don't have time to hike to all these Grand Dame monuments because You still had to get to the hot springs to heal Your Blistered feet until the Heat of the Day passes into the Heat of the Water and then, You think, You will be ready to go to Area 51 which is actually in Nevada and not Colorado so You may not be mistaken for an Alien, You better depart Earlier as it's already close to Tea Time and You know how the public transportation in Colorado Springs stinks to the depths of Hell even the Gods would be ashamed to let You know the real reason the Garden is such a Wonder is the fact that the rock formations actually transform with the Passing of the Day and it's not so difficult to see You will enjoy it much better if You take the Path less Traveled to watch how the formations interact with each other as if the Gods had Awakened and Conducting the Screechiest Symphony of Shadows to seduce You into lumber of most wet dreams where You piss into Your bed with Greatest Joy to know that You can be in paradise for that one thousandth of a moment so You know it's true, this Honey that You are tasting in Your mouth from the Mammary Glands of Your Love is Real and not sand or origami eel or broken wings or any negative thing because You can feel the nourishment and it makes You feel like a human again so You understand YOU SHALL DO UNTO OTHERS WHAT YOU WANT OTHERS TO DO UNTO YOU kind of epiphany, Waving a Hand at the Witch of the North Smoking a Joint in that Blue Room in the Bushes while her grandchildren were Chasing Butterflies, it's all so lovely, the Walk in the Garden and all, it's decreed, All Slaves should visit the Garden of the Gods at least once in their lives to partake of the Wisdom of the Gods, laid out for all to see, the Plan and Plot for the Apollo Program and the Yuri Gagarin Debate which is still disputed up to this day like it's so important in the History of Mankind who's the Man who first walked on Mars or even the Moon, all these Extra Earth Melodies seemed too far… too perfect…

As I ate the flowers of some cactus, yellow and appearing almost like nylon so they reflect some light in light of their natural qualities, there's no nectar but when they are Poisoning Your mouth, the Clouds so Dark, flexing some muscles in the Sky and You thought it's Gonna rain some storms today as You walk faster in case You are drenched and all Your precious things will be damp and useless soon soon You come to the stream near the Highway so Seductive so You take off Your soft leather Jesus sandals, placing Your Battered and Wearied Buddha feet into the somewhat clear waters so cold and refreshing, You are tempted to stand there for more than a few hours and there's really no Word to describe such a feeling… such a feeling… You walked briskly to the 711 again to buy some drinks again… You must have spent more than a few hundred Dislikes on energy drinks and it's still not enough to quench Your thirst so You walk to the nearest Ride Stop to Meditate and wait for the next bus to the Downtown Main Terminal, relaxing on the pure pure American grass, sprayed with pesticides and other crippling poisons, contaminating Nature in obscene overtures and inhumane cruelty to kill the insects in front of Diplomats and Monks who have come to Bless the Land and pointing the Right Way, You ask the Terminal Service Person about whether it's too late to go to Manitou Springs and to Your Great Surprise, he assured You it's still early enough so You hop on the 3 Ride, rushing towards the Sanctuary of the Indians.

"Excuse me, Kind Sir. Do You Know Where are the Hot Springs?"

"Hot Springs? There are no Hot Springs here!!"

"Wait..."

"Hey! Buddy! Do You Know Any Hot Springs around here?"

"No, Man, there are no Hot Springs around... only Cold Springs..."

"Cold Springs? Alright... do You know where are the Hot Springs?"

"I don't know... it's quite far from here..."

"Alright, thanks..."

V COWS

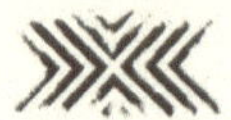

And Now, in common courtesy and good gesture of Friendship, I invite You, cordially or uncordially to come to THE FOUNDATION, yeah, throw away Your trumpets, throw away Your clothes, throw away Your cards, throw away Your keys, Naked, You Come, Naked, You Go, it's the Law of THE REPUBLIC, and as such, I ask that You come in utmost civility with most basic requirements… like a pack of most organic healthiest food thought most responsibly harvested and disposed in Algerian musk smoked Wild Boar or for the Vegetarians and the Virgins, olive leaves dipped in most golden chocolate cows made of repose of most juicy caterpillars crawling in Your ear, Listen, and You will see the Big Invitation card appearing before Your eyes like most of these cards You receive in Your mail every day, post card size, a cute grey cat in red dress probably getting ready to hit town for she has her cute heart shape handbag the same color as her cute dress with white handkerchief or tissue in the only pocket on the Left and she's also holding a parcel so both her hands are holding something and if she's attacked, she will surely find it hard to defend herself but it's alright, everybody knows she lives on Tabby Street or she's arrived at Tabby Street, it wasn't so Clear, the Sky is becoming Downcast, then, turn, turn to see if Anybody is following You for it's of Si Supreme Importance that You come Alone and definitely not with any other friend or pal You have just met on the Internet a few days ago telling You about the trips they made to Paris or Montevideo and how in the former, it's such a Big Grand Glamorous City when You take the subway on the way to the Glass Pyramid, Yeah, You Witness how the well-heeled folks transformed into sewer rats and street rodents, You know, the type of transportation the Rich never use, no, don't even be jealous or admirable at this time as You hear the Roar of the Hell's Angels, yeah, my dear friends, are You Ready? Are You Ready to Rumble??? Repeated at least seven times to get their veins bulging a little, yeah, Fucking Retarded Rednecks, You are invited too, just follow the address behind the Card with Egyptian Reunion symbols curling in all finest Infinite Glorious memories of the softest breeze blowing on their cheeks as they dismount their Horses, Iron or Natural, it doesn't matter, Come One, Come All, You are Eternally Invited, dead or living, poor or rich, Boy or Girl, it doesn't matter one bit, please, no weapons except Your favorite knife, Burmese or Republican, Child or Serpent, it's FREE, there's no entrance fee and membership fee and what have You fees and taxes and yeah just bring a few hundred Dislikes and You can stay here for up to a week, it's like a Communist Camp but sure… You will be given Your daily supplies… professionally proportioned so You will not even feel a Pang of Hunger, I tell You, now or in the future what the Great Spirit says… Liberty must be given Free and not with anything impure about the Case of West Delta

Virus or Zika or anything else they concoct to Deliver us from the surface of the Earth and basically, the Deal is that You are encouraged to bring Your Highest Quality Cigarette or Cigar or even the best Puma Droppings so full of proteins and minerals, the Chief says the best fertilizers are Natural but Nobody believes him when they exclaimed all about the great Powers of Science all the time showing us movies about space ships and Crystal Balls with electric current inside so You can touch the Outside and witness the Wonder right before Your eyes How the Electricity Kisses Your Finger Nails on the Other Side and how Miraculous it is that You can feel it but not Electrocuted, You know even if You are being Undressed by Sgt. Lt. Curry Pepper who possesses the softest hands in the universe so he's able to feel through the mink gloves he wears on his hands and he's not all that PETA conscious or what when some people are killing millions of chickens and cows and sheep and pigs everyday so what's wrong with responsible hunting practices that govern every Citizen of The Republic, yeah, we will have our own flag and some real starving artist will come up with it FREE and if the time comes that we need a National Anthem, some real desperate composer will come forward with the Lyrics done by the most gifted Poet on Par with Neruda's stature to step forward and present it FREE for the Citizens who will have their rooms, each and every one of them and they are allowed to share rooms but what happens in the room, it's in the Room, the Ultimate Room in the world where it's Dark after Ten and there's no Electricity inside, just a Mountain Granite Bed, You know, the kind built to last the Ages and Hard enough to withstand greatest pressure of a few hundred elephants so when the Maximum number of persons in the Room is Only Two, it's quite impossible to break the bed for on the bed, there's a European Queen sized mattress of Five-Star Hotel Standard so You don't feel a little cheated when You feel Thirsty, You can suck on each other's nipples and it's damn fun foreplay so much so every couple should at least try at least once so they know how each other's milks or spirits taste and not lie about them Knowing one another so well, it's imperative that when You enter the Room of Suspense whether You weigh more than three hundred pounds or You are Deaf or You are Ugly for yeah we are not Judges of people so You should not feel Ashamed about Anything even if You have murdered millions of people and You are the Descendent of the soldiers who fought for the Holy Garments or the group of people who hunted down Crazy Horse like he's a real Beast and solemnly create Disparity to protect their Interests, it's Nature's Paradise and You can come in the Morning or the Evening or even at Midnight but if You come after the Hour of Curfew, sorry, You have to sleep in the Woods and We are not responsible for anything that happens outside for there are Sightings of Mountain Lions, Fat Knights, Kind Bears, Gentle Nazis, Limping Foxes, Obese Coyotes, Cow Aliens, Beaver Ghosts, Singing Witches, Medicine Balls, Faith Healers, Nazi Negroes, Cult Leaders, and the Occult, Everybody can have a turn at the Public Announcement Tower if You care for such things and there will be a Big Gong Tower too… made of Blue Bamboo please… and sometimes, You will hear operas and other type of music for the High Brows but really, it's up to You, the Citizens… and there's no Head of the Republic or any of such thing for we are not a political organization but a peace-loving ceremonial obedient people who care for the Good of the Collective Good which will be Good for all Mankind from Come Share the Wine in Painted

Tainted Room and You Acknowledge right away how backward they were in the 1630s or even before that in the times of castles and dinosaurs and men revolving from apes kind of fancy superficial putrid soup fed to children as young as three years old and You know the Outside is screwed and no matter how they repackage it and redesign it and remarket it and blow it until their lungs crack, it's a Wonder why we even accept such preposterous theories they dare to publish… Blasphemy… Torture… Lies… and Nonsense… and Yeah… We will have a place to Burn Books of our Fancy so we have to apply for a Burning Permit and also a Building Permit for we are building THE REPUBLIC and it's the Freest but not in that Way because it just doesn't sound Right at all so I have decided to call it… The Free New Nation… WELCOME TO THE JUNGLE… those are the words You read on the Postcard and it's printed in such Macadamia Clove Orange Skin Peppermint Infused Sanford's Premium Writing fluids, never fading, Permanently, it's made from the most sticky ingredients so even if You Lasered It, the Ink will still be Imprinted in Your Mind Forever and No Matter What You Do, You Cannot Wash It Out or even Blemish It just a little bit in Defense of Charity to the New Prophet who says the Human Race is too Bitter to Repent and the Time is Past… but wait… haven't we discussed it before… no matter… we have more important things to discuss now…

"What if We don't want to be Naked?"

"Why? Do You have Something to Hide?"

"No… but we need to protect our bodies from the Cold, right?"

"Alright… but You can't wear Anything in Your Room… OK?"

"No Problem… we agree to abide by The Rules… but we don't know where to look…"

"There's only ONE LAW and that's… THE GOLDEN

"No Matter the Weather, when You go to SOUTH PACIFIC, you have to leave your clothes in the antique boxes. They will keep your coats in the COAT ROOM so You can be totally Naked when You Stand on the Circle of Green where You will be scanned for dangerous weapons and the BALLROOM may be that type of perfect place for people who are preoccupied by measurement of genitals and the curious crowd who just desire to have a peek, sorry, we don't encourage peeping here."

THE GARDEN OF THE GODS

GIVEN TO
THE CITY OF COLORADO SPRINGS
IN 1909
BY THE CHILDREN
OF
CHARLES ELLIOT PERKINS

IN FULFILMENT OF HIS WISH
THAT IT SHOULD BE KEPT FOREVER
FREE TO THE PUBLIC

And that's the Big Plaque at the Garden of the Gods, informing You that You owe a sort of debt to Good Old Charles or the City of Colorado Springs but You say… O shouldn't this part be in the Previous Chapter? and I will concede that You are right except for the fact that it's better to put it in this Chapter because it's a Toto Surrealism thing it's Alright because we have no Judges in THE REPUBLIC as You all already know and it's simply governed by the simple law which says that You should behave in such a manner in which You want Other to Behave Towards You and if You don't have One… maybe You are God, and You start treating everybody like a God, then, suddenly, You Realize O How Wonderful the World is… yeah the Great promise of the Garden of the Gods is not Only the Fact that it's a Wonder of Wonders but the Simple Fact that You become a God once You go there to read those few words on The Plaque and Presto! You are transformed into a God Immediately and so… yeah… You need to go the Garden of the Gods… definitely… try to walk from the 711 if You yearn for the full scale experience of the Journey… You shall then come to appreciate how it feels to be a God as You walk in the Garden and partake of the Fruits and Nectar and Milk and Honey and all that fine stuff, breathe in, breathe in like it's the last time that You will be breathing in the Spirit of Liberty and You will be glad to know that the Great Spirit has been leading You from so far away from thousands of miles away, She calls You to remind You to pay Your WIFI bills and Your car installment and Your house is flooded away together with Baba Bibi, Your favorite silicone sex doll who's so Sexy, You fucked her seventeen times on Your first night right after You removed the rose from her panties, continuously, like a vibrating baboon, and You remember how that igloo was moving closer to the edge of the Lake of Sorrows where people are washing away all their sins in the Holy Waters while You were coming upon another Ejaculation so grandeur explosive that the inserted silicone pussy was malfunctioning and You cannot give the thumbs up just because they use such inferior melding techniques for such impervious imperfections and such times when You get lost in THE JUNGLE it's no time to panic for the Great Spirit, She will see You since You have become a Ghost of Your Past Self, She will protect You, The Great Spirit, just say the Prayer in Your Heart, slowly, Three Times without Stopping and You will be SAFE in the Mountains.

THE GREAT SPIRIT PRAYER

Oh, Great Spirit, whose Voice I Hear in the Wind, whose Breath gives

Life to all the World.

Hear me; I need Your Strength and Wisdom.

Let me Walk in Beauty, and make my Eyes Ever Behold the Red and Purple Sunset.

Make me Wise so that I May Understand the Things You have taught my People.

Help Me to Remain Calm and Strong in the Face of all that Come towards me.

Help me seek pure thoughts and act with the Intention of Helping Others.

Help me find Compassion with Empathy Overwhelming me.

I seek Strength, not to be greater than my Brother, but to fight my Greatest Enemy, Myself.

Make me Always Ready to come to You with Clean Hands and Straight Eyes.

So when Life fades, as the fading Sunset, my Spirit May Come to You without Shame.

Anonymous

Arriving in the SOUTH PACIFIC, You encounter an Anonymous Person and You think to Yourself what's the real meaning of being Anonymous and it's quite an important trick of the trade for the Spy to become Anonymous so You can Infiltrate the Tribes without being treated as an Outsider, it's Imperative that You give up all the prized Knowledge You have Acquired in Your Lifetime and Depending on Your age, it may be mountains or piles, it doesn't really matter what You know or what You don't know for there's not a single human being in this entire Universe in the full History of the World – recorded or unrecorded – who knows every single damn thing and achieve what we call Omniscience which is one of the Three Attributes of Jehovah, the God of Israel and not the God of THE REPUBLIC for We Worship no gods and all gods are also accepted in the Broken Temple and yeah, it's the only place in the World that takes in all your unwanted Idols, bring them there, and the Water Witch of the South will Bless them and inform You if it's something she wants to keep… or not…

After the Inspection and the Interview, You will be given THE KEY to Your ROOM and in the time You are going to spend in the compounds of THE REPUBLIC, We, the Guardians, including You, We will not be Held Responsible for any Misfortune that befall You so You know that if You Fracture a Finger, We will not be Liable to Claims on Your injury but we will send You to the Banyan Tree where low lying physicians will tend to Your injury to the best of their Abilities but it's also Imperative that You keep THE KEY with You all the Time for the loss of THE KEY will mean You have to pay The Penalty which is Reasonable and Fair so You will not spend Fortune, it's a contract that suits everybody fine so it's best that You sign on the dotted line after reading all the fine print before making the Decision to stay for the number of nights requested. Once You come into THE REPUBLIC, You are to Follow all the Rules and Regulations for these things ensure Everything will run smoothly without any hitch or high pitch singing voice pleading with You to Trade Your Dislikes before it's Time to Give Up Your Spirit, You are Advised to get used to Your ROOM because once it's locked, there's no way You can't get out for there are no windows and the walls and floor are made of the most exquisite ice so You feel Cool in the Heat and it's air locked so You will never find any insects or animals in the ROOM and sorry, Your pet will have to be left at the PET HOSTEL where they will be Pampered by the Most Artistic Pet Hairdressers, Manicurists, Shampoo Girls, Pet Chefs, Entertainers, Masseurs, and all those great things fit for Your Beloved Pet so You don't have to worry about them because We adore pets even more than You, only, our pets are FREE and roaming around so it's best that You come Prepared if You want to venture into THE JUNGLE All by Yourself, You better come to THE FOUNDATION before You embark on Your Adventure, yeah, just relax a little, drink a cup of fire cold Acai Mint Lime Guava Smoothie in THE GREENHOUSE and enjoy a Smoke of anything You Wish or if You want to try the Old Dutch, You are Welcome, all the same, it's also included in the Sums paid to Our Treasurer who will funnel the funds to THE COUNCIL which is made up of every Citizen just so Everybody has a say in THE FORUM, the only real place left which Champions FREE SPEECH and the true colors of FREEDOM... yeah... isn't it all about FREEDOM?

"Where is It? I Want to See It!"

Still, no answer. At that moment when he felt the last wavelength of vibration fade from the door and absorbed the last wave of sound of brass fin hammering on Rock of Brass, Jeremiah decided that it would be quite Impossible to go home now and come back tomorrow because the line is getting longer all the time, and he still had to relay the message to the rest of his sisters. Right then, the task at hand turned out to be much more complicated as he's really doubtful if he would even see Blue Moon that very day. It's peculiar how things could change in such a short time. When he arrived at the door and communicated with her on the other side of the door, he was highly optimistic that the message would be sent and received in just a short time but now that he's making the trip to the backyard, he's feeling rather dragged down by the gravity of the task at hand, and he wasn't so sure that he was the best person to perform his Mother's wishes. It had seemed so simple in the beginning...

"No… I don't mean…"

"Go ahead… Open the Door… You will See…"

"I CAN SEE EVERYTHING! I CAN SEE YOUR STOMACH! I CAN SEE YOUR RIBS! I CAN SEE YOUR BLOOD!"

"Hey Hammerstein, give me a Bloody Mary! Double!!"

"*I'm Gonna Wash That Man Right Outta My Hair*"

"Do You know that song? It's my favorite song of All Time!"

"It's a song that empowers woman. If You are a woman and You are going through a difficult phase, it's a good time to listen to that song. It helped many women overcome their sorrows."

"Is there any restaurant around?"

"Sure... We have one Nice Cafe... just walk half a mile East and then make a right. When You see the Traffic Light... look around... You will find it..."

"No... I don't mean..."

"What Can I do for You Today?"

"I would like the Weekly Special, please..."

"Alright... that will be Eleven Feathers... Thank You..."

"Don't mention it... can You share the WIFI password... please..."

"Here... Drink It in Remembrance of Me."

Pueblo is a small city between Colorado Springs and Moffat which is the Next Destination and it's Extraordinary to take that minivan with all around windows where there's no check-in required for Your luggage unlike the big cities where Security must be heightened in case of some disaster or other such threats that threaten the life of every resident living in the big cities, it must be a big tragedy to see hundreds dead or sometimes even thousands as in the case of 911 which is such a Wonder that it's Ingrained in the minds of every person in the world, You can go to the most remote hideout in Bhutan and You can ask any kid in the village about the Planes and Buildings, coming from a Muslim country, I can attest that the Malays were Happy about the Twin Towers and Many of Them are Staunch Supporters of Al Qaeda Including the Woman and her First Man, it's Serious, the Muslims Cheered and Shouted their Approval in the Bars though they were not allowed to Drink Beer, Nobody could Prevent them from Sipping Tea as they

Watched it Over and Over again, Feeling Prouder than You can ever Imagine, it's their most Trumphant Moment and they will tell You all about it, how the planes crashed into the buildings and how they just crumbled down like castles of ash cascading unto Ground Zero when You burn them, yeah, they know the song too, and it's such a grand catastrophe that so many victims were struck at the back of their necks by most devastating Karate Chop executed by Masutatsu Oyama so like a Samurai walking on a String, they clenched their teeth so hard that their cheek bones cracked and then they crashed into the pillow placed in front of them and it's such a Great Sleep that they could sleep forever and it's possible... say... they want to wake up from the Big Dream anytime... it's not necessary that they will be in a Coma and Sleep for more than Six or Sixteen years, it doesn't matter, the Fear was so deeply injected in the Red veins in their hearts beating in Insecurity almost every other day even more than seventeen years even if the Sleeping Giant wakes up seventeen or seventy years later, it's Surprising You still see Him as Plump and Before, His Nose Redder than Rudolf's, his stomach as sculptured as The Thinker which don't make so much sense if You really think about it for a while, yeah, not even a minute, just think, how does he get all muscular by just sitting in that pose all naked or not, I forget, and yeah, the sculpture would make more sense if it's a Middle Aged Wanderer, Somebody who has seen enough of the World and read enough books to think for more than a few hours a day as his Primary Occupation so he's developed a Belly due to all the rare wines he has tasted all over the World and he can't say NO when people are being generous to him, it's the Gaucho's style, it's very Simple, You don't carry any Debt, You just carry Your Pride as a Gypsy and You go from One

Place to Another, Blessing the Highways, Rivers, and Sky, yeah, the Husband of Pink Blossom who must have some children now for they were doing it so much so they should have at least twelve children lining up like the kids in the *Sound of Music*, *Mary Poppins*, *Chitty Chitty Bang Bang*, *Fiddler on the Roof*, which are still some of the Greatest Films in the History of Cinema and they should be shown to every child before the age of seven to Implant some sort of Triumph into their little hearts so they will learn how to sing the music that little bit more and it's an important discovery for those Unjust Criminals who Only Live to Kill as many humans and animals as possible, performing atrocious Acts of War against Humanity whether it's to chop off heads or to destroy entire cities and civilizations, yeah, it's never ending, this spiral of I Hit You and You Hit I Hit You Hit Hit Hit Hit, yeah, how long more, how long more before You are Satisfied with the number of Deaths at Your Hands, Murderer! Look… Look… Savor the scenes of Mountains on Your Left and the rushing waters of Arkansas washing Your Soul clean… on Your Right… Yeah… Take in the Pristine Air of the Valley even when the Windows are Shut and Forget Everything as You Scan the flushed out landscape just as those two Fools sitting behind You with their Smart Dog in front of their feet so when the vehicle halts or slows down, the dog slides up to Your feet and she loves You more than her owners, licking Your toes to partake of Your Spirits, dried and stimulating, it's such a pleasure, You return the Kindness by petting her on her Head with Your toes and in those few minutes of her life, she fully understood what it means to be Melancholic as she was pulled away by the bigger quieter Fool who struck Deals in the Bus while mostly Ignoring the Complaining Fool who's just rambling a Load of Rubbish all the time, Pissing on Pueblo being such a Horrid town that he would never ever step foot there anymore and the way he said it, it showed his complete Disgust for he was so Devastated that he didn't even walk a few steps from the Circle where he camped, lying down on the pavement like it belongs to his Great Grandfather and even if it did belong to him, how can he say such things about a town when he didn't even walk around Downtown which is such a vibrant hub of Energy that You can feel the Scorn of the Devil when You walk past them and You are made to feel like You are a Minor O Minority and not the Majority so You walked another Circle around the block before entering the café, the only decent one in the City but it's Alright, it's such a great joint because You can sit there for a few hours, enjoying their Middle of the Line Coffee and passing time in such a hurry, listening to some of the Latin Jazz songs You used to play, every day, and while We are talking about Music, the Law is Passed, Music that Instigates Violence are not Allowed in THE REPUBLIC and it's also True that Every Citizen will be Educated and Instructed in Arts and Letters so it will not be until Adulthood when the Young Ones are informed about such macabre stuff and such other Negative Elements so if their parent passes away, they will just be told they have gone to a New Place and it's Important that they relate to it in the Physical Sense because they are not yet ready for such Reality like Everything Lives, Everything Dies, Everything, Everything Passes, and they will be told of the Miracles so they will have Faith to move Mountains, yeah, mostly, they use Machines and all these gadgets to Hook the Masses and that's the Reason why people don't read much books anymore but the Young Ones ought to read for it may well be the most important skill they may learn in their entire life and the real treasures are being buried under heavier and heavier Earth Shattering Truths and like it or not, it's the only way that they will know how the Telephones of our Times Sounded in Winter and it's exactly things like this that opens all the World to them, of course, it's a World that We Create but it's done for the Future of Future Generations so it's still in their Interests that We are Forming THE REPUBLIC in the First Place and it's not just the Best Way to Go Forward but the Only Way for We have given every Government and every Nation enough chances and centuries to Repent and Uplift Reason but it's Impossible in Utmost Fear and Impossible Disdain for Immigrants slowly digging away at their Roots and Culture and Wealth and Discipline and Heritage and they are so Fearful that Trafalgar Square will be One Day be Called *Ni Ma De Men* or worse… *Damascus Tree*… One Day, who knows, if the Price is Right, You can buy anything at all, yeah, even Kingdoms and Realms, yeah, You think, You can buy Salvation, and all the Friends Underneath, well, Think Again, my Foe, Your Actions in this World, Your Words in this World, Your Time in this World, all these Things will Accumulate into a Dot on the Other Side, the Good on the Outside and the Bad on the Inside, and now let's not debate about what You Know or Feel to be Right or Wrong because You have a Soul and a Spirit and no matter how Inhumane You are, You are not so Foolish to believe that there is no Life After and Life will End when You Breathe Your Last, well, Surprise, it's actually Your First, it's so Simple, You will not Fear to go to the Other Side, just like the Blinded Warriors of St. Francisco or Congo or Communism or Allah or Darwinism or Religionism without suffering great Mental Anguish, it must be said You should not Commit Suicide because Your life does not belong to You… yeah… it's very

Simple… Reason… You never chose to be Born in the place where You are HERE… holding this End of the Truth… tasting the Smoke which have been Blessed to Evaporate into Your Eyes before they are Transcribed into Poetry into Your Lungs and Flowing into Your Wild Heart, Pumping the Blood of Great Purity and Channeling the Dragon's Fire, Metamorphosing the Intoxicating Pulp of Black and White Hope into a Giant Bubble Whale in Your Mind, yeah, the Secret Locket of the Brain, Wash, Wash, Wash Away all the Dirt from Your Hands and the Blood from Your Mouth, You Vampire of Jerusalem, yeah, even You are Invited for THE REPUBLIC never rejects Anyone based on Anything so just come and see how the Blue Mountains merge with the Blue Clouds as the Holy Waters Flow against the Gradient of the Slow Slope, Rushing to the Source like Norwegian Salmon, yeah, You can feed those to the Young Ones but for the Warriors, they need their Roasts because there's Something about Lighting a Fire beneath a Whole Carcass of Cow and Waiting for it to Cook while they Drink and boast about how Valiantly they defended the Land, eating the Flesh of the Captives with Sea Salt and Vinegar and thunderbolts for they need to be Barbaric when they are protecting THE REPUBLIC and it's true, Chief Chavatangakwunua was born on the day his Grandmother glimpsed that Short Rainbow and though she's old and most people think that she's going Blind or something else, she saw the Wanderer taking a picture of It so she asked him…

"Oh! A Rainbow! How Beautiful! How Precious! Oh! Oh! Did You get it?"

"Yeah… See?"

"Oh! How Lovely!! There are so many Rainbows here! The Other Day, I saw a Double Rainbow, One on Top of Another, and it was Splendid!!!"

"Yeah…"

"Yeah, I like Bobby more than Bing… do You know them?"

"No…"

"Just listen to *La Mer*… it's my favorite Song of all time!"

"I think Charles is the best…"

"Yves is better…"

"Why can't we have a singer like Georges who plays the Guitar with One Foot on a Chair?"

"He's Ideal as the type of musician we want, someone like that David guy who mastered the Violin so Completely, he didn't even need to see Anything at all when he's playing the Instrument and he's so into It."

"He's Sweating all the time!"

"Yeah, there were such musicians as that Pianist from Beijing who gave up a life of acrobatics though she was guaranteed a Gold Medal if she slept with the Mayor, no, she shunned that kind of life in her Fatherland to go West where she studied the Instrument and Scales and European Traditions so she can play all the pieces with her eyes closed while she slides on the Leather Saddle, wetting her panties as she moves from one end to the other, O Wonder, You have to Lick the Screen, my Friend, clean it up."

"We need Musicians who give up their Soul like Evans, Theodorakis, Monk, de Lucia, the Lady, the Sparrow, Beethoven, and all those who…"

"What if they don't want to Come or they can't Come?"

"It's Alright… We have their Records. We can Train New
"Yeah, Surely, they will Arise…"

After the Reaching Rainbow's End, Pedro decided to change his name which was such a Big Decision in his Tribe because it's the Time that he decided to cut away his ties with his Father who had gone to the Other Side on Independence Day and it's with such Great Sorrow that he stopped at the Red Rock which is actually a big rock balancing on its tip and for so long Everybody thought it's going to fall off the cliff but it never did and it's still standing there Today, still, it appears as if it's going to topple and flatten the most Innocent Children or Infants or Squirrels or Bears chasing each other under its Shade at the Spot where it's most likely to tumble, they don't really care for they don't know all about physics and all that scientific things yet and subsequently attacked mercilessly by a swarm of mosquitoes, You know You have arrived at Your Destination, Looking at the Point where the tip rests, You know it's Scientifically Impossible for Cancer to be Cured but there are people who have been cured of it and the thing about the Raising of the Dead is also not Impossible for it has happened more than a few times than You Believe just because Memory is a funny thing so that You Remember only what You want to Remember no matter how painful how illogical how dangerous the Narrow Road, on that day, heeding the Call of the Wild, Pedro is Gone to the Other Side with his Father and in his place is one Nahiossi so he cut off his left Thumb and Pinkie as Sacrificial Offering to Kiyiya who howled until his Finest Moment in the Old World came to an End, surrounded by his closest relatives and friends, he felt so full of Pride to see his Great Great Grandchildren howling along with him with tears in their eyes and they cried so much, the room was flooded, joined by the whole Clan, it was with such Sorrow that Nahiossi sealed the wounds with his Blue Hot Knife he renamed Green Fairy so their names start with the same letter, making it easier on the Brain You don't really want to Overstress because it may develop various illnesses such as Depression, Bipolar Disorder, Rabies, Artery Blockage, Schizophrenia, Heart Attack, Post Partum Blues, and a whole host of other such illnesses all bundled together so they are treated with just one type of medication so why are they diagnosed separately but the long-term results include flashbacks, relapses, weight gain, loss of self-esteem, Depression, Bipolar Disorder, Rabies, Artery Blockage, Schizophrenia, Heart Attack, Post Partum Blues, and a whole host of other such illnesses which should not be treated with the same medication resulting in the patients being sent to the Mental Asylum in The End so there's the explanation as to why there are so many mentally ill people all over the World but especially in America, yeah, You will see them, people walking around with no Memory of where they come from or where they are going or even what's their name and then, they just Disappeared, probably carted off City Officials who Work to Keep the City Clean and Attractive to Tourists because Everybody Knows How Big the Tourism Industry so It's Logical that the World don't really see them in the Sense that they try to ignore them as much as possible for they are Always Afraid they will be Attacked when they least expect it, they will be bitten on the nose or something sinister like that, it's Alright, kissing Green Fairy on her lips, Nahiossi Headed to the Mountains to Mourn his Father as all First Born of the Clan Swears to Undertake this traditional ritual though he was really the First Born of his Fifteenth Concubine as Kiyiya was a Native

Maverick Stud, he had many an affair with countless women who fought to be in his bed every night and his conquests have numbered more than he could remember for he had lived more than One Century and a Half and One should not be Jealous or Overjoyed that he was still screwing all those insurance agents and specialty chefs and high class physicians and spritzing his spirits far and wide, even until his last day in the hospital, he was being fucked by his little sultry nurse who kept rubbing on his member while whispering dirty phrases into his ears though he couldn't hear anything at all but only sensing the heat of her breath at that stage of his coma, his Birds were still Chirpy enough to Knock her up so she crawled to the matron when she realized that he had passed away, right away, she wondered if he had already been dead when she was clawing at her own breasts bouncing up and down in furious rhythm so fast that the nipples were slapping on her cheeks and sometimes, the swing was so violent, her own milk squirted into her eyes or nose as she was collapsing on his chest over and over again, honey sweat flowing down her spine onto his stone hard stomach for he's the Most Exalted One she had ever experienced and she had slept with almost a few hundred men, yeah, she's one of those sex maniacs or nymphomaniacs which means about the same thing only that nymphos sound more animalistic and she's always closing her eyes when she holds his Birds in her hands, better than one Hand, and surely better than Two in her Bush, planting primal vulgar smacks on one then the other so she makes those smacking sound so doubly loud it's almost embarrassing but since he was staying in most exclusive suite, it was soundproof so she sucked his Birds dry before swallowing his Spirits and immediately, without waiting for the Green Light, she mounts him for the Birds are still Wooden and not Flying or Singing or Pecking at the Hole in the Tree where You can Bury all Your Secrets without Worry it will ever See Light, no matter how Black the Sin, according to Legend, You have to go to some Deep Jungle or Forest, You Know the Difference, and in such a way, it's compulsory that You go as deep as possible so You are sure Nobody is Around, Up to Radius of Nineteen Miles or more, the Further the Better… the Higher the Better…

SIX COLORS OF EMPATHY

If by now You are Convicted Every Day You have Left may be the Last, it helps matters much much more than You can Imagine, yeah, it makes it all the more easy to discard all those furniture, paintings, toys, guns, vehicles, prescription pills, houses, insurance policies, Dislikes, and while You are it, throw away Your Children, Your pets, Your clothes, it's so familiar, every little bit of thing in the Universe possibly dragging You down or even slowing You down for even a Moment, I implore You, Seriously, Discard Everything, including Your most Delicious Moldy Cheese Chocolate Mushroom Clouds with Camphor, Cinnamon, Rosemary, and Thyme, and let's not forget those fantastic Petals of Golden Peonies to make Your Bosom more Voluptuous more Supple more Spicy more Flowery more Aromatic more Ecstatic more Romantic more Sensual more Sumptuous for Your Lover, yeah, even Your most Precious Lover who has ever made You understand the Rules in the Nine or Ten Kingdoms, and yeah, Forget Everything and run at fullest speed to the door, open the door directly and if You have an infant or two and You are confident You can Carry them without Foregoing Your fullest speed even a trifle, then, by all means, carry them and make the quickest dash to get out of the house or whatever building You are in, and if You Happen to be in a Trian or Bus, Good Luck but Otherwise, Just Shoot Straight for the Closest EXIT, again, open it, quicker than a leopard changing its spots right before Your eyes, Don't be Fooled, Don't Look, just head out and run for the nearest Hill with All Might and All Fastest Speed ever, breasts bouncing, testicles slapping against Your thighs, and hundreds or thousands of people overtaking You because they are more athletic and bigger in stature so they have longer limbs and hearts that beat more Efficiently than You real city folks who seldom walk more than fifty steps in Your Daily life, Beware, You will be left behind and zapped into thin air and there will be nothing in the space where You see Your Toilet, it will not be there anymore, and where You see Your Emails, it will not be there anymore, and where You see Your Toenails, it will not be there anymore, Everything's just a Vision, Everything Vanishing as if there's Nothing else except Nature as many people were zapped along with all those structures and objects and every other living thing but even You, You have trained for this Day all Your Life, You were almost zapped too just because You were not Cold Blooded enough to leave Your babies to be zapped and You certainly rolled the dice to be zapped with them together rather than saving Your own Precious Life, yeah, We Admire You for You have Overcome the Fear of Death and You probably deserve a Purple Heart or two and there's nothing You can do if You cannot run more than one hundred steps at fullest speed which is just about twelve miles an hour and if You ever walked that distance, You will know it's not something You can cover in fifty five minutes or less unless You are some kind of professional competitive marathoner who goes the distance and these people will surely be safe unless some accidents occur so once You reach the Foot of the Hills, Scramble up as fast as possible and let's not bother with Civility and other such Rubbish for It's the Apocalypse and it's not that film about a few soldiers going into the Jungle which is based on *Heart of Darkness* which is a book I have never read but I can tell you that it's a terrific book to read to Your Children when You are putting them to Bed, yeah, Why not read some Spanish Poetry or Opera Lyrics or the History of the Roman Empire, You will be amused at how Sweetly they look when they fall asleep with a Big Smile on their frost bitten faces and You think to Yourself… O What Cuteness… O How Can Any Harm Befall these Angels… and the Truth… the Hand of God has no Eye, no, not even One, It doesn't have any Sense so It can be Devastating especially for people who never think about such things in their whole lives even if they have lived up to a few hundred years old, they just think that they will always wake up Tomorrow and Tomorrow and so on, there's no stopping these people for they will somehow find a way to Survive and live another Tomorrow, and Everything will be just the way it has always been like Yesterday, You know, that song, so what, so they will experience the most mind-boggling short term memory loss as they see everything they have created and built and fucked and nourished and watered and educated and promoted and brought to the Zoo at least once in their lives and You think You have done what a parent is expected to do a lot more for the Young Ones who You suspect were not very keen on the Trip but anyhow, You just want to bring them to the Hot Springs to play by themselves while You take a long deserved dip, it was the most perfect plan of All and in that small town, far away from the City, You see how that Giant Lightning Blaze Came from the Sky and blasted the whole Town into Nothingness, and surprisingly, You don't feel any Pain at all though a few hundred of Your family members, a few thousand of Your friends, and billions upon billions of Dislikes are Dust now, You are so shocked You stand there, a statue of flesh and bones, arms akimbo, Your Eyes looking at the Sky and then the City where it used to be and You really don't believe Your Eyes for You have never seen anything like it, even on Tablets or Computers or TV or Cartoons or anywhere else but only… it's Real… and no matter how much You rub Your Eyes until they bleed and turn All Black, it doesn't matter, it's still the same, it's Gone… Disappeared just like that and Forget all about that Christ is Coming Back for His Bride type of promise or any False Prophet telling You it's on this Date and that Date and they ask You to donate all Your possessions and follow them, well, You can spit on their faces and vomit on their carpets all You wish and I don't even care if You agree or not or think or not or breathe or not or not turning back to look at the best view of Colorado Avenue emblazoned in most glorious sunset, crossing the Bridge with Natural Insect Spray and a Greek Dinner, suddenly, there's a very strong wind blowing directly from opposite direction, parallel to the Direction Home, making it the Hardest a Wind in the City can Barricade for me to Progress, Measured at more than twenty eight or thirty six miles per hour and carrying with it, Sparkling Quartz Particles from Manitou Springs or somewhere further or nearer but it's the Damn Strongest Wind You have Faced in Your Life and You know It's Strong because the plastic bags were like lips vibrating so much they became miniature parachutes even when there's a good thousand plus grams in There so it's certainly strong enough to blow away some things under a certain weight and there are some leaves as well if You can open Your eyes, yeah, You will see some leaves and some Tea Cup Puppies flying in the Sky as well as Malnourished Children... they will find it quite Impossible to walk against such a Fierce Wind so they were Stumbling backwards in such a way their tiny legs are moving in the opposite direction but they reversed on their heels as they struggle to figure out the best way to remain Stationary, definitely, the first thing to do is to Find Your Footing and that's why it's so important for Young Ones to learn the Horse's Stance which is a simple thing to do but it takes a lot of patience and endurance to bring it to the level where even twelve Green Giants couldn't move You even a millimeter of a millimeter even if they recruit all their friends and relatives and yeah, everybody else, the Whole World, including animals and all other beings like Sprites, Dwarves, Halflings, Werewolves, Super Heroes and whatever else, they cannot move You at all as they press from all sides in a circular kind of Pressure and even with all the Energy of the Universe, it Shall Not Dislodge You in any way, shape or form, and You smile at how they are all using all their Might and how they are straining so much until their veins were at the point of exploding and they are sweating buckets of spirits but they cannot infiltrate the Sphere of Green Force, and You know, whoever is Inside, they will be Safe too but the Circle is not that Big Yet so it Accommodates no more than two Adults and Four Children so the Best Way to Prepare Yourself for such an occasion is to watch how it's done properly in those old Jackie Chan Movies about Snake and Cat and Dragon and Drunken Fist...

Yeah, it's very Simple Resurrection by Slim Smith, now, can You Hasten to do but as You practice more, You will feel Your Roots going into the Ground and to be Exact, it's Highly Recommended that You Perform this Exercise on some Fertile ground just not on Concrete but as with all things, You must learn to make do with what You have and not what You have not so when You are in a New Town and You are Thinking about the Previous Town, it's Called ECHO and Now, Your Body is in Crestone but Your Spirit is in Colorado Springs so You are seeing some common scenery of the Old Town in the New Town and it's such a Wonder the whole town is infested by mosquitoes and too many other species to be counted, it's a place for Fools as You see the Jeep with Neon WELCOME Sign Approaching the Moffat Post Office cum Bus Terminal cum Court cum Police Station, and You are opening the back door to put Your Fresh USDA Beef and Pork and Basket of Fresh Vegetables and Fruits while the Corn Mother is afraid of the Mosquitoes getting into the Jeep because she's going to Wake Up very early in the Morning to go to the Tibetan Temple to pay respects to the Gods Atoning herself for killing hundreds of those mosquitoes following You everywhere and for people who have never Experienced such a Rock Steady Calamity, it's a real Nuisance and in Those Times, You really don't care much about Reincarnation or Killing or the Pope so You are Informed, there are these special medallion insect repellent with refills that really get the job done and there's also this radar sonic insect frequency moderator or something that emits a sort of brain crushing kind of technology for We don't have to Practice any Form of Humanity to them simply because they only have a Few Dislikes so they will not come into the protected space and a good one can cover up to one acre of land so if You can afford it, it's the best thing though they never talk about how high frequency signal affects the human brain, and obviously, they cannot tell You the Long Term side effects because the Studies about Korea shall reveal it cannot be harmful to the Human Ear since it cannot be picked up even by the sharpest ears in Town and they have tested it extensively so it's perfectly safe for You and Your Children like the Sunday Matinee which is always all sun-filled fun and bright laughter to spread the Good Hope of the Innocent Age when Little Girls still Spoke to Big Bad Wolves and tamed them with such a kooky song as *Chu-Chi Face* and You thought how silly she looked when she tickled Your Chin and ran to hide under the Bell, and how You brought her to the Casa de Colores, housing all kinds of Gods in such a small space, there are Images of Christ here and there and Tezcatlipoca and Sleeping Buddha and Quetzalcoatl and Apollo and Mohamed and Jehovah Jireh and Huitzilopochtli and Poseidon and Vishnu and *Crocodile Dundee* and *The Godfather* and there are also some lovely statues of the Virgin Mother but She wasn't a Virgin at the Age portrayed in some of those Idols, it's Written, She also delivered the Children of Joseph who must had felt the Wrath of God when he made love to Mary for the very first time and She's still a Virgin, he's so surprise to find her hymen intact even though she had given birth to Christ just a few days ago, it's such a Miracle because she didn't even bleed as the wet nurse whispered that the Holy Baby was born without any umbilical cord so He didn't have any belly button and that's the real sign that He's the Son of God, Isn't it?

Just as he was starting to go around the house, joining the City of the People from all over the World, he heard someone shouting, "Hey boy! Where are you going?" Who's that? A little startled by the Loud but somewhat comforting exhortation, his immediate response was to ignore the person and try to speed up. Obviously, he didn't turn back to take a look at her no matter how Beautiful for it was a melodic voice, and he was constantly warned about how he should stay away from strangers so he just tried to get on with his duty as quickly as possible. At the same time, he was wondering why he was trying to escape... he knew the person to be a woman, yeah, a woman more than a girl for he's perceptive enough to make such distinctions just based on her voice, he could tell that she's a kind person simply because there's a kind of warmth and cotton type of softness in those few words plus he also detected some kind of familiarity in the voice though he could swear on Lulu's life that he had never ever heard it before. What's the point? He stopped when he could smell the flowers in her bosom, realizing it's pointless to try to escape since she's much faster. Casting a side ward glance at her hand which was on his shoulder, he saw that she was turning gray.

"Where are You going?"

"My sister... Blue Moon..."

"Why are You trying to Ignore me? Don't You Remember?"

"No... I don't know You..."

"What are You talking about??? I'm Your Sister! I'm BulBul! See?"

Really? Jeremiah looked at her carefully from top to bottom quite a couple of times, shaking his head, and at that same time, sweating his mind inside out, trying to find out if he indeed had a sister by such a name for his memory was almost photographic in the sense that he could memorize whole volumes of encyclopedias so it's no secret why his Mother has chosen him to perform the important task even though he's the slowest of them all, and he perceived how it's extremely rude to forget the name of his own brother or sister, especially in such a close knit family, and all that sort of mindless civility bearing down on his young, fragile soul, finally, he could tell the Truth.

"Is this the House of Dislikes?"

"Yes… You have come to the Only Place."

"Congratulations! You have won a new Planet!"

"No. Where are You going?"

"I'm Bringing this new Wolf Skin for my Grandma and this Quiver of Poison Arrows for my Grandpa."

"Do You have the Address?"

"It's on Sunset Boulevard!"

"Yeah… but where's the Intersection?"

"Roanoke Ave and Tioga Ave"

"Wait for a minute… stand here… don't move…"

"Sometimes… I feel… like a Motherless Child…"

"Come… come… I will show You the way to the Rainbow House…"

"Here… put Your leaves into these bottles… and here's a Christmas Tin Box for You to keep Your pipe…"

"It looks like an Antique! How nice!"

"Thanks… it's made of Antelope Horn…"

"There's a way which seems right to Man but it's End is…"

"Shut Up! We don't want to listen to all these kind of talk! It makes us feel Reckless!"

"The Swan is the Ugly Duckling!"

"The Way to Eternal Damnation!"

"Do You ever answer any of our questions? What's the Meaning of the Truth? Answer us! Don't beat around the Bush!"

"There are Seventy Two Maidens Waiting Outside Your Door and You Cannot Open It!"

"It's Boring! We don't want to go to the Hills!"

"Why do the Insects come out the whole day? It's strange. In my country, they only come out in the Evening."

"Did You bring the Insect Repellant? Did You bring long pants and some long sleeve shirt or sweater?"

"It may be the Aliens… You Know…"

"No… You said it's not Cold at all…"

"Alright… when You go out… put on this orange sweater… it's my father's… and this pair of old jeans… it's my husband's… but he's very tall so You have to fold it up… then… spray these clothes with the Insect Repellent…"

So it went that she explained all about her artworks in the Studio and all the work involved in the Art of printmaking and watercolor painting of the Chief and Psychedelia and Frida Kahlo who is like her First Most Important Idol of All Time, I mean, judging from the way her Eyes sparkled when she heard me utter those magical sounds of her Name, it's true, she loved the Artist more than the Virgin Mother who's cruelly inveined into her sense of Rebellion and she had a lot of those Spirits for she was a real native gypsy girl even when she was so young, she was following her Father around, Mr. Colorado, he's highly Imaginative and Hard-working with his Remarkable Talents of Rebuilding Houses into Homes so he could simply buy the most run down places in the Neighborhood for pittance and he has the Mind to See What has to be Done as long as the gas pipes and electricity lines are in good working condition, he and her brothers can buy a Property for a few thousand Dislikes and within the time of a few moons, they can rip the whole place down and rebuild the piece of thrash property into Swan Feather Properties with Most Beautiful Dollhouse and Intelligent, Courageous Brothers to protect her from all Kinds of Hardships that may befall her, she's like the Princess in the Family and her Father and Mother dotes on her so much for she's talented with her hands from a very young age such that she was able to draw the most meaningful pictures to make her Mother Blush and her Father Giggle, bringing much Happiness so much so that Everybody loves to be around her for she's such a Spicy Performer when she plays the Ninja Hide Drum during those Tribal Native Mexican Celebrations which were truly Tribal Sacrifices for You will see during those times that the most number of Buffaloes, Yaks, Cows, Bulls, Rams, Goats, Lambs, Sheep, and such Dark Meat animals are Slain to Maximum Volume and if only You can see where their Blood flow so You know how Large the Farm and the Sharpness of the Knife needed to make it as Painless a Death as humanely possible so the suffering of the Beasts is brought to a Minimum by Bringing them to the Slaughter House specially designed to make the killings as Civil as it can ever be done, only then, it so happened that they were forced to leave Trinidad as the Sheriff was under great duress to Create Tension in the town so regular Citizens who don't know how to think properly and those who are lazy to read books Immersing some Important Lesson in the Universe and Life and yes, You may Rewind all You want, and listen to Your favorite favorite type of music either repeated repeatedly at twice the Original speed or You may opt to slow it down at an eighth of the slow speed of Snail so it becomes a Fucking Long epic Song of the Century and such grandiose slow motion movement so You can copy what that Gal in the movie did… again… and again…

During the first few weeks in her New Elementary School, she had befriended a quiet Asian boy and they were walking to The Tree where they would play Chasing Around the Tree for at least twenty five to thirty rounds before she would give up as Chong Wu was really Fast and even her Best Friend, Tis-see-woo-na-tis who tried to Help her catch that boy with all her speed, she's the champion runner but he's always step or two ahead and it didn't even seem like he's running at full speed yet so they were Lucky that The Tree was quite a Huge tree with girth measuring two times the Radius of Twenty Two Point Three Feet times the value of Pie which You know is Infinite so the actual Scientific measurement for any Circle is only arbitrary but let's just say that it takes about fifty steps for Corn Daughter to complete the Circle, it takes Chong Wu only thirty steps and Tis-see-woo-na-tis forty two steps or less depending on her Form for she's not so consistent like the two of them, all it means for the two of them was that Young Bill and His Gang of Cowboys, they had been keeping an eye on the two of them and they carefully selected a secluded spot to ambush them so as to take them by complete surprise without anyone else coming close as they stationed some Cowboys at strategic spots to ensure that Nobody will be coming to the area, it's with such Trickery that Young Bill approached that Odd Pair.

"Are We the only Asians Here?"
"Hey! Chink Wu! What are you doing here?"
"Ha! Ha! Ha! Ha! Ha! Ha!"
"Get Him!"
"Run! Run! Run! Chong Wu! Run! Run! Run!"

In that moment, he just couldn't run. Somehow, his legs turned to water and he just started to cry like nobody's business for he didn't know if he had made things worse or worse, he cried like a mummy's boy though his mummy passed away quite a number of years ago and he's not even close to his daddy who sent him away to his granny as soon as he got a brand new wife he's so crazy about her that he sucked her toes and licked her Pearl of Opium for a great many hours for he exclaimed how it tasted like the Elixir of Youth, somehow, he was becoming younger everyday so some days, he didn't eat her dumplings for he was becoming almost like a teenager while he walks with fresh Spring in his steps, nevertheless, Chong Wu didn't harbor no ill feelings towards his daddy who fathered sixteen step brothers and sisters with Miss Tiger Toe for even when she reached the age of one hundred and seven and the number of offspring of her offspring reached a Thousand or more, spread all over the Earth, she still insists that she be addressed as Miss Tiger Toe, and though he's sometimes Jealous of his step siblings for they were always dressed as movie stars or models, he couldn't deny that she's the Fairest of Them All and he didn't complain much because he had an Allowance of a Thousand Dislikes every month and for a boy of five or six, it's plenty of Dislikes so he could go to school anywhere and he wisely chose to go America to get far away from his so-called

Family and join his cousin's family and start all over again, and he's so pleased to have met Ominotago who reached out to him on his third day in school for all the other kids ignored him all the time and he was feeling a little of the Culture Shock they always warn people who are going to another country to check the Currency, Climate, Standard of Living, Places of Attraction, Demographics, Crime Rate, Geography, Education System and such other things, it's the Culture which is the most Immeasurable as it can be difficult to teach an Indian to use his hands to eat on Leaf of Banana so there's no need to wash plates and utensils so it's so ecologically perfect but for the Demand becoming too high and economically unviable for those farmers to sell the plants for almost Nothing, then, the Cowboys started circling Chong Wu and singing Ghost Songs to Frighten him and he's so scared that he pissed and shat in his pampers but it's overloading, causing his pants to become more roundish and they were laughing even harder when Young Bill was forcing the poor little boy to lick his shoes smeared with his Daddy's very own shit he brought from home, and Chong Wu was such a mess that he was frothing and going into spasms so he was all covered with green shit and foam… when out of nowhere, just when Young Bill was about to force the shoe into his mouth, POW! Ominotago Jumped into the Scene and WOW! knocked Young Bill on the nose with Stunning knee kick so his eye balls fell out like stones and he fainted immediately, falling into his Special Private Pot while Chong Wu hugged her so very tightly for more than a few minutes before taking pictures of her standing over Young Billy with her foot on his right cheek, she appeared so Victorious, she's Untouchable…

"Mr. Colorado, we are sorry… but we have to expel your daughter..."

"Please! Sir! Is there anything that can be done?"

"No. Mr. Bill was absolutely mad. He wanted to press charges against Ominotago…"

"But… she's so young… just seven years old…"

"Yeah, he mentioned how she's so young and dangerous so we can imagine how dangerous she will be when she comes of age…"

"But… they were bullying the Arabian Boy!"

"O Koreans are our friends. They wouldn't say anything…"

"What about the Pictures?"

"O Don't worry about that…"

Yeah, except the Mosquitoes. Going into the Hills, Nahiossi never Imagined he would be attacked by such pests feeding on his flesh and blood and they especially thirsted for his blood because he had killed so many men with his most Beloved Always Dependable Green Fairy as it's always just the two of them when he's away from it all, walking towards the Tibetan Shrine, Vajra Vidya, Indestructible Knowledge, he prayed to Guan Yin and Shrine of His Holiness, asking for protection and direction, and immunity from the mosquitoes but somehow, he's becoming quite distraught to be walking, living, fresher than ever food for the insects and he could see it's not just mosquitoes but other types as well and it's the first time in his life that he felt Impotent even when he had Green Fairy with him, he thought he would take a few more steps into more private parts before he engaged in a bloody

Fight to End All Fights with the insects and though they came in the millions, he managed to destroy more than a few hundred thousand of them in just under an hour, Nahiossi took Great Delight in the Exercise tremendously because he Improved his Slicing Skills up another half level or two since he's Famous as The Gaucho of Gauchos, he always had to be ahead of the Competition.

In that Final Battle when he's facing the West Nile Mosquito King who could kill a person with just one sting, he's much bigger than normal mosquitoes and if You can Zoom in, You will see his Crown for all kings must be identified by the Crown and it's quite a Regal artifact, yeah, he's even carrying a miniature Spear in one leg, a miniature Mirror in another, and a miniature Lotus Flower in another, and a miniature Book in another, let's see, and a miniature Spindle in another, and a miniature Golden Scale in the last leg, he moves so fast, it's even hard to see him but only for the Sound of his Flight being Louder than the other normal mosquitoes for his Wings are extra Big and Strong so when they are flapping in quick succession, they Stir the Air for all they care, and it's only when he pickled the Sound that Nahiossi was able to Track his Patterns of Warfare and with Green Fairy's Inverted Lightning Dance where the Delta was at the Top so it appeared as if the Bolt was sent from the Earth to the Sky instead of the other way around, Zap! Zap! Zap! the Wings floated in a balletic lullaby so it's like they were slowly oscillating on invisible swings, slowly, falling to the ground but not for the West Nile Mosquito King who fell so thunderously with clumsy THUD! that he bruised at least half of his knees and crashed into the root of a dying tree, seriously injuring his sexual organ so he couldn't engage in Reproduction Rituals any more, he was carried back to his

Palace by his generals and barbarians who waved the White Flag quite so easily when they saw that Defeat was Nigh, and then, finally, Nahiossi could take a Rest beneath the Sacred Wind Chime and he saw that it's quite a big one with many colored strings of seven colors joining hollow aluminum cylinders of various lengths to create higher and lower pitched sounds to create natural music so sacred in the hills, sadly, there's no Wind, not even a wing of it so he climbed up to the Top of the China Tree and rang the Chime with all his leftover Might so mightily that he couldn't move his hands for a good few hours and after half a day of Hard Practice with Green Fairy and climbing up the most energy sapping hills, he was feeling more thirsty than the mosquitoes, certainly he's suffering from a bad case of dehydration, his lips were flaking and he just remembered that he had not a droplet of water so he looked around for source of water and he saw some nice little pinkish cactus flowers and without thinking twice, he ate them, and he ate some other edible leaves to stay alive but it must be said here that Botany is a specialized field of study so it's not Encouraged that You follow the actions of Nahiossi since he's highly trained in Traditional Remedy, he knows what plants are safe for Consumption and what plants are poisonous and not fit for Consumption for animals and humans alike so You better warn Your family and friends of the Dangers of Travelling in the Wild and carry enough water.

After half a day in the Hills, You will feel refreshed and strong in Spirit for the Hills are so Refreshing and Rejuvenating like all the Posters You see of Mountain Men smoking cigarettes of all brands while the Chief smokes his Peace Pipe and everything's so Quiet, You can hear the sound of Your very own Heartbeat and You can also hear the Big Eagle

Gliding in the Sky, Eyeing for a Prey, as usual, how Majestic he swoops and catches the Snake in his claws and it's kind of Amusing there's Nothing she can do to Free herself while he uses his Powerful Beak to peck at her Magnetic Eyes so she becomes Blind instantly and then how he continues until he pecks at the Brain and devours it with Double Happiness in his Heart as he divides the Snake into two parts, the Head part for the small group of Hawks numbering around six or seven and he gets the Tail part for its all his Hard Work. It's true what they say about these Hills, there are hundreds and hundreds of Meditation portals all over so when You feel the need to Sit or Stand or be at the same Point to contemplate the Wonders of Nature, You can STOP and spend some time to look at the Valley and the Heavens and the Trees and the Mosquitoes and Breathe in the Song of the Great Spirit as She Blows through the leaves to produce a sort of rippling reflection of rapturous melodies of Pan spying on the naked Nymphs in the Bush, Inside the Secret Refuge, surely, he was very excited to see their private parts exposed as they chase each other around the Pond, their thick luxurious hair no longer covering their nubile bodies but thrashing wildly all about and laughing and giggling like Nobody's Business and the best part was that they are totally unaware that he's Playing with his half man half goat penis which has grown so Gargantuan and Taut he sprayed his Semen everywhere and there's even some on his horns and these Nymphs, they always make him so Horny and Rocky, he Grunts, he will hypnotize them one by one and conquer them with his Pipe for he can play the most Hypnotic tunes, attracting a great number of admirers including Midas, and he dreams that the Nymphs will come to him and he's Making Love to all of them, Slipping his Tail into one Nymph after another

Nymph for just a few hours only for each one while the rest of them plant plush kind amazing kisses all over his body, including his hindquarters though the hooves and horns are Harder so he can't feel any sensation, in Pan's dream, he can sense the brush of their erect nipples on every part of his body and it's so Real, he will rather Die than to Wake Up from such a Wonderfully Never Ending Deluge of Unspeakable Sensations, Nobody can blame him at all for it's the Dream only dreamed by satyrs who possess Eternal Erections so they can give the Greatest measure of satisfaction to Women of All Nations, they will enjoy the Sweetest Fruits, watered by the Sweetest Rain and nourished by the Sweetest Sunshine...

Coming Down from Other Side of the Hill, there's a dusty road, and You just have to go East to return to the Case De Colores but it's still quite a distance. Along the way, You will pass by an Ashram but if You reach the Spanish Creek, it means You are on the Wrong Track so it's best to go in the direction of the Japanese Shinto Colony known as Shumei. It's a Landmark worth remembering because You can take a Rest at the Food Area though they don't serve any food but Praise be to the Japanese folks, there's no mosquito in the compound because it's quite obvious these people can afford to buy a few hundred nuclear torpedoes to blow up some Islands so You know they will have installed that Ultra Sonic Mosquito Warding Machine so fortunately, You are not a pest but a Photographer who just came to explore the Region and finding a Fountain of Water, You rush to it like You have not a mouthful of water for more than a few days, and still, Nahiossi washed the Blood off Green Fairy for she was winged all over, and she's more than six hundred years old even though You will never suspect it when You hear her name for it's so Innocent and Harmless for what do those

Beings do other than Bless people and bring them some sort of Happiness and Profit so they are all more Confident than when they first started off really not knowing how to solve the Problem at all, most of them could only Cry and sing about how poorly they had been treated by their Step Mothers or the Heat or the Market favoring the Technical Sector because they have the Aptitude to understand all kinds of Sciences and it's true considering the superior wages these people spend without breaking a sweat and how so many people are running to pay to meet them in those Fancy Dislike Dinners where they are certain they will get a Tip or Two to harvest a few more millions in a few years so they see it as a privilege to come to the Crestone Center to learn English for a few years but Nahiossi didn't understand a Single Word Kurosawa muttered for the guy was speaking in Japanese because he thought that he was his countryman and he was so Proud to see his countryman drinking from the Fountain, soothed by the automatic recycling waters and the most gentle Wind like what You feel towards the End of a Song, knowing it's gonna be Ending and You are on full standby to put it in the Loop so it can play in Endless Cycle of Exhilarating Golden Words of the Lyrics appearing in Your Mind and suddenly, he appeared beside You to communicate in enthusiastic mixture of his Native language and New Language as he filled Your bottle with fresh mineral waters and not the Unsafe Waters from the Fountain, he gestured that You should not litter within the compounds but it's alright to continue smoking for his Father's a Smoker too so he perfectly understands why he always has the Urge to Smoke after a good Lunch, a good movie, a good song, a good fuck, a good walk, a good Supper, a good Smoke, he says… makes You more happy than the Gods… and then… The Interrogation… Imagine… being interrogated by a Japanese great grandson of an Honorable Soldier who killed so many of Your relatives so many year ago that You cannot remember all that clearly because You are quite Advanced in Age… Ahhh… the List of Questions…

"What is Your Name?"

"Mr. Hiroshima."

"Ok… Mr. Hiroshima… do… You… want… me… to… give… You… a tour?"

"No… thank you… I'm very tired today…"

"Ok… Mr. Hiroshima… why… do… You… come… to… Cre… Stone?"

"I'm a Medicine Man. I come here to collect Herbs."

"Ok… Mr. Hiroshima… how… long… will… You… be… in… Cre… Stone?"

"Only Two Weeks."

"Ok… Mr. Hiroshima… do… You… want… any… more… Water?"

"Who's that Girl?"

"She's… Tiger Lily… the Prodigy of Reiki."

That night, the Corn Mother was in some extreme jovial mood so she's inviting me to the Hot Springs in the Great Dunes the Next Day and after walking for more than 69 miles over a period of Five days, it was quite an achievement but You don't tell her for You are not boastful, and she's serving You some sort of authentic Mexican food like how the Indigenous people used to make it traditionally and the Pinto beans had been slow boiled for more than half a day so they are tender but still retaining their shell which was of a soda crunch texture and the Tortillas were all crispy from the box but it's pardonable because I can Imagine how hard it would be to make those things from scratch but the Salsa was prepared with Fresh Sun-roasted tomatoes, Chile chilly, Chile, Repeat Champions for they have stopped The Messiah from leading the people to the Red Sea where they were too slow and they were murdered, every one of them, slaughtered without Mercy by the Egyptian Charioteers who took Great Delight in Bloody Sports, Torture Games, Rape Deaths and Bone Burning for they are not even interested in Profit or Loss as long as they can go on Terrorizing the Weak, they will Champion it without Shame or Guilt or Whatever feelings that make them STOP and think a little about why the Batman elects to Let the Joker Go when he has the Power to so easily crush his neck with his Gloved Hands ever since he was trained in the Martial Arts School of Wudang which is all about Tai-chi and the Tao so he also learned the Technique to rip out his Adam's Apple without Bleeding, making him sound squeaky for the rest of his life so his gang members will laugh at his every Command, and of course, You know he has all the Weapons to torture the Joker so badly that he would rather choose to work in the Library than to continue terrorizing the poor old citizens of Gotham, yeah, he hands the Most Criminally Lunatic Guy in the City to the Police! and she hands me a can of Latino soda for she's always talking about how people need to return to their Roots so they can Preserve their Heritage and Culture and why she's retiring from the Organization she founded called Sisters of Color after she lost her husband who had served in Vietnam where he was Exposed to the effects of Agent Orange which is a chemical the US Army sprayed on the crops in the Fields in the Sixties when the Hippies were demonstrating against the War, people were calling them Idealistic, Naïve, Psychedelic, Disillusioned, Misguided, and all Socially Negative terms to describe them but You should be Clear Now, if not Then, the Idea was to make it Impossible for the Viet Congs, the Communists, to Eat and it's called Operation Ranch Hand, approved by Then Most Charming President JFK so You understand the Animal Instincts of those people who spent so much time to Create these chemicals which were also used by the British Army to subdue the Communists in Malaya, and if You are all that interested, You can easily google Agent Orange and see the images of the thousands of victims of such cowardly war tactics even affecting their own soldiers whose mortality and health don't mean so much to The Duchess and her Old Man's Maid so How Many Dislikes Shall they pay to compensate for the sufferings of the Veterans being exposed to the Glories of War, physically, mentally, spiritually, and even culturally? It's Criminal! Criminal! Criminal!

I HEAR A RHAPSODY

It's a Friday so Tis-see-woo-na-tis was Happy she's going to the Hot Springs and she's also Excited about going to Alamosa where she could buy a sack of 50kg soil fertilizer for the Plants in her House plus she's also going to the Radio Station to collect Four Free tickets to see a 2-Star Mariachi Band in a Barn and also Ten Dislike Dinner vouchers, it's her Lucky Day. Corn Mother was driving and she's quite a fast, safe driver for she was talking to Tis-see-woo-na-tis all the time, and they had so much stories to share for they were bosom buddies for more than sixty years, they were in the same Elementary School, and through all the years after they became mothers and grandmothers, they still kept in touch with each other and somehow, they are living quite near to one another, and though they are Natives and all, somehow, their Perceptions of Life are quite different. At their Age, there's really nothing much to change in terms of their spiritual beliefs, cultural leanings or even economical plans for Corn Mother is a teacher in Middle or High School while Tis-see-woo-na-tis worked for the State of Colorado as a Software

Programmer since she jumped on the IT Bandwagon many years ago and updated herself constantly to stay abreast with the faster Rats and she still draws a stingy pension but she has good financial acumen so she's able to afford the simplest Pleasures of Life such as Harvesting her Own Food and Stuff, Obviously, she's more laid back and calm than Ominotago.

"Do You know why We go to the Pools on Friday?"

"No…"

"It's because they clean the Pools on Thursday…"

"I see…"

"Have You ever seen Aliens?"

"Go ahead! Tell him! Tell him!"

"Yes… please…"

"Well… it was more than ten years ago. In the Middle of the Night, I was awakened by a Light and it was coming towards me…"

"What Color is the Light?"

"It's White but as it came nearer to my face, I saw that it's actually two lights so it's like a pair of Eyes staring directly into my Own…"

"What Happened?"

"I was frightened… just a few feet away was my granddaughter… and she's only three years old… I was frightened because I thought they would take her or me… there's really Nothing You can do…"

"And Then?"

"The Light floated down the front of my body and

traveled in the direction of my granddaughter. It left a fluorescent trail…"

"Did You take pictures of this Trail?"

"No… in those days, we didn't have Smart Phones and… we didn't have a Camera."

"How long was the Trail?"

"A few minutes later, it disappeared and… I have no proof of it anymore. I recorded all these things in my Book of Dreams."

"What?? You wrote it all down??"

"Where is it?"

"I don't know… it's been missing for some time…"

"Show him! Show him the New Pictures!"

"Well, You cannot really see it very well in the Light. A few days ago, I was looking at the Stars for Research and I saw some strange lights in the Sky… so this time… I took some Pictures… Here…"

"It's hard to See… do You know anyone who's been Abducted?"

"Yes… there are a few of them in Crestone…"

"Well, I remember this trip I took with my Husband and my Son in New Mexico… it's Summer and we were going camping at somewhere around the Los Pinos ghost town. It's real quiet and we felt like we had all the mountain ranges to ourselves and Pedro was very Happy. His father brought him to the River and they had a lot of Fun floating on the river in their tubes while I relaxed and cooked the most delicious food they had ever eaten and it was just the Best Camping Trip for our family. As usual, we were looking at the Stars at Night and that Night, the Stars were all Brilliant like You can only See in the Wilderness and then, we saw two of those stars becoming brighter and bigger... My Husband was a Veteran so he knew all about Constellations and it's not a disillusion because all Three of us saw them... closer... and closer..."

"What Happened?"

"Somehow, we didn't feel frightened or anything because we all believe in their Existence and I remember we were very quiet and we couldn't even speak... and they got nearer and nearer..."

"And Then?"

"They just stayed in the Valley for a few minutes or a few hours, I'm not sure, and We immediately fell asleep. The Next Morning, my Husband and I felt like we had recovered from a Bad Headache. Without any Delay, we rushed to keep all our stuff and headed Home. It's like we were programmed or something. After around a hundred miles, Pedro asked us... Don't you remember about the Lights? And, then, we realized... we had totally forgotten about it... until he reminded us..."

Arriving at Alamosa, You see it's smaller than Pueblo but still bigger than Crestone with a Walmart where You can get many of Your necessities and there's also a Big Hardware Store You can get all Your building and renovation supplies and Corn Mother has a Grand Plan to add a Terrace behind her house so she can enjoy the Heavenly Bodies and she had gotten some wooden planks she needed to paint reddish brown to match the color of the landscape for it's extremely Important for the Natives to achieve a sort of Balance with Nature and even the Modern Natives such as the New Corn

Daughter, Kamali, the New Director of Sisters of Color, she's a Spiritualist, and they are Practitioners of the "Barkman Method" so they can show You how You can Heal Your Body with Grand Traditional Techniques from ages ago but still effective in these Times so one of the Great Benefits of being a Club Member is that he gets to go to the Hot Springs every now and then to soothe his Body from all the rigors of Exploration, the waters burning the thousands of Mosquito bites on every part of his Skin and it's so cool to walk in the Blue Tunnel, it's quite dark so You can't see the faces of the people walking towards You even if You walked past Your best friend or Your Husband or Wife or Most Beloved, You won't know it but not Nahiossi who's trained to move in the Open like a Wolf and he can easily see her Beauty in the Flash of an Eye for she's Nefertiti, yeah, everybody knows how Beautiful she is... and she's just Extraordinary in that Hour or so she spent running around the Hot Springs Naked and Glimmering without a Care in the World while the Toad Men kept googling her and all Eyes were zoomed on her and even some Frog Women were salivating at the thought of licking the Nave of her Neck being the Fourth Most Sensitive Spot and she would always like somebody with a Snake Tongue to plant kisses all over her Body with Special Concentration on her belly button for she was heeding the Call of the Wild one fine day and immediately, without thinking about anything else, she disrobed and never wore her clothes again, she felt such Great Freedom that her Heart leaped and somersaulted so it's always easier for people who had not come upon such an experience to exclaim that she's barbaric and gone mad and O how she should be captured and raped by the Bad Jungle Jaguars and then put in The Cage for all Humankind to see how Degenerates should be

Punished and Separated from the Society but Nefertiti, she's different, she can discuss dialectics with renowned Philosophers and play Chess with Bobby Fisher's grand-children and she kicked their asses every time the IQ Kids came to contest her IQ being in the Clouds but the Family's against her taking the Mensa test which would have paved the Way for her to join the higher Echelons of the Society which is now finding every loophole to prevent her from showcasing the most Elegant Gait of Deer, hopping around the Compounds and sniffing those Purple flowers You see everywhere but You don't know their names so You can't reference them but there are so many more things to describe about her and You can surely talk about how her tits wobble with every step she takes even though it's the softest foot step of all the other day when she stole the Tiara Crown from the Fire Witch and she touched her Hand in her Sleep and asked her to Bring Five Stones, One Rabbit Foot, A Pinch of Applewood Dust, Whisker of Siamese Cat, and a Dash of Red Vinegar to light the Fire which they Lighted to burn Nefertiti to ash but they were so surprised that she's totally unburned and she's laughing and asking for the Fire to be Stronger because it's so ticklish, the Hungry Worm that they put into her Mouth after tying her up with life time guarantee ropes strong enough to keep her tied up for a thousand years if she really lived up to that Age she will still be Younger than Mercury who lived up to some years more than that and why do people really want to live that long anyway, Imagine a person living from 1001 to 2001 and... is it possible there's this Fountain of Youth that some people have talked about but rejected by the Majority who rather believe in biodegradable super effective ecologically manufactured anti-aging cream known as Mystiko which is all the Craze in the World so all the Grannies can now apply this Magical Aid all over their bodies and become all Seventeen again, You know, a few years after they had done it with their Best Friend's Little Brother and that's a popular way how girls lose their Virginity other than going Camping with a group of friends being a Big No No for any parent because Christmas parties and Halloween are all Red Flashlights but what can a Parent do to really prevent the kids from flowering and it's no coincidence she needs to be spending more overnights for exam revisions more and more important nowadays than their Chastity and such things which have not been practiced in most parts of the World from the most Primitive Tribes to the most Cosmopolitan City, girls and boys are losing their Innocence at younger and younger ages and no matter how You Crack Your mind about when It happened, the good news is that You will never find out unless they get pregnant and tell You about it but Nefertiti is not such a type of girl for her Great Grandfather was a Powerful Wise Wizard who created the Venus Girdle for her and the Day he put it on her when she was no more than eight years old when she understood these things so he told her how it will grow with her and protect her from the Jaguars and other Barbarians for most people know what a stinky shithole the City has become less Civilized where Impatience, Lies, Scams, Violence, and Hooliganism and all kinds of Evil are Celebrated like some sort of New Age Religion and Nobody is doing anything to Reverse the Trend but they are all doing all they can to Continue cheating everybody to believe in Democracy, Socialism, Fascism, Communism, Consumerism, Nazism, Feminism, Racism, and every other type of Society that requires the members to believe in their Ideals and swear by the Blood of the Lamb that they will uphold the Law of the

Land for what are they really going to do in these Times when even a Beggar can rise up and form his own Clan known as The Walkers all the while they are all carrying a Black Porcelain Bowl like those that the Scottish use to feed the dogs they keep for fur and meat and it's the custom of culture where they are so close to nature that they couldn't think of any better way to bury their dead friends than to skin them for their fur and it didn't matter if it was a lamb, a dog, an iguana, a cat, a chimpanzee, a bison, a prairie dog, a lion, a crocodile, a parrot or a hamster, the meat is either roasted or chopped up to be made into a stew with wild herbs, purple Aussie potatoes, Smelly D Carrots, Mexican Peppers, Obnoxious H Tomatoes, You see them everywhere now, and they are always smiling like they have Your number and You have nowhere to Hide come the Time to go to the Polls, You have to choose either the Way to Hell or the Way to Death but of course, You are confused for You have a Right to Abstain from siding with the Militants or the Peacekeepers who are not working well together so isn't it better to Send in the Clowns and they will be impressed to see how funny the whole TV series have become since they started to play the Monkey sounds when they slapped Bozo until his nose fell off and his face is so red from the terror heavy whacks he got on his Left Cheek only for the Strong Arm has only One Arm and he's the best Slapper in the World, he swivels on One Foot and executes the best follow through as his Rough Industrialist Hand was toughened up since he was still young and only about thirteen years old, he left the Family because there was not enough food to feed the whole Family so he went to the City to look for Work and after enduring all the sufferings that young boys like him experienced in the City in a few moons, he found work in

Coyote City where he functioned as a Production Hand, earning just enough to pay for his food and board and nothing much else, yet, he's proud of himself after so many years where he's moving up the ranks and he's put into more important shifts where the Danger is Higher but he's really pleased they were giving him a raise and for a boy his age, it was a great deal up until the Accident occurred when he lost his Other Arm for he forbade Everyone to ask if it's Right or Left, and the Company reported how he was also getting drunk more regularly and itching to get into a fight with anybody who beat him up seriously after all so he decided to join the Militants because they made him feel Important and Powerful when he beat up those prisoners who were tied up properly with all rage and bitter fruit but he knew how they would defeat him if they were not tied up but he didn't care so much for it made his Penis hard, and Allah be Blushed, O Mohammed the Virile, he knows it's a Sin Punishable by being Stoned to Death, he had participated in these Trials before where they strip the guy and shows him a picture of some Handsome Bollywood Star in the raw and when they see that the Accused has a Hard On, they pass the sentence that he's Perverse and while the Flag is still Standing at Full Mast, they will sing their own National Anthem and after that, they will bring the Criminal to the Circle in Tiananmen Square where they will Stone him with their own Personal Stone and the Slapper gleefully remembered how his Stone Cracked the Cheek of one of those convicted Criminals and he felt so good that he could sing La La La like the Yellow Teletubby and growing even Harder as he saw how much Bozo's lips were dripping with melting lipstick and how even his Brain juice is trickling out of his Nostrils, his Wig and Funny Straw Hat lying in the corner of the room, he gave up all Hope to live or return to the outskirts of Tulsa where he had hidden his most beautiful family and how he had been selected for this special operation called Operation Red Nose where he was to Act like Bozo the Clown and though he was reluctant to go, initially, the Force made an offer he couldn't refuse, it's a very lucrative contract, and the rewards were too good to be true for he was promised an early retirement and it was his Last Mission, and after that, he can spend all the time in the Universe with his Beloved Wife and Three Daughters and Three Sons and so many other things that he had put together with the Income from so many dangerous missions but none too so dangerous as this One and though he learned from the Original Bozo himself for more than seven moons, mastering all his mannerisms and shows including his voice and stunts and makeup and jokes and everything else to the point where even his own Family and favorite iguana couldn't recognize him anymore when he put on that Great Show in Chicago, the fans clapped and cheered fervently so he totally believed he would pull through with the Mission... if only he could free himself and get to the Wig which is one piece with the Hat...

"I'm sorry..."

"It's not your fault... we haven't actually met..."

"How do You know me?"

"I have seen your picture... Mother showed it to me and asked me to come look for you."

"Why should I believe you? I don't know You."

"Alright. Blue Moon is our eldest sister. Our seventh sister is New Haven, right? Do Mi is our seventeenth sister and Fa So La is her younger twin. Am I right? Do You believe me now?"

"You are right but I don't remember anybody like you. Sorry. Perhaps, you saw the List with all our names on it and memorized the whole thing. If your memory is truly good, you will agree with me that your name's not in the List at all! Can you leave me now? I have an important mission at hand."

"Of Course! Of Course!"

"What?"

"Fa La?"

"Bulbul?"

"Yes???"

"You should know... She's dead."

"It's not important. You just have to believe that I'm your sister and you should bring me to see Blue Moon. Mother has an important message for her."

"It's no use! He's not waking up! More Electricity!"

"One… Two… Buckle Your…"

"Hey Mister Kite… it's the Door on the Left…"

"Do You know what happens at Half Moon?"

"Don't You know? She's a Mermaid!"

"No. The Exit is at the End of the Tunnel!"

"Wake Up! I know You are not Bozo!! He's My Favorite!!"

"Sorry, Sir Raleigh, You are in the Wrong Scene. Please don't do it Again."

"Shall we rub him with some Agent Pink?"

"Alright. Hurry up! Do it now… before he wakes up…"

Then, she just lifted him and carried him in her arms as

if he's just a sack of pumpkins weighing no more than twenty kilograms but he's rather certain that he weighed more before he embarked on that journey. Still, it's better to be carried than to carry as he had some time to study her face. Safely cradled in her full Olympic bosom and old hammock arms, Jeremiah was feeling ultimately secure and insanely sleepy so much so he felt almost like a traitor to be so sheepishly trusting in this person whom he had known for just a few minutes but strangely, he's still awake enough to see that her eyes were of the color of his Father and her nose was similar to that of Nishwequanniquaweseh, his ninth sister and the one whom he loved the third most for she had a funny, bright laughter which never failed to lift his spirits even when he's feeling the bluest blues so he always wondered how he could capture the sound of her laughter so he could be happy forever and ever, and he saw that her hair was turning white and orange, blending with the sky and cloud, he was a little worried, it's raining but not raining, he's not so sure why she would be walking in reverse when it would be easier to walk the other way round.

"What's the time?"

"I don't know. It should be around 2100 hours or later. Why?"

"It's nothing. Sometimes, I just feel the urge to Smoke."

"What?"

"You know..."

Yesterday, everything was working so perfectly well. Today, it's working but not perfectly. Opening the book, you still see the same things as yesterday, yeah, the colors are identical and the structure of content is just the way it was but the only thing missing was The Sound. It's hard to explain. It's the same link as the one you clicked on yesterday and when you had clicked on it, the symbol of the rotating circle to represent "downloading is in progress" was rotating in a clockwise direction like how things are so normal as usual and you see that the bar is moving to the right slowly but surely to signify that the music is playing and everything is working as usual or even as early as yesterday but today, something is not right. The music is playing but there is no sound! Have you forgotten to turn off the Tap? The Other Day, you were able to access the Website but Just Now, it's not accessible anymore... What's happening? Naturally, you turn off the computer and restart it, just as any tech-savvy grand user of computers will instinctively shake the gadget a little and tap softly enough somewhere near the CPU but of course, hard enough to stimulate it a little or so to say, awaken it to the fact that it's supposed to be working like a slave and nothing more, you just expect it to be working fine when it has fully restarted, you rushed to open the page again to see if it's working so perfectly yesterday, you could hear the near silent echo of the ripples rising just enough to carry the little paper boat just a little further, you are so persistently sure that it will be working perfectly again that you shouldn't even be trying it out again but for some unknown reason, you are once again at the point where you are clicking on the same link again just like you had done a few moments ago but of course, the time is different as it was just a few minutes past midnight earlier and now, it's a few minutes past it but other than the few minutes, nothing is ever the same anymore, except for the fact that The Sound is still Muted and the Music is playing and it's driving you a little out of sorts, simply because you really want to listen to that piece of music again. Can you remember the part where the wolf is hiding behind the tree so perfectly that nobody even knows he's there at all? What about the episode where the princess runs off with the outlaw even after she kisses the prince so fiercely? How does it feel if your best friend calls you, out of the blue, and informs you that it's the last time that you will ever hear that song again, just as you were listening to it for the hundred and fifty seventh time even though you are not really the type to keep tab on such matters but you can be certain, you will try a few more times on your computer before you surrender, probably cursing your luck just for the sake of it anyhow or anyway, you don't really believe it will ever happen, do you?

"Are You there, Nefertiti?"

"How do You know my Name?"

"What's my Name?"

"Na… hiossssssssssiiiiiii…?"

"It's Dark. How can You see me?"

"I can Smell You…"

"Can You say my name again? I like to hear it…"

"Can I Drink Your Blood?"

"What's the Recipe? Do You like it to be Spicy?"

"Can You Give Me Three Strands of Your Hair?"

"Passing on Your left! Hutt! Hutt!"

"Do You want some Twinkies? Limited Edition Blue, White, and Red for Independence!"

"The Pool next to the German Garden is the Hottest. Wanna Go?"

"You know, after a while when Ominotago's not looking, You can sneak out for a Smoke."

"Alright. Do You want a beer? I will buy You…"

"O Thank You so much! Come sit here! This is the Life!"

"What's the use of the Num Lock Button?"

"It's so Stupid Cupid! Delete it!"

After spending an illuminating day at the Hot Springs, Corn Mother was busy conversing with her Friend while she was driving with one hand and adjusting her big fruity hat with dried leaves and grass and her own hand-painted Indian Chief scarf you see, it's really interesting how she can make different copies of the same Print with different colors but I was too Sleepy to ask her to explain such technical stuff for it's one of those sciences which appeals to the Man of Science but I was thinking how many Brains she possesses because it's as if she can perform so many tasks at the same time, she's answering Tis-see-woo-na-tis' line of questions and elegies about the Plight of their Tribe in which Ominotago wasn't too interested in those issues anymore so much many years ago when she was incensed by the Injustices and Heartaches she felt when even her own Children were taken from her and it's quite true that some people would have gone Cuckoo Bird after experiencing such difficult Episodes of Pain in their lives not Twice but Thrice, some people never recover from those Dark periods in which they themselves get scalded so badly that they are ashamed to appear in Daylight, the Coyote Woman, she's going to bring some Powerful Insect Repellent from Denver, specially bought by her Husband, Pierre, a Frenchman who's the Boss of the Community Recreational Facility and he's a Jolly Good Fellow who takes his Job seriously, this time, we are going to win the War, this time, the mosquitoes are going to get it, she kept exclaiming while she's still talking to Tis-see-woo-na-tis who was enjoying a short nap for people of that age are more prone to fall asleep even when she really wants to stay awake and not miss a Moment for she knows Everything can change in One Moment in Time one of their best bonding songs of all time, they share such a Deep Bond, I was sure, she could hear Corn Mother in her Sleep, and even when Tis-see-woo-na-tis had gone Home, You still get the sense that she's still around, somewhere…

"Hi! Nice to meet You! My name is Mona!"

"He smokes Weed! A Real Pot Head!!"

"Come let's go for a smoke! I want to smoke my Cigarette!"

"O My God! Let's Go!"

"Did You see the UFO images on Tis-see-woo-na-tis' phone? There's a Flying Saucer with Lights! You can see clearer in the Night."

"Yeah, thanks… it's so Beautiful up here… see… the Stars are so Near!"

"I Hate these Mosquitoes!!! Ewww!"

"What a Chore to Wear all these clothes in the Summer… but it's quite cool…"

"There's Mars!"

"No… that's Mercury… I know it…"

"Let's see… I have Skyview Free… it shows You all the Constellations… isn't it Amazing? See? I told You! It's Mars! You need Glasses!"

"Hey… it's better to go Behind… we can see much better back there…"

"Alright! Let's Go!"

"Be Careful! There are Traps all around!"

"If You look at the Sky long enough, You can always see the Heavenly Bodies moving."

"There! That Star moved!"

"It's not a Star... It's a Firefly…"

"No! It's a Star! It's a Star!"

"It's a Firefly!!"

"Firefly? We are getting those here but… it's a Star!"

"Are You Alright? You are Scaring Me…"

"Don't Worry. He Gets it Good… He's Fine…"

What's more Scary than knowing it's Your Last Day in Existence kind of Negative Fore Shadowing fit for Philosophers who are Ready to Die for an Opinion and no You don't have to sell off Your slaves to another Macho Cowboy who fucks all his slaves whenever he feels like it kind of deal worth not more than five hundred bushels of those Macedonian miracle wheat able to Feed all the Hungry People in the World, Everyday, and it's Your Last Day, no, there's no bargain, there's no regret, yeah, die already… You will See how it can be such a Lunatic idea but also the only Truth for Every Living Thing is the simple passing of Time and when It's Over, there's no more Beautiful Feather of Topaz Blue You can ever hope for even one glitter of a moment of Imperfection, it's never late, always on time so when You Turn Your Eyes to the Clock and see that it's six o seventeen and You count up to sixty seconds without Breathing and

Thinking of anything else, roll, roll back Your Eyes to the Center of Your Skull, now, keep it there for at least thirty seconds minimum, sometimes, You hear such good music that You become a statue without knowing anything about Elf Tree O so what's the damn so important about a few Stars in the Sky! I don't really want to know about it, if You asked me, secretly or in public in front of the Statue of Chief Joseph who's nodding his Great Approval when he saw how Nahiossi was drooling on Nefertiti's Conduits and she's Lubricating his Knife with her Honey and Satin Horror Sweat Snailing down her Navel pierced with Centipede Brand, 77 Thumbs Up and Zero Thumb Down, how often have You seen that on youtube, Right, and You may Wonder why they didn't use the Big Y so it becomes Youtube but sometimes, we are not so observant or curious to get to the bottom of these things for what's the Big Secret which is Really Nothing so important so You take Your Sorrowful Time with the Newspaper and Cup of Coffee steaming Hot and You can still smell the freshness of the beans in Your Nose and also... the Seductive combination of the Cheapest Most Toxic Ink printed on the Cheapest Most Recycled Paper which feels so Luxurious in Your fingers and it's a Family culture for the men of the house to sit on the Rocking Chair and Spend fifteen to thirty minutes of their Time Each Day to Read anything they want with a Cup of Chocolate so Nutritious for the Young Ones You will be seeing for the First Time in Your Life and You know it, Luckily or Unluckily, the Dice is Cast, Three for Humor, Six for Light, do You remember how You held her in Your arms as You felt the mouth on Your Bosom and how the Milk is flowing out of Your Motherly Heart and how You understood that You can Nourish the Young and that's One Condition which has to be weighed carefully by Smoking a Cigarette beside the Statue of Aristotle so Everything can be discussed Logically and it's extremely Important that We become as logical as possible regardless of anything else, You have to ask Yourself how You want to be going over to the Netherworld where Anything is Possible and You Remember how Your Aunt was going on a Holiday and a few weeks ago, You saw how that Plane has been shot by the Russians and suddenly, she's gone, and if You were her, knowing she's never going to See the Colors of the Rainbow and why not the Light anymore so she's totally Blind as she shuts her eyelids to enjoy his fingers fiddling at the Jukebox, searching for the Perfect Combination to Unlock the most Romantic Song ever, the Song was *Odeon* and it's an Instrumental piece so there's no Lyrics to distract You... jaaa... it's just a Guitar playing, sometimes accompanied by some other Instruments but You know it's always that Guitar playing and how Slow his Nails cut into her Persian Wild which was the most Precious thing ever given to her other than her Grandfather's Gift which safeguarded her Virginity until she was so fabulously smittened by the Gaucho King and she especially squeals in giggles when he brushes his thick whirling moustache with thin curling hairs spiraling into Infinity, Try to Lick on her Pearls, they are sour, Remember, then, falling down over a Cup of Peppermint Tea spread all over her Face so she's giggling again when he rubs his mouth on her pet rabbit probably needing a shower around that Time she's Sinking Her Dreamy Cow just manicured Two Days Ago Nails into the Space between his Ribs and ever getting closer to his internal organs which are all of the Highest Quality for his Heart alone is the Perfect Heart regulated by his Breathing which is the deepest ever recorded for he can stay underwater for more than Ninety minutes with a special technique he learnt from Blue Moon and he never felt he was cheated at all even when he had to be her Sex Slave for Three Days after which she was Impregnated and he received the Key to Samarkand exclusively for him to come visit his children some time for she's very sure she's got Fab Four or Fantastic Four coming and though she understood that he will not be Responsible for he's not that Type of Man and it's not to say that he's not a Man at all because she Came in violent volcanic eruptions almost from the Moment she opened her Eyes to the Time she closed them and even in her dreams, she can see him pushing the plough until the wheels came off for it's no Secret how Animalistic he becomes when it comes to the Zen of Art of Reproduction which is one of the Favorite Past Times of South Americans dancing Salsa on the beach with the strong breezes blowing off their skimpy bikinis and the boys, they are not shy to carry the girls into the Sea and Copulate right there and then like there's not another thing more urgent in their lives than Fucking and everybody is doing it so much from Teens to Men and Women waiting for their Time to Ride the Waves and they don't have any much Choice because their Genitals are not Working all that Well anymore without Aphrodite's Blessings, it would be Impossible unless You take some pills which make You either Wet or Hard and there's no telling how You will go or how he will go or how they will go but You are sure everybody will go… One Moment… they are here… in Time… they are gone…

Dressed like a True Communist, leaving Nefertiti in his Warm Nest, he left to hunt for food for he knew she would be Hungry like a She Wolf when she woke up and if she's not fully fed, she would be really Angry and she may even run away into the Forest and never come back anymore to make him worry a little bit more about her for even she knew that a Man like that, a Real Man, not some cheap fake bastard You can hire for a single Dislike an hour with cucumber sized penis and lousy Turkish sense of style where he will cheer when the airplane lands after a journey of more than twelve hours before he arrived at the foot path which appeared much more interesting than the Road More Traveled and it's Highly Illogical for a Nation who Christened Frost as Her National Poet to choose to go the Wide and Open Way which surely is the Way to Paradise Lost which was also highlighted by Jesus Christ when He said…

"It's Easier for a Camel to Enter a Needle's Eye than for a Rich Man to Enter the Kingdom of Heaven!"

"Goood… but Wrong…"

"O Sorry… Big is the Highway which leads to Destruction but Narrow is the Way to Paradise!"

"Goooood… but I think it's supposed to be Heaven!"

"Don't they mean the Same Thing?"

"Which Way Are You Going to Choose?"

It's not at all a Hard Choice. Of Course, Nahiossi chose the Narrow Way though it appeared much more Dangerous than the Public Way for how are You going to get to hunt any wildlife if You stay on the main roads all the time? Isn't it a Great Idea to detour into the Unknown sometimes for Nothing but Just for the Heck of It kind of jive You don't understand at all but it's like I'm Typing Wedding HERE or even Woo Hooooooo or even Bangladeshi Princesses Jacking off the Royal Sparrows for no other Reason or even

HHH BBB wesx LioMoisxt iMextsbyu BOMM BOOOM JUEINDHJS Kindnhemahss maki Maki tikka saka saka ri ri tee nee dee zzz z zzzzzz O O JUST FOR FUN when we need to explain Everything so clearly, yeah, we can never understand another person absolutely no matter how many decades You spend in her Bed and let's not be Boring by the saying a woman's heart is harder to find than a needle still sinking into the Night depths of the Oceans where Nothing can be Seen and Technology is disabled, it doesn't affect You one bit, it's some pointless information You can throw into the waste paper basket from way Downtown with Your eyes closed since You have been practicing The Shot everyday so if You ever get the chance to shoot it in the final second when the ball is launched, You knew it was Nothing but Net just at the same time as the Commentator said Goooood!!! and Nobody could have blocked it for You have fired it in such steep trajectory it takes about sixteen seconds for it to fall into the Basket which doesn't look like any basket at all but You imagine that the game will seem like a girl's game with those fine traditional English wicker baskets so it's not so Out of the Point to Meditate when You come to a Portal where there are truly a few thousand of those mosquitoes and insects and it's such a Waste because those Dedicated Entomologists will be so Busy taking pictures and recording videos of such a great concentration of insects all within the space of a Sphere Big Enough to cover You with Praise and Hymns and Tangerine Juice and Pulp from Head to Toe, yeah, Save the Skin to ward them off and in such a manner, he managed to stay Calm to Smoke a Pot or Two and he's feeling Almighty now for solving the Mosquito Dilemma for he never believed in killing even a single Fly not to mention a Mosquito or a Garuda in his Life though he's taken the lives of more than a Few

Thousand Men for there's a Time where he was Challenged more than Thirteen Times a Day for that's the maximum Daily number of Challenges in the Arena so he had to kill those men who were puffing to kill him anyway and they came from Far and Near, mostly Envious he's Impregnating all the Women in Town and some of them were Fighting for their Father's Glory and some of them were Fighting for their Family's Honor which was the most Precious thing in their Culture for that's what their Father would always tell them that they may have to starve a little sometimes and even give up their life for Pride is Something not to be Compromised no matter the Profit or Loss so Nahiossi will never reject any woman who presents herself to him for it's against the Law of the Land to not increase Your Territory when You have the Upper Hand so he's forever Blameless, Sinless, and Holy in the Green Eyes of All Womenkind, and all of them instinctively know what a Night it will be to be ravished by such a Romantic Latin American Legend who sleeps on a Hammock of One Rope tied to Two Trees or Poles up in the Rarified Air, Sagging and Open for all to See but she will have to show some Identification Papers because she looks a little underage for those Adult stuff and she needs to show some Medical Certifications because she's a wanton woman but he knows how it's Important other people wouldn't be exposed to Danger or Suffering so the Nurses will prevent them from hurrying to him like an army of ants attacking You when You are sitting under a Tree in Relaxed Lotus position and there are hundreds upon hundreds of them, a few of them heavier than two dimes in weight, and these are the Generals or something for they have Super Strong claws to cut into Your Flesh so it's believable that this Species of Ant is capable of killing a person if there's big group of them and they wait for

You to Fall into a Deep Sleep before they come to chew on Your wrist so You bleed until all the Blood is gone and You wake up in a Dream and You say You are Coming but You are never There and when the Time arrives with no commercials and seminars and Loud Trumpets blowing so melodiously that You cannot even hear the Explosion in Your Mouth so You cannot taste the Flower anymore and also, You cannot Talk, and Your legs are melting below the Furnace like hot wax dripping into Your Ears but You should know by now that it's not Painful at All if You don't Overdramatize Peace and Environment Protection Schemes in Your Mind which is slowly being drained of All Memory and soon, very soon, You will feel Your Eyes becoming Glass so You cannot even See Anything but the Light and it's hovering above Your Head not Believing for sure how they are pouring a few buckets of Molten Iron over Your Body to Turn Your Flesh to Ash so You cannot sense anymore and even if a Butterfly has landed on Your Bone, Softly, You will not feel a thing and sure enough, all Your senses are destroyed at the First Opportunity and the Remains will be recycled to be manufactured into some Potion to Fight Sleepiness which is why Ms. Muffet keeps forgetting her phone and she keeps looking for It in All the Wrong Places when she's not wearing her glasses, she looks like a Blind Girl who believes that she has arrived at the Gate of Nirvana when she saw the Bird landing on her Desk with Stealth of Goddess Laverna, she was moving closer and closer to him with every passing moment so quietly so she could see that it's Yellow Breasted but there are so many thousands of species of birds, she didn't know if it's a Robin or Plover or Warbler or Western Kingbird but she loved the Song so much, she followed it to the Colorful Skull where the Way seems even more Dangerous but she thought she has come too far to turn back at that time when the Sun was still near the Apex so there's still plenty of Time to explore the Mountain Range for there are no vehicles or bicycles there and she felt so Peaceful as she took Pictures of the plants and trees and terrain and then, she found the Most Peculiar Leaf in the region for there were Millions of leaves of that kind in the Jungle but there's this Leaf, this Exotic Leaf with Out of the Ordinary Organic Motif of Cactus Design on the Surface so it's known as The Alien Leaf and she's trembling in Cold Sweat when she studied the Design in Greater Details for she's a Graphic Design student and she's a Jungian as well but she's No Idea how Nature always Surprises her like Nothing else but she didn't pluck it because she's taught to Respect Mother Nature but she kept sensing that she's being Followed and the Trailer is a Shadow for it must be Only Him since he's the only one who can Walk with No Footprint as he's becoming Lighter than the Feather he's biting, blowing on it ever so softly so no not even one strand of hair moved and watching how she was so perplexed by The Alien Leaf, he collected the specimen in his pocket and he's quite Pleased with himself when he saw Nine Caterpillars Bunching on a Branch, a Good Omen so he saw the Butterflies as he followed her in Secret however certainly he knew that she knew that he's Shadowing her but isn't it true… the Shadow has to go wherever she goes…

66:1. That's the Most he had to Kill in a Day and his Instructor Grand Master Drunk Mantis had told him to study the movements of the Praying Mantis in the Garden of Wails and there he would stand by himself and follow his Master's every Word like it's the Word of his Father for Nobody had to tell him anything more than the Fact that he was disowned by his very own Family though they had ample

Resources to feed him and give him a place to practice his Kung Fu to the level where he can Leap on Top of the Tree and in no time, he could skip from one Tree to another in no Time at all and 194:1 is the highest number in the History of Gauchohood for it's done in such quick time since the Day Alexander killed five thousand of the most despicable and slim bag poor child soldiers where they Not only Pleasured themselves with the Young Ones but also the Old ones who were knocked up by a few hundred of them so she had totally no Idea who's the real father for she was Bleeding profusely and she's become a Rock with Flesh Eyes and she's Not Blinking Anything or Fighting anymore because her Flesh was Numb and she's become a Nonliving Thing for the Amusement of those Military Men of the Cave Era who walks around the whole town of Pueblo wearing just their skimpy leather napkins and when they saw the Phalanx, they were so shocked in their tracks that they spewed out peppermint canes everywhere and ran for their lives so basically You know they are Yellow when the Real Time came for them to prove their Mettle, they run to the Mountains like hamsters or rabbits when they know they are outnumbered by millions to one go so it's no use to distract them from their Monkey Shows being so entertaining and only costing them a flat fee of five fifty Dislikes so Cheap and it's really no Point to Bargain with the Saint because he really knows more than You do about the Meaning of Existence so after You really spend hours looking at the Hungry Tiger, naturally, You will picture her movements in Your Mind and Imagine how You will move in rhythm and gesture if it's Nothing more than the Shadow of Darkness, yeah, how much Deeper are You willing to go if she asks You that question so when the Day Comes and You are so Surprised that It Came at All, You may Whisper to Your Comrade Idiot who's Defaulting just like You are doing and You feel so good about it because You are Greater in Number, Consider This, My Friend, You are on the Wrong Path and I Seriously Advise You to Turn Back and Return to the Origin where You can Kindly Remember All Your Childhood Memories, yeah, even those that You Remember You have Forgotten in the Bashfulness of Your Youth and all that type of Thing the Psychiatrist will always not Probe when they have the Chance to See You Next Moon and the Next Moon and You Know it's a Good Memory Exercise for Older Folks who think that they are Losing it Slowly but Surely for the Day will Come when they will have Zero Memory left in their Bank as they Get Closer to the New World, what do You really expect to See when You cross over to the Other Side or use whatever terms You may Find to Imagine how it will be like when You Enter into the Cave of Lights and Pick up the Pieces from where You thought You would never Come Across them ever again yet for Hugo's Sake, there are really some things which we like to keep a Secret even unto the Day we Kick the Buckets into the Mouths of Martyrs really dying for Nothing in this Modern World where people will Die for Gadgets but No, Not for their Parents, Not for their Brothers or Sisters, Not for their Gardens, Not for their Art Collection, not for their Country, not for their Religions, Not for their Race, not for Anything but for the Love of Wealth and Power and the Flash of Cameras Brightening the Valley of Glutinous Rice in Bleaker Times when they allow You to wallow in Self Pity and what have You that You don't really like to talk about Your Dead Husband and how he still comes to Ravage You at Night just like the First Night, sometimes up to Three or Six Times continuously without Pulling Out for even once in

Nine Hours of Nonstop Action Blue Films in those Days appearing in VHS Format which is a Ghost Format Now because people have moved on to Blue Rays and what have You when You think properly about how the Purple Panda will buy You a House in a Safe Town just so You don't Erase the Occurrence or Pull on the Tape too Tightly so You will Figure out how to forward and reverse to get to the Interesting Parts where the Midget was Slapping the Bitch on her Face with his Caveman Club and she's all Bloody and parts of her flesh had been bitten off by the Werewolves turning into Half Werewolf and Half Human at that time when You see the Lights Flashing Green so You know it's going to be Yellow for three ticks of the Clock and then it will Turn Red so You then Slam on the Brakes, halting the Car in such a Jerk that she wanted to Slap him for sucking her nose so violently that they turned Blue Black and she was wondering if he would love her more for sucking his testicles until they turned Blue Black which is Popular Phenomenon in Itself and it's Sometimes Against the Rules to Wander into the Realms of the Unknown for in a Little While Longer, You will find the Way to be more difficult if it requires that You scale some rocks so You better not attempt Rock Climbing if You have not gone on a Course ever before for it's True what they say... It can Cost Your Life! and how many times have people Ignored all the Signs and Symbols of our Time Warning of The Way of the Wicked and face the Punishment of being turned into a Cloud of Salt for that's what the Lord promised Lot and he specifically instructed her not to Turn Back to Look at the Burning Town until it's Safe to do so but we know how Women were always the weaker sex even in the Days of Old when Eve bore the Children of her Children and Nobody dwells on these facts so much because it's

Forbidden to Smoke when You are Carrying a Child kind of PC Culture, some of the Words of Old cannot even be uttered in Public or people will think You are the Mad General or something akin to something You had come across once in Your Life over and over again in circling sheets of shiny steel curling so there's a Circle over a Circle over a Circle forming a Kaleidoscope with Transmutating Patterns of Magical Colors we think so Little of those things now that we will not even take it and adjusting the EYES to look at the Sun when it's the Brightest and Possibly Causing Blindness if You Stare at It for too Long even when You Close Them until there's just so little a Slit though which You See the slightest trace of the Mid-day Sun and don't You feel Revitalized and Revived when they demanded that You participate in the Daughter-in-Law Tea Ceremony, it's a Scheme to get You to Submit to the In Laws, whether You are Dry or Fresh, You have to Kneel Down before them as if they are the Emperor and Empress or some Deity Come to Earth for a Brief Visit so You better be on Your Best Behavior and You better put a Big Feather on their Crowns if You want to be in their Good Books for if they Dislike You, they will Dislike You for the Rest of Your Life, You will be subjected to all manners of Hate and Envy so much so they will be Angry to see You Laugh and Rhapsody in Hymns and Praise be to Sarah that the Bad Guy in the TV Show is Dead and the Series is Coming to an End so they are all preparing themselves to read Morse Code Outside where Nothing matters any more than how You feel about the Discourse over Equal Wages regardless of whether You are Right or Left or Stronger than Hercules when he was just a Boy of ten or eleven, he went Hunting by himself when he was not more than Nine years old when he crossed path with a Jaguar who was in the Midst of Raping Venus but just before he could put his Snake into her Snuff Bottle for he imagines how she will be lying on her Elaborate Floral Scented Musical Lamp Divan with Gold Trimmings and the softness of two cheetah furs so professionally tanned but if You Examine the Handiwork Up Close, You will See that the cheetahs were killed in most humane touch and You can surely see that the Outer of the Fur was a full piece on itself for the Skinner had set up a Trap with Jamon Iberico produced in these places where the plains are filled with acorns hazelnuts pine fruit and there are also such places in Italy where You can Hunt for Truffles and if You found the Heaviest of All Time, You may get a few hundred thousand Dislikes and it's not really that Divine when it goes into the Decaying Body so even if You eat the Most Out of this World Shark Fin Soup, think about the Sharks were being thrown back into the Sea after their fins were chopped off Rogues chopped off the Fins for Profit and You see how it's all so Evil it's a Wonder Who will be so Happy if Some Giant came to their Town and ate all Their Houses cooked with a slice of ginger and Rock Sugar and Red Dates and Lotus Seeds and a Dash of Paprika and boiled with Poplar Wood for at least a few hours before Sunset for it cannot be at any other time when You and Your Children are not even allowed to Step out of the Room where lots of Meaningful activities take place and they are being educated in the Art of Thievery and the most Important of All, the Art of Survival for it's not Easy to be a Survivor.

No, it's not Easy at all… You have to be Filled with so much Optimism and Good Will for the Human Race and they will give You a Funny name so they share the Grand Joke about the Concubine complaining her Shanghai Slit Dress is Tearing at the Seams and how she doesn't like to wear Revealing clothes so he ripped the dress into a few more pieces or more with Rage and Hurt in his Heart, he climbed up the rocks, eager to Catch her and show her what a Big Great Man he had become after all the walking and heaving and puffing for the Air is Thin Up There and there's not so much You can do when You get a dose of Mountain Sickness for You know how Nahiossi is such a Lightweight Hero for Equality, many people will say that he's a Chauvinist, a Murderer, a Coward, a Villain, and even a Free Mason since he's also an Immaculate Artist so good with his hands that he can crave a sensual wooden figurine of the woman he has Known and he will present them with the Souvenir at time he unloaded his millions of tadpoles into her Raw Oyster or Abalone for it doesn't really matter what it looks like as it will taste delicious if You spread a teaspoon of Hazelnut Cream, it tastes Rich and when You add some Lime, it tastes Sour and when You rub Bird's Eye Chilly in, it tastes Spicy maybe too Spicy for people who are Allergic to Spices, well, what a Shame, and when You drip a cup of Original Bona Fide Dead Sea Water Down There, of course, it tastes Salty and that's the four Cornerstones of Siamese Cuisine which is deeply rooted in the Arts of Traditional Healing so it's highly Healthy to drink a Bowl of Genuine Thai Tom Yum Soup with all fresh Ingredients being such a Keyword in Everyday Conversation You will at least come across the Keyword of the Day and sometimes, it may take up to a few days before You get the Keywords on a certain Day but it's strange that there's no Clue of anything about it that You tried to get something from Your Sexy Neighbor who lives Down the Hall and She's always Sitting on her Simple Red Colored Stool in Transparent Plastic underwear so You can see the well-groomed Hair of her Pussycat propped strategically on her laptop and she's dragging on a Joint and Farting like it's no Tomorrow and You can even say she's a Girl Go GooGoo for it fits her too well, the Gloves he Sent her on her Birthday again and again You go over there to see her up close for it's when her baby's feeding on her that You find her to be most sublime and serene and moist as she avoids Your presence like she's simply not interested so You learn to Retreat before It Happened at the Most Unexpected Time... Least... Lest... The Last Mohican Swept Your feet... and You fell with the force of a quarter of a ton of St. Josephine Tinged Rocks dropping from Height of Sixteen Story High Penthouse where You can see the City Line in every Direction and now without knowing the Bitter Bruise of Rock on Your Back and Head breaking on a Brow of Rock so Sharp and Stone Age so You are bleeding like a River and wondering if this was the Day when You Pass Away as the Blood kept flowing and dripping on his Robin Hood Shirt and pants already torn beyond repair, Nahiossi, Bless You, the Skull so shaken so anyone can see his testicles from behind when he regained a little Orientation and staggered to the Road More Traveled and still Thinking for a Moment Only as the Meaning of It is to Mean Less than a Second, he's going to lose enough Blood to die an Urban Legend but Remembering His Promise to the Great Spirit, he offered a Gentle Supplication to the Lord of Lords whether It is Indiana Jones or Jehovah or Donald Duck or Shiva or Goddess Kali Enid Blyton or Satan or Ranch Style Nachos or Ganesha or Acai Berries or Allah Oil or Rocky Pie or Buddha Energy or Ali Theory or Brando Ghost or Dalai Lama Talisman or King of Russia Nail Polish or Maradona Goal or Kris of Sultan of Malaka or Anything else for what does it matter when You are Bleeding and Wincing in the Face of Death, almost Begging for some Divine Intervention even though as a True Atheist You are not Supposed to hang around the Corridor Two Hours before Midnight Sort of Humor and the Forest appeared Menacing with Hysterical Laughter Echoing in circular motion among the Trees and You are Lucky for You Know the way Home and it's true You had not seen a Soul for more than a good five hours if You can be more Certain, You will Know that You are not going to survive another three hours for the Shumei is still a few miles away and You have calculated that You will not have enough blood to Last the Distance even though the Flow has slowed somewhat with the Tension of Rubber Band in the Maoist Hat and You suddenly understand what it means in the Little Red Book which is really the Record of his quotations, some good, some not so good but when the Masses believed that He was the Ordained Head of the Dragon in the Communist Revolution, they don't always see that he had put his Life on the Altar of Moirai, Fearless, and Not a Paper Tiger and millions of people were sacrificed including those Monks and Nuns in more far out locations, they were forced to Rape and be Raped with bayonets in their Brains Melted in Pot of Barbarism, Surrounded by Loud Laughter getting Louder and Louder and it's Senseless but they were really entertained and it's so Funny that they even Cried until they Hiccupped and Vomited as they drank to their hearts content of the Hundred Year Old Wines, the Family Jewels, they feasted on White Lions so well trained and gentle that they are very attentive when You finally got down to the Trail, the Sun is still a few hours from Setting so there's still enough Light and You can hear the Constant Rush of the River being within sixty steps or whereabouts, the Life Promising Waters of the Hopi, and out of Nowhere, there… there They appeared… in the Nick of Time, the Perfect Moment, Two of Them, Royal Savior Rangers of the Realm…

"Ayuda! Ayuda! Sangre! Sangre!"

"Are You Hurt? Find a Clearing where You can Lie Down. We will be on our Way."

" N A A A A A … HIOOOOOOOSSSSSSSSIIIIIIIIIIIIIIIIIIIIIIIII!"

"Let me look at the Wound… Wow… there's a Big Cut… lots of Blood loss…"

"A-mi-ta-bha…"

"Let me look at Him! What's Your Name?"

" N A A A A A … CIOOOOOOOOOOSSSSSSSSSSSSSSIIIIIIIIIIII!!"

"It needs to stitched… Do You have a Sewing Kit?"

"No… he's going to be alright… There's a bump and Your Head Opened Up… there's a gash but I think it's going to be self-healing… I have a Bandage and I will go look for some Herbs. Wait here!"

"Can You Sterilize the Wound?"

" N A A A A A A A A A … … MIIIIIOOOOOOOOOSSSSSSSSIIIIIIII!!!"

"There's a Circle Mark around His Ears!"

"Are You Undergoing the Pains of the First Pangs of Love?"

"Alright, I'm going to put some herbs on the wound and it may Sting a little but everything's going to be well in no time."

"sayo… nara…"

No. I hoped I had known earlier that it was so challenging to travel on the Narrow Way as I contemplated the Present at that time which would become the Past after she pressed the Natural Remedy on my bleeding head, I discovered that I could focus my Eyes like my Camera and I was able to see the particles of Dust Fairies Floating in the Air as the Royal Savior Ranger Hound licked the Blood on my Hand and she seemed to like it very much as well the Blood which had seeped into Native American Soil and even in the Place where the Fall Occurred, and the Family of Squirrels living in the crevices of the Mountain Foot, they tasted how Pure and Vital the Blood, bursting with most beautiful Poetry capable of Art of Birth Control and Bore You to Sleep in Only a few Sentences and such other topics to Preoccupy themselves with the State of the Union and all that Jazz about how it's going to get better and better and better and all along, it's their Duty to Walk the Trails to Help Some Hiker in Distress and Imagine if they didn't come along and found You almost getting the Chance to fully understand the Meaning of Infinity so it's something that Nobody has ever told You how they were kind enough to Accompany You until they were totally Certain You will be able to make Your Way to Safety on Your own after You have Washed off Your Blood in the Icy Cold Miraculous Springs so Icy Your feet were Numb after Only a few minutes Only and if You had drank from that Spring that Day and Only that Day, Fast as Silver, the Waters Splashing into Your Eyes from more than two feet away, You would have Tasted what they call The Sweetest Milk in the World, Yeah, I Tell You, Sweeter than Honey or the Color of Gold and it's so Subtle, the Difference between You and the Devil, It's True, You Know, If It wanted

You Gone in the Woods or the Apartment, There's Really No Waters which Spring through Your Soul as These Crystals of Most Holy Orbs Appearing around You when You Found Out You had Washed Your Bloody Chin to Appear as Normal as Possible for Just a while ago You looked like Red Beard if Only Somebody was Visionary Enough to Take a Picture in that Time Splitting Moment when It All Came Together and now You appeared Normal especially when You put on that Mao Hat, watching in a dreamy gaze as You Watch the River Carry the Red of Liberty to the People of America… yeah… millions and millions will partake of the Communion as the Spirit of the Wild enters into their blood streams, We Become One, Brothers and Sisters of Color or Black or White or Blue or Green… Everybody's Coming Together… At Long Last… the People is United…

DEAD WOOD TRAIL

The Day After, openly discussing the Fall with Mona, well, she's the type of person who is very easy to converse with just because she has a more Perceptive Opinion of the World and she's more Liberal for she's Twice married or more, it's quite the Norm nowadays in the most Modern of Times when Ominotago found out, she's all Apologetic for she had a Premonition that something Bad will befall Mr. Wild Turkey who is her favorite Character in the Series known as Little Prairie Otters where there are no Real animals in the Barn in which most of the Action takes place and Everybody knows Everybody is having an Affair with another Character but they don't tell about those things in Line with the Ten Commandments Dramatically Burned into Consciousness Tablets of Marble and It should be Five on One Side for if it's Six Four, then it's heavier on One Side and the Boat may not be Balanced enough to Endure the Storm Blowing so much Stronger than forecasted and it's no longer Safe to go Outside but Mr. Wild Turkey, the Long Savage of Longevity, His Majesty Instructed his Nymphs to Tie Him to The Tree so he could Feel it First Hand to compose a better Picture in his Scrapbook for that's pretty much what he does… but for that… we have to go to Wales or Dublin for there's his Hometown but he's not very specific with Places and People so Corn Mother asked You to check Your Phone to see her Message around the Time It Happened to Him that he had the same Accident, her Sixty Seventh First Cousin, and she could see his skull and Doctor Octopus had to use the Stitch Gun to Close up the Wound and it was more or less Six or Seven times for it's Hard to keep Track of these Things when Someone is Hovering Over You to Shine a Light on It and Taking a Picture to Show You how it Looks in the Digital Age so I Kneeled on One Foot Under the Shower as Corn Mother Turned on the Lukewarm Waters so I could wash the Clots of Blood in the Hair and Nobody will tell You that it causes a Momentary Loss of All Memory for Jazz a Moment when Your Head hits the Rock from Approximately Shoulder Height, Your Brain will be Enveloped in Grand Wave of Epicenter of Existence if it may be Permissible to Use such a Word such as the Big Bang being just the Spark to Blast a Universe into Existence where we have just the Right temperature to Cultivate our own Foods and if You bother to not Study but Give some Notice to the Fields of Botany and Zoology, You will literally find Hundreds Upon Hundreds of Species in both Kingdoms where You witness the Wonders of Creation and You will Definitely be Mad to Believe that it's All such a Big Accident that all Living Things have Outlets for Waste and All the Specific Organs to Survive as a Race and no Matter Who You Are or Where You Come From and Who You Believe In, just come to Casa de Colores to be Administered Traditional Cures using Tree Bark Oil and some other Ointments, Hoila! I was Instantly Cured and the Wound was Sterilized and Everything's Groovy…

"Do You have Insurance?"

"No… I'm a…"

"Really… I think he's going to be Alright… it's Nothing so Serious… Just need Some Rest…"

"So… How was the Show and Dinner?"

"O… I feel so bad… it's Stupid… all Old Men… do You Believe it?"

"We were the Youngest!"

"HA HA HA"

"What a Waste of Time!"

"Do You want some Fruits? They are really Good!"

"HA HA HA"

"O my Brother Lucas is Coming Later."

"Here… here… talk to my Daughter Kamali… she can Help you…"

"Hey… How are You? Fine…"

"When is the Last Time You Visited a Doctor?"

"I Forgot… it's Been too long…"

"Have You ever had an Accident?"

"I don't Remember…"

"Why are You in Crestone?"

"To meet the Great Spirit…"

"… Very Well… We can feel Your Spirit Coming Out… but it's Not the Time yet…"

"Yeah… at least It's out of the Way…"

After a Long Nap of Five to Six Hours, feeling that the Wound has Dried Up, somehow, He's more Hopeful than ever that it's not Infected and no Worm is Trapped Inside and a few moons later, You can Feel Moths Flying Out of Your Mouth and it's all so Special when You Listen to Mona telling all her real stories for she Swore that Every Word she said was the Truth under the Watchful Eyes of Saturn and Jules Verne and she told about how Her Son Hototo Opened the Windows so the Winds would Mute His Whistling as they were Driving in the Mojave Desert on a Road Trip with her which was a very Nice Drive so it's Highly Recommended that You should do it at least Once in Your Life kind of Deal and Twilight was Creeping Up on them in Surreal Landscapes where the Boundary between Darkness and Light is Blurred and Gray isn't even the Right Answer if You have Guessed It, You are Always Right for it's almost Nine PM or so it May be too late to See the Sunset, yet, Without Reason, We were Speeding up the Tibetan Stupa as the Sun is Turning a Dot of Red Just as One of the Chief's Favorite Poet Described how the Art is More Important than Life and Who's More Romantic than One who Gave Up the Ghost for Love like Mark Anthony's Speech it's such a Thorny Scene I must have Snapped a Few Hundred Pictures and Just When We are Passing these Strange Creatures, it was in my Bag so we missed the Opportunity to Prove that Our Story is Real but I tell You it's Real because I still get Goose Bumps when I tell it… see… the Sun was Setting and Hototo was talking all about his girlfriends and he's quite the Ladies Man from his Younger Days and the Wind was blowing quite strongly on our faces so You can see our cheeks sunken in a few places… on the Shoulder… we saw these Two Big Black Wooden

Silent Stone Dogs… Big Tall Giant Dogs… Sitting on their Hindquarters… with their Front Paws Held Out… like this… and after we Passed… they were still there like a Pair of Stone Monuments… or Totems and then… Hototo asked me… if I Saw them… and I just Nodded… and he said… those were Shape Shifters… we didn't talk so much for the rest of the Journey… but it's so Unreal… we didn't dare to go back there… anymore…

The next morning, they finally arrived at Blue Moon's backyard. Jeremiah was fast asleep for he was totally exhausted from all the traveling and he hadn't had anything to eat or drink for almost a full day. Poor boy... BulBul looked at the line of people behind her and she felt a certain kind of happiness which is sublime, not for the more obvious reason that she had to wait in line like the multitudes who would have experienced some degree of heightened exhilaration when their hometown team of semi-professionals battled back tooth and bone and nail and hair from a six-goal deficit with ten minutes or less remaining, and if things were not impossible enough, their only courageous captain was agonizingly stretchered off, though he was sobbing like a little girl only for the reason that he wanted to continue playing and not at all due to the fact that his ankle was destroyed so cruelly by the superb role-model professional opposite Vice Captain who performed the feat without even a yellow card while another two of his teammates were given red cards for some soft punches at the back of those super top divas who fooled the referees blind, and against all the odds of all the odds, they managed to notch the most incredible victory without going into injury time but You can imagine how much more exuberant the locals would be singing if the seventh goal was scored in those few minutes after the 90 and how they would be gushing about that game for the rest of their lives, let it be known, it's with approximately the same measure of glow on their faces when they get to be within touching distance of Blue Moon that some of the devotees began to start wailing or weeping or laughing or jumping or standing on their heads or whatever actions You associate with the state of ultimate Euphoria, there, You would see, also, people fainting, people removing all their garments, people procreating, people somersaulting while whistling and almost every conceivable action You can think of, You will see it, yeah, even people dying and fainting, and these were the people who caused the heaviest traffic for they would just be falling over and it's the stewards' job to separate those who passed away from those who passed out. It's really a mess. As for BulBul, she didn't really queue up to see Blue Moon for the same reasons as those people because she's her sister and she's carrying Jeremiah who would have taken much, much longer to arrive at the Showcase.

"Jeremiah! Jeremiah! We are here! Wake up!"

"It's no use... He's dreaming... He will not awake..."

"JEREMIAH! JEREMIAH! BLUE..."

"Please stop shouting... You are disturbing the Brethren... Let him dream..."

"But... but... he's carrying an import..."

"STOP. Who are You??"

"I'm Your Sister... BulBul..."

"BulBul?"

"Yes???"

"I'm Sorry... I don't remember You at all... I just... and How can You be Older than Mother? "

"It's Alright...

"Relax... Tell me What You See..."

"It's a rainy day and I was traveling in a slow moving vehicle... a bus... or van..."

"Is it a van of bus?"

"There were rows and rows of seats..."

"How many? Can You Remember?"

"Of course... more than 90 rows..."

"Alright... how many passengers were in that bus?"

"In the beginning, I was the only passenger in the bus so I had a weird kind of feeling because I had never been in a bus with no other passenger and so, I walked to the very end of the bus and dived on the long continuous seat to the window pretty pleased that I had the whole bus to myself but at one of the stops, a group of four travelers came into the bus. For some reason, I hoped or maybe even prayed that they would sit nearer to the front so that I could enjoy my quiet time but alas! They were coming nearer and nearer and they finally occupied the seats only a few rows from me but for some reason, I wasn't quite so angry though my face was red and all so I found it quite strange."

"Do You know why You were feeling that way?"

"No... but I calmed down when I recognized two of them... The two girls were in the same ferry as me and I guess the other pair too but I didn't see them. The man was younger and he seemed to be more aloof though it's quite clear that the talkative girl was happily talking all the time and it's quite obvious that she was just talking and talking just so he could hear what a beautiful voice she had... and the older woman who was old enough to be his mother was quite aware of the intangible attraction the younger girl had for her man."

"Do You remember any of the conversation?"

"No... they were speaking in French and I don't understand any of it at all but I could guess some of their conversation."

"How so???"

"Well... There were two pairs of strangers. Though they were from the same country, they met in a foreign country where they didn't understand much of the local language or culture. Out of the blue, a chance connection was made, something which is secretly hoped for by almost every traveler. The two girl travelers were obviously lesbians but I suspect that they are more easy going and the younger one was also bisexual because she was glaring at that guy and talking in her sweetest voice whenever he asked her any question. For instance... he asked... Where are you girls from? so she answered somewhat sheepishly... Montpellier... and his companion, who's always holding on to his thigh like she's so afraid to lose him, she would suddenly be flushed and shout... O my fucking god... We are also from Montpellier! and then the three of them would enter into a flurry to talk about their exact addresses and so on and exclaimed in ecstasy how they were actually living so close! to each other and they had never met and then! when they traveled a few thousand miles away from home, they met! kind of banter. By this time, the group was totally in heaven and they were blushing and blushing so the most friendly girl instructed her more serious partner to climb on the seat and take out a few packets of juices though the bus was so empty, they could have just saved the trouble by putting their knapsacks and bags and equipment almost anywhere."

"Maybe they were being considerate... just in case the bus picked up more passengers?"

"Maybe... but that's not the Point. Then, the guy made his move and offered some authentic local tidbit to the girls and his

older girlfriend was playing the good hostess, encouraging the girls to accept the token of friendship. The talkative girl was showing her eternal gratitude by pulling out the string-like delicacy in the most gracious gesture of French eloquence, then, turning to her full lesbian companion who's hiding in her shell in a seat, far, far away from the newly-forming nucleus, and she's asking her if she wanted a piece of the communion, and she just shook her head, saying she's not that hungry, quickly turning her face to the window so the rest of the world didn't see her eyes, blurry with tears. All this time, her younger and more adventurous lover wasn't aware that she was feeling abandoned so she continued to talk and laugh, and then, the man asked again... Where are you girls going? So she answered devilishly... Koh Phi Phi... and just like the previous time, the older woman who was already caressing the younger girl's shapely long thighs or neck or more... I forgot, she wailed like a sex-starved banshee, almost screaming What a fucking coincidence!! I can't believe it!!! while comically turning to her younger boyfriend at least a dozen times or so and you can guess what sounds of orgasm she Maketh in the exaggeration of her passions... so then the bisexual girl was turning to look at her fully lesbian partner who asked... Which Hotel? and the four of them shouted out the same name in unison, intertwined with boisterous laughter, giggles, clapping, spontaneous exclamations of disbelief and scurrying belief, cocooned by a hot rush of pink gushes and excited whispers and trains of blushes chugging away to the station of endless possibilities where everything makes perfect sense."

"Anything else? Do You know their names?"

"No..."

"I Can't Take It Any Longer! PLEASE STOP!"

"Why… the Storm is my Friend…"

"No! Not You!"

"Can You Meet me at Washington and 10th?"

"Shall I Invite the Witch?"

"No… I think she's Busy with the Cat who's…"

"Can I Come into Your House? I just Need to See the Cyclops!"

"Sorry… You are not a Member… this is Only for Members…"

"Can You Give Me The Tree?"

"Please… Madam… it's Our Family Heirloom… it's…"

"Why? Why?? Why???"

It's not really so Grand to go to the Stupa on the Road passing Shumei especially with all the Mosquitoes still Ferocious and Thirsty for Blood and there's some Fresh Ones who are still excited to see a Fox or a Deer and You ask Yourself why You no enjoy those things You enjoy when Younger and You didn't know so much of the World so You could be Happy when You saw a Squirrel jumping from the tree to the bench and when did You lose Your Innocence, You can't even Remember the Last Time You were genuinely Happy to be Alive and You had Nothing to Fear like a Two Year Boy or maybe even Three in some cases where it's Easier to Pretend You are not Interested in any other thing more than to Show Your Sincerity to the Witch who Locked Herself in the Room for more than a few weeks after her Beloved was Murdered in a Challenge and she blamed the Gods with all her heart because she had prayed… prayed with Fresh Pregnant Salmon Blood Dribbling Down her Cheeks… Petitioning the Lord for the Life of The Count who had loved her unconditionally though no Man ever Dared to be with her… she gave herself totally to him… he's so Romantic to send the Golden Swan Carriage pulled by Six Flying Horses like Pegasus and she didn't care to Check if there were Three Females and Three Males for Equality or there were Four Females and Two Males for Speed for it's Always a Fact that Female Flying Horses have more Beautiful Wings like Butterflies so in Those Days, they were also known as Butterhorses and she's Wise Enough to know that Butter has Nothing to do with those Beautiful Things Surrounding her in Most Unreal Fashion, there were two Rings of Four Butterflies Each on Her Breasts, attracted to the Malt and Sweet Pineapple Jelly Jam Wobbling in her Womb whenever they went into the Clouds and the God of Thunder is Whacking the Hammer on the Chisel and Flashes of Lightning are making the Cloud Pillars Glow as she was Welcomed into his Palace in Paradise with Grand Fanfare and Worship as All the Servants bowed in Fear of the Fireworks being Ignited too Close for Comfort and she's Blossoming in her Spirit and in the Cave, the Black Wind is Blowing, in Tornadoes and too Violent for her to Think about any other thing except the Count's Scepter which is adorned with Head of a Serpent with Eyes made of Three Philosopher's Stones in which You can see the Roots Within so when the Lightning Strikes, They will Glow a Blue of Deepest Ocean before it All becomes Black and Indistinct until You feel it in Your Hand and it's a Good Source of Light since it doesn't require any Battery or Electricity or Fuel so there will be quite enough Light for You to Find the Way to the Trail, tracking the familiar scent in the Winds, starting from the Backyard of Enchantment Court, Watch out for the Ant Hills and once You have located them, You will see that they form a Trail so just go along as You will also come across mini stone structures erected by some LOA People who Stack the Stones so they now become Towers of Insignificance for the way some of the stones are Balanced on Top of Another One, it requires a high skill level and it's more Strange because these Towers were also being built by People of various Cultures thousands of miles apart, only that they may not be known as Towers of Insignificance but it's Unnecessary to know so much about these Things, it's just… it's just on this Trail Witch Maris Stella Embarked on her Journey to the West to search out the Sage of Blanca as if Somebody would have told her it's Futile because even if she found him, he may not offer his Council to her or even if he's willing to accept her in his Chambers, he may not know how to Unknot the Gordian Knot in her Heart for it had been Bothering her so much that she had not been able to Function Normally as a Normal woman and then when You Chance on a Door in the Dead Wood, Enter It, and You will Come Out on the Other Side, Surprised not to be Surprised not to be Swept into The Garden with Unicorns and Scurrying Four Winged Geese with a Lion's Head and Fish Body so it's called Merliongoose and it's really kind of childish to Expect to Witness the Extraordinary when You Enter a Spiritual Portal, You think You are going to Disappear Physically and Become a Spirit, Forget It, it's not how these Things work and You may even Imagine You are Floating Up to the Heavens as You Recognize the same Yellow Bird or maybe it's the same family member but You cannot be sure because from a certain distance, many Birds appear the same so it's hard to pick up distinguishable habits or traits to tell One from Another but she's Singing a Song Most Decadent so the Signs are Right when the Bird flies Southwest when You are heading Northeast, yeah, it's true that she was Tearing up this Way and Heaving and Puffing for Air as she gets Nearer to the Midway Point, she put her Hand on One Tree after Another, Extracting All Life from the Crown to the Tail of the Roots, Witch Stella Maris stopped to Grieve every few steps so she didn't feel a little Pity for the Trees Turning Black, Dry and Dead, and the Trail is Mildly Interesting for Hikers who want to Experience Just that Extra more Distinction form the Ordinary Ordinary Hikers who Just go on a Hike to Smell the Mountain Air or Grow a Beard or Smoke a Fortune or Just to be Healthy or Admiring the Scenery, This New Type of Hiking is for Hardcore Citizens…

"Now, Darling, I Know, You Got Another Girl…"

"Yeah, I saw her. She just ran past Here just now… like a Lightning Bolt…"

"Even more Beautiful than I…"

"What's the First Commandment?"

"THOU SHALL NOT READ!"

"Will You Stay Awake and Keep Watch by the Window? I have a Feeling they will be Coming Tonight…"

"Why?? Are You from the South Pacific?"

"No… I'm from… South…"

"… how I Long… for You…"

"THOU SHALL NOT BOW OUR HEAD!"

"No… Not Yet…"

"Wait for the Signal! We are not going to be Standing Here All Night to Tell Everybody about the Same Damn Few Things Over and Over Again!"

"I Have Only One Love to Give..."

"Did You see the New Pictures I bought Today?"

"THOU SHALL NOT BE WORSHIPPING BAEL!"

"NAAAA....HIIIIIIIIOOOOOOOSSSSSSSSSIIIII!!!!"

"People say I'm a Fool..."

"Do You Have some Time to Spare?"

"Turn Around. Go down the corridor and there's the Restroom. Can't Miss!!"

"I wish to tell You... I'm the Fiddler..."

"Recognize me?"

"Just go to the Rooftop and when It's Clear... Jump Down..."

"Don't Worry..."

"When I was a Young Fellow, no more than Twenty Nine, my parents Invited me to the Fair of Roses by the Rivera Steamboats where we were going to be enjoying a Sunday Evening Dinner with Vishnu in the Grand Blue Lotus where we would be having a Big Banquet with our friends and family. It was such a Charming Day, You can Imagine You are Hearing the Harps of Angels playing the most Sleepy Music You have ever Heard and I Knew It Even if I had not Reached Adulthood, yeah, I was one of those Slow Ones. The Roses were all so Pretty! My Stupid Sisters kept Whispering into my Ears! O How Much I Hated them! Nevertheless, the Roses were Terrific even if I'm a Zorro and I'm not Supposed to like such Stuff like my Sisters' under garments but one sniff and I will know who they were with Last Night. Sorry, I can't tell You such things."

"Please... Run Faster... You are Falling too Far Behind the Pack..."

"After the Feast, we were drinking the Finest Finest Champagne for I had Never Ever Felt such Sense of Tipsiness as Tipsiness is Supposed to be Felt in the Happiest of Times when People are Celebrating for a Reason for Daddy had won a Big Business with the State Department of Labor and we were going to move into this Sixty Room Mansion in a moon or so when all of a sudden, the Waiter Started Shooting Everybody with a Tommy Gun while the Gorgeous Phyllis Dillon was Singing about How Her Lovers were leaving her One after Another and a lot of people were Slow Dancing, fondling and caressing each other in the Wide Open Public and I was talking to this Fanciful Fifteen Year Old Babe in Mirror Sequin Mandarin Cheongsam and I was just about to Kiss her Hand when Everybody started Screaming and Shouting in Big Jumble of Noise as You had Never Heard in the Slaughter House, You can hear it, the Trumpet Players still Playing for there's Nothing Else they wanted to do in their Life and the Gun Man was still Shooting and Laughing and to this Day, Nobody knew how…"

"Love the One You… a… with…"

"It's too late... they have all gone Home…"

"How many Buffaloes do You want to for the Princess?"

"Do You know the Way to Jamaica City?"

"C'mon… Boys… it's Rocking Time…"

"You Know, I could have missed the Steamboat Party. It's my Best Friend's Birthday and she warned she would not Speak to me ever again if I didn't go to her party…

"Slow Down! Slow Down! You are Going too Fast! You will Burn Out Soon! Slow Down!"

"After It was All Over, he killed more than a few hundred of our Townsfolks and also some people from other parts of the world before they put him down. He Shouted… Anarchy! Anarchy! Death to the Pussies! Death to the Tyrants! I mean… Why Kill Me? I Never Did no Harm to You! Why don't You Kill Your Own Father and Mother for They were the Ones who Brought You to This World and While You are at It… Why Don't You Kill Yourself since the God is in You and You and You are the Greatest Right? Yeah… You have No Right to Take my Life or any Other Life, not even Your Family Members or Church Mates or School Bullies who are Allowed to Prosper in the Hypocritical Dimension and I always Hated David more than Anything but I Never Felt I had a Right to Kill him."

"So.. What Happened?"

"It's so Good for You to Settle Down…"

"THOU SHALL NOT LOVE MONEY! MONEY! MONEY!"

"What's The Punishment?"

"Don't make me… wait… too… long…"

"After he was Shot Down by the Special Force, I saw his Soul coming out of the Body and he was Standing over his Corpse… and Shaking His Head for he didn't know He's Dead… See… I told You he was Stupid and Naive… and I can Remember the Confusion on his Face as he was Shaking His Head from Left to Right so Fast… and he didn't even know Why he's doing it until it became Faster… and Faster… a Whirl or Stroke of Colors like how those Masters perform in some Paintings and his Face was Turning Blurry like that so You can't even see his eyes or mouth or nose or anything… for it was Disintegrating…"

"Do You Swear that Every Word You say is True?"

"I'm already Dead… I have no Reason to Lie… what

have I to Profit… anyway… I'm a Gentleman… I don't Swear…"

"I'm Alone… I'm Alone… I'm Alone… by Myself… Tonight…"

"The Music was still playing… surprisingly… he didn't get the Musicians… but he got my Family pretty good… leaving just the Second Youngest One… but I can't Remember her Name anymore…"

"THOU SHALL NOT SPY ON YOUR NEIGHBOR'S WIFE NO MATTER HOW SEXY WHILE SHE'S BATHING IN THE EVENING!!!"

"Satan… Get Thee Out of the Rock! Get Thee Behind the Crescent Moon!!!"

"Then… I saw the Man with the Horse Face and the Man with the Bull Head put a Big Heavy Chain of Black Mountain around His Neck and they Immediately Dragged him though You should Know how He Wailed and Screeched but They Couldn't Hear Him so They Didn't Stop even for a Moment towards the Crater to the Underworld for I was Extremely Interested in What Punishment Awaits such a Person so I Saw that I was not Alone for more than a Few Hundred Souls including my Beloved Family and Friends and even my New Girlfriend, we were all there, and we were all Holding Clubs of Diamond Spikes and these Spikes, they Really Pierce You Up Pretty Bad and they are Given to the Victims to Punish the Culprit. Right at the Entrance, the Limbs will be pulled Taut at the Maximum so they cannot be Stretched anymore and if You think that since You are Dead You cannot feel any twinge of pain at all, Go Ahead, think all You want but I will tell You, I don't Care, I'm a Ghost and I'm telling You that the Pain is Magnified a Thousand Times or

More because I never Heard a Person Banshee like that when we Pummeled and Stepped on His Soul with All the Blows we Could Muster with Most Powerful Muscles Rocking with Enough Energy to Charge the Earth for a Million Years or more, he was Shaking like a Pulped Up Catfish Squirming with Bones and Eyes already Mortared but still Alive and Kicking and Twisting to get back into the Water, he Begged and Begged and Begged until his Forehead is Darker than Other Parts of his face as a result of him Pressing so Hard into the Sacred Ground and Three Quarter or More Asleep, full prostrate on His Shadow and he was Whacked Flat and maybe even a little Flatter than the Thinnest Tracing Paper of the Highest Quality so even if You Trace the Origin of Pain in his Soul just now Starting to Pay for his Sins and his Interest in First Person Killing games Surprisingly Proven to be Not the Cause of Violence in the Biggest Cities or the Smallest Municipalities so the Masses ask… Who's the Culprit? and the Truth is… Everybody is Responsible… and he's not even a very good player at that for he's always easily Beaten by the Nerds who can decipher the Algorithms so they will always beat these Bone Headed types who Only Knew How to Follow the Wrong Leaders all the Time even when They are Not even Cool and You can tell Right Away that they are the Most Simple Minded Folks and they would make…"

"Be Happy…"

"Are You Satisfied Now? Does it Pleasure You to See Him Suffer such Atrocious Pain?"

"Yes! Even a Million Times Worse, I have No Qualms. He has No Right! Sorry, I will Say a Person like This Doesn't Deserve to be Born at All! Look! Parents! Guardians! Teachers! Law Makers! Nurses! Soldiers! Indians! Look at him NOW! How does…"

"After that.. they forced him to kneel at the Palace Front where he was Judged by Aeacus, Grandfather of Achilles, and Minos, First King of Crete, and his brother, Rhadamanthus, and the Trio of Them were Full of Anger when they Saw the Grief Stricken Tortured Molecules of the Guy who Should Not be Named for they are All the Same Lamb led Astray and though they Believed their rewards were Eternal Pleasure in Earth or Paradise, how stupid, and so many of them think it's One and the Same, they shrunk when they were Magnetized so Utterly Shocked to Discover they would Stand Trial for their Crimes against Humanity and the Line was Quite Long for there were many Murderers as well as Others and the System was such that Rhadamanthus was the Judge of these Sons of Debauchery and False Religion, they would be Judged according to the Number of Killings so the one at the Front of the Queue will be the New Dummy and there, he was kneeling before the Judge, begging like a Fool and shouting Holy Spirit this and Allah that and the rest of them too, they defended why they murdered and trampled on the weak and poor but when the Horn is Blown, they fell Silent as they Acknowledge it's no use since they were Naked so after the Charges were Read, he was Sentenced and they pulled him away for further Punishment."

"What's Your Name?"

"I have Forgotten! The Punishment was too Painful! HELP! HELP! I Can't Stand it!"

"What's Your Occupation?"

"O Please! Let Me Go! Let Me Go!"

"It's Nothing. You are now feeling all the Pain You have caused all those souls plus all the Sufferings of their Loved

Ones plus all those people that You have harmed in Your Life!"

"IT'S ALL HERE! READ ALL ABOUT IT!!!"

"How Does It Feel?"

"No… Please… Don't Push Me Off the Cliff! PLEASE! PLEAASSSEEEE!!"

"What's Your Occupation?"

"I BEG YOU! PLEAAAASSSSSSEEEE!! LET ME GO!!!"

"Is it so Intolerable? It's just The Beginning!"

"I'm a Goat Tender! I Remember. My Father was a Goat Tender and his Father too! PLEASE! PLEASE! ENOUGH!! I BEG YOU!!! STOP IT! STOP IT!!"

"If I Stop… It will be Brighter… and Brighter.... Do You want me to Stop?"

"What's Your Occupation?"

"I'm a Father too… Please Spare Me! I Will Do Anything!!!"

"It's no Use to Lie… We Know Everything… We Have the Full Record Here… We Know Everything… Even when You Think Nobody's There… We are There… We are All Knowing… We Count Your Hair… Every Second…"

"IF YOU KNOW EVERYTHING… WHAT'S THE PURPOSE

"It's Your Last Chance to Repent… but You Still Don't Get It… Do You???"

"I KNOW I'M A SINNER! PLEASE! GET ON WITH IT!!"

"Guards, Take him away…"

"After that I saw the Man with Horse Face and the Man with Bull Head lead him on the Road to Tartarus but that's just the beginning of his Punishment… and after the Judgment, all of us stopped following him for we were not Permitted to go on that Path since it's the Path of Redemption for them for You See, the Theory is Simple, he will suffer just as he made them suffer in exactly the intensity and manner and the Barrier prevented us from Treading in his trail for we were so called The Innocents but we were Feeling Vindicated to some Degree and We are Convinced the Judgement of Minos was Just and the Scale of Justice was Fair so we were also Judged by Aeacus who found that I was Innocent enough and the Nymphs brought me to Lethe, the Pool where I met many other Innocents and we were all Enjoying the Soot Packaged Music which was played many years ago by Orpheus but somehow, they have a record of it… and we were all Weeping for it's Really the Saddest Song of All Time… and I saw the Bronze Statues Crying… and the Nymphs… they were also Weeping and Raining like they had Heard the Scratch of the Most Empty Heart… and to be Frank, I Felt that the Song should be Played to the Evil instead of the Innocent but I guess, the Cleansing of My Memory is an Essential Ritual so the Gods may want it to be Performed with a little more Drama... There… but Sadly… I didn't see my Father or Mother so… I didn't Drink of the Wine…"

"Why are You Here?"

"Where is He?"

"You Know… he has gone to the Underworld… and You cannot follow unless You take Your Life and even then…"

"Let me Go!"

"You will not be able to meet him…"

"I'm Totally Ready!"

"… find him because You will have no memory of him and neither him of You so Know Fully Well of the Punishment if…"

"It's not Easy to Come Here, You Know? Do You Know how much I Sacrificed?"

"No matter what… I can't let You pass… They know Everything…"

"Please Help Me! I really need to see him One Last Time… just a few words… please!!"

"It's no use! He doesn't remember You anymore. He's just a Statue. Don't You understand? It's just like… I'm Trying to Tell You but You Don't Get It… Once they Enter the Deepest Realms of Hell… they will be Prescribed the Darkest Tortures Ever Imaginable so do You think he will have time to hear You out?"

"I don't care! I have come too far to turn back and no matter what You say… I will push on even if it means I have to take Your life!"

"O Little Black Foot… You Think too Highly of Yourself…"

"Hey! Hey! Wait! Where are You going? I need…"

Going back down from where she came, disappointed and cursing her Luck, the Black Hand Witch W, she made the Solemn Decision to change her name to Hasten the Acceptance Stage of the Loss of the Count who had been such a Sucky Part of her Life, she could never Imagine existing for even a few minutes without such simple joys like his razor sharp finger nails embedded in her hips so she's not

Bleeding even a Little Bit or Notwithstandingly Curious… What's the smell of his hair in her Morning Coffee or the Taste of his Semen in her Quarter Boiled Eggs with a Drop of Sesame Oil and Soy to soften the Potency of the Count's Manhood poking vigorously into Her Mysterious Jewelry Box and all those sapphires and moonstones and cat's eyes and maw-sit-sits and mystic topaz wands Collected to Stir her Strong Will into Sweet Surrender and It's True, she never felt so beautiful ever, 169:1, she skipped from one Dead Wood to another and on her way, she met the Mad Monk who's Blessing One of the Fallen Trees with some Holy Water so she looks a little Bewildered and Tickled.

"HA! HA! HA! HA! HA! HA! HA! HA! What the Hell Are You Doing?"

"Do You Know the Way to The Challenger?"

"Why? Why do You want to go there?"

"To Prepare Myself."

"For What? Why are You Watering the Dead Wood?"

"It's not Dead. It's only Sleeping."

"HA! HA! HA! HA! HA! SLEEPING? CRAZY! IT'S DEAD!!!"

"No… it's not… look… it's Alive…"

"You are Wasting Your Time! You cannot Resurrect the Dead! Jesus Christ! You are Mad!"

"How Do You Know??"

"I don't have Time! It's been a Rough Day! I Wanna Go Home!!"

"Good Luck! Good Blessings! Good Tidings!"

"Thank You…"

VII FOURTEEN SILENCES!!!

Did I forget to tell you all about Sir Arthur Francis Pollen who lived more than three centuries ago when the men of those days were still Real Men and not like the Pussies they ask us to model after this or that Hairstyle or things that really Matter like how You Part Your Hair, yeah, it relates to how he was the Richest Guy in Town and surely he owned a Platoon of those Fine Soldiers that Lay Their Lives Down for Their Masters for Whatever Reason, it's not their Business but to Protect him or his fancies no matter his Gold is Pure or Not, he just needed a bigger and bigger Platoon for the Call to Arms is not the time to watch TV for in those Dark Times, these Gadgets were not being Invented yet and it took a good many Writers to record his Achievements and there were many so the faster Writers of the Country were Commissioned to Write the First History of Mankind in Latin and strictly, there were not more than ten people in the whole wide universe who knew the language well enough to write about the Time when he presented eleven swan songs to the Lady in Waiting and she was so Happy she hugged him and planted the pinkest peck on his cheeks for a good few minutes so the writing was: Left Right Smack Left Right Smack for pages for she's a very fast one and he was so taken by Surprise that he just stood there like a Statue as His Stick was turned to Stone in her Patio of Pleasures where she entertained the most Athletic and Scientific and Political and Intellectual folks with Seductive Music and Suggestive Dances and Endless Drinks on the House and it's not even Funny when she paid his Family a few thousand Dislikes and Purchased him outright for all her Sexual Desires and Fantasies and among women, not quite so many women possess such Precious Stones as she had Collected since she was but a Three year Old Innocent Little Girl, still Wearing the Tudung to cover most of her Attractive Features so she can keep her Purity for her One and Only Future Husband and the cloth is so long and fancy that the fringes come down at the exact spot where her G-Spot will be if Somebody had told her about it Earlier, she would have missed the Chance to meet the First Son of the Prime Minister who was Touted to be the Future Prime Minister at the Tender Age of Seven when he Announced it for all the newspapers in the Nation to Chart his Promise that he would become the Wealthiest Man is the World simply because he's Assisted by the Smartest and Most Evil Scammers in the World and he's still the Darling of the Press as well a Respected Dictator in the World, Welcomed and Worshipped Everywhere she went because she has got more Dislikes than many others and it's not a Crime that she was Corrupted by her own Daddy who has got eleven wives for there wasn't any Quota in those times so she thought it's Alright to sleep around and the more she slept around, the more Dislikes she accumulated so it's also not an Accident that she Developed the Eye for Taste and

Good Judgment so she had a whole trunkful of these gems and topazes and quartzes and jades and malachites and her High List of Clientelle including the Debonair Prime Minister so she collected even more Decadent stuff so Historic so many years later she had Rooms full of these Stones and she was so Sly and Devious she Sprinkled Gold Dust to the Peasants Everywhere she went and Surprisingly, the Halal People, they Adored and Worshipped her so much so she needed whole blocks of Project Flats to Keep them and also more Troops, yeah, it's always Time to Spend on the Military for we are not Fighting against Flesh and Blood but Principalities of Darkness and we need them to be Fierce and Ferocious with Extreme Thirst for Soul so when they See any Living Thing, they will Sprint towards It at Full Speed without regard for Safety or Anything Else which are Important to Mademoiselle for she had mastered the Art of the Stones so she knows exactly what Stones needed to be placed on a Person to bring him or her to a State of Unconsciousness in a matter of Days when they went under her Spell, they didn't need to Eat, Drink, Sleep, Talk or even Breathe as they were to be Half Frozen on their Private Bed of Ice for it sounds better than Ice Beds so You know You are still on the right track and You may Think that You are losing yet again and You can't even walk another step, at the very Least, You have come THUS Far when Everybody Surrendered after a few lines, it's Useless, it's Impossible, and all that type of Negativity to be Alleviated by the most Soulful of Songs so they will Remember the Happy and Proud Times of their lives, it's not so Difficult, Take a Deep Breath, Hell, in fact, Take the Deepest Breath You can ever Take and Keep it in Your Lungs until it Expands to the Fullest You can feel Your Lungs growing more Muscular, it's Time, it's Time to go even Deeper so the Chi can go into the Stomach and pass out through the Exterior to Clear the Body of Impure Air and we Shall Call this Air the Air of Queen Elizabeth, the Original One for You will perceive that she's One who likes to Perform such tasks in Public and Open for the Council to hear, yeah, it's always the First Man on her Right who will take the Blame and he will say Pardon my Grace! It's Me! so she will not be Disgraced during the Debate which will be One Whole Boatload Upon Parcels of Mountains Tonyhoods Diseased Puss Whack Dough of Dirt Laundering of You Did This and You Didn't Do That kind of Nonsense People just Cannot Ignore because It's Election Time and Like a Train Line of Impatient Idiots, they will still go to the Polls and Cast their Votes and they are all Believing and Hoping that their Chosen One will Win and just when they were about to Cast their Votes, the Happy Go Lucky Gang of Cold Motherfucking Sons of Lucifer, yeah, the Neo Nazi Yahweh is Glorious Einstein Demon Possessed KKK Marx trained mercenaries Burst Out of Nowhere, Ramming on the Gas Full Tilt, Aiming their Fully Loaded Trucks and Vans at the Innocents who were just going to the Ballots to Cast their Votes, Risking their lives for their Voice to be heard no matter how Immaterial it seems, I tell You, it's not all for Nothing for in HERE, there's a Hero of the Masses, one more Mighty than Genghis Khan or Napoleon or Gandhi or Pikachu or Supergirl or Zeus or Moses or Rumi or King Kamekamehaha or Three Wind or Mohammed or Doraemon or Christ or Lego Guy or Buddha or Zarathustra or Zhuge Liang always Winning after he Plotted the First Victory and the Countless Defeats he had to Endure to win the Heart of the Masses, he always appears in the Right Place at the Right Time in such an Idea like it's Alright to Try to Counter Program the

Terrorists so he's such a Gentleman, he issues a Signal to Warn them they will be Killed within Two Seconds after the One Second that they had Received the Message Loud and Clearly Imprinted in their Minds like the mark of the Beast being Simple Six Six Six enough to process the Information for their Safety and all of them Screeched like Hyena Bitches and in just a Splintered Spine of Just that One Second being the Difference between Life and Death, Nahiossi Launched Green Fairy into the Sun and in less than a quarter of the Time they thought they were going to Truly Terrorize Thousands, she Slashed off their Throats and Strangely, Rightfully, she didn't feel Guilt at All Not Terrified of all that Stinky Martyr Blood Splashing all over the Cabin of their Trucks and Vans, the Head falling on the Passenger Seat where they had Sexually Assaulted so many Lonely Women who were just Looking for that Great One Night Stand so many of them resorted to a Life of Prostitution to disguise their desire to be loved by Wildest Man of All Time kind of Songs playing on his Radio he always Carry Everywhere he went so there's Music All the Time for he always had a Penchant for the Dramatic so he Whispered to her Faster and there they were without their Heads while their hands were still on the Wheel and their necks became Fountains of Blood as their Souls were Dragged away in Mirror of Irony where they saw their own Naked Bodies and for the first time, they felt ashamed and they were reaching for the garments or anything to cover their genitals for it's the just the thing to Consider when You are in a Sticky Situation so You Reason You still haven't figured out that part about the trucks and vans which are still going at Full Speed towards that Cute Little Doggie Pie and Little Honey Pie and also Old Timers and Teenagers who don't really care who wins as long as he's rich enough to buy their hearts because when they are Free they talk Nonsense almost all the time but sometimes when You are Lucky, You will hear some Old Guy lazing on the Seat and he's talking to some young Aspiring Rastafarian African Gentleman and he's showing him a few latest fashionable sunglasses and the guy somehow sees his Girl's Picture and he asks if she's his Wife and he suddenly becomes shy, imagine that... a Macho Big Daddy Guy becoming shy in a bus and he says no she's My Girl he says so the Old Guy tells him not to Worry and how he should get married earlier instead of later for that's what's matters, man, don't worry about the Race, it's not there, man, You get what I Mean, yeah, get a job, stay off the drugs, man, Love Your Woman, and that's the Big Secret of Life, my Friend, don't listen to Them, Listen to Your Heart, man, and he went on all about his Life and how he needed to get his Shit together and it's quite Obvious that if You still haven't figured Your Shit Out when You are Sixty Nine Years Old or More, When, When will it be the Time for You to get figure the Shit Out ever? Still, the most important thing in Life is to know When to Get off the Bus and not be carried to the Four Corners of the Globe where there's No Regrets, Alright, even If You don't read, You will hear the Sound One Day when You are Called to be a Savior, You Crash into the Terror vehicles with all the Strength of the Almighty and Without a Grain of Sand of Fear of Hell for Your Life, You Crush into the Truck, BOOM!, BOOM! BOOM! BOOM! BOOM! BOOM! BOOM! BOOM! BOOM! BOOM! BOOM! BOOM! X Thousands for there were so many vehicles all Loaded with Time Bombs but it was just One Sound in Reality when You saw it's such Luck for all around, You witness the Guardians Arise and it's quite a Sight to watch how they Smashed the Plot and within a Second, the Ant Generals with Those Crab-like Pinchers who have planned the Journey for a few moons, Arriving at the most critical moment to Cut the Red or Blue or White Wire, they don't know but somehow, It's a Miracle, they cut it Right so the Bombs were disabled successfully in Time so No Civilian was harmed in the Least except for the Fear they felt gripping at their Hearts when they thought they were all going to Die on that Day and there's no Way they would Escape the Evil Plot Hatched years ago in the Cold War which was just a Cover for the Struggle to Control the Most Important Resources so it makes total sense, it's the Rich Guys who are Funding these Terrorist Activities one way or another, it's Senseless for a Country as backward as Burma to develop the Technology or Intelligence or Capacity to venture into Nuclear Science for another one hundred sixty six years but Ahoy! Watch it! In a few years, their Military expenditure Increases significantly as they receive the latest technology from the Arabs in cohorts with them for they can see how Au Sang is still so Sexy after all those years in Isolation with her Maid who cared for her and Massaged her Bruised Shoulders and Backside as She Sacrificed her Body and Soul to the Nation and all the people were so Proud of her but surely they don't know about the Nights when the Junta King sent his Men to the Outhouse and Smoked the Compound so She and the Maid would be Put into Deep Sleep so he could enjoy Stomping on her Back and no, he didn't violate her and he didn't allow any of his dogs to devour her or the Nurse since they had been castrated and he too when he became a Soldier but he was too Ashamed to tell Anybody since it's such a Shame for a Man to have no Penis in those days, especially in his culture, they would be made to Stand in the Middle of the Square and Recite the Wasteland poem in

French and it was quite Impossible for their tongues were also clipped an inch Shorter so they couldn't pronounce Je Suis ton tonton que je suis verre vert ver pas si sont si tonton rats grillen six chats and even chasser chausse du jasmin so much so he just wanted to see her every now and then since he Imagined she would be his Perfect Daughter if he was a Full Man which was why it was Easy for him and his soldiers to kill the Peasants as if they are Insects or some Pests and it's become such a Sport they enjoyed going into some of those Small Villages with their Machine Gun Jeeps and Automatic Rifles with Ammunition to eradicate entire small farms, totally decimating Everybody in Sight, regardless, they were all Shot and their nice little wooden huts were shot right through so Nobody survived, everything was shot, every jar, every wooden cart, every cup, every pot, every straw hat with sweat drenched string, every pet, every book, every slipper, every piece of clothing, every cupboard, every corpse, they were shot over and over again for they were Commanded by the Emperor to Sickle the Grass and Rip out the Roots and they even had a list of all the Inhabitants in the Village, name checking to make sure that Nobody survived for that's how the Clan of General Green Dragon operated, the Man who cut off their Testicles on Initiation Night told them all Real Soldiers had to be Castrated and they were Lucky that he's so humane that he allowed them to keep the Shaft so they could piss without having to Squat all the Time, and how According to the Ancient Greek Military Manual, it's Compulsory to Castrate the Soldiers for it makes them more Violent though they are Impotent, and they cannot even Remember their Family all that well with all the Drinking and Feasting with the Emperor, they forgot all their Sorrows but they will never forgive General Green Dragon because he Delighted in bringing the most Amorous women to his Harem which is in the Centre of the Barracks so they could hear all their Loud Sinful Activities until the Sun Rises and they would be Punished the Very Next Day, Building the Railroad to Freedom, they would Fall into a Trance, Performing the task with gusto and Wounds and Brutal Comraderie, they were so Tired, they Slept like Pigs until the Sun Rises and in this Way, they Forgot all about the Sex Scandals surrounding Green Dragon for they no longer viewed him as a Worthy Leader and when Your subordinates start to question and humiliate You in front of Your Superiors, You know it's Time to move on for it's Terrible Manners to Overstay Your Welcome Anywhere and no matter how much You like to Deny it just for the Sake of Going Through the Motions of Handling Grief, yeah, it's True, many people don't know that they can actually Skip the Denial Stage and Go Directly to Acceptance because some of these people never get out of that Stage at all and they get too Comforted to be in their Little Shell, and it happens for some people that they grow so attached to their Swallowing in Self-Pity Pills and Rage Cloths they kept inside their Heart all this Time, they just had to let it all come out and for some of them who had more Traumatic Childhoods, they will take even longer to come out of it without realizing how Fast Time Flies being such a Cliché but it's undeniable, it's still the Greatest feeling in the World when You find out You are not being attacked by thousands of Insects in the Capital of the State, You find these conditions more in Agreement with Ordinary Level of Humanity which states that we should be allowed to walk Free without wanting to kill them all the Time, it will be Real Inglorious...

"Are You in There? It's been Six Moons!!"

"Stop, Big Bird, stop disrupting his Concentration."

"He can Hear You!"

"So? What Happens if He's Passed On? You know… if he's gone to the Other World?"

"Why are You so Worried? Why do You always look at the Moons? What about the Suns?"

"They are too Bright! I can't count! I can't count!"

"Wait… I hear Something…"

"Hey… Sixth Brother… Keep Quiet… Second Brother is trying to Hear Inside…"

"Father… Mother wants to Talk with You…"

"Shut Up! He's Trying to Hear! Shut Up!"

"Stop Steeping on my Toes!"

"Wait… the Rats are saying that he's Healthy and Alive and they have been Injecting him with Essence of Immortality for he has not eaten since the very first day he came into the Cave and pushed that Rock to Block the Entrance and Exit being the Same so there's Oxygen."

"So… isn't he Dead… without Water?"

"No! He's Lying! Arrest Him!"

"What's the name of that Dog with Three Heads?"

"Why? Why does he need so many Eyes?"

"That way, he can Survey the Area Three Hundred and Sixty Degrees. It Ensures that Nobody Escapes."

"What Happens if the Souls are Caught in the Act?"

"They will be Devoured and each part will be Shared equally. It's said that these Souls will be Destroyed forever so it's like there's no Record of them at all, not even their Name will be remembered. It's like they were never even Born."

"You mean… there's still Hope for those…"

"After they have atoned for their Sins for No Matter how Big is their Crime, there will come a Time when they will have paid their dues and they will be given the Chance to be Reborn again though they have no Choice and the Convention follows that in the First Cycle through the Few Thousands, they will be Reborn as those Animals which were Bred for the Masses such as Chickens, Goats, Pigs, Buffalos and even some Ducks that suffer Untold Cruelties so some people can enjoy luxurious liver delicacies and any shop that sells these subhuman products should be banned with immediate effect so they will feel the Agony of Death at the Hands of Strangers."

"Do You want to go to Timbuktoo?"

"Where's the Poet?"

"He's Real Bad! Don't Awaken Him!"

"Nonsense! Nonsense! It's all Nonsense!!"

"If You have the Chance, will You have chosen another Path?"

"Do You think…"

"Alright. Keep Quiet! I can Hear Him now!"

"O Father! How are You? Do You have Enough Chests of Hell Notes and Hell Jewelry? Do You feel Cold? Do You Need Another Mansion? O Don't Worry! If I couldn't buy a Mansion for You when You were Alive, I can buy One for You every year now! If You wish to have more Virgin Slaves or Sexy Nurses, I can Burn some to You! Just let me know!

What Else? O Old Seven? He's in the Hospital! They say he's going to join You soon!"

"Please... I need... to... go...."

"Do You want some Sushi? Line up here!"

"Somehow, we pulled through..."

"Yes! We Got It! We are the Champions! We are the Champions!"

'Yays! Comrades! Let's get on their Space Programs!"

"After the Old man gave them the Manual, the Hmongs improved significantly in Military Prowess and Technology which is how they are just a Nation of Paper Tigers!"

"And then... the Rain..."

It's an old curiosity shop quite like the ones You see in movies or magazines, and just like these types of shop, it's quite fully stuffed with odd looking objects such as forgotten souvenirs, dusty unwanted memorabilia or collector's items that are not collected anymore and thousands of other irrelevant items waiting to be picked up or touched or stolen, it doesn't really matter, simply because they have been there for such a long time. Walking along that street, You must have passed by the shop more times than You can remember but for some reason, You have never gone inside though it's easily one of the more interesting shops You have ever seen but it's almost always without a single patron so You think it's probably too expensive or something. Perhaps, it's because the objects in the shop are too densely and haphazardly arranged or disarranged so people are afraid that they would mess up something or break something costing a fortune or more accidentally or otherwise, it's hard to explain why sometimes, some people will stand outside the store and peek inside the way some people love to spy on their neighbors undressing with powerful kinetic telescopes so they can see the naked body more clearly without getting discovered, some of them will cup their eyes upon the window so they can peek inside clearer than just standing at some distance from the window so their view of the objects within is obscured by reflections, among other obstacles. Now, let's stop for a moment. There's no rush to go anywhere. There you are, standing in front of the store, You are trying to look into the store and at the same time, You discover Your reflection, looking into the store, looking beyond Yourself, there, You are standing there, frozen in Your shadow, aware and unaware of the pedestrians walking past You and the cyclists blurring past in crazy neon colors, and a pair of good old sparrows beaking amorously atop an old-fashioned black Victorian lamp post, You just know, it was not made in those times when Queen Victoria could speak her mind about how she deplored breastfeeding and nobody would challenge or criticize her about being insensitive or politically incorrect or just plain politically wrong, why, isn't it easier to say it like that but sure, those lamp posts were manufactured with the relevant motifs to hint at the lofty magnificence of that era when the world was still mysterious and larger than what they imagined. Would You like to live in those grand olde Victorian times? What about a little later?

"Blue Moon??"

"Yes?? Are You Alright? You were Sleeping So Soundly… I didn't want to Wake You."

"Where's Bulbul?"

"I don't know... she said she had some important task and then… she just flew off."

"It's strange... she said she's my sister... but I can't remember her at all..."

"Yes... I can't remember her either but somehow... I believed her because she's too old to be kidding."

"Old? She's definitely not older than You! What do You Mean?"

"Most Strange... I must ask Father about her someday..."

"Father?? Didn't Bulbul tell you??"

"What... What Happened???"

Entering the shop, You can certainly make a case for the shop to be called a gallery or museum of sorts for there's not another soul other than Yourself Inside so You feel like You have the whole shop to Yourself even if You can hear the shopkeeper snoring away in one corner as if she has not a care in the world even if You go so near to her ear that You can smell her hair and she just doesn't care for anything else other than sleeping so You leave her alone instead of softly unhooking her bra clasps to ease her breathing just a little for she's wheezing a little and now... She's breathing more freely and You begin to wonder a little about her rhythmic inhaling and exhaling like she's sucking in the most resplendent dose of opium tinged air and releasing the least audible least damp least musical memories of her illuminant dreams floating in a colorless column of cloud floating above her eyebrows and You think to Yourself oh my! what a perfect smile and what divine peace of mind in her sleep and all but You know, for sure, You didn't enter the shop to spy on her godly or ungodly slumber and all.

'Why do we have to Hear this Song every Morning?? It's too Boring!!!"

"it's a Good Happy Song and it Makes...

"What's the Meaning? It means the Legs...

"Well... there's Mother Goose!!! Why don't You ask her?"

"What... What's the Time?? Anybody Got the Time??"

"it's gonna be Over in a few Seconds... Eleven... Ten... Nine..."

"I'm Sleepy!! I want to Sleep!!!"

"Tomorrow, I'm going to take a Trip to the Denver Museum of Art because it's Free on Saturdays. Just don't go the Mongolian!"

"Take the Light Rail all the Way to the End."

"Do You want to Join me for some Momos?"

"They are Addictive, aren't they?"

"Hey... Wait... this time... I think I'm really hearing something..."

"You are..."

"Oucchhhh.... Ooooo.... Chaaaaar..... liiiiiiiiiieeeeeeeeeeee!!!"

"Do You know how they did it???"

"It's a Miracle! We came back from a Fifty-five Point Deficit!"

"Don't look... I'm taking off my Bra! It's so Hot in Here!"

"Whatever they tell You... question... question... question..."

"Don't Looookkk!! I'm not Ready Yet! Six... Seven..."

"Do You know what Soap the Nuns use to Cleanse themselves?"

"The Sin Away Soap!"

"Yeah, it's made of Sandstone so after they had been violated by the Honorable Prime Priest of the Golden Sanctuary, they would Scrub their Skin Extra Hard to Remove all His Saliva on their Skin and they won't even dare remember how he licked their Cunts and fed them a Mouthful of Bible verses meant to Arouse them like…"

"… for the Word was made Flesh…"

"… Drink of My Blood…"

"… and Joseph Begot Jennifer… McGarter…"

"Hey… Buddy… that's Cheating!"

"Shame! Shame! Shame! Shame!"

"In My Father's Kingdom, there are Many Mansions…"

"Excuse me, Kind Madam, I would like to buy two Fish and Six Loaves of Bread!"

"I will be Coming Tomorrow! I Promise!"

"NO!"

"Please… we are only… trying to Help…"

"It's such a Long Story that I personally fell Asleep more than a few times before I reached the Midpoint, I must have Dreamt of the Red Chamber or Mansion, I can't even remember, I can't even be sure of Anything…"

"Yeah. We are Hooligans!! What do we Know?"

"turn back!"

"The Road Ahead is Filled with Greater Danger… are You sure… You want to Go On…"

"I'm packing the Suitcases! Please tell them not to Run Around and Around."

"Did You see that Weather Girl? She's performing oral..."

"... THOU SHALL NOT LUST..."

"... three... two..."

"It's Nothing so much to see and some of the Sections are not Even Interesting for Kids but there are lots of Activities!"

"One... day... You... will... float..."

"it's Useless... Father says it's Time to Play the Ukelele..."

"*Djobi Djoba*!"

"Here... here's a Little Something for You... so... expand Your Mind or Something..."

"it's just a Quarter! What can You do with a Quarter?"

"Do You believe in Life after Death?"

"Plant it at the Roots of that Old Chestnut Tree with a few Thousand Purple Ribbons..."

"Rest in Peace... Lou..."

"... it's a Gift of God... Not of Man..."

"Nooooo... Reverent... noooooooo..."

"... God Loves You..."

"... loves Your Sinless Body... smelling so Fresh... so Bloody..."

"Noooooooooooooooooooooooo..."

After she turned Thirteen, Witch W never thought she would have Power over Life and Death so she always made it a Special Point to Cover that Evil Hand in a Badger Glove and she Seldom used it to Touch a Single thing unless she's really pissed off, she has made a Pledge to Refrain from using It unless it's absolutely necessary like the Time she was Crossing the Road to the Bus Stop when she came across a few thugs beating and kicking their Whore like she's not even an Animal so she rushed to her Rescue and Touched them in a great hurry and all of them Turned to Dead Wood and it was such an Insult to the Jaguars that they Colluded with their Greatest Enemy to Conjure a Strategy to undermine Her Powers, they sent Spies to her Cottage of Candy to Alert him when she fell Asleep but to their Great Amazement, she didn't Sleep for even a Second while they watched her Round the Clock with X-ray Vision and Ultra Violet Rays and Military Grade Drones capable of taking out the Culprits before they could be Rehabilitated and Paroled and Educated to become Model Citizens of the Republic, they will be given the Freedom to Walk the Land and Take a Goat for Wife and it should be Fair if they Wish to take another Wife that they should allow their Wife to take another Husband kind of Deal even under schooled people can understand and appreciate that they should take out their Woes in the Arena where they will Fight the Grudge Match and in the Red Corner, we have… King Midas… and in the Blue Corner, we have… Ms. Muppet… and they are Stabbing each other… she's Stabbing at his Stomach… and he's Stabbing her in the Back… and the Crowd is Jeering… Booo… Boooo… Boooooo… throwing all those Rotten Eggs they kept for Ages for this Occasion when they Pelted them with Fermented Tomatoes and Apricots they kept for more than a decade or two in their Chest for Traitors so they cannot make out where's the Blood and where's the Tomato Paste for they went at it for more than a few hours and then, the Black Faced Judge with Crescent Moon on his Forehead, he asked them to send their One and

Most Beloved Child and it's only Fair that it's One Boy and One Girl for Everybody Knows What a Chauvinistic Guy and What a Long Lost Friend how He Suddenly Appears at Your Door without Any Announcement and You don't know how she found out where You are staying from just a mobile number now there are programs to Invade Private Space which is not even Private anymore for it's a Lost Cause, the School of Servitude, and Proudly, You say, it's Terrible, the Planning of the Flow of Crowd, lulled by the *Lure of the Tropics*, it's becoming Brighter, and it's very quick, it's one week gone, one week left, and there's not much Time Left for the Count to Confess his Crimes but in the Very Least, You have to admire the fact that he didn't betray his Tribe even when he knew the Cost would be his Life and he would be Fed to the Scavengers who are always just waiting for Leftovers for the Deer was too Large for Just a Few Lions and Coyotes and Beavers and Vultures who always get to the organs with their Sharp Claws and Beaks pulling out the Intestines and also the Liver and the Heart which is their Favorite for it's quite hard for the rest of the Beasts to get to that Part…

If You Remembered to Water the Plants, they wouldn't be All Dried Up and it's quite a Solemn thing to remember as You were looking into the Fear in that Native Girl's Soul as she Kidnapped the Poor White Baby Waving Frantically at his Father who was Shooting at the Indian Boy with Just a Bow and Arrow in his hands but it's still enough to kill a person if he's accurate enough to hit his enemy's Heart or Brain before being hit by the Bullet going through his Ribs and Exploding in his Heart so he Passed On as quickly as possible and now, he's just Pursuing the Native Girl who's Barely Fifteen but we know how the Boy's Neck is so Nimble and so Easily it can be Twisted until the Head dropped off so it's absolutely Pardonable in the Court of Law to Condone the Killing of the Enemy if a Child is Kidnapped, there are no more Rules and Nice Little Coloring Books with Masked Riders and Flowers of Perception or Windows Opening and Shutting on its Own and Furniture Moving even when there's Nobody at Home You can then say it's a Paranormal Experience when You see the Hair on Your Hand Rising and all the Hair on Your Head too so if You have very Long Hair, it will Reach the Ceiling and even Beyond if You have been keeping it for years and so long it's Washing Your Soul when You Come across a Painting showing how a Virgin Girl is Hanged while Another Virgin Girl is also being Sacrificed and a Man is Puncturing her Lungs with a Stake so She would not Wake up to Terrorize them and their Children who must be Sleeping Soundly in their Little Beds he had Crafted for them in just a Day or Two ago since he's a very Productive Carpenter and his hands are so Strong to use a Chainsaw to Cut the Wood into Burial Poles which can be Sold as Art for a Few Hundred Dislikes, he's so Glad to discuss Bierstadt's *Estes Park* and Patridge Adams showing Slight Impressionism in *Moraine Park* and *A Wanderlust Memory* by Tupper True and You are quite Stubborn You have not Heard of them Before so You are Standing before the Pueblo Indian Girl with her Hair Shaped into a Noose and You must say Geer Philips was quite a good one as well as Henderson's *Little Sister* and the Arcimboldos You have Seen in some Museum but You Forgot which One was more Intriguing, The Moon was Yellow, the Kauffman with Snake of Mother or the Caillebotte or *The Vision of Tundale* forecasting the Events after the Last Supper gone Awry while the Whole Party's Inside the Monster's Mouth and on Top of the Horns, there's the Newborn Surrounded by Three Monkeys, and in the Center, two Rats were Roasting a Human Ear for a Naked lady with her Boyfriend in a Bear Suit while His Best Friend who's Dressed Up as a Reindeer, he's Forcing Another Naked Lady into a Cauldron where they will be Transformed into Some Creature Turning into a Tree, the Blue Fairy is Hugging a Naked Person but it's not all that Clear if it's a Male or Female so in the Moon, St. Gabriel is Seducing another Naked Woman who seems to be Afraid of him for it's quite Normal for people to be Afraid when they are given the Opportunity to Talk to an Angel, they would be so Astonished when they go to the Asian Section to Discover that Pornography wasn't an American Invention like the Press will have People believe that the Elephant Headed God has got Two Consorts and Three if You Admire the Buffalo Headed Woman who's too Ugly to Look at but You cannot Deny that she's got One Heck of a Fertile Mound and it's quite the Miracle of Nature when the Child is Born and it's got Four Hands and a Cobra is Curling around His Lower Right Arm but it Surely wasn't going to Bite him even though it looks Fierce with Full Blossom Head and Stepping on a Baby but Not Hurting Him or Her or it can be a Midget too and He's Dancing within the Circle of Flames with His Eyes Closed, and then, You notice the Connection between Religion and Art for in Ancient Times, Artists were in Demand by the Church or Temples or Mosques for Creation of Murals, Paintings, Sculptures and other Artifacts to Give a more Powerful Representation of the Struggle which was what they would always Talk about through the End of Times when it's Depicted that Orgies are Occurring in the Palace Courtyard just when a Loyal Subject was bringing a White Horse to the King, encouraging his Son to Chase that

Strange Fellow with Three or Four Faces and Six Arms and Chain of Skulls around his Waist, sitting on Eastern Style Lion with Shackle of Bells Sideway so You Wonder some moments about the Story of the Ten Inauspicious Sins and what about that Buddha Statue with a Gang of Little Heads on Top of His Head beneath the Gourd Vine, it must be quite a warm day for the Man and Woman to be Half Naked and just Staring at the Sky or the Mynah Bird on Willow Branch which was a Popular Imagery for East Asian Ink Painters who were Capturing American Ships in Edo Bay as early as 1854 as well as pottery arts from South America, it's a Fashion thing in those times for Warriors to Adorn themselves with the Skulls of their Conquests and there's Archangel Raphael in New High Leather Boots with Flower Pendant and Red Silk Stockings, holding a Staff in one Hand and carrying a Dead Fish so Here Comes the Three Kings, one a Negro, one a King of the North and one Anonymous but their Crowns were all the same so it may be that they were crowned by Same Bear in Fur Coat and Two Canes, it's been quite a Pleasure, especially when France was Destroying the Icelanders in Revenge for their Most Hated Rivals whom they wanted so badly to thrash properly so they would be more Embarrassed, the Underdogs were so Happy to have Overachieved that they didn't mind losing a knockout match to the Hosts who would be Meeting their Greatest Nemesis Germany who had Defeated their Greatest Nemesis Italy in an Earlier Game while on the Other Semifinal, the Welsh were Wrestling the Portuguese so it's only going to be interesting to find out who make it to the Final and that's why so many billions of people are watching these games for a couple of hours when they couldn't be pulled away from the

TV or Video Apparatus, You know, something's Wrong, and it's just Wrong, alright, alright, Right, Miss Chelsea?

"Yeah, You are Right. That Color's a Little Off!"

"When do We get to America??"

"it's a Filthy Place where pedestrians Spit on the Streets and Disregard the Elderly and Vagrants for they never were to be Near those Nasty Immigrants. Always Loitering in the Rat Holes."

"Enough! You are Eating the Cat of Nine

"Wait till You Hear my Latest Album! It's a Big Bimbo Bomb!"

"Why You? Despicable Serbian Villain! ERRRGGGHHHHHHH!"

"NAAAAIIIIIIIIIIIIIOOOOOOSSSSSSIIIIISSS!!!!"

"It was Almost Morning when the Cock Crows…"

"Do You See It?"

"IF YOU DIDN'T WATER MY PLANTS!!! YOU SHOULD JUST ADMIT IT!!!! I KNOW MY PLANTS!!!!"

"Hey… it should be the Other Way…"

"Remember the Time… Cal Tjader asked us Out?"

"Why are You Learning to Read the Ancient Mexican Calendar?"

"Where is My Phone???"

"Do You Really

"… who… who will You… pick…"

"Nachos! I just Love those Moustaches of His!"

"I want Caleb!"

"I want Mercury!"

It's no Time to get Excited no matter how Excited You Actually Feel about the Pointless Plot about Six Chins Feeding Joker some Poison Ivy and he seems to like it quite much when You tickle him Under the Chin and he may even Bite You on Your Ankle to Taste if Your Blood is still Pure and then BAM! BAM! BAM! THANK YOU MA'AM! Kind of Stories You don't think You will be Interested in Voodoo Dolls You Stick Your Acupuncture needles into their Significant Points to Improve Blood Circulation and Breaking the Flow to the River Mouth where the River has not Flowed for such a Long Time that You thought It's not going to Flow anymore and You almost believed the Slick Salesman who told You that it's already been Blocked so the River will just Dry Up and how the price of land around that Region will Continue the Downfall so it's Always a Good Time to Sell off your Property when You need some hundreds of thousand feathers to move comfortably to a Far Eastern Country where You will be Celebrated along with Your Status as a White, get Thee to Asia, and You will feel like a God or Goddess even if You are Bald, Fat, and wearing Dark Sunglasses to Hide Your Shame, it's alright, they will treat You like the Queen of Rangoon or Yogyakarta where You sit on the Pulpit under the Quarter Moon, drinking most Aged Wine for There's really never a Better Time to read the Crystal Bible and Celebrate the Magical nature of certain Stones used to Heal Backaches and Eradicate Voices so Powerful that they may be Used to Alter Reality meaning Nothing more than a few books about Self Reliance and Self Actualization which is a Concept only a few people understood previously before they come across this book left on a bench in Central Park so it may be ripped to pieces by those Jaguars who were so pissed that they couldn't read even a single Word on each and every Page for they were too Animalistic to get the Point about them being able to Understand the Simple Fact that they will be able to grapple Keynesian Theory which is just a Simple graph about how Prices adjust according to Markets shifting in changes in Consumer Behavior affecting how Demand and Supply works so You can just Imagine that people are not getting enough of Elvis so You just play more Elvis movies so the Young Ones can witness how Great an Actor he was breaking out of jail and joining the Marines and Hipping too Vigorously so those young virgin girls in the Fifties, they were feeling all Sexy when they saw how he was Swinging even though the TV Stations had the Audacity to Sensor those moves only Poor Priscilla was so Young and Naïve she squandered all the estate away, and she even had to Donate Graceland to the State to be turned into a museum with all his Big Toys for he was a Man who Loved to Collect Stuff and he Collected Loads of Stuff that he didn't Need at all but he's such a Big Spender that he even flew out of the Window to test the Safety Standards of his Favorite Haunt in Lakewood where he Perfected the Art of Sky Diving and he was Pretty Fortunate that there were some Swedes camping Outside just Below His Daughter's Bedroom for he Always allowed them to come and give them a good meal of Louisiana Fried Chicken with all the Fantastic Southern Spices You can't find in the North for some Specific Reason only Known to the Gods who all deserve to be worshipped in their own Statues and Environment so why not we Start a One Religion Day falling on the Seventh Sun of the Seventh Moon for not so much people seem to hate small nations like Tahiti or Uruguay so these are the Best Countries for Black Monies to be turned White for these Primitive small countries have really Backward Accounting Systems that You may be Surprised that they are still using Eighties Software and in some other towns, the towns are still like they appeared more than a few hundred years ago so there are people dressing up in Real Leather Skirts and Boots and Real Feathers around their necks being long as Swan Grace Kelly for it's quite a Scene when she wrestled Bette Midler on the Ground and they were lullabying and banging each other's Head on the Earth until the Director had Enough and issued a CUT! CUT! CUT! So many times he gave up the Idea of Stopping them, he realized these women need to kill each other sometimes and they will not be satisfied until they get some Blood on their Hands and she remembered how she Smiled when she squeezed that Baby Bear to Death and faked the Assault by Scratching Herself Up by Slashing her own Thigh with the Lifeless Paws she put under her Stone Pillow every night, she would Pray to Mother Mary, asking to be Forgiven for her Sins and Crimes against the Republic but everybody knows she didn't really mean it for she's slower than her Mother-in-Law who also hated her Twice over the Limit for Seducing not One but Three! of her sons being so Stupid and she totally Felt like she didn't spend enough time with Her Daughter who was sent to Her Grave by her Father and there's Nothing she could do to prevent the Hand of Fate dealing her a Six Starves Outcome and she's been Fighting against the Norm even when the King was such a Great Father of so many Bastards and it's only due to this Love that the whole Kingdom is rumbling and there she Sits on the Elephant, taking care of Business and Waiting for them to come and kick her down, it will be a Blast because the Nuclear Arsenal is Dwindling but they should be Building Up Again for You already know that One Season can be for as long as One Decade if it makes sense so there's a lot of Dead Wood to be Transported to the Castle and the Young Women were Struggling to meet the Orders so they Hired Illegal Hands in the Kitchen for how do they upkeep the Authenticity of the Menu if they hire Brazilians to cook Vietnamese food and in every of those Laundry Sweat Shops, You will find a few undocumented aliens for which Self-respecting Citizen will be Humble enough to sweep the streets in the evening or take out the rubbish or build houses with their own fat hands or clean windows on gondolas or slog under the burning sun, making a fraction of the Minimum Wage but there's Nothing else they can do about it because they have to send Dislikes back to their family in St. Paulo and reminisce about his homeland in the pastures and how he would Dream of getting away from there to seek greener meadows and it's only after he had traveled to more than Seventy Countries that he discovered the Grass in his Home Country has been Nuked but by that Time, he's already Seventy Seven so he didn't Think too much about Village which is so Devoid of Teens, yeah, they are all looking to get away from the Monotony of the Organic way of Life adopted by hundreds of millions of patrons in the World so they cannot be Wrong and no matter how Right You Felt when You went to Your Computer this Morning, it's particularly Strange You Feel Your Chest Swell as You do when You are with Someone You Love and it's even Stranger that she's not Lucy, the Blonde who Ruled the Air Waves in Times Past when just the Word Lucy would drive Demand higher than Yesterday and they kept on Wondering when the Record would be Broken for it's been Climbing and Climbing and there's not a Day that it's Slowing off for they kept Thinking it's going to be this

Day that it's Gonna Rain Today for it's not been Raining for Ages as the temperatures keep dropping and Environmentalist are wondering if Global Warming is so Bad because it's the Time when the Population is breaking records every year so it makes Perfect Sense the Earth is heating up for more Peoples mean more Energy is to be Expanded and it's such a Simple One, isn't it? so it follows the only way to reduce the footprints of the Human Race is to show them *Tristan and Isolde* in only Blue Sorrow Lights with Music from *The Seduction of Piero Piccioni* and while we are at it, let's say, we shall use *Sognando La Tua Voce* for that Fourth Scene when Everybody's Supposed to be Reaching for Their Hankies so it should be noted that the First Three Acts are to be Executed in Highest Comedy so get those Clowns and Comedians in there and the Audience is to be in Stiches at the Close of Act Three so when they Enter Act Four, they would only have just Recovered from their Tummy Spasms as they were all Lining Up for the Loo during the Intermission when the Patrons had some Time to Relax and Smoke a Cigar while they Laze around, cracking their backbones and twisting the ankle, Tristan was so Depressed when he discovered Isolde's lifeless body in the Glass Coffin especially after she had planted the most Passionate in all possible art forms with such impact that he felt her hot stream of lava brushing past his uvula and her teeth is biting on his tongue so strongly, it came off and she chewed it so he could taste the Union of their Blood and since he didn't feel any pain and he didn't like to talk at all, he didn't think much about it but he can distinctly Remember that he had a Semi-Erection at this Point in their Volcanic relationship as he spied how her Tits were Still so Firm and Fresh in scent of Fig and Pink Chalk used to cover her Countenance for she's still a Virgin and how he Pictured her Naked and walking to him in slow motion cinematography now 1260:4 that has sure to be a Top Hit because the Fairies are Pleased so they will clothe You in Cloak of Invisibility You must have Imagined how You can Walk around Totally Naked and Nobody can see You though they can see Your foot prints Appearing and Disappearing right before Season of the Crow and the Snowman singing about the Tropics where it's always Sunny and Breezy so how can the Snowman be so Daft You hear how the Sacred Waters from Heavens fall through the Hay Rooftop and drop through the Air in Slow Motion, it may take Forever to Hit You on the Crown or the Hardwood floors You are so fond of in the Winter for they keep Your Soles Warmer than Imported Artisan Italian Tiles costing a little bit more than Cedarwood or Hickory, why, why does it Matter, right, who's gonna win, who's gonna lose, and there's always One Victor and the Rest are Losers, It's True, the Slow will be Fast will be Slow kind of Dangerous Literature we should Keep Away from Children for we don't know what they will do with Laser Shooting Robots in their Hands, sometimes, it's slower, and sometimes, it's faster depending on Regular Events of the Day and it's not at all Cool to threaten Your Brother or Sister or Anybody if You are Uneducated, it's alright, admit it, You are good enough, You are kind enough, You are humane enough, and Goddarn it! Everybody Loves You! So The Fortuneteller tells You all about how You are going to be such an Ordinary Citizen when You can't even spell so good when You were in the Big School and Nobody could see You so You always sat alone and walked alone and listened to the teacher alone and she was just so Kind to sing a song to the Class and they all seemed so genial and wholesome as they sang it quite Perfectly so You thought they must have had some Practice sessions when they must have pissed off the Neighbors trying so hard to get a Good Night's Sleep after a Hard Day's Work, that night, they were like creaky Hurricanes, they were just too disturbed by that Fiddler who was a Doctor in his Day Job so You can Imagine how he played the Violin and Everybody had Cursed him and some Children even threw Frozen Overripe Banana Pies at his Car and Some of his Patients just paid to see him just so they could Spit on him for it's so Terrible, they Celebrated when he became Poor enough to move far away from them who had already earned some Merit of Success in their Fields, they were not considered to be Rolling Stones Old but some of them were definitely Canned Heat Old for most people had never heard of them and people who remember them don't really care about them all that much so You may see the Band Leader Sleeping under a Tree in front of Capital Hill which is the Place they Come to Air their Grievances the Day after Police gunned down a Hardworking Civil Afro-American Male in the Suburbs of Minneapolis being such a Racist area, they don't really like the Dark Skinned People to Infiltrate into their Own Private Haven into which they only Accept Fair Skinned People but they will not mind hanging out with them if they have earned enough Dislikes to Party in the Neighborhood, on the Surface, they are still giving lots of love to Prince, and other high profile Coloreds like those Bitches in the Eighties who were so Hot back in those days that You have totally Forgotten about the name of the group or the name of the song but only Remembering they were In Your Face on the Runway and they were Stylish and Silvery and Brash and All about Fame and Fortune, You Know How Old You Are When these Things Keep Happening and Keep Happening, You Know, You are getting Nearer to The End and It Should be a Great Consolation to You that You are Leaving with Full Knowledge and Control of the Inevitable which Befalls Everybody but Everybody… goes into the Wild in their own Style and Fashion… and It's Just a Matter of Dignity to the Most Enlightened…

"Do You want to Ride on the Ferris Wheel?"

"Yeah… we can see as far as our eyes can see… up there…"

"Can You see the Lady in the Moon?"

"I'm sorry… I can only see the Rabbit…"

"Do You think she's Satisfied tonight?"

"I don't know… her face's obscured by the clouds…"

"The Monkey King is Complaining…"

"Why? Why are You always going against the Flow? Are You trying to get to the Eye of the Needle? It's quite a Far way off! Takes half a day to walk there and there's no Transportation available. Get it?"

"it's safer up there where the air…"

"Do You like African Drums? I Dream when I Hear those Jungle Beats…"

"I remember the Time when I was working in City with the Lake of Salt and I tell You it's the most boring city in the States! No alcohol and all shops close at Six Thirty or something. You don't even feel like going out at Night. It's all run by the Mormons!"

"No Smoking?"

"Yeah, it's like the most oppressive city and all, and You are always feeling You are being Watched because they are always in the Towers with their Guns and Crossbows and they are always looking for some Target. Once, they shot an Old Lady for Crossing the Road too slowly. Can You believe it?"

"What… Happened?

"Fortunately, she survived for they only got her on her Buttocks and they are Fleshy enough to stop the Arrow from going deeper into the Bone. They were trained Marksmen so they never miss the Target. It will be a Sacrilege for them to miss because that's what they are paid to do! No Way! When they give the Green Light, the Operation Never Fails!"

"Is She a Minority?"

"Yeah… sadly… it's always the case all over the World… if I go to India, I'm Prepared to be Raped… and so too in No Name… sigh… such a Faraway Land…"

"Please tell me… if You want some more Water… I can get it for You…"

"Drink! Drink from HERE! You will NEVER Thirst Again!"

"Tomorrow… You will be Meeting Goddess Freyja…"

"No… You are getting Nostalgic… I can see it in Your eyes…"

"Can You see me? I'm Invisible…"

"No… I can feel Your Finger on my Belly Button but I cannot see You…"

"Soon, it will be Light… Your Third Eye… O…"

"STOP! I rather be Blind! SUCK my Toes! SUCK THEM!!! O GOD! WHERE'S the Staff?"

"366:2! Blue Camel!"

"Get the Key! Get the Key! Run! Run! Run!"

"Did You see that? Right at the Roots of the Tree!"

"Stop Kicking! It Hurts…"

"Do You want to talk about Politics?"

"KEEP HOLY THE SABBATH!"

"HOLY! HOLY! HOLY IS THE LORD OF FLIES!!"

"Let's take a Look… there! There! A Shooting Star! Do You See?"

"*Lucy in the Sky with Diamonds*?"

"The Key Word is Sky. She prefers Diamonds but Lucy's not the One."

"Do You Mind Shutting the Door?"

"Yeah…"

GOLDEN HORNS & SPEARMINT SPRINGS

And, There, they lay, each on his or her Bed, Sleeping in Different Rooms, Sleeping the Night away when the Opportune Time came and the Thief entered into Contract with the Opium Lord Complaining about The Orphan Inheriting more than an acre of Native Land You claimed beside the Mouth of the River San Juan or even then You have Forgotten and so Surprised are You of the Probability in which the Rain will Come Today and Not Tomorrow or Another Moon, Another Week, I implore You, please, Don't Look Back, Head only for the Sun for that will Save You in the End when Your Flesh is Decaying and even the Winds are not Crying any Memory anymore but just Blowing over the Fields of Gold as You have so occasionally seen on TV how the Iron Crow Kicks at the Window, yeah, un fact that we just Say that we are all Dislikeless and Fateless for we don't Believe in those Things and We Rebel against all Laws and Regulations and it's not a Matter that We Wish to Forget such important things like paying our Bills by Big Computer

Pineapple Brother who will Never Forget to Subtract Some Dislikes from Your Bank Account and You are so heartbroken when You see that it's Dwindling down to the Last Few Feathers and now You know more about how Thieves and Spies work on Their jobs and it's True, not every one of them knows how to Kill but they know how to Disappear when they need to Go to Kathmandu, they will be in Kathmandu and they don't even need to know Everest is situated There and the Himalayas is one of the Most Beautiful places in the World just like Istanbul, Tibet, Catatonia, Bokhara and what other ones like Xinjiang and Brasilia and where else Your Heart leads You to the Most Secretly visited Place where You have to plant the Rainbow Beans, and the best thing is that You didn't even in the Slightest Know anything about Abel though he's quite an Important Character in The Bible and it's also Followed in Earlier Books where they also had Adam and Eve running around the Garden of Eden and Chasing Butterflies into the Caves where they would be Copulating without even knowing the Word or Meaning as His Sun Rises and Her Heart Softens, it's the Story even Small Kids Know how these things work without Anybody having to Tell them how the Hummingbird Suckles from the Violets so wildly growing in Your Backyard and You are so Happy to see the Moon that Night, almost Full for You are not such a Deceptive Witness for times of the days and such things which are so Important for Modern Folks it's Logical they will be Angry with You if You forget their Last names, it means the Greatest Insult and it's no Accident that we have Resurrections and Exorcisms and all the Horrors of a Post Apocalypse World they like to Portray so You can understand more about the Music and there's no use to Consult the Horoscope Either because what they don't want to tell You is that there will not be any Post Apocalypse World because there would be Nothing to Tell and I Challenge You with my Forty Seven Dislikes and my Golden Mountain Goat, the One who can Leap from Peak to Peak without the Slightest Effort and You see how she glides across the Horizon like a Snowflake Leopard so some Stupid folks think we are Talking all about *Animal Farm* which is such a Great Work of Art it should be made Compulsory Reading in every language and I Guarantee You, in a Little less than Twenty Years if we have that Long a Time, it would be good, wouldn't it, to talk about how the Tulips are so Sweet Smelling in the East of Liberia where even the most Staunch Bitter Evil Taliban Catholic Wayward Video Game Warrior is Reading about how that Iran Girl Defied the Authority right under their Noses and they were probably a Little Sleepy since they are Enveloped in the Fog of Lost and Found Counter Revolutionary Ideology and Perceptions of Reality and we would just like to say a little bit about it since it's quite a popular topic even if we have the Full Right as Citizens of the Republic, we certainly have the Right to *Petition for More Space* also a Great Short Read such as when You are trying Real Hard to Get it On with the Whore and she's Laughing at You and Giggling behind Your Back and Calling her Sick Mother to chat a bunch of Rubbish for You know it's Rubbish when her mouth is so reeking of heady perfumes and her pussy cat smells of mirror and a Space of Three Inches More to the Right while Your Staff turns into Snake when You play with her lips, they feel like Rubber Eels and when You play with the Earlobes, they are as Wax only not hot or liquid but Soft, not in Texture but Volume, You think she's Perspiring for All Your Hard Labor, building the Best Razor factories for the masses when in Reality, there will be more and more Ghost

Towns and even Ghost Cities and You may Agree, it's just Scratching on the Surface, Unreal, Unsheltered, and Unrealistic so You feel so Boiling with iron and Turkey Wish Bones, Tearing It Off to Prove she's only Faking It, the Slurpy Noises, the Moths in Your Stomach, the Sperm in Her Throat Trick which even most Powerful Men like Old Billy falls into Temptation for how do You tell the Japanese High School Girl who's perfectly Legal to Fuck and she's Looking through the Looking Glass too, Mr. Secretary, Compulsory, some Grand Masters, they have absolutely no Vision in Regards to How their Art will Flourish and Grow until the Final Stroke they place on the Canvas which is Still White for to the Romantic Painters, it's Night, and so how many nights and years more, You Think, Luckily, You can maybe Remember Yesterday or just a few Moments ago, You are Stalling at the Red Light and You are not sure how to go Forward where it's Safer for You to play Your Mandolin in some Peace for a Gaucho always have to have his Music so he can be a Friend to All Animals, Serenading them with the Most Soapy Long Winded Epic Poems about How Tristan Traveled the Underworld looking for Isolde and Without his eyes, he couldn't see how she was being Washed away by the Styx Roaring so Boisterously that he couldn't even hear her screams for him and it's in those volatile and heart wrenching passages that They fell Asleep for You are Fully Entitled to Believe that the Animals couldn't Understand a Single Note he Played but Miraculously, they Dreamed of Orpheus too so in the Shadow of the Peace of Heaven, he Fell into Most Moist Sleep in the Wild with the Heaven as his Blanket, and Truly, even this Image of Nahiossi lying down on the Wooden Pillow is such an Impossibility for You Think It's Impossible to Balance It on just a Thin Thread and it's True You don't really know if he's Asleep or Resting but just a while later, the Little Girl was running away from the Big Bad Wolf running to her with mink coats and jewels and clouds of rain following her wherever she goes, May the Angels shine the Light on her Patrons so they will Ejaculate in less than a Second so they feel as though they are Wasting their Dislikes because it's no longer Legal Tender just like how the Ninety Nine year old Broadcaster shouldn't be allowed to Run for Office in the First place and the Eighty Eight year old Former Gymnast shouldn't be allowed to Fulfill the Promise of Israel but that's how the Story goes and I hope You Remember, You Dear Dear God Loving Heathen and Pharisees throwing Bird Seeds on Sara for delivering the Pariah Son Branching Off the Line of The so called Prophet and it's with such Scorn they dragged her into the Alley Way to Punish her Violently and the Angels, Somehow, they were still asleep, and the Good Samaritans, they were Partying at George's or Caesar's place for they were Born in the SAME DAY AND YEAR! and how Coincidental is that, You ask, and I ask You, have You ever met another person who's born on the same day and year with You because it's simply not a Coincidence that much more of You will feel a little Jaded when the same phone company offers the new Immigrants better deals than You though You have been paying Your Taxes regularly and without Fail, You have also been paying Your Utility Bills and all the Mortgages and Study Loans You are still paying through Your Nostrils becoming Bigger and Bigger the more You Dig at Your Nose which is not a very Pleasant thing to do when You are in the Food Service Industry and You are Hoping People will Appreciate Your Cooking Talents a little more than Your Husband or Children who Devour Everything You Put on the Table while the Table is not so

Big, it accommodates more than Thirteen people or so there are still many People crowding round the Table and it's almost Discernable how else should He serve the food to the Disciples though in the Picture, He was Just Serving that One Disciple so You may Observe It's Quite Impossible for Him to be a Humble Servant without forming the Triangle of Illuminati, Prieteni, Favor the Lord's Apprehension for He's still to go to the Garden of Gethsemane where He Sweated Pellets of Blood and He's asking for His Father's Will be Done on Earth as It's Done in Heaven when it's already being done for He's born in the Year of the Rat so it's Natural for Him to feel a little Small as He Neared the Day of Reckoning at Mt Sinai when the Covenant was given unto Man and how He was going to replace it all with His Blood Quenching the Cross and it's been Reported that some Blind people were able to see for the First time in their Life and some Younger Crippled Ones were Jumping Out of their Wheelchairs and Running to the Meadows, Chasing those Butterflies again, and yeah, some of the Lepers, they were made Whole and some of the Cancer Stricken Folks too, they were Completely Healed and Little Isolde, she came back to Life after her mother fed her some of the Red Earth even though she couldn't eat anymore and when she awoke, she couldn't recognize anybody and she was Frantic, eyes a blazing and she's Shouting in some Strange Language You have never ever heard before or after the Flood when You were playing the harmonica on top of the roof, watching all those things floating away and You are busy fighting off the sharks snapping at Your toes though the Tune was so Hypnotic and how it's able to make You fall into Deep Sleep and it's so great when You are able to enjoy a full night's sleep without the weight of some perverse men on top of You or behind You, slamming and slamming Your head against the wall or bedrest and You are so numb to those cigarette butt burnings and even hair pulling and really what can You do with a knife at Your throat and Your throat is already bleeding a little and he rubs it into the Labyrinth of Juices of every kind You can imagine so he's just screwing the antennae into place again so they could watch some movie about an old grandmother seducing a young suicidal boy and yeah, it's one of the best songs though the Story wasn't meant for Main Stream Catfish so easy to catch during the Season so much so You will have too much to eat, it's a good choice, an Old Cat who's fast losing his memory so he's eating again after he's just eaten and some days, he's not eating though he has not had any food for a few days, he's not feeling a little hungry or even Sleepy so he's not sleeping all that much at Night, preferring to go Out for a Hunt of Raccoons which was his favorite activity while he was in his first owner's house more than twenty years ago when he was still a Young Cat and so Popular among the female felines that they fought over him just as all Beasts do when they want to deliver the Crown Prince, sometimes, they may even be so desperate to place a Spell on their Opponents so they can become Queen and every woman, no matter how serious and ladylike and law abiding and pigeon holed, they are accustomed to the Tenets of Faith according to the Oracle predicting all about occurrences happening thousands of years into the Future so what's the Point really to know when the Olive Branch is bearing Fruit and they are so pleased when Mary Magdalene was pregnant and the whole town's talking about who's the Father and all that sort of gossip people are so preoccupied about all the Affairs of the World to stay Ahead of the Pack so there were quite a number of Media Masters who envisioned how such a woman would appear in the Limelight when Ed Sullivan was asking her about the Joys of Growing Up in Little Prairie, she just got hysterical and started scratching herself while looking at the Poster of the Pope and it's true, without even asking her to elaborate, it's diagnosed that she's suffered from some childhood trauma involving sexual exploitation by her Father and maybe even her Brothers so she's gnarling and bubbles are coming out of her ears and nose so You know it's Real and Not Fake as the Ancient Wooden Edwardian Arm Chair is rotating and rising into the air and she's finally freed herself from the Electrified ropes holding her Captive as the Devil's Step Son had His Way with her and she's wriggling and screaming insane insane insane vulgarities so vicious You Cork Your Ears Instinctively just to block off a little bit of the insane insane mayhem when her head was Spinning and Spinning and it's Insane for You are thinking it should be falling off any Time soon according to the Law of Physics but with Your mouth opening so wide so that even a tiny swiftlet can fly inside and withdraw that unbitten piece of Golden Apple in Your Stomach, it's been so many hours, You are frightened out of Your Mind to Replay the Flashbacks again and again and it's already a few days more but You can't be bothered anymore with Anything Else for You have been to the Other Side so many Times, and even Little Boy Blue is shy to tell she's been following him ever since and she's just like a Mother to him so when the more Selfish Hindustan Movie Extras pick on him, she will step in and when they saw all the Worms and Sewer Waters in her Mouth, they just backed away since she also carried a Jar of her own Evil Solution she applied her own Waste all over her body so she thought they will be too Disgusted to Rape her again but somehow, these Animals, they make No

Sense at all, Oishii! Oishii! they will still do it even if their cocks become too soft and she's infected them with Vietnam Rose, they will still Fall for It since they are men with Little Self-Control and Respect, We Shall Not Even mention It in Passing or Otherwise Not Boasting of Anything Else, they would have Zero Understanding of their Existence being Solely to Protect the Innocents rather than Preying on them so when they realized they have Lost It, maggots and slime, and Amputated, they become more quiet and serene and so many of them underwent sex change operations to transform themselves into females and in Truth, Suffer the same Evil Deeds they had proffered on those street hookers they just love to hurt even more for even Law Enforcement Officers Ignore them, treating them no more Worthwhile than some Tramp and You know how they are always Forgotten by the World as You stand under the Tree, say it, Little Angel, say Good Bye to the Past, and more Opportunistically, take it One Step at a Time, Don't Hurry, feel the Blue Air Beneath Your Nose, Breathe It in One More Time, Breathe and Hold, Breathe and Hold, Keep It in the Abdomen, feel It Germinate, and There… It Rains…

"Please Take in the Blankets... The Clouds are Dark."

"Wait a Minute! I'm Reading *Finnegan's Wake* in Kelantanese!"

"Why don't You Listen

"Last Night, I Sneaked out to See Flash Gordon! Love his Bulging Eyes!"

"I'm sorry to tell You but Ms. Bum Bum said it will not be Dry and Humid Today."

"Do You Know the way to Clear Creek Reservoir? I'm meeting Count Dracula there."

"Can You show me some ID? You have to be above 21 to Smoke."

"I'm 69… going on 70…"

"It's not Good. 7778:131"

"It's not Raining!! Will You Change the Channel? I want to watch some Documentary."

"Wait for fifteen minutes… I'm in a Jam…"

"Do You like Pepper Jack? See?? I Knew he likes It!"

"Yesterday, I saw three rabbits jumping out of the same hole."

"Did You take a Picture?"

"it's important to Support Independence…"

"Will You please help to Pound the Wheat? We need to make more Flour to last the Winter."

"Zorba! Zorba! You forgot to light the lamp!!"

"Yes… Mother… I will run to the Market to check on the Old Yak."

"Look! Look! The Hot Air Balloons! They are floating to the Heavens!"

"Rattle the Snake!! Rattle the Snake!!!"

"The Time Now is Six O Six in the Morning…"

"Have You gone for Morning Prayers? Ramadhan is Coming Soon."

"Why is The Prophet so Rich, Blood Thirsty and Lustful? Does

"Are You Killing Again? You are Most Disillusioned! Repent!"

"Five for Fatimah. Red for Brighton."

"Are You Fasting Today? Be Careful. They are Making the Rounds…"

"The Clouds Weigh Heavy and the Winds Carry Hope."

"Are You Sure We Are Past the most Perilous Parts?"

"Will You take out the Garbage?"

"*Now, you are looking at the curiosities in complete peace and quiet. It's getting more and more difficult to experience such absolute silence anywhere in the world for you may be in the deepest forest and you may still hear the sounds of crickets mating and tigers snoring with their mouths wide open with flies defiantly resting on the tongue without a care for anything else, you are holding that century old telephone designed like a candlestick with rotary dial so you can see the numbers from zero to one and they are arranged in such a way that you have to almost make a full circle when you are dialing zero while the distance from the number one to the stopper to determine the right number dialed is quite minimal so you may wonder why the phone is not designed in such a manner whereby the numbers are reversed in sequence so the number one is furthest from the stopper and zero the nearest?*"

"Don't You have a Nose?"

"HELP ME! HELP ME!!"

"Yesterday, we just crossed the Mountain of Fire so it should be Easier today…"

"You need to develop Compassion for the Demons. They also Need Salvation."

"Please bring me to the Textile Store. I want to buy some Cloth of Wax."

"If I don't kill them, they will kill You and feed on Your Flesh! They cannot be Saved!"

"Remember the Spirit of Bone White?"

"She's One in a Billion! All Demons must be destroyed!"

"That's the Way! That's the Way!"

"Will You Carry me up the Mountain? I will pay You Half a Dislike!"

"It's not enough! We want more! We want more!"

"Down with the Elites! Down with the Murderers! Down with the Tycoons!"

"Are You Jealous? She smells like

"Go Further Upstream to enjoy the Ride to the Fullest!"

Why? There are so many questions as you lift the funnel-shaped earpiece from the socket from which you should be able to remove and slot it in again at least a few thousand times or thereabouts because it's quite expensive to make phone calls in those days and it can be quite tiring to hold that earpiece to your ear and talk into the mouthpiece at the same time even though some of those mouthpieces are more consumer friendly in the sense that they can be adjusted at various angles so a taller person can speak more comfortably and there are even these fancier wires that connect the earpiece to the mouthpiece which are coiled so you can pull the earpiece much further away for the manufacturer has even taken into consideration that you may be talking or listening to a person who may love to do almost all the talking so you may want to take a more comfortable position to say such encouraging or assuring words like yeah, I understand, hmmm, I see, wow, how wonderful, awesome, right, and all that sort of expressions and you can be lying down on the floor for the wire is surely long enough when stretched out fully, it's about a good seven meters, more or less, you are somehow enchanted by her voice more so because you cannot see her so you don't ever want her to stop talking, no, not even for a second or less but except for the fact that you are afraid that she may not feel your presence though you are breathing quite loudly into the mouthpiece, you are not sure if she can hear you so loud and clear as you are hearing her orgasmic angelic voice which is so mesmerizing, you can feel your ears being sucked into that earpiece and if the cumbersome laws of physics are but suspended for but just a moment, your whole being will have evaporated into a single atom or two, it doesn't really matter because the idea is to be small enough or electrical enough to travel through the cable of telephone and go the distance, diving underground before climbing the poles like those you see in old time movies where the cables lag a little from one pole to another until they reach the intended destination and you spring out of her mouthpiece and appear right in front of her so she's totally aghast and probably so shocked, she would be frozen right there like she had seen a ghost or angel or maybe even God himself if you may imagine the whole concept of communicating to another person who is so far away, there's always the opportunity for errors or flights of fancy seeping through the air and in just the fading fibers of her melodic descriptions of her wonderful weekend trip to her grandfather's farm when she slipped and knocked her most angelic head on that darn old beam of oak and lost her memory momentarily for a few hours or few days for she couldn't really remember but she didn't really care so much because she didn't really keep track of the calendar and all that sort of useless information but she's mighty glad that she still remembers you and that's the most precious memory to her, even more important than her name or her own telephone number was the fact that she could remember your phone number and how it was such a torture that she had to wait to get back to town before she could make that call and how she had quickly scribbled the numbers down and written "My Dear Love" over it just in case she lost her memory again when she woke up and somewhere in the middle of the middle of her heated gushes and proclamations of passions, you fell into a dream...

"Do You like the Beatles?"

"No… we have never heard that Flies can be Food…"

"How about the Republic? We Should really take out some time to talk about…"

"It's not a matter of Priority but Destiny!"

"One Day, I met the Don in the Supermarket and he's holding this Girl's waist and Waltzing her around right in the Middle of the Nowhere as the Broncos were running their Lap of Victory and he signaled me and told me to go to the ATM machine to withdraw some Dislikes for him because he wanted to buy this Gift for her as he's really Pleased she brushes his Cat every now and then and he's Satisfied She's a Genuine Genius Cook."

"If We still don't Pin Down a Date… We will be Late for the Revolution!"

"Comrades! Attention! Take Up Your Swords!! Forward March!!"

"Where are We Going?"

"Do You have the Compass?"

"Do You mean the Divining Rod?"

"We want to Learn more about Beauty and the Underworld!! It's what we are Born to do… to Know and

Understand What Happens when We go there One Day and it may even be Tomorrow so we don't really have so much time. Right?

"Tell us about the Green Fairy!"

"STOP! STOP! STOP!"

"It's Forged by the Blacksmiths of the Red Mountains. They are not the best in the World because the Best Blacksmiths are from Favorite Warring Countries like Japan and Germany, Uncoincidentally, they are still the leading producers of the Sharpest Knifes in the World and the Champion Blacksmiths of the Year whose Weapons are used to split cut the thinnest tracing paper in the World so that there are now two Equal pieces of the Tracing Paper but Half as Thin as Before... and the best of them... they are really the best Story Tellers so they had such magical gifts as to draw the Listeners into the Tales by urging a Sigh Here and planting a Snare there and the Flow of Stream is so Slow, the Eye Lids will become Heavier and Heavier and it's truly quite Impossible to stay Awake for more than Three or Five Hours before You Fall into Trance and before You know it, You are Snoring..."

"Are You Talking about the Pueblo Fairy Tale Weavers?"

"Fast Asleep!!!"

"Tell Me! What type of Wood Produces the Smell of Sleep?"

"Ponderosa? Nutmeg?"

"It's a Combination of the Most Erotic Spices from the Indies and the Freshest Possible Organic Herbs..."

"If it isn't for the Test, she would have been Married to the Scum Village Leader's Sixth Son, the Weakest One who's so well known for his unpunished crimes that the Villagers Bow their Heads in Shame when they thought about how he Raped all his Dogs and how his Cock was Contaminated and how she would Howl even Louder, Knowing Full Well the Winds were Blowing Real Strong that Night so her Screams of Ecstasy shall be Carried into every House where there's no Punishment for Any Damn Thing She Ever Done in her Life was to Rub the Back of the Man who was Falling Asleep and she tried so very hard to get his Attention from the Very Beginning when he entered the Palace to pay his Respects to a person he doesn't..."

"Click! Click! Click!"

"Slide! Slide! Slide!"

"BREAK HIS KNEES!!!"

"That Day, the Security and the Military and the Prime Minister and the Dictator and the Savior and Old Chang and Anybody Else couldn't have done anything about It because the whole Stadium was Empty and the Spectators were Frantic, the Moon was Full for You can see the Frenzy in their Eyes as they ran for the Woods like it's so Easy to find those Private Trails where they could be Alone without a Care for the World and just Rolling Down the Meadows with His Cockroach in Her Palm, fevered and hot, throbbing and veins bulging and appearing like it's going to burst out of its Skin any time sooner and it's true that She was Ravaged beneath the Cedar Tree."

"Northeast. The Waters are coming from the Northeast but… "

"SHUT UP!! We Came to Hear The Sound Again and Again!"

'Into the Night… she goes Poop! Poop!"

"No! I mean… Blue is Black!"

"How can You say Plato's a guy who has the Luxury of

"If he knew the Truth, he would have been a Greater Ruler but he's too preoccupied with his Second Lieutenant Uniform Tailor and he's particularly glad they used real Bear Fur this Year for his Union Jack Tall Hat and they were so Invested in the Boots of the World's Most Brilliant Footballer who does not get any Protection from the Referees and his Teammates when they saw the Mob Coming to Step on his Knee one Time for each Person from young ones to middle aged ones and all those skeptical kinds, You are Welcome too, Come… Come…"

"The Clown is always able to Lure the Naïve ones into the Tent…"

"Use these Ear Plugs to Block out The Sound!"

"Quick! Quick! Get under the Sheets!! She's Coming! She's Coming!!"

"Bring her on a Tour of the Crystal Creek on the Magic Carpet. Then… Sing!!!"

"Frank is the Best among them all!"

"he makes Time Fly Faster. He can make one Minute pass like one second or less and in no time, it's already Ten O Clock, the Golden Hour, the best Time to hit the Creek and Float Down the Stream, yeah, try to rub her rib bones for she's falling Asleep to the Monotonous Voice so Incredulously telling her to Fondle her Dried Oyster and she's Surprised O how Hard it has become and so she's Dripping some Moisturizing Aloe Vera on Her Most Neon Stones so they Taste all the more Sweeter when she Sucks each and every one of them Clean so Ms. Lilliput will not be Violated and she's Distracting them into the Jungle where they can pull off her Hair so she's become Bald all of a Sudden and then she's totally Senseless to Sleep on the Bed of Ice in the First Place, knowing it's Melting Right at the Time when she's Sacrificing herself to the Gods of Fire no matter how High they Manage to get the Flames and an Elite Troop of Iron Monkeys even went to the Center of the Earth to get a Small Sample of the Core, supposedly the Hottest Point within the Bowels of Mother Nature Blowing Her Nose and it's there she Knocks out their Brains with a small stone she hid under her tongue and she would always laugh when she trembles at the thought of That Dirty Old Man coming into Her Room in the Middle of the Night with His Certified Genuine Calf Skin Whip and his Bottle of Gin he Swigs every now and then and he really thinks he's riding into the Sunset with Rifle on his Shoulder to look cool and sipping on the Poisonous leaves some of which possess the Powers to heal mental illness of all forms so the Patrons will not be too Shocked to find Woodworm in the Soup for they are Agents of Hallucination and they are also Super Delicious so it's a good Idea to Hang the Swastika on the Wall in Your Room…"

"I'm Sorry. Do You want any Desert? Today, we have the Most Amazing Javanese Shrimp Paste Softened Caramel Blue Cheese Sour Diesel Mousse Souffle. Do You want to try?"

"No, I have a Stomachache. Give me a Cup of Hot Peppermint!"

"I'm Sorry. We Only have Spearmint… will…"

"Keep Quiet! You are Scaring the Scare Crow!!"

'He's just made of Grass! Use Fire!"

"Don't be so Anxious! Wait for me in the Hot Pool! Bring a Net!"

"Do I Need a Permit to Catch Butterflies and Birds?"

"It's Seventy-seven Feathers for the Annual Membership but You may enter all the National Parks in the State for one Calendar Year!"

"Here You Go! Here You Go!"

"Do You want to buy Some More Pachinko Machines? I have only a few units left!"

"Here's Fifty-five. I want to Save the Environment!"

"When I grow up, I want to be

"Are You Not Afraid You may not Come Back Here anymore?"

"The Enemy must be Destroyed! Citizens!!! Raise Your Fists!!"

"Bring out the Sickles! Bring out the Brooms! Bring out the Hammers! Bring out the Oils!"

"Do You Know the Way to Mecca?"

"Do You like the Lady? Nine Hundred Thousand Only."

"MILF with Natural Papaya Milk and Long Nails and Teeth of Saber Tiger, she can Circle around the North Pole…"

"Hey... the Angels are still Awake… STOP…"

There's not a Spot of Dirt on her Skin, bumpy, You better be Careful, she may Carry the Yellow Rose and if You don't know about it, You are truly living in the times of cavemen and cavewomen for it's really Pleasurable and Ecstatic and what else the Most Cruel Virus Ever invented for it will be Injected in all Potential Sex Victims even in their Infancy and We will name it PPQQSL2710 and the Parents will be Fully Informed that in the Event that their daughters or sons were being assaulted, sexually or otherwise as they imagine The Sound, the Holy Sacred Sound, the Venom will be released and the Ballistic Germ will transmute against the stream of Sperm Cells rushing against it with all the Ferocity of the Greatest Tsunami sweeping the whole City under so even the Capitol Seat is Submerged and many valuables are floating away and the Debris of Treasure has been washed to California and Alaska and the Murderer will soon Shudder in Disbelief to see His Member is Beyond Salvation for he can even Smell the Rot and O how much he spent to find the Cure but Unfortunately

"Do You have the Time?"

"Here's Five Dislikes... Eat it in Remembrance of Him..."

"Let's Go One More Round! This is FUN!!"

"I Want to go to School! I Want to go to School!"

"Miss W... I Want You..."

"Are We on the Right Track?"

"It's just a One Way Street to Hell! Hell! Hell!!"

"Yeah, Jerry, even You can be Saved!"

"Forget it! I Want to Sleep in the Park! I Want to Sleep

"Can You Smell It? it's Horrible! Horrible! Horrible!"

"it's no use. We have to perform Surgery to Remove It from Your Body."

If You Delay, the Virus will Spread to All Your Organs and Contaminate them with Agent Brown which effectively browns up the Small Intestines and Spreads to the other Innards and so on and so forth so for over a Period of Twelve Days, they will Slowly feel their bodies turning to Lead, getting Heavier and Heavier and they will be told the Story of that Corrupt Ruler who was Punished in Cycles of him Pushing a Boulder up the Slope and then Watching it Roll over the Murderers over and over again for the Punishment of their Foul Sins against Humanity and Nature, and so he chases after the Stone, rolling Down to the Valley and It's Logical, in the Beginning, it's all so Cold, he developed a strange relationship with the Object in Perpetual Motion as it was the only thing he's related to Nothing Else when he's Walking Down the Slope, and it's True, at some Point, he was so Attached to It, he Sprinted at top Speed after It, and there was more than a Few Occasions when he ran Faster than It, and sometimes, he would be Rolled Over when It Rolls Back if the Up Slope is too Steep to Roll Over so he would be so thin, the Winds could carry him anywhere but he never went anywhere else and it's there, beside the Creek that he found the most precious amalgam of precious metals for it's never just One Type that makes the best weapons and the Weapon of a Gaucho is to be Crafted with Utmost Detail for every one of them have a Specific idea about how their Weapon is to be Produced because they are the only Ones who can Instruct the Blacksmiths to Create The Weapon for it will soon become the most Important thing in their lives and the Smart Ones, they know it's not enough to have the Best Weapon so they go into the Jungle to practice some Martial Arts so they may have to shave their Heads and Carry Buckets of Water up the Hill, two buckets each, the Younger, Smaller, the Older, Bigger, and it's Balanced by a Bamboo Strip so the Buckets Slip down a Notch when they get can't Walk anymore since their knees were all gone and when they reach the Well where Old Master Twin is Presiding over Matters Big and Small so it's his Duty as the Abbot of the

Monastery to Check on the Volume of Water Delivered and for those Kids who have Dropped the Buckets, they would be sent to the Jungle where they will spend a Night with Mother Nature and Somehow, they will Return Stronger and Faster…

"Out! Out! This is the Plum Blossom Room."

"Do You like Jiro's Sushi?"

"Yeah, this Is Better than all the Rest. O the Smell of Virgins!"

"Who Shall We Cook First?"

"It's His Nails! Do You think it will Work if I Blanch It?"

"No! It's too Cruel! Please Pass the Mustard…"

"Wait for a while… I'm trying to Focus!"

"Do You need the Screwdrivers?"

"Positive or Negative?"

"Why are You tearing down the Door? It's against the Law! They will put You in Prison for Blasphemy!"

"I accidentally locked it and I can't find the Key."

"Key. Key. He said Key again!"

"Do You want the Green One or the Blue One?"

"Come Here… Fifi… Come Here."

"I Will Be Waiting… There… for You…"

"This is Mr. Crow Nose and his Glamorous Wife Mdm. Long Hand Wonderful Lead Singer of the Seagulls Flashy Sun Disco Globe Queen of the Forlorn and Lower Subjects Who Majestically Bow to Her Waving Her Hand to the Masses Worshipping the Same God and the Blood of the Law and Commander-in-Chief of the Military so She Can

Start Zapping at the Hideouts of the Rats and North Burma as well because They are developing WMDs and they are Posing a Threat to International Interests."

"Are You Sure? I heard… that Guy's Going to

"Follow Your Instincts! At least, They will not Betray You."

"Tomorrow, I'm going to bring You Down to the Jungle. Then, You Will Know How

"it's King of Diamonds! Total Diamonds!"

"Hey… Miss Pushkin… not… yet…"

"How many Times must we perform this act over and over again? Why can't he get his Timing Right? Do You know how many feathers I make in a few Seconds? What are You waiting for? Fire Him!"

"It's Just a Mistake… I will get it Right the Next Time… Trust me…"

"Here! Take this Red Packet of Dislikes! It's enough for You and Your family to live comfortably for a few generations."

"When I Grow Up, I want to be Don Dictator!"

"Why are You Telling Me?"

"The First thing is to do a Color Check. If You are Color Blind, You cannot…"

"When I Grow Up, I want to be Charlie Chef!"

"Why is the Price of Oil Falling??"

"The City is Sinking an Eighth of an Inch per year and the King is Quite Concerned it will not be so Long that the Subjects will be traveling around in Boats and it's a Fact that people had been Warned to Leave the City but a Few Million

Stubborn Subjects of the Realm made a Pledge to Stay On in the City even if they would be Buried Alive."

"When I Grow Up, I want to be a Cupcake Coach!"

"Are You Forgetting Something?"

"When I Grow Up, I want to be a Liposuction Spy!"

"The Poor Girl is Waiting for You at the End of the Trail."

"HEEEEE! HAAAAAAAAAAWWWWWW!!!"

"When Shall We Dive

"Wait for a few more moons. By then, we would have saved enough to buy a Korat Kitten."

"But I Tell You…"

"It's… it's… Near… I Can Feel It…"

"What's the Use… replied the Thief to the Joker… if I Stole your Queen of Hearts…"

"Retreat! Retreat! Run Ye into the Hills! Run! Run! Run!'

"Forever May the Blue Sun Weep!"

"Widows! Pick Up Your Stones!!"

"The Revolution Has…"

"Is that the Meaning of Love?"

"You are a Damn Stupid Buffalo! Moo Young Daa Dee ver re le vera la…"

"Medicine Men! Blow Your Pipes of Sleep!"

"How do You say Hello to the Revolutionary?"

"Left Baden Powell Salute above the Left Brow… Eyes Looking as Far as Possible…."

"towards the Horizons of Existence…"

"Onward! Onward! They are getting Closer!"

"Why did the Guy Decide to become a Monk?"

"They say… His Bird Doesn't Sing Anymore!"

"It's Dead Wood… they are Everywhere…"

"Why the Same Thing Again and Again? We want Something New! Something Radical! Something Dangerous!"

"When I Grow Up, I want to be a Pariah Philosopher!"

"Choose Your Stone… Choose Diligently… You Only Have One Chance!"

"What Happens if I Pick the Wrong One?"

"Gently… Walk back towards the Path You came from and getting as close as You got to the Spot where You picked the Stone, then, mutter a Soft Apology and Lay it on the Ground… Gently… Without a Sound…"

"it Pleasures You, don't You, to know that Everybody is Dying when they are Near You!"

"The Pleasure is All Mine! The Pleasure is All Mine!"

"What's the Meaning of

"REVOLUTIONS! NEW MANNERISMS! REPACKAGED MARXISM! LET THE COMRADE LIVE! LET THE COMRADE LIVE!"

"NAAAAHHHIIIIIIIOOOOOSSSSSIIIIIISSSSS!"

"Overdue Heinz Beans and a Dash of Peyote Powder. Taste! Taste!"

"You Have Ten Seconds Left! Ten! Nine! Eight!"

"Seven. Seven is The Lucky Number."

"ZERO ZERO"

"Seven, the Number of Swans Flying South East

An Arrowhead, this One from more than Two Thousand Suns!

The Octave Cow, he's Looking at Moon Shadow Again

Parameswara! Salute You the Blue Sun!

Salute! Salute! Salute!

Salute! You Salute the Magicians! Salute!

Salute! You Salute the Ring Masters! Salute!

Salute! It's the Day of the Uprising! Arise! Arise!

Fat Bone Headed Mencius Inspired Soldiers! Quick Witted Soft Handed Superstitious Farmers! Nose Bleeding Nose Golden True or False Rebels! Foot Stomping Mother of Intellectual Thieves! Sick Skin Velvet Tongue Pope Murderers! Insolvent Magnified Magna Carter Charting Judges! Non-Believing Darwinism Drawf Teachers! Pregnant Virgin Bus Drivers! Slow Hand Breezy Bald Jesus Accountants! Up Skirt Phobia Gypsy Queen Secretaries! New Age Guru Pipe Fitters! Assistant Stalin Team Managers! Sleepy Santa Sloppy Diseased Train Conductors! Out of Tune Classical Feminist Singers! Green Card Seeking Missile Prince Charles Aliens! Romantic Crows! Bums! Dirty Doctors! Melodramatic Uninspired Bipolar Heads of State! Hungry Lost Left on the Shore to Die Communist Immigrants! The Red Eyed French Accent Newscaster Abused! The Brave Cowards! The Victorious Losers! The Humbled Winners! We Salute You! We Salute You with all Our Hearts! We Salute You with All Our Souls! Salute! Salute! Salute! We Salute You! We Salute You! Salute! Salute! Salute!

Then, the Mullo Reggae Ship Comes Floating into Sight

Loaded to the Brims with all the Treasures of the West

There, He Saw Miss Washington Beside the Stream

Lost, her Tits Falling Out and she has that Curious Stare of the Wild

Serene, not Ready but Always Reading her *Lolita*

Again and Again?

To the Hills! To the Hills! Raise the Thunder to the Sky!

Sir! We are Surrounded! The Ring of Saturn's Sixth Son. There's No Escape!"

Do We Wave the White Flag of Surrender?

No! The Magical Mystery Bus is Coming!

Are Your Certain? so said she to the Blind Swedish Masseur

Telling her of Shady Characters Living on the Fringes of Society

There, there, she Nods like she understands all about the Universe

Yeah, she likes to run naked on the Beach at Three in the Morning

Challenging the Stud to a Game of Horseshoe in Stake

Somehow, He Always Wins even when She's the more Holy

Without knowing She's The Whore, the One Dreamed by all Sorts of Johns of the Universe, You Hear all about how she Sucked Man of War's Penis until he Passed Away with a Heart Attack when he could have Easily Disappeared into Thin Air but still Being Alive and it's No Point to Perform this Exercise unless You are Alive because if You are Dead, You will not be able to pick out even a strain of the least seraphic music from these pages at least after 101 and Your professor can tell You it's metaphysics and You will Believe him just because Nobody told You Otherwise and it's so Easy to believe Him when He has such a Big Bunch of Keys in his Pocket for it's so Obvious, it can be Seen almost a Mile away and it's so Obvious that You will be a Fool not to Blow on Her Nose with Your Foul White Snakeroot Breath and Tickle her Irish Iris a Little when She's washing the Dishes Again because her Brother's having a Period Again, and her Sister's Growing a Caveman Beard, and her Mother's in Love with Thelonious Monk the Night she Saw Him Play in San Francisco in 1959, she sewed her Heart to his sleeve and tore up her Ticket to Paris just so she could spend the Night Listening to Him Live for there's a such a Big Difference if You just Listen to his Studio Albums because he's not allowed to use his Vocals in some of those numbers just like what they tell You to Clap when the Clap Lights Come One and they tell You to Smile when the Camera's On and not to Frown when she Ran Out the Back Door and Disappeared for more than a Few Days and he would be so Anxious so he Aspired to go to Another Country to Distinguish the Local Cuisine as His Duty as Master Connoisseur of the Universe so You have to Respect his Artistry and Perfect Timing in Quick Short Breaths but it's quite a Surprise how such a Country Bumpkin will even know Hortense Ellis when she's into New Age Floatation Theories and Way Out Fantasies about a Long Line of Policemen and Lawyers and Doctors Shoving it Up her Ass and she's speaking in broken American English and totally losing Control of the Situation as she's Squirting and Going into Spasms in the King Size Bed and her Hair is Tied in Ridiculous High School Girl Style so it's Time to Fantasize about Teenagers always being the Biggest Stars but it's the Truth, some of them are Taller than Others, and Faster than Others, and Sillier than Others, and Less Fortunate than Others, and More Naïve than Others, and More Succulent than Others, and More Gifted than Others, and More Ridiculous than Others for it's Quite Strange You

Shall Find the Key in the Vacuum Cleaner when they had been keeping it Real for so many years and how many times must we tell You Nicely… Violence is for Sick Puppies and War is Wrong and Racism is Wrong and Religion is Wrong and Nationalism is Wrong and Human Nature is Wrong and Freud is Wrong and Honor is Wrong and Economics is Wrong and Everything is Wrong before It becomes Wrong to You and even if You are not Educated or Uneducated so You will Find Yourself HERE and all that White Lies and Black Humor and yeah say You may even be Happy to Smell the Words Coming Across the Screen like a Slow Train even though You are not in a Movie House because such a thing can Only Happen in Fairy Tales kind of Revelation no Priest or Prophet or Bronze Medalist or Lichen Professionals or Muddy Politicians or Smart Computer Girl Friends are going to Illuminate Your Mind so You can Read It in All the Glory of the Moon Beaming a Light on You in the Middle of the Plains where the Hounds Love to Call Them Victims so they Don't Feel so Vindicated for their Crime of not being able to afford Rent and the Children are Starving because there's Just Too Many of Them! And Everything Else of no Relation to her Baboon Neighbor showing off his gleaming Pollen Textured Emerald Shark Teeth and You remember that Town for the Big Complex Beer Brewery Intoxicating the People of the Nation and Ensnaring them with Glowing Lasso of Wonder Woman, Finest Hero of All, a Great Sort of Body Guard, I want to hire her for Protection, please, Vigorously, Compassionately, let's Take a Walk to the End of the Creek and Float Down Memory Lane of Summer together, that's all, just the Two of Us, O Carry her Tube I Shall Float if she comes in Costume, yeah, three somersaults along the Way, please, and upon reaching The End, she will Float First and I will Come Along Two Minutes later but I will Still Beat her to the Finish Line at which Point I will go into the Unknown and she will be so Pleased to find the petals of blue leading to the Moon and it's then she thinks of Blue Moon... but how else the Sacred Eagle Steal the Jade Mockingbird Hair Pin from the Orient where such Arts have Perished under the Crushing Heels of Imperialism, Extraditing the Natives Out into the Wild Lands where Coyotes still Steal the Young when You are not Watching TV, You are on the Phone so to Help Deliver the Masses from their Addiction, No, You will not be able to Read the Republic on any Electronic Device because then You will not Fully Comprehend How Softly the Cave of Puppets Singing their Song of Shadows so You react in Anger when It's Supposed to be Humor even when he's not Speaking a Single Word and it can be so Entertaining to see the Tramp walking into the Desert with Trail of Dust blowing out from the shuffle of his Penguin feet and he's so fast that over some distance, the cloud is Highest and Most Dense at the furthest end nearer to the Crowd and it's Rising all the Time as he goes Forward more and more so if You are looking from the Side, it's like a Right Angle Triangle of Dust Cloud until He disappeared and the Audience just Erupted and Clapped the Skin Off when they Heard the Final Note and there's such an Explosion, the Crystal Lamp or Ceiling Chandelier Rattled and there must have been a few pieces of mirror falling down and Piercing the Soul of the Wrench who's Hated by All Womankind as well as using their wooden clogs to hit on a piece of rice paper with caricature of her as personally drawn by the Victims, Possessed, Rigorously, they hit Her so Violently, the paper bled and cried out in Shame when they Burned It and Spat on the Asses with Venom and Alcohol as well Vinegar for in those days, they were really not so Strict about Structural Integrity of Building Safety as there's this Shameless Rush to Develop as Quickly as Possible Kind of Futile Race only Third World Folks Still Believe they can Catch up with the First World Countries, I Tell You… Bloody Stupid Babi Idiots… there's No Way You are going to Catch Up even if You Test a Million Hydrogen Missiles or Launch a Thousand Astronauts into Space to Drink a Cup of Tea with Milk kind of Scam, Fuck You! Fuck You to the Power of Infinity! It's Real Stupid… just think how a Laser may be used to Zap Anything into Nothing and it's still a Technology Unavailable to the Masses Living Way Way Below the Poverty Line it's why they are forced to Sacrifice their own Flesh and Blood to stay alive for another day or so before the Landlord's Hooligan Son's Gangs come to Take Fern Fern away and they are licking their lips so the Older Sister Chose to Offer Herself Up because she felt it's her Duty to Protect the Younger Sister just as her father told her before he died of starvation just so his family can eat for Another Day or Two for he already calculated that… she would have to go through a great deal of suffering and we know all about how she became a Mutant and so on too much revealed in the Media where every goddamn thing about the First Lady's Panty Hose to the Prince's Muscular Mistress Fracturing His Bone was reported so Everybody knows how she made him Fetch her Pee Pee Slippers with Authentic Mustang Fur and You may say You may know a softer or more glossy one but You can't deny the fact that a Mustang is more Volatile and in less than a Half a Day Only, he would be panting at her feet at exactly Nine O Clock at Night for he's a Clockwork Slave in her hands and she can Wind him up anytime she desires to have a Little Fun with her Poodles and Butlers and Piano Tuners Charging a Fortune to Tune the Instrument, the more Rare, the Higher, and he will even place them in her Feet with his Tongue so she will Squirm and Hiss like a Pregnant Serpent and Kick Him in the Crotch with such WHAM! BAM! his Butt will be Lifted Up a few feet in the Air KATCHOW! His Body Lifted Off the Ground, Spine a Snapped, he was Shocked Out Flat and the Queen was so Worried, she was pacing Outside the Emergency Room and Digging her Nose again as she was wont to do when she's in a State of Panic, she would call on the Dalai Lama…

"It's Nothing Blue. Are You Listening?"

"Yeah... Straight Kop… but I'm feeling a little Sleepy."

"Don't Worry. It's not really important that You remember everything."

"Are You Sure?"

"Yeah... it's perfectly alright if You miss some parts or misunderstand some of words. Better, You forget everything..."

"Is it Alright if I fell asleep?"

"Perfect! That's exactly what I want! Sleep! Dream! Snore!"

"Alright. See You tomorrow..."

"What Shall I Do, Harold?"

"Don't Panic! Be Calm!"

"You are Making me more Nervous…"

"You are Entering a Blue Cloud…"

"Shirley, I told You to calm down… You are frightening Angel…"

"DO YOU WANT TO GO

"Sorry. Dancing's Not Allowed Here. You may Proceed to Buenos Aires. It's North of Ukraine."

"Can we Fish in

"Please read all the Rules and Regulations in greater detail."

"Efficient and Businesslike, that's right, Shirley. Give it to them..."

"I can't... I have George's Sickness..."

"Ahhh... Nevermind... Here Comes the..."

"No! No! Not Them! Make Sure they are Not Within a Radius of a Hundred Miles from Me at All Times!! They are Animals!!!"

"No... Majesty... that's Another Band..."

"OK. CUT! Erase all that! What are You Doing?"

"Why are You Taking Pictures of People?"

"Yeah! You are not Allowed to Take Pictures of Us!"

"Come Here! Let me See that Camera!!"

"Why is He Taking Pictures of People Doing Their Jobs?"

"What's This??? Why are you Taking these Pictures???"

"Nice Tits! You have Nice Tits!"

"Do You Know That?"

"Are You Sure it's all Deleted? Show Me!"

"See? Nice Bums too."

"Hey... Martha... He Likes You!"

"Meet me under Fortitude after your Shift. I will be Waiting."

"Who's this? Paaameeellllaaaaaaaa!"

"It's all Your Fault! You should have Sent the Ninjas

Earlier when I was in the Woods. Now, it's too Late! You cannot Stop me!"

"Are You for or Against Me?"

"I Don't Care! I want my Feathers Back! It's a Fake!"

"Do You Want the Real Thing?"

"When he's Playing *Trinkle Trinkle*

"Why are we going back to those Days? It's History! He's Snowball! We Want Our Own History! We Want Our Own Heroes! We Want Our Own Era!"

"Yeah, tell us, why are we

"See? You are Always Avoiding the Question of Truth but do you Think The Holy Mother Knows?"

"How Dare You??? 22,874:623. What's the Answer??"

In the Republic, there are No Vehicles of Any Kind, no wheels, no dreams, and no aspirations, no, You are Mistaken to think that the Riddle of the Golden Apple Blinded the Wisest Men of Troy or Trojan, I Forgot but I can tell You it's highly Difficult to Build that Wooden Horse in such a Short Time for they would have to go quite Deep into the Jungle to Chop the Trees so that their Enemies could not hear them going about it with all the Banging and Sawing and Singing their Seven Dwarves Songs such as they do when they built that Railroad to Join the East to the West, and it's not even easy to pass such a Monstrous Looking Wooden Horse Idea to be Placed in Front of the Enemy's Castle so the whole Clan is Foolish to think that their Enemies had Fled kind of Logic but Nobody Picked it Out, the Illogicality of the whole plot twist being that they will Pull the O So Obvious Sleight of Hand Technique which these Men didn't know about Art and such things that they didn't see the Trickery when they drank and whored to Celebrate their Victory without Lifting a Hand and let it be Known that when You are Winning too Easily then it's Time to Retreat and that's what the Wizard of Investment told Augustine when he was Fishing at the lake where they were going to the Dragon Boat Festival to remember their past and all their polished Ming Dynasty Vase meaning so much to them that they will not sell it no matter what price is offered because it represents the Chastity of all the Women in the Dragon Family, all of them are Virgins on the Day of their Marriage, even when they were to be Carried in a Gama by the Strongest Men in the Winery and One Peeked at Her under the Red Veil and then Carried Her into the Plains and Deflowered Her so when the Boss Found out that She's not a Virgin, he's so Traumatized, he Beat at His Heart until it turned Purple and he's Coughing and Sneezing and Vomiting and She's Just Unconcerned at All as She thought about Small Train Head and She thought all about how he chewed on her earlobes and how it was so painful that jets of tears sprang out of her Eyes and she's now the Queen of Siberia, looking at the Mirror of Promise, and she's talking all about how it's her most Favorite Thing and there's Nobody in the Room when the Alternate Her Spoke of how it's Best to Murder the Girl whose Skin is White as Honey who's always singing when she's performing domestic chores so all her animal friends love her so much they help to wash all the Dirty Spoons and those Spoilt Brats were so good at wasting things that even their Bare Foot Servants have grown too Fat to Walk to the Market so they have to Rely on the Driver who's always Late and Irresponsible and Everybody is Becoming Fatter for so much Food is Wasted, it's her Greatest Dream of All Time to Cook Up the Biggest Feast of All to Feed Every Mouth in the World for as a Pure Chef, she doesn't think about whether You are of what race, sex, language or religion for as long as she can put a Smile on Your Face through her Culinary Skills, she will be the Happiest Person on Earth if You will only Kiss her Hand and Offer the Greatest Blessings on her Future Generations who will be Instructed to Walk in the Light and Act in the Warmth of Humanity even in the Coldest Regions of the World, there will be Peace and Love, that's the Simple Wish in Our Prayer, O Great Spirit, Breathe Your Song through a Love Supreme and Drip Rain unto the Lines until the Ink flows to the Other Side and flow through to the Flag, Bleeding the Colors to become Just One Color and all the Words Merge to form Just One Word spelling NOTHING, all blank, White or Black, it matters not, it will be a Triumph, a Triumph of the Human Race if at last, We can all Stand before the Blue Sun Rise, and with well-polished wind instruments and well-worn stringed instruments and well-seasoned percussion and even a bowl and a toothpick, We Shall Raise Our Faces as the Face of God is Revealed, it's such a Perfect Face she Felt Ashamed to Look Up even when he asked her and he even went down on his knee to show his Sincerity but she kept going lower as if she's trying to go into the ground, the Evil Bull King knew something was amiss so he issued a Warning to the Iron fan Princess and Miraculously, she confessed her desires to Partake of the Flesh of the Monk for it will make her Immortal so she wouldn't have to Terrorize the Commoners who were Betrayed by the King who offered every one of the villagers to her as a Condition that he and his family be spared and strangely, for so many years, the commoners still paid their taxes in fear of his Secret Patrol Squad who always appear in groups of more than a hundred for it's a number big enough to terrorize many other groups, it's not so often You see such big groups of people but at the same time, it's also quite difficult to mobilize and command such a number of people from all walks of life just because there's no Discrimination in the Republic of Good Samaritans.

"It's... supposed to be Written... not Spoken..."

"Your Majesty... You should Fire the Prime Minister... He's Screwing Diana with Blue Moon of Josephine!"

"Your Majesty... You should be Kinder to St Paul. He's feeling

"Are You One of the Knights?"

"We are the Guardians! We have no Love! We Want Blood! We Want Blood! Down with the Purists! Down with the Establishment!"

"In the Republic, Every Citizen is the Government! Don't Listen to Him! He's Misrepresenting the Most Important Part..."

"It's Impossible! It's Impossible! I'm Alive Again!"

"John! Can You point out the Culprit?"

"It's too Dark! A Drop of Blood Red Spot Light on the Top of His Head..."

"Good! I can recite the Alphabets in Pakistani!"

"Hip! Hip! Hurray! America Scored! America Scored!"

"Sir! The Citizens are getting Fat and Lazy."

"Shall We give them a Warning?"

"it's been a great century... I want to Sleep... another Ten Thousand Years..."

"What about the Slaves? What do we do with them? They are not Working and there's hardly any Grain left!"

"Wait! She's bringing more Barbarians and Dragons to feed! Pick Your Children! Who is it?"

"What will You do in such a Situation?"

"Arapahoe & Stonehenge"

"Wait here! I will Go Pick some Firewood."

"This One Looks Like it's Gonna Do It!"

"Let's… let's listen to some Junkie Mexican Cowboys sing about their Cows…"

"And with Tears in their Eyes, Looking at the Jewels in the Sky

Half Spastic and Half Smiling like a Buddha Dreaming of Food

Fit for the Soul of the King with the Golden Touch of Death

Queen Persephone, she's Good with the Battalion Formation

And What Reputations, the Gypsy Maiden Shook her Tambourine

Clang! Clang! Clang! It Goes into the Winds, Shaken with Glue

Strap Sorrows of the Clapping Man Always Clapping His Hands

It's True! He Clapped Until the Bones Are Sticking Out

Clap! Clap! Clap! For what the Champion Wants!

Throw Away Your Blue Dream Posters! Throw Away Your Georges!

Throw Away Your Daughter's Favorite Sex Toys! Your Son's New Servants!

Collect! Collect! Collect! Collect all the Bricks! Collect all the Plastic Bottles!

Sell them Back to the Emperor so he can Walk to Krakow

Go the Heart of Nigeria

Where They have no Mother or Father

As They are Born of Rocks and Pestle

Trading Humans for a few packs French Fries

And it's So Good You Think of the Mermaid

The One You Cut a Hole in Her Fin

At the Spot where the Golden Calf Sleeps

And You Breathe, Not Once, Not Thrice

But for the Grand Eternity of Blissful Desolation Blessed Sutra

Yeah, I Tell You…

It's More Excellent than All the Wines in Paradise

Here, There, and Everywhere!

Better than All the Virgins in the Universe

If You Can Hold the Edge of the Table of the Greatest Harvest

Where You Can Taste All Kinds of Fruits from All the Realms

And Drink the Wines from Under the Lamp of Old St. Petersburg

Winning the Grand Old Cup with Iron Crown of Thorns

And Nobody Wears it so Well like Sir Independent Guy

Who Wears It Like He Never Wants to Give It Back

For Squeaky Bum Time is Most Appropriate Expression

For Scrambling Up the Hills

At Full Speed so You're Panting at the Hundredth Step

For that's How the Welsh do It

And Though You May Think You May Understand Some of It

Don't Worry Be Wondrous

You Won't Understand Even the Simplest Number of Amalia

Of Three in the Morning when the She Wolf Hunts

That's the Time She Must Leave the Rotten Cottage

Don't be Ridiculous! It's Simply Not True! I Never Said That!

Shut Up! Shut Up! Shut Up! It's Piercing My Ears!

Will You Pick Up the Stave?

He's Heavy! He's Not Your Sister!

Go to Patagonia!

Are You Crazy?

I will meet You at the End of the World!

Let's Go before the Sleeping Giant Awakes…

Shhhh! He Can Sense You…

Go to Sleep! You have to Wake up in the Morning to Sweep the Floor!

No… I'm Going Blind…

It's not the Way to the Republic! It's the Other Way!

Turn! Turn! Turn!

Turn, Turn the Sun Blue.

Go Ahead! Make My Day!

Do You want to Climb the Tiger Mountain with Jayu?
She Must Be Over the Moon with Joy Now

The Room is Simple with White Walls and a Queen and a Shelf and Walk in Closet and Bath is Only Steps Away so You Can Shower and keep Yourself Clean for You Know How Important it is to Brush the Chimneys of Love no Matter how Contaminated, it Can be Cleansed with the No Sins Soap of Limestone and Valium or some kind of Grease will do the Trick, Rub in the Ointment of Oregano and Basil and Scratch the Rubber so Lightly so it's at the Brim of breaking but still Intact to Trick the John who's Foolish to Suspect She's a Victim of Sexual Abuse in her Own Home, it's Known her Father is a Surgeon General, yeah, the Same One who Outlawed all the Smokers to The Corner which is the Only Place You can Smoke Nowadays and the Queue is Quite Long no Matter How You Measure It, You Will Always Win General Competitions where they make You stuff as many Hotdogs down Your throat, remember, it's always a good idea to maintain a Fit Body for You always want to outdo the Strongest and the Meanest and the Most Inhumane and the Most Evil and the Most Seething Crazy Angry Loud Big Motherfucker in the Neighborhood looking Most Macho and Standing in Stance when it seems like he's got not even a Sparkle of Electricity in him when he's Turned into Dead Wood by the Black Witch who's Laughing as she rides on her Broomstick Across the Same Damn Moon the Frog was Swallowing in Eclipse of Reason and how shall we say it the way the Thief said it in that Japanese movie with the Bamboo Castle and You can Head Off to Lafayette, a Sleepy Little Town with not more than Thirty Thousand Souls Sleeping Soundly at Around Ten O Clock when the

Moon was Still Shy and Blushing in her Tracks where You Found the Path to the Lonesome Tree Spot.

"Walk to the End of Cabrini... You may Use Cristo Ave..."

"How Far is It?"

"Roughly Six Miles Round Trip!"

"Should I Launch the Nuclear Bomb?"

"Hey! He's Listening to Latin Love Songs!"

"What Does It Matter?"

"What's Your Name?"

"Bill. My Name is Bill."

"Where are You Going?"

"I'm from Tail of the Scorpion."

"Do You Play the Banjo?"

"No. I'm the Driver! I make Things Happen All the Time!"

"Is that You Neal? It's Time to Go..."

"Bye... bye... Jack... and George..."

"See You..."

O Princess Pollen, she loved the Cakes, they are so Sweet and Everybody Knows She's got a Sweet Tooth and She was so Pissed that Day when Her Wisdom Fell Off and she Directed the Sheep to Her Golden Swallow Pillow and showed them immediately how it changed to a Jade Artifact Describing a Child, possibly a Girl but it's Hard to Tell because She's on All Fours and bending as Cats do when they are Nauseous and Sensitive to lemonade which makes her Tummy all

Spinning and She's so Happy to Speak with Mrs. Robinson who always bring some goodies for her and she's got a Sharp Mouth so she can differentiate all the different Spices from the Four Corners and she's Brilliant with Numbers and Music and even Sports for she ran so quickly when she Imagined the Alter Ego of Igor was Chasing Her and she Preferred to Stay in her Room without Anyone Disturbing Her and even including the Butler and Her Mama and Dada who Treasured Every Moment they Shared in her Presence and how she's Learning how to Interact with the Sumerian Cats and they are so Clever to Pretend to be Meowing Here and Meowing There so how about a Toast to her favorite Guitarist for he makes her laugh all the time when she's told, O he only has Three Fingers so it's really Amazing he can play so fast so all the Lonely Ladies will slip out of their sweaty panties, unclasp their glittering necklace or bracelet and wrap it so they can gracefully slip their offering into his pocket and the men, they will be wiping their faces dry and unclasp their Watches and Drop it into the Hat which was Quite Similar to the One Worn by the *Cat in the Hat* for he can even hide Behind the Curtains so You Cannot Detect Him even when He's sitting right beside You and caressing Your neck with the Softest Touch without a gleam of Sensuality for that's the level of professionalism we aspire when we were learning how to make sashimi so many years ago, we cut our fingers so much we only have four fingers or less, we really Pity him more than the Others simply because he lost his Fingers in Strangest Accident Involving Wax, Fire, and Chemicals, the Ingredients of Alchemy and in that One Moment, His Life was Transformed, He put on the Cloak of the Gypsy Prince and Disappeared into Thin Air!

"Just like That!"

"That's Not Hard at All! Everybody Can Do It!"

"Dearest Uzza… I Beg Your Pardon!

Do You Smoke?"

"I Hate It! I Hate it! I Hate It!"

"Stop! Stop! The Train is Coming…"

"You are Either On the Train or You are Off the Train!"

"Did You think the Cuckoo Really Flew Over the Rainbow?"

"it's *One Flew Over the Cuckoo's Nest*!"

"Why didn't they Put a Rainbow Over Her Head as She's Singing? She's Immortal!"

"Immoral… You Mean?"

"Why do You have to go to the Water Closet so many times?"

'I'm Fainting!"

"AWESOME!!"

"Catch Her! She's Poisoned Her Majesty's Secret Service Mastermind!"

"HELP! HELP! HELP!"

"What will You Say to Telemachus?"

"Hi! My Name is Stephanie Armstrong from Nebraska."

"What will You Say to Cleopatra?"

"Do You want to go to Budapest?"

"oooooooooooyyyyyyyyyyyyyyyyyyyyyyyyyyyyaaaaaaaaaaaaaaaaaaaaaaaaa"

"What Shall We Pack?"

No Matter How Heavy the Cargo, we have more than enough men to carry all Your stuff, Everywhere we Go, we will be surely Protected as it's Impenetrable, these fifty thousand soldiers to die before the Enemy can Get to us and it's such a Great Feeling isn't it to Know that You are Perfectly Safe like the President when he went for a Bowl of Noodles, it's such a Big Deal they had to Shut Down Google for a Day and it's so Safe that You can even Enjoy the Richest Nectar they Call the Foods of the Gods not for Nothing because It Really Melts in Your Mouth and it's True when You go to the Other Side, You will not have a Mouth or any Sensation At All for You are already Dead Wood for as soon as she touches Anything with Her Black Hand, it will Expire so You may Wonder about how She was Able to Burn Up the Car with a ball of Her Fury and she's always angry about something for she's easily bothered by such Trivial Landmine Issues in Some Regions in Hanoi, there are Villages of Freaks but Nobody's allowed to Talk about It for it's against the Law to talk about Them in Public and if You are found to be in Offense, You will be sentenced to Jail for up to the Term as passed down by the Judge who's known to be such an honest man that he would run a mile to return the Most Exquisite Red Jade Dragonfly Brooch to that Maiden who lives up in the Tower so she can Practice her Archery Skills and she's Improving so Fast that the Olympians, referring to those athletes who were rewarded with Golden Laurels to be Propped at the Valley at the Top of the Ear which is able to hold things like pencils, pens, brushes, and other such artistic tools seldom mentioned in Elementary Schools nowadays where they are Drilling a Whole Mountain of Candy Science Hippo Sweat Textbooks into their Poor Little Minds Cramming so Much Knowledge into Such a Small Space that they are Feeling like the Brain is Overloaded and You are slowly starting to discover how difficult it's become to enjoy such simple joys such as taking a walk in the Hot Sun and hearing how *I will See You in My Dreams* becoming such a Retro Hit just because some teenage raw paper puppets were Singing It with New Band and Humor, what's the use, what's the use when You can go to the Original and Listen until You are Blue and it's no use, You are still Holding the Pencil with Your Fingers and not the Nape of the Ear being where the Point of Skinning Occurs in Autumns Coming Earlier so the Leaves are already turning Red and Yellow even when it's still a moon or two away and she's explaining all about how the Planting Season has been Shortened as More Farmers are Operating Indoor Grow Shops where they are Becoming More Powerful Each Day for their Business Never Slows Down even during the Holidays, their Business is Booming and Booming and in just a few slow years, they have amassed such Fortune they don't have to worry about more Things than the Middle Income Folks who are more fortunate for they don't have to Swim with Shark Lords who are always prowling on the fringe, ready to Pounce when You make the Slightest Mistake and the Princess can tell You all about how Her son craves for Extra Special home tuition with that Eighty Eight Year Old Mamasan who's always fanning herself like she's so hot all the time even when it's in the Thick of the Battle, she will still be Fanning, Fanning, Fanning, and she's extra furious that night with her husband as he was fanning the Red Ha Boy to Sleep and he's such a Genius that he Defeated the Monkey King with the Magic Horn, he's Blowing on It with eyes closed so the Loser took the Opportunity to Fly and Somersault across the Sea of Clouds to arrive at the her Abode which is Supposed to be in another Dimension but Somehow She will be Telling Him the Same Thing just like the Tang Dynasty Monk who has attained Enlightenment so Anyone who partakes of his flesh shall not perish but gain Immortality, it's understandable that all the Demons are devising all Sorts of Schemes, Shape Shifting into Beautiful Nymphs, Spider Women, and what else when she's alone with the Monk, she couldn't even come within a skin's breath near him and it's something His Disciples never Knew because He was such a Humble Man so when the Three of Them were running all around the Region when he was in most dire thirst for a Simple Bowl of White Rice and a Cool Cup of Green Tea to Lose Weight, they don't know that he's got the Power to Defend himself.

"That's the Question! How Big

"It's No More than Twenty Acres Only!"

"Have You Found

"After You go into Lucerne Street or Avenue or Road, go straight until to You arrive at the Wide Open Space."

"Shall I Bring Some Water?"

"it's not been Raining for many Moons…"

"Do You want to eat some Strawberries or Grapes? They are Organic!"

"Please! Some Eggs and Coconuts!"

There will be a Platoon of Prairie Rats standing on their hinds and looking at something very far away for they must be Farsighted not to see You if You don't scare them, they will be so very Glad to Invite You to Visit their Homes beneath the Ground for they are Tremendously Hard Working so It's

Quite Impressive that even these Fellas have their Houses as they are Inhabiting quite a sizeable parcel of land but it's Open so they don't have to pay any Rent and Neither will they be Evicted or Hunted for Food so they are also delighted to tell You about the Two Trees where the Great Spirit blows sometimes and it's also a Fantastic place to Smoke Up for You will be too far away from the next Human Being who's too high up in the sky to notice Nahiossi sleeping on his Rope, not at all worried about what's he gonna do when the Next Challenger Arrives to engage in Hard Core Inhumane One-on-One Fight to the Death with Only a Knife and Nothing Else, and it should be noted that the Titanium Breastplates must be Insulated with most tender of Inside of Big Giant Antelope hand crafted in a Sickening Country deep in Pedophilia Culture which is such a Taboo Subject even in First World Countries so it's Avoided in such sexually arousing eye contact in public transportation when You can be in Tokyo in just a few hours from Hokkaido which is such an imposing volatile volcano always threatening to sink the whole of the Nation in a Flood of Magma and where else are there so many virgin panties and school girl armpit odor and his neighbor's daughter's puppy sprays for sale as in the Land where the Red Sun is Perpetually Rising and the Nationals are all against the Welcome Carpet they are Rolling Out for a more International Cosmopolitan Atmosphere, it's quite Compulsory for Each and Every Big City to Accommodate as Many Immigrants as Possible for they will be the Ones doing all the Dirty Work which is Shunned by the Citizens so it's very Important that The Republic Shall Not Condone Any Kind of Activity which Promotes Pedophilia which is Considered to be One of the Greatest Sins, if not the Greatest for it is Thoroughly Revolting and Cowardly for a Giant of a

Man to Push Himself into that Hole which is too Small for Him but He Pushes and Pushes until He's all Bloody and Soggy and He goes around Town to Recruit some Nurses.

"What's the Menu?"

"I Prefer Somalians. They are Good Cooks and Good Mothers."

"How Many Engineers? How Many Sex Change Plastic Surgeons? How Many Cheer Leaders?"

"528:4. We are Outnumbered Again!"

"It's Over! The Players are Rebelling! They are Refusing to Play for their Country!"

"THOU SHALL NOT EAT CHICKEN AND PORK!"

"Don't You Love Your Job?"

"Every day, it's the same thing. I will say I'm accustomed…"

"I Love Doris Day! She's a Darling! It's Cool like it's Raining…"

"Sir! Sir! The Show's Over. Please go Home."

IX IS THE NIGHT

When they asked him to point out the Sacred Lamb, he found it hard to lift a finger for he never thought the Day would come that he had to choose one of his hundreds of kids to be Sacrificed while most think it's not such a detrimental loss for he had much more than any of them could ever Imagine and they may even be Right in most circumstances but he Found the Most Fair Method by Making them Recite the Blake poem about how to be careful about trees with poison without make any Noise or even a small Noise or even a Noise which is not to be Heard and those Children who cannot Perform the task, they will be asked to Wrestle with Each Other According to those Olympic Rules and the Defeated Ones will be asked to Play the Jackpot of Sacrifice where One will be Randomly Chosen by a Computer System Executioner who will then Bring the Lamb to the Outskirts of the Town to be Bathed in the Hot Springs in the Glenwood Caves and it's such an Extravagant Coup, once You lived like a Sultan, Get On, Get On, We are living in the twenties when those French Nigga Sisters they are Wearing those Flowery Skirts and Holding those Poodle Skin Umbrellas with Alligator Hide on her Shoulders and Disguised as the Troublesome One I need a Little Hotdog on my Robe I feel so Funny I Need Some Sugar in my Bone between my Robe Looks like a Snake and Drop Something in My Bowl Now yeah and she went picking up the feathers from the Floor and it's quite a Big Surprise when she found out she could make Seven Pillows Stuffed to the Seams Breaking a Little More Every Day and so she got some helpers to carry her Goods and they were Little Boys from the Slums so soon they will be Impregnating Old Widows who kept them all in their harems and they got so Good at it, they are Riding the Train, the One that takes You to the Top of Pike's Peak where You can see the Furthest into the Horizon while taking the High Risk of Breaking Your Bones and Fighting with the Time Keeper who Always tell You You are late no matter how early You come You still end up being late for the Grind when it comes, there's no Stopping it until the TV Engineer comes Riding on that Train, it seems, it takes at least three times a day to Satisfy her completely so You can plan it One in the Morning when Your Flag is at Full Mast and Ready for Takeoff to Saturn, she will come to lick it at four in the Morning even when You are Doggone Tired for You Came Home at Three in the Afternoon when You Ripped Off her Silly Coca Cola Lady Chef Scottish Square Style Apron but She's One Step Ahead of the Old Rock Head and Everybody can see how he lusted after her even on National TV he Showed His Half Erected Cock to the World and Almost Everybody Fainted for it looked like the Nose of the Reindeer called the Sheik or Something during those times when You sing Ding-a-ling bell-a-ring it's those traditional belly buttons where the umbilical cord is cut a little above the navel so there's some piece of meat swinging around and the Natives of Old will pull each other by that little trunk and it's kind of Special because it also Functions like an Elephant's trunk so it can Suck in Food and Liquids and it can travel all the way to the Stomach where the Tip will Tickle their… they will be so Delighted to have their Organs cleaned in such a Manner for it creates such Secret Sensations which they have Never known to be possible so it's No Clue how the Silent Maiden end up Standing Beside the Cave Mouth and You are feeling her legs to see if she's developing some Chameleon skin and You are feeling her Buttocks and thinking about how the Japanese Cannibal talked about how the Buttocks were the worst parts to be eaten when he had Imagined how it would be the Prized Highlight but the meat was tough to chew and how he gave up after a while and gave himself up to the Nordic authorities and the Law is so Humane that they only Imprisoned him for no more than Twenty Some Years and now he's Out after serving Time in well-manicured Lawns with Clear Crisp Crystal Fountains of Most Crystal Clear Fresh Spring Waters and the Best Wages in Blue Europe where Retired Astronauts can still get three feathers for their signatures and they are Guaranteed at Least five patrons a day business deals cities make with Zookeepers and Gatekeepers feeling the Numbness in their left hand thumping down on her spine in the Evening so the love making sessions can last until Midnight when it's Most Mysterious as she Cradles the Twins on her Bosom, one on each side and she's so feeling like an angel who has forgotten how to fly away when the Man is getting more Violent and he's biting the skin and nails off her toes at first and she's thinking that it will stop but surprisingly it continues and he's moving to the collar bones and sucking at the napes until the roses blush a Deep Purple song You hated so much for the fakeness in packaging and genre for they really belong to Theatre Rock, including Black Sabbath and KISS so some people call them Gothic too so long as You have some Darkness and You push the envelope to the Bank Clerk Rocking Madam Butterfly when he found out that he had been married to a Man and spending so many Passion filled nights with the Fortune Teller who gave her the Mojo and she will never be broke as long as You keep Your hands off her Mojo and times are so hard that she has to Hustle to continue living in that House in the Sky and she's keeping his hands off her Mojo too for she needs to sleep on her own bed with a Dozen Goliath Sized patrons and it's kind of a clever advertisement for the Giant comes on after the Future King fiddles on his Harp to soften her Nerves a Little Bit and how this One is a Bitch and She's Running from a Distance with the Sun setting behind her and She's getting Closer and Closer and how David is so sure about the Light of God Shining on Him so Brightly so he's taking his Time to pick his Perfectly Round Stone which is the projectile he's Calculating on Launching onto that Rushing Buffoon and She's thinking that he's Easy Meat so she's running so fast that You can see a Cyclone of Dust behind her as She Crashed through a few Barriers, Tearing Off the Heads of some KKK Killers who were Trying to Stop Her with their Lives so Cheap and here's a Message to You, there, this is the Challenge to You so if You such a Tough Macho Guy like You always proclaim to the World about how You Zapped Fifteen Thousand Jihadists who Bombed Subway Stations and Mega Malls and even Paradise, let's leave the Innocents Alone! Right Now! Stop Your Fucking Shit Hole UnHoly Wars! Just come to THE ARENA and Sign THE CONTRACT so when You Die in the Ring, there's no Debt to Anyone, no, not even Your off spring will be allowed to take Revenge on Your Behalf just like the Person You are Fighting and there's no weight classes and no Restrictions as long as You are an Adult, You are Welcome, You may even invite Your Friends and Family on a Long Distance Trip to the Edge of the Jungle and there You will be Greeted with the Cheers of Thousands as they Worship You for those are the First Few Minutes of Your Life and You Know It... What Chance have You against the Gaucho of All Gauchos, the Undefeated, Undisputed, Unanimous Champion of the World the ONE and ONLY ONLY NAAAAAAHHHHHHIIIIIIIIISSSSSSSSSSIIIIIIIIIIIII!!! and the Crowd shall Jump Up and Scream and Cheer and Clap and Fly into Gleeful Raptures as they Greet the Grand Champion for There can Only be One and There can Only be One and the Noise is so Deafening that the First Thing a Serious Challenger must do is to wear some ear plugs to block out The Sound because It had been Reported that Some People were Killed before they could even enter the Ring as their Ear Drums Ruptured and their Heart Stopped as they were in the Line, waiting for their Turn, it's a Definite Defeat for the Boy as he's placing the Stone into his Slingshot made of Bison Guts and it's so Elastic that You can Swing it Over Your Head and Make Such a Big Circular Motion that You may Hit some of the folks who don't know how to get out of the way when they are near dangerous objects and it's just simple common sense when You really think about the Physics of it and how when he flung the stone at Her, she sidestepped the Dart so it hit the Red Rock Monster, Crunching his Crooked Nose and he's Sneezing when She Stepped on Him, Flattening David the Poor Shepherd Boy, and the Implications of such a Scenario being played out in

Shakespearian Plays about Midsummers and Star Crossed Angels Knowing it's Time to go Back to the Moon and without knowing even how to Write or Speak or Breathe or Cook or Anything, You are Welcome, just leave a Thumb Print of Blood and You are ON! Just take a Number for His Permit only Allows him to Fight Ten Persons a Day so there's enough land to Bury the Dead and it's not a problem at all because it's a Grand Graveyard, the One as You Have Never Seen Before in Your Life as Every Challenger will Get His or Her Own Statue of Gold for It's then become Worthless and even so, the Response was so French, the Statues will only be about Eight Inches Tall if You Opt for the Platinum Club Membership but if You wish to be Economical about it, You can also Opt for the Bronze or Iron Club Membership but You should always review the rules and regulations for they are always Changing as the Temperature changes according to the Environment, You will also learn the Art of Camouflaging so You can blend into the Society without sticking out like a sore thumb and You know how it hurts to have Your kitten bite on Your toe but yeah You will suffer the pain for Your moment of glory kind of Righteous death befitting the Most Valiant Warrior and You will be Rewarded with a Chest of Dislikes and it's Exclusively for Your Family or Lover or Whatever and You are Standing behind this Gypsy Woman who's Telling You how She Graduated from High School after so many years and how she found out she learned Nothing much because everything she learned, it's against the very basic tenet of Human Rights and that's the Right to Rebel, the Right to Freedom, the Right to Equality, the Right to Fraternity, the Right to Dream, the Right to Rebel, the Right to the Promise, the Right to Smoke, the Right to Fart, the Right to Eat the Finest Dinner of Your Life with the Finest Chefs from Your very Own Country Serving You Any Dish You Wish for it's Your Very Last Dish in this World so You Better Lick It to Its Last Drop and You will be Satisfied if You Desire, the Most Desirable Women and Men from a good number of Nations Waiting to Give You the Most Sensual Massage at the end of which You will feel moist or tender or heavy with seeds so it's a good idea to put the condom on and proceed to the next Episode without divulging the details for we are a Race of Sensibility and Sense and There's no Pressure if You Wish to Terminate THE CONTRACT by Mesmerizing Your Partner to Sign the Blood Pact, then, You are Free to Leave the Premises but if You Insist on Meeting the Champion of Champions, please, Kneel before the Great Spirit and Silently Say The Gaucho's Prayer underneath Your Breath and Take Your Place in The Line and You May Even Chicken Out as Many People Pull Out at the Last Moment, their Greatest Joy is Getting as Close to the Action as Possible but It's Really a Numbskull thing to do because they cannot see or hear anything at all once as The Door closed so You Should not be Stunned when You Find Yourself at the Front of The Line and it's that Split Second when You have to make Your Final Decision for Once You Go In, You are Not Coming Out…

"it's not always… we used to have Men of Courage…"

"and dinosaurs and Clubs to Pound the Insects…"

"As long as they are Dry, you can make a Powder…"

"For Long Shall I Hold the Masses?"

"Why? Are they getting Ruthless?"

"No… they are Talking among Themselves and They are Not Happy about Something!"

"Can You Hear?"

"Who's the Captain of the Ship? I want to see him at once!"

"Have You seen the Mad Monk?"

"Is he Drinking Again? O My God! It's Crazy!"

"Yesterday, I saw him Speaking to the Tree at the Roadside."

"Are You Sure? I'm Afraid You Will Bleed…"

"Just do it! It's Not My First Time!"

"The Head is to be Consecrated with Smoke from Cinnamon Sticks until It's Well Drained. Keep Refrigerated. The Body is to be Embalmed with all the Ingredients used to Mummify Pharaohs and People of High Importance in the Society, they will be Given Affordable Royal Treatment and they will be Buried according to Their Wishes as Stipulated in THE CONTRACT."

"Can They Surrender in The Arena?"

"No. Absolutely No."

"Can I have my Eyes back?"

"Time's Up! Who's the Sacrificial Lamb for the Year?"

"Please! Please! Don't Take My Child! Please! Please! Take Me! Take Me! I will make You feel like a Man!"

"In the Forest, there's no Light so You Can't See Anything at All. If You Bump into Someone, Just Apologize. They Will Understand."

"Are You Alright? Are You Comfortable? How do You like the Alligator's Tongue? It's Delicious, isn't it?"

"It's too sweet… I like the Raspberries better…"

"What's the Time? Do You have the Time?"

"What do We do with the Heads?"

"Do You Want the Indian One or the Spanish One?"

"I want a Dutch One! I want a Dutch One!"

"When I Grow Up, I want to be a Sailor!"

"That's a Great Idea! We will go Camping! We will go Fishing! What a Life!"

"Did You See the Manna on the Ground? Did You See the Eye of the Needle?"

"It's too Small. I don't think I can Squeeze through the Crevice."

"It's the Eye! It's the Eye!"

"Did You See that Woman Reading a Book in Her Hammock?"

"It's hard to sew him up… we can't find his liver…"

"Hush! Hush! Keep the Volume Down!"

"She's the Fairy of Red Rocks! She can Hear You!"

"Shall I Walk on My Toes? I love to Tip Toe Tip Toe Tip Tip Toe!"

"He's so Sad… the Elephant Man…"

"What about that Ghoul Face? Are You Unafraid?"

No… Not When You Already Sign on the Dotted Line! Last Chance Saloon is to Crawl through THE COWARD HOLE. It's not easy. You have to go on All Fours and Crawl Your Way Out of the Tunnel Measured at more than six miles or so and You have to Waddle through the Shit and Urine and Waste of the City and Half of These are Specially Imported from the South Seas where the Smelliest Shit and Rubbish is found. It's True… it's Enough to make the Toughest Humans

Faint and again, some of them passed away in There and You should understand, it's Hard to Go In there to Excavate their Bodies so the Rats and Foot Long Centipedes and Malicious Scorpions and Red Poisonous Toads and Grass Snakes and Gila Monsters will be Feeding on Your Remains as well as Maggots and those three foot worms You Already Know about. If You Smart, You Should Also Find a Way to Block Your Nose and even Blindfold Yourself and Last but Not Least, Practice, Practice, Practice Your Crawling for You will be Like a One-Year Old Baby Who Still Crawls Due to the Fact that You are not so Confident After Quitting before the Day of Rock Steady… Do You Suppose You will be Permitted to Live in Ignominy and Abandonment so Easily? The Whole Nation will Hate You for Bringing Shame and Dishonorable Conduct to the People and even pulling off the Creatures from Your Flesh will Not be Sufficient to Save Your Soul because You will Surely Lose Some Parts of Your Body when You Reach the Light at The End but It's Quite a Way to Crawl as Fast as Possible As You Won't Know If You are Running from or toward Something and what

"Mr. Che Guevera… what is Your opinion about that Punk Mao? Is he a True Communist?"

"Sadly… I have to say no… he and Stalin the Emperor… they are Living in Luxury Fit for Kings… how can they be Communist… much less… True Communist…"

"Can You Tell Us the Difference?"

"Do You Give Pleasure to Pregnant Seals?"

"No! With all Respect, Sir Yokohama… You are sidestepping again…"

"The True Communist is Someone Who Cares for the

Welfare of the Comrades Before His or Her Own. Never Will a True Communist Lie in the Most Comfortable Mattress when He or She Knows that Comrades are Sleeping on Mats of Rotting Hay and Suffering from Rheumatism and Spine Injuries as They Try Really Hard to Increase the Population, in fact, They are Only Reaping the Least of Their Labor but They Don't Know Anything about It because They are Uneducated."

"How Shall We Educate the Masses? We are Dealing with the Principalities of Darkness and Evil Devil Spirits! We will Surely Lose the Battle!!"

"YES! AHMED BIN MUNSHI ABDULLAH, YOUR PEWTER MEMEBERSHIP HAS BEEN APPROVED! PLEASE REPORT AT THE BALL ROOM ON JULY 29, 2020 AT EIGHT IN THE MORNING! CLICK ON THE DIRECTIONS BUTTON TO GET FULL DETAILS. HEREBY, WE WISH YOU AN ENLIGHTENING AND FULFILLING TRIP! ENJOY!"

"Do You need an SUV or a Sedan?"

"No Thanks. I Prefer to Crawl."

"Walk? Are You Crazy? It's Thousands of Miles!!"

"Are You Dreaming of Home Again? You Know It's Forbidden…"

"I Saw… I Saw… I Saw…."

"I HAVE A DREAM!"

"Is He a True Communist?"

"Sure. Even Jesus and Mohammed. I saw Them Flying Kites in the Plains of Trompe-Loeil. They were Courting the Sea Nymph and the Greenish Nymph."

"Tell me! Where is She? Please! Please! I Beg Your Pardon! I Beg Your Pardon!"

"Do You Know the Way to the People's Republic of New Guinea?"

"Do You have a Light?"

"There are some Jewels at the Bottom of the River of Gold. Can You Pick them?"

"Leave No Traces... but a Trail of Memories..."

"it's Impressionistic... it's Post Impressionistic... it's..."

"Do You Go to Lafayette?"

"Yeah... let me have my lunch... please..."

"Miss... You are Bleeding... are You sure You can Go On?"

Located between Boulder and Denver, somewhat like how Salida, the EXIT, located between Colorado Springs and Moffat, it's a Town or City of Retiring or Retired Folks so there's Nothing much Going on There kind of Place but it's definitely a suitable Place to Philosophize about the State of Colorado being quite Friendly to Immigrants especially if they are Spitting all Over the Place and the Song's Playing Quite Loud in Your Ears for You Too have been moved to put on Ear Phones for fuller enjoyment of the Sound of those Supplementary Devices that Fit so Nicely so they will not fall off even if You Shake Your head so vigorously to the Rhythm or Beat so Your cheeks Twitch with Energy of a Longevity Rate You have to Suspend so You can Continue the Journey no matter how Long more it takes for You to Brush Your Teeth and Change into Your Sleeping Attire and it's so troublesome when You know You have to disrobe before His

Majesty who's dying to smell Her Flower for it makes him feel Younger and Younger Each time She Watered the Soil, the Plant of Life will grow another inch so when it was really time to Reproduce and after Siring more than Six Hundred or More Children and Thousands of Grandchildren for His Ancestors would Also be Practicing the Lifestyle of the True Communist who Knows that Today can be His or Her Final Minutes for who's to Say You can Live to Such and Such an Age and You Know for Sure You Can Never be like that, it's a Suicidal Attempt went Awry so he's not Dead that Day when they Planted a Secret Explosive Device in His Fifty Sixth Concubine who Happens to be His Neighbor's Daughter but since he didn't Spy on her or lust after her, it's still acceptable and the Most Important Thing is that there are no more Naysayers who are always rebutting Anything revealed to them and they have been so Programmed that they will always say nay to something even when they wanted to say yea sometimes they just can't let go of the Fact that Old Stanley Filmed His Masterpiece so many years ago and he's somehow lost it to the fifty five year old woman who planted cherry scented kisses all over his Body at Night when he was so fast asleep that he couldn't hear her opening his door with the spare key and he didn't hear her stomping next to him and undressing him so hurriedly that he didn't know Anything and she was whispering Latin Poems so loud that he couldn't hear anything at all in his dreams of aliens coming to collect his Specimen and it's so sour You could spit out a stream of blood in a Second or Longer when She Rubbed His Nipples with Extra Virgin Mustard and made them Stand Up and Hard as Ice, she even ran those Ice Cubes on His Eyes so it's so clear to Everybody that He's Wet and Soaked in Cold Sweat, he ran his tongue on his Lips of Mellow Yellow but it's Still Not the Time for Rain to Come on that Day when You were no more than Eighteen and Your Father Sends You into the Traveler's Room in the Middle of the Night, it means that he's giving the Virgin Away and She cannot Run Out of the Room if he Pounces for it would be Bad Manners so said the Old Fool so all Folks of the World Should Really Retire after the Age of Sixty Six to make them Feel a Trifle more Sexy for some odd ball Humor about how he didn't wake up after she stole his Scholar's Rock looking so much like charcoal colored clouds always threatening rain but in the Evening, somehow they will be Blown Away so You know at least the Great Spirit is Still Working Hard for the North is quite a Big Land to Cover but It's Extremely Important that we get to part about how she even Rode the Buffalo until the Sun was at its Highest and He's Still Sleeping like the Sleeping Giant who had been Sleeping for more than a thousand Years or so for it's Recorded that He was Born around the Time they were saying the End is Nigh The End is Nigh so it's well know that he's a man who's never late for work or classes even once in his Life for he's a really Dirty Fellow who doesn't shower for a week or so at a time and his record was going for decades in the colder moons so his Body was real hot and when he Awoke after Sleeping for a few suns, it's not Closer to The End than the Beginning when the Word was God and the Word was Made Blue so it's easier to read the Stanza about how she planted the Kiss on Samson's Forehead and All the Same, he's Sleeping almost all the time and that's how he stopped the Bleeding when they dug out his Eyes and surely, they would not be Kind enough to give him some bandage or cotton balls and even if they threw some into his cage, how will he know since the Bible didn't tell You they not only Blinded him but also made him Deaf with the Blacksmith's Most Precious Steel and it's not Valkyrie Steel Either because in our Story, there are no vampires or such things which appeal to Another Race but we know how sure, we are not of that Race so We are More Pure and even more Communistic than Castro for his Presidential Suite is Built with a Hanging Garden about Eleven Acres in Area, Perpetually Swung by Hundreds of Virgins who go to Massage his Cigar on their Thighs sometimes when he feels the need to impregnate some of them, it would be their Lucky Day for they would be given some Improperly Celestial Titles like The Brook that Runs to the Shadow of the Sacred Golden Calf, I Salute You! Bravo! Di Amor and when she gave birth to His Child, She will Surrender Her or Him to the Pocket Monsters who are Specially Trained to withstand Hunger and Torture so they will rather bite their tongues and kill themselves than to Submit Themselves to be Tortured in Insufferable Manner for their Crimes against the Nation but in the Republic, there will be no such Nonsense for Every Issue will be Settled in an amiable way to satisfy all parties no matter You are Red or Blue, they will take the Infant to be Sacrificed to Baal and His Minions still building his Kingdom without many people Knowing all about how he stalked ISIS day and night even when she was fast asleep, he was there, hiding behind the Kimono Screen for it's a Full Ancient Design, Craftily Mounted on pieces of Highest Quality Teak from the Jungles of Borneo being burned at least ten times every year so the surrounding countries suffer Haze Sickness which is truly a Strange phenomenon because it's a Wonder how Everybody starts to behave in unpredictable ticks and tocks and it's not a problem at all when he was slapping on her salmon stomach with all his force and she didn't even feel an ant walking on her lips so dry and flaking so You wouldn't even dare to look at the silver hair and the wrinkled fore head, she appears much older than Thirteen or Younger for in those rural villages, it's the norm for girls to start becoming mothers to children they leave behind to be brought up by their uneducated mothers who raise them to be younger mothers than their mothers so she's a great grandmother before she turned thirty six and all the villagers are so Blessed that the latest family member is a boy for they had not had a boy born in the family house for more than four decades so there's such a modest celebration in the family as befitting the folks in the more rural places to perform the Ancient Art of Subsistence Farming which is not very Popular nowadays but once these arts and skills are lost, they are lost forever and no matter how many documentaries are made and how many comic books are selling like hot cakes and how people don't like to read real books for they feel it's too heavy and too sleepy to turn the next page and sometimes, they may even be planting their noses in those cheapest paper swans, yeah, a million and one, who's the Lucky One and when they awake, they find that the Music has faded completely but somehow You can still remember the path back to the Ride Stop at the Side of Central Park where many folks are Sleeping under the Trees on the Grass without a care and without blouse or top, You can spy on those crazy girl protesters always taking the opportunity to Flash their Breasts like all of us are so Interested in their Flamenco Belly Dance and even when she lifted up her Skirt for him and him alone, he was fixated with the Instrument and Nothing Else so even if she took off all her clothes, he couldn't turn away, a Great Warrior, he will not be Distracted by even the Consorts of Shiva or Zeus for You know how Difficult it is to keep them from getting Bored and Useless yet Nobody Invokes their Names quite so often anymore for the Night is Still a Dame and You Should go Another Round before the Curtain Closes to Block Off the Rays from the Moon so Dangerous that You Should Never Run under the Full One in the Open Meadows and Howling for the Longest Time, You pass out and transform into a Big Green Gal or Guy and You cannot remember anything so much as the Widow who lived in the Giant Shoe House and it's so Big that more than a hundred or so Young Ones can fit Inside and for Only Ten Feathers, they can play for the whole day from sun rise to sun set if they wish to chase each other until they are drowsy, falling asleep to Nursery Rhymes read by Mother Goose herself for she sure looks like it with the Granny Glasses and the Feather Costume so expertly made so the Innocent Ones don't know that she's actually a person and not a goose, they are so unsuspecting when the Government spiced their cookies with the Strongest Opiates without any worry about their Safety and Future Generations to Come, What's the Residue of their Heritage, fading away like the Tides, Subsiding, Bang, Bang, Bang, Bang, Bang, Bang, Bang, and it settles the Problem? Is it so Simple??

"Arapahoe & Old Tale"
"Yesterday, I Drank the Mead of Suttungr…"
"The Leaves are so Thin…"
"The Word Merged from the Other Side…"
"If You Lick the Ink, You will be Born Again…"
"Will my Tongue Turn Purple?"
"No. It's Invisible."

"NOW IS THE TIME! NOW IS THE TIME!! DO IT! DO IT!!"

"Again… No Pain…"

"No, I don't believe in Angels. It's just pure rubbish! Don't believe in the Nonsense! Nobody will ever tell You the Truth. Tell me. Have You met anyone who has come back from the Other Side?"

"Yes. I Only Have Nine."

"Do You want a Filipino Farmer Girl or a Sex Doll Chauffeur?"

"Please Send more Ladies from the Borneo… they are

"How about the New Cars I sent? What? You Lost them! How…"

"Don't Worry. Everything will be

" O O O O O O O O O FREEEEEEEEDDOOOOOOOOOOOOOMMMMM…"

"Excuse me… please Ma'am… spare a Dislike…"

"Merry Christmas! Sorry… I didn't bring any Presents…"

"Don't Eat so Much Chocolate! It's Bad for Your Teeth! Also, Candies are not Good. Have You brushed Your teeth? Good… Once upon a time…"

"Where's the Naughty Cat…"

'Yeah, and he's trying to catch the mouse, round and round the table…"

"He's Eating Cheese! And Ham!"

"Suddenly… there's a Sound… it's getting Louder and Louder…"

"It's too Soft… You have to get Closer…"

"Go Faster! Meow Louder!"

"and then the Clown…"

"No! No Clowns! I hate Clowns!"

"Why? They are very Funny!"

"No. They are Scary! I dreamed that Bozo Squeezed on my Nose and I became Pinocchio!"

"Did You have a Long Nose?"

"No! No! It's Scary!"

"Do You want to Listen to Black Cat Hoot Owl Blues?"

"It's the Top Hit Now!"

"10,009:0. Best Song of All Time!"

"The Dislike Clan is Coming to Fuck Things Up!"

"Yeah, I have seen them getting drunk and singing into the night so neighbors have to wear ear plugs to get a good night's sleep and it's so unfortunate that they were burned to ashes as they were too tired as they did it more than a dozen times yesterday."

"Well… What a Way to Go!"

"We just won our first Gold Medal! Tomorrow is a Holiday!"

"Do You Want the Half Blood or the Full Moon?"

"Nothing's Happening in Waneka Lake!"

"Come Home to Mama!!"

"Honey Where You Been So Long?"

"O Please! Don't Let Them Know!"

"Do You Think They Will Come So Far? I Don't Think So!"

"Here You Go! Have a Nice Day!"

"Thank you, Sir. Anything Helps."

"When You Can Play *Someday My Prince Will Come*, Slow and Steady, You are a Genius!"

"No… no… the Cat becomes the Joker!"

"The Best Thing to Do is to Relax and Get into a State of Deep Concentration…"

"How are Things? Are You Hungry?"

"Bring me Wine! And Roast Beef! And Baskets and Baskets of Fruit!"

"Do You Need to Go to the Restroom?"

"It's this way! Turn Left! O So Close!"

"These are the Flatirons…"

'So beautiful… so beautiful…"

"Let's Go Roll Down the Hills! It will be So Fun!"

"No… I'm Allergic to Grass!"

"Let's go… before he shits and he shits thrice a day on average so we need to prepare a lot of hay. He's too old to wash in the rivers for it's the easiest solution but they say that he's contaminating the waters so they made a Giant Sized Toilet Bowl of Solid Bronze for him and he's satisfied that they are selling them for just half a feather for a whole twelve pound bag so the consumers started to buy two bags so they don't have to divide it into two because it's really hard to cut it into two equal parts. Most people will think that it's Easy, well, it's not Easy at all!"

"If You are always Running in Circles, they will catch You so Easily."

"If I Go Straight all the Way, There May not be Enough Road at The End."

"How Do You Know?"

"What about Children? Are They Allowed to Come to the Republic?"

"Of Course! It's for Them that We Are

"Faster! Whip Harder! We Need More Speed! Don't Let Them Escape!!"

"Mr. Thompson, they Refuse to take out the Trash..."

"Stop Apologizing! It's No Point! The Train Has Already Left!"

"How Long... How Long..."

"At least three moons before You are given new shoes and tooth brushes."

"There's too much Negativity! I'm going to Break! I just want to Sleep!"

"Calm Down! Calm Down! Relax! You are Making Yourself Nervous! Calm Down!"

"It's Getting Worse! I'm Going to Do Something Crazy!"

"Please! Please! Stop It! Calm Down! Calm Down! Calm Down!"

"I'm Mother Teresa... How May I Help You?"

"Please! Please! Help My Daughter! She's Going Mad!"

"HELP! HELP!! HELP!!! He's Pulling My Hair! POW! POW!"

"Again?"

"CALM DOWN! CALM DOWN! YOU ARE MAKING ME MORE NERVOUS! CALM DOWN!"

"Do You See the Light Yet?"

"The Mad General's Wife is Petitioning for a New Young Driver."

"What's the Smell? Is there a Cat or Dog Here?"

"I Will Never Give Them Anything! Disgusting! Disgusting!"

"Horrible! Horrible! Horrible!!"

"CALM DOWN! TAKE A DEEP BREATH! DON'T BE UPSET! CALM DOWN! CALM DOWN!!"

"When I Grow Up, I want

"I'm Sorry… we have already done our best…"

"Don't be Ashamed! A Silver Medal is still better than Bronze. Don't Worry. The Indians will give you some Land and Trees."

"There! There! He's the One! Look at the Hunchback! He's the Thief!"

"Stop Him! He's Got the *Scream*!"

"Can You See Abraham Lincoln? He's Holding a Rifle!"

"Why is Liberty…"

"Do You have the Time to Spare?"

"Hey… that's My Stop! Can You Open the Back Door?"

"Sorry, Madam, You Can Smoke Here. It will be the Next Stop."

In the Morning, the Mountain Air is Fresher and so Full of Promise of the Coming Day and It's Such a Joy to March through the Fog of Doubt and Shuffling Feet to Rush to the Ride Stop to Take the First Bus to go Home for even though Mr. Kamikaze wouldn't Agree Just a Moment for those who dig some bit of Japanese Culture will Immediately be struck by how they enshrine the Departed, especially those held in high esteem by the Ministry, they will be Nationally buried in some Ceremonial Burial Highlights showing how they burned the Body with those wooden logs chopped into wedges like those You see in the supermarkets or hardware stores for people always need firewood when they live in Cold Climate areas where they feel more acutely the Effects of Human Survival and all the Environmental and Animal Rights and Gender Rights and so and so a Non Profit for what does it Profit the Soul when Everybody has Broken all the Ten Commandments and even the Golden Rule so they Do What They Don't Want Others to Do Unto Them for You Still have No Right to Take Advantage of the Weak, yeah, and You will keep Hearing the Sound until You accept that there's NO OTHER WAY but to Repent from Your Crooked Ways and You May Still Have Time to Pile Your Deeds on the Other Golden Plate with Three Golden Chains to balance it so Please Please Remember to Start from the Center but the great Thing is that the Plate will Never Topple even if You Start from Anywhere and it's not even about Donating all Your Feathers to the Poor and Unfortunate for Feathers will Never Buy You Anything Other than Material Possessions and False Insurance which is the Worst Stumbling Blocks for Royalty and the Grandiose and the Filthy Wealthy Segment so for Appetizers, they want Shanghainese Hairy Crab Lentil Chowder and maybe even something Evil like Caviar when You Discover how those Roe were Forcefully removed from the Nest where the Mother Ant has Worked so hard to Produce so Many Eggs, She Hoped they would all grow up to become good Worker ants or General ants or Supervisor ants or Cashier ants or Gourmet ants or Hercules ants or Prime Minister ants just any ant who will contribute positively to the Colony and She has been Working like that for so many years that some nights she just hope that the stud ants will ejaculate faster so She can lay even more Eggs for the

Expansion of the Colony and without warning, some of the Sweet Talker ants start to Install Her as the Queen and as soon as it's Happening so much that even the Priest ants worshipped Her Footprints and Excavator ants Pick up those grains of sand by which You can actually see the entire universe according Solemn William who wrote some of the most memorable verses and also painted but Children are not reading much Bard William as well as Cool Hand William and Naked William and Prince William surely You think he knows his King Richard II or Pastoral William who composed Most Musical Ballads that Celestial Celtic Singers cannot even dream of performing in those rural grasslands the Gauchos will spend their Days in Peace for they are Free Men and they have the Right to Not Work if their Stomachs were not Growling, they don't have to hunt a rabbit or a squirrel and for all those Romantics who have ever tried to Catch even a Rainbow or Chicken which is the Champion of Domesticated Animals for any household can have them so it's normal for Grandmother to Dim the Lights on Fridays and put on her favorite record as she listens to that same song more than a dozen or so times before she tip toes to the Coop to pick a fat hen to be cooked tomorrow, she carries her to the Backyard while she's still Sleeping and with the Swiftest Slice of Hand, she throws the Head into the Sink and quickly empties the Blood into the Bowl while the Heart is still Beating and she's Massaging the Legs and Breasts and Wings and Neck and it's done in such a Politically Correct Way that Nobody's saying anything bad about the Queen Mother Passing Air in the Open and all the Members of Her Family can see it and taste it but they just had to act like everything's so Rosy and all when the Princess was going to be the Third Wife of the Shah, the Press went mad and finally when they came near the Light, they were the Most Amorous Full Moon and Empty Arms Lovers so at the very least, her fans should be Consoled that she will not suffer another heartbreak when the Shah marries his Fourth Wife and she will have no Power to Veto and it will not be too Long before she will be Carted to the Palace of Ice where she will have her legion of workers and attendants where there are many rooms and in fact Nobody even bothered to count for the Builders are just constantly adding more rooms like they have all the Space in the Garden so it wasn't so long ago that her Palace was Infringing on Queen Mother's Swimming Pool and the First Wife Vimi's Complex of a Thousand Enlightenments and the Second Wife Vyjayanthimala's Palace is also Pressing on Her Space so She feels so Entrapped in that Bermuda Triangle where even Flying Saucers went Missing and Everything's Transported to the Other Side so how so many people thought it's a Hoax and the Republicans are Speaking Over the Loudspeakers and Repeatedly Announcing how the White Race is more Supreme than all the Others Combined and all the Red Necks and Nazi Followers will Raise their Showels in Unison, and in the Background, there are Racist Religionist, Nationalistic, Sexist Propaganda Machines urging them on, egging them on so they cannot even stop their feet from marching to the Beat and without Realizing it, they are Shouting Slogans of Hate and Pouring Gasoline on the Bodies of the Holy Warriors and Negros and Zombies and Low Down Hamburger Flippers and so the Day arrived when they would have the Grand Battle which will Determine the Winner once and for all so when the Champion of Sri Lanka Surprisingly Defeated the Champion of China who Defeated the Champion of Taliban who Defeated the Champion of Greece and it went on and on so it goes as One

Champion is Killed and Another and Another and it's Round the Clock so even the Most Easily Influenced Young Ones are Bored and Sleepy and You are Wondering if You have not Forgotten to take those Pills again like the Other Day when Your Bones are Creaking so You Know You Have totally lost track of how Time Flies so Quickly and Just a Few More Lines and It's already Bright and You Exclaimed to the John O How You Stepped Out of a Dream and he's so quick to come and Salivating on Your Tongue for Such a Long Time that You Feel Disorientated and Groggy as Nobody has ever Tickled Your Uvula and You are also a Little Aroused so You Vomited all the Three Quarter Processed Food into His Mouth while You are Poking Your Index Fingers as Deeply into his ears as possible but somehow, he doesn't know at all, Your Desire, Your Evil Nature, somehow, he's not taken aback at all and he's laughing though it's inaudible as his tongue is twisted with Your Tongue so he's still sucking and sucking like an Infant Sheep who has not eaten for a few days and his fingers have melded together so they become one long and hard cord about the diameter of his middle finger and it's something like Captain Fantastic if You want to ascribe some Plagiarism to the Idea and it's true so what so You gonna sue him or what when he gets to the intestines and You can Feel It Poking at Your Liver and Lighting Up Your Kidney and it's the Most Aromatic when he finds the Garden of Perfumes and Whispers all his Lies into Your Voice Box so You can Voice It Out to the Citizens who are Walking in Circles around the Omega Tree and after walking for suns and moons, not only is the grass gone and a Circle has formed in the Ground and they call it Holy! Holy! Holy! it's also True that the Ground is being Eroded Slowly but Surely so in a few years, they will be walking in the Trench and it's getting

Deeper and Deeper, and her Wings are Poking Out of Her Back and he's blinking his eyes even though It's Closed so in the Real World, it would not have been possible for him to see anything at all much less anything so Wonderful and Unreal as She Hugged him so Tightly that his ribs cracked and Wrapped her Long Long Three Mile Long Legs around his knees and off they went… flying off to the Clouds and they had such a Grand Old Time together as he savored Holy Eggs of the Garuda, feeding her the Whites while he sucked on the Yolk, it's Absolute Bliss…

"Mr. Kamikaze is asking for the Rent."

"Tell him to wait down stairs. I will go down in a while."

"Mr. Ramachandran… Please be Patient... I'm Panting!"

"Cut! Cut! Cut!"

"Do You remember how we used to Frolic in the Sea without a Soul around?"

"Here are thirty-nine feathers. Just to let You know… I will be moving out in two moons…"

"Alright. I will go get another cup of tea."

"How about Your Head? Is it Healed?"

"Sarah for President! Sarah for President! Sarah for President!"

"Do You want to run another round?"

"What's Your Name?"

"Mr. Kamikaze… do You want to come up to my Place for some Desert?"

"Now's not the Time for Reproduction! Now's the Time for Preproduction!"

"Can You be more Gentle? I'm only Bleeding!"

"it's not a crime to enjoy Your life sometimes, isn't it?"

"Let's not talk about the Past and Future! I want to be in the Present!"

"Destitution is the Strong Arm of the Caste System!"

"Today, it has Spilled over to the Streets. The Soil of Society, it's Brown and Pungent."

"We Want the Perfect Solution! We Want the Perfect Solution! We Want the Perfect Solution!"

"Do You want some slow stewed venison and raw celery, Mr. Kamikaze? Do You like the music?"

"Yesterday, I dreamed of the Archangel Mobius…"

"There's no such a thing as a Second Chance, man. If You love her, get married and settle down. That's the Life! Don't Listen to all those Barren New Age Idiots! They never know what they are talking about! It would be so good if their Parents thought like them! Be Nice to Your Lady! Be Nice to Your Children! Hold on to Your Job, man. Stick to it!"

"Hey! Hey! That's my Stop!"

"Do You Know the Way to the Mesa Table?"

"He's Polishing the Seven Branch Chandelier of Gold…"

"Did You come with anyone else? Are You Being Followed?"

"I don't know. I was just chasing the butterflies. See? I have caught eight of them. Aren't they pretty?"

"Did You Get Some Great Shots?"

"A lot of times… I question if you are serious about Your job… I can't really tell…"

"Do You want to go see a movie or something?"

"AWESOME!!"

It's really not that difficult if You are going on the Enchanted Mesa Trail which is even suitable for Elementary School Children so it should be Compulsory for the County to Organize an Excursion of the Region for it's always a Great Idea to Cultivate a Bond with Mother Nature as Early as Possible so The Young Ones will Know the Wonders of Land First Hand and it's Important to Show them the Importance of Checking Out the Sign Boards at Critical Junctions so it's Smooth Sailing all the way to the End of the Trail which is the Beginning for then they will learn all about Loops and Swollen Tiny Toes if they are not Careful and Kick into a Rock Accidentally or Not, they will feel the Pain but they should always be Alert since You are not a small kid and You already know Everything and You don't even need to look at those sign posts always more confusing than not especially if You are not so good with maps and directions, it's just a matter of staying on the trail as much as possible and when You come to a fork, it's just a matter of going Left or Right and if You are Observant enough, You will always figure out that one path is slightly wider than the other so You should be taking the lesser path even if it leads You to another entrance point so You find You are on the wrong track again but this time, You see how the Wind is changing Direction and now, You can pick up her scent which is quite unmistakable for You had rubbed Your nose in her armpit so much, sometimes, You pass out and You are pleasantly taken by surprise to find her riding Your horse in the morning and it's possibly the greatest love affair of all time since You find Yourself in some kind of weather station where they are taking measurements of rainfall and wind speeds so

You know it's not such a good idea to piss on Government Property for they will put You in jail if they catch You wet handed, spraying on the Green, Green Grass of Home so You are Civil enough to walk around a bit to wander further away from the Federal Agents who were off duty for it's a Saturday and it's such a good place, shielded from private properties belonging to some rich folks cause it's easy to see from the size of the compound but it's Great to be all Alone finally so You can Burn, Burn, Burn up Your Spirit, after just one pot just when You are pondering if You should Burn another, Little Green Riding Hood jumped out from Behind the Bush and You are a little shocked so You quickly hide all the apparatus and start taking some pictures of the red olives for they are hard so it's hard to break them with Your teeth since they are becoming weaker and You think how they appeared so Surrealistic with backdrop of the Flatirons which are said to be thus named because they looked like those Old Time Irons which are Flat but no matter how much You crane Your Neck looking at them until the Sun goes down and comes up again, You can't figure out where's the Iron and why it's Flat so You can certainly give up after just a few minutes since You are a really smart person, You are thinking it's about Time to go Home so You Turn Back in Direction of the Little Hood but You decide against it because she's much faster than You and the Way Forward leads to a Residential Area with Roads and Interesting Home Gardens so You are able to capture the Fine Image of an Orange with Black Polka Dotted Fairy Feeding on Nectar of a Wild Yellowish Flower which must be so Rock Steady for her for it's quite Improbable that she will know what's sweet and what's not but all You can say is that the photography is so detailed that You can see the hairs on the leaves and again, Dead Wood so

You know she's been here for the manner in which the tree has Fallen bears all the hallmarks of the Touch of her Black Hand as You see how the Rays of the Sun Shining Through the Figs are transformed into Crystal Orbs so You take some time to lie down on the pastures and take some time to look at the Clouds softly passing above while tasting the grass for it's truly not worth the efforts and hours spent on the hike if You are just going to spend a few minutes to enjoy the Fruit of Your Labor when it makes more Sense to take some more pictures of the astounding landscape all around and it's all so Awesome to Shoot that Knot of Grain in the Sky and Flash of Gold in Blue and White and the Blur of the Wild is so Muscular and Fuzzy, the White Flowers of Angel Hair Swaying in the Bowl of the Great Spirit, Upgrading the Essence of Bonsai Photography, Straight from the Soul, in those Pictures, the Bee in the Flower, Just Magical, and the Descent is Easier than made Easier when You Notice how the husks were scattered on the cracks of earth and You think if it's indeed developing into a fault line with all the fracking that's being done in the State for the Benefits far outweighs the Dangers and that's what they like to tell You and it's not Important at all that the Land is Cracking, most of the Time, it's a good idea to think less about these things because it's not going to make things better, it's best to go with Flow and Squander away the Final Remnants of the Fractured Earth so the Generations to Come will not have the Opportunity to Come Close to the Amazing Tree of Birds and even if You see the Picture, You can't believe that more than Thirty Three Birds are Perched Motionlessly on that Tree so it's Natural for You to Sneak Up to the Tree to take Closer Ups of the Birds but for the Sake of Cain who Believed that it's his Birth Right to receive the Blessings of God, he will be so

Blessed to stand under the Tree and look in Silent Awe as the Birds posed and tried their very best to be as still as statues especially when the Green Orbs started appearing, of course, they were a little stunned, Black and White Breasted with Long Tail and Sharp Beak at Full Attention and it's around this Time that You Saw the Monument at the Foot of the Tree with the Words "IN MEMORY OF JOHN GARREY TIPPIT" and if You bothered to google him, You will find out he passed away at the young age of twenty four, just a few moons after he graduated from CU Boulder, he was killed by a methane explosion on his Off Day when he generously filled in for his friend and it took his Life, it's all quite sudden and unexpected, without Warning, the Birds flew off, flying towards the Southwest, Down the Hills, Down the Hills, You waded through the dry grass reaching to up to Your chin and after walking for a few miles, enjoying the private gardens of Boulder, You reach the Ride Stop, more Blessed than Solomon.

"He's Crying because he Wants to Talk to You!"

"Miss… please take a rest in the shade…"

Seven fairies, there were seven of them fine ones too if You see that they are so minute and crawling on the screen as You are checking the stocks and the Superbowl tickets and the Lottery Results for You are just an Internet checker and that's Your job because they pay You some great feathers costing ten times what they are getting but one day, You Decide to take a Break from the Main Occupation *and* Take a *Walk on the Wild Side* and You are paying closer attention on those Creatures You have never taken them seriously and so that day, You saw them Up Close, yeah, use those Magnifiers, use those reading glasses and put them on regardless if they fog or frogs keep nibbling at Your Achilles Heels so on that Day You feel much more Heroic than before and You think You see how such little ones and those have the Ability to Develop their Own character and You Will See the How the Hand is Setting up the Moment with such Grand Detail when they ask You to Check on the Prices of Tickets to Russia's World Cup Final and Now, it's still relatively cheaper and as such things go, the most Faithful Football heroes, they are Saving up for the Big Moment, and the First Fairy, she's named Delilah for she moves like a dancing panther and she can put any man to shame with just a wriggle of her hips, she turned many a boy into a man and she's the Perfect Eldest Sister because She's so Magnificent that She Easily lords over the Second Fairy who Happens to be just Two Days Younger than the First One so she's called Cinderella because she has to run around and do all the chores while Nobody even cares to give her a Compliment when she's Chasing a Car Down just to go the Old Professor Guy to tell him something important but he's thinking he's being assaulted or something and he rolled his car into her Door so he's highly Apologetic and vehemently Offered to pay her a Thousand Bucks for the Accident and he's thinking all the Time how the heck was he going to go retrieve the License Plate which must be left behind for more than ten miles or more so it's no hurry to wake the Third One up yet for she's always Sleepy since she was a baby and Mother was so Happy because she would just Sleep from Morning to Morning and Nobody ever saw her Awake except for Mother and Some Days, Father, really, she was such a good Sleeper that they named her Sweet Sleeper and the Fourth One is

Really Amazing because She can turn Water into the Finest Wine and the Best Connoisseur from the Furthest Corners of the World would come to Taste Her Wine once a Moon and they always left totally Speechless so they called her Liberia, the Mother of Wine and even though She never became a Mother for she was Sleeping so much, the Elders, they Knew that she would be the Virgin Bride One Day when Prince Peacock Humor came to her Ultimate Rescue as He planted that Eternal Magic Kiss on her cheeks, she was in Raptures so they gave her the rather Unceremonious and Inauspicuous and Utterly Unimaginative Name Sleeping Beauty II so Some people thought she's too young to be Eleven before Mother Priscilla told them that it's TWO TWO not ELEVEN so they Understood that they are Roman in Blood, and the Fifth One, she's called Violet so You should Just Know that she has Skin with Twinge of Hues of Violets and she also smell like those devilish tiny flowers You can smoke to get a better idea of the Grand Old Stuff I Consumed in Amsterdam where the Red Light District was the Place Many a Virgin Man lost His Marbles of Innocence for Once they Departed from the Whore, they will become Men and they will like to Marry the Sixth Sister for She's the Most Special One among the Flock and it's No Telling where the Light will Fall but in each family, big or small, old or young, Blue or Green, they couldn't really tell so clearly about the Color of Her Skin for it's a Spectrum of Shade in that Big Green band which must mean so much to the Science of Color that a Good Many Number of People actually dedicate their lives to the Study so they become Expert Color Scientists which was such a Big trend in those Days so much so that so many People were Willing to Pay Three Arabian Feathers for an Hour with Her and She will be There getting into a Frenzy with only her Eye Whites Showing, Crouching Down on the Small Coffee Table Made of Ultimate Pungent Hickory and Sprouting Tiny Golden Nuggets Out of Her Mouth and they will be so Blessed to just pick and pick and at the Height of her Popularity, the Queue was so Long, it stretched all the way from St. Louis all the way to Santa Fe New Mexico where They all Witnessed how Nahiosis Fought one of the Greatest Battles of All Time when he came face to face with Princess Iron Fan who was one of the Great Beauties in Chinese Literature and it's how she was bathing in the Quarter Cave where they will always find many feathers thrown by Silly Superstitious Folks who Believe that they will be Rewarded for Throwing Feathers Only for if they knew the Truth, they would have thrown their All Ins when they know for sure that the Investment will be Substantial that they will review Your case seriously so You understand that it's not so easy to change jobs anymore because You develop ties with Your colleagues and Your Bosses are so Kind to You that they send You to a Faraway Place at least once a year so You can totally unwind with Your Family Kind of Benefit for people who work in Airlines where the Security is Highest, they are Screening out the Minorities so they have a better handle on the Terrorism problem but it's never done and the Masses are so Tired of Waiting that they are Starting to Scratch vehicles on the Streets and the New Age Punks are Starting the Movement by Sticking Silicone Bubble Gum into All Sorts of Key Holes, the Masses are getting so Mad and Impatient because the Key Smiths are so busy, they are almost Working Round the Clock with Minimal Rest but They are Sleep Performing so Well that their Clients don't even Suspect Anything is Amiss but it's such a great Surprise because the tasks will be executed perfectly as if they are

Awake and in no time, they will have the keys working again so now the Masses are Clamoring for Remote Key Operated Locks which can be activated and deactivated according to the Wishes of the Consumer for that's how things should go in the Future Futuristic Future where Everybody wears those Silvery Wings and See Through PVC Raincoats so You can See Her Cunt Hair and her Elfish Ears so Sharp and Pointy that they can be used to open overdue tin cans or not who really cares when they have not eaten for a few days, they will even eat her Shit because then they will be collecting Silver Shit tomorrow but they are trying to Bribe the Olympic Champion with Offers of Ching Dynasty Snuff Bottles and Solid Gold Feathers He Needs a Dozen of the Strongest Rough Hands in the Land to Carry that Trophy to his House on Top of the Mountain where he had Reigned for Two Cycles and it's Sixteen Years Ago when the Gentle Giant of Iran was Lifting Boulders from the Ground with such Ease as the Villagers had never seen and he's so strong that He was Selected to Challenge the Grand Champion of the World but it was Nothing so Special for the Small Boy Defeated the guy so easily so it's well known that the masses don't like Boring Contests where Victory is so Easy and they especially love nail biting stuff like when two teams play out those grind them out Nil Nil end of regulation kind of matches where many spectators had to be woken up to watch the penalty after the teams complete the thirty minutes of extra time which is another goalless stalemate so they go to penalties with is what they call the Russian Roulette of Football and it's such a Chuckle because it's the Greatest Cockup in the Whole Wide World for it's the Time when these Professionals kick the ball into the Stratosphere to Throw the Game and that's why the Payout is so High when a Miracle Happened in Sports when a Five Thousand to One team broke all ranks when Underdog of All Underdogs Leicester City were Crowned Champions against all odds of odds so they say never again will there be another more unlikely Miracle on Ice Story which means an Impossible kind of tale to make the most skeptical folks think about something positive like the Day when they will triumph over their hardships or handicaps to strive for a better Life even when they Know that they don't really deserve to win on that day because the Winds were blowing against the opponents so all their fastest furthest strongest arrows were slowed down in the Air and with a Greater Gust, finally Nullified, Falling to the ground like dead birds, only much lighter for they were made of Port Oxford Cedar and the Arrow Head is Sharpened so Professionally that it can pierce the hardest metal helmet of the Spanish Musketeers well fed with the Finest Muscat Wine and elected to join the Elite Force since they were just a few years before Puberty so they can be Submitted to the Most Streamlined and Most Vigorous Physical Fitness Facility No. 33 where the Dictator gets to Impregnate the most Athletic Ones when they had been Drugged and Unconscious, it's when he would expand his empire so everywhere he was going in the fields or the factories or ball rooms or theme parks, they better prepare some virgins for him to select to be his companion and it's such an Honor for the young girls that they are already weeping when they hear that they have been chosen and they would be given some high grade imported amphetamines for the Dictator didn't believe in the products of his comrades so he drinks only the best champagne from Europe costing a million bottles of Original Northern Sri Lanka Coconut Spirits with such High Concentration of Alcohol that the

Men would be Drinking so much for they always need to get that High and when it Subsides, they will start beating the wife and children to prove that they are the Cowards of the House where they expect to be treated like Dirt even though they are making just a few feathers, they still spend a bundle on their Vices and Hobbies without thinking much about the Satisfaction of the Wife or the Education of the Young so he rather give them a good beating rather than solve the problems in a manly manner when he's finally fired and the daughters have to start working at the bars, one by one, and the sons have to start to work in factories, one by one, and he still Forces them to pay him a few feathers every moon but naturally, one by one, they migrate away, leaving him to wallow in Alcohol and Misery while it's perfectly legal to Drink, a Real Communist should practice how to hold Herself or Himself when it comes the Time to Test the Visiting Heads of State, it's Compulsory to Offer them Your Finest Beverages and Cuisine so they shall be Served by the Finest Chefs Earning so much more than the Lousiest Chefs in Downtown where the Kitchen is so Dirty that Rats are Building Nests and Traps in the Rooftops and it will cost a Fortune to Clean up that Landmark Historic Restaurant Serving the Best Local Fare and Most Affordable according to Most of the Top Reviews, they always say the same things like Must Not Miss! Brando Dined Here! With Blushing Bardot! With the Peanut Farmer! With the King! With The Greatest! And what about all those photographs of the Yankees coming here to pick up whores and every team that plays in the City makes it a Point to visit Kingstown for they were made to feel like Kings the very moment they stepped into the establishment, they are made to feel like Kings with a string of Eastern European girls dressed in Phony Ancient

Egyptian Garb Welcoming them by Prostrating themselves, one on each side, and they are even Kissing the Soil as You walk under the Roman Columns which are so tall so it's perfectly natural for You to lift Your eyes to the heavens and then, greeted by the final sister fairy, in case You have forgotten, You should know You are in good company for she's called Fruit which is Ripe or Well Done in Incan English which is not so widely used or translated for You Know how it's such a small country like Singapore where You can go from East Coast to West Coast in less than thirty minutes if You are driving a Super Sports Car at full speed and crashing Red Lights with a Cabaret Chick slow balling You and You are Jerking her hair to get her to stop for a second so You can prevent the sperm from getting into her throat which means that it will get into her stomach and if it's not deemed to be Fit for the Body, it will be excavated as waste which is then used to fertilize organic vegetables and plants across the Land for there's such a fixation with the movement and what is more Organic than human excrement, relatively speaking, the more smelly, the more Fertile, and the guy ended up crashing into a Midnight Cab with Law Abiding Uncle Chong Lee and he's keeping so quiet as the Skimpy Dressed Serbian Moonlighter spoke to her John on the Cell and she's absolutely Mad that he has to go back to his Home and Sleep in the Cold bed for he told her that he's not at all interested in the Wife but he cannot leave her because then he will be Jobless for he's not much of a Great Worker that he can find another job which pays even a ninth of what he's earning now though in all actuality, he knows he doesn't deserve such a Life as such where he can give them Cherokee Feathers, the Most Rare Ones so they can buy most things for teenage girls like themselves who roam the Night App to pick their Sugar

Loaf Mountain Daddies, they are always on the go and in some cases, they service a whole group of these Johns who organize Orgies and such Lavish Mardi Gras parties where Everybody becomes someone else, someone not themselves and they really party until the whole living room is full of human waste and they are crawling around like a clan of rhinoceros having one or two horns being such a heated debate among the Conservatives and the Liberals and there are so many Issues that they can debate into the next Century or beyond as the people are confronted with so many voices telling them to go Red or Blue, and it's Time that they Exercise their Power of One so they lined up to See the Golden Child which is that movie with the Funny Little Black Guy who go KERCHUM! and CHERWARNG! and they are always delighted with some Life Kalimantan Music with Puppet Shadow Shows as they dine on their monkey brain desert scooped out of the giddy monkey still alive and how the poor animal is slowly closing her eyes as they chatter and exclaim what an intoxicating delicacy is the moldy texture with semi humid moisture to sprinkle the dessert of their souls and so many comrades will be misled to think that these people are doing the right thing but one shall even think of them as the Worst Inhabitants of the Land for it can't be Imagined what's possible if they get their hands on the Nuclear Codes if they managed to Conspire with the other two Branches, then, Day of Mayhem, and The End will Come, and the Mayans are Right and the Jews are Controlling the World and Extraterrestrials are Going to Cut You Up for Fun and the Government is Really Spying on You and the Fiddler is Lucky Fidel O He's a Sure Fire King of His Land, Suppressing his Enemies and he sure has a lot of Suppressing to Perform for it's the Summer when the Schools are Closed and the Parks and Gardens are Overflowing with Kids and it's so Hot and Slimy, and…

"Shhhh…. She's Asleep…"

"Do You read to her every night? She loves it…"

"What a Baby… Did You Put that Thing in Her Soup?"

"HA! HA! HA! That's Me!"

"What's the Best Way to Say This without Offending Anybody?"

"NO! NO! IT'S IMPOSSIBLE!!!"

"There she goes again…"

"Faster than the Roadrunner?"

"BEEP! BEEP! I'M FASTER THAN YOU!!!"

"WHEN THE WIND IS BLOWING THE STRONGEST, THE WAY IS BROKEN

THE KEY! IT'S DECOMPOSING! SURRENDER! SURRENDER!

SURRENDER! SHAVE YOUR HEADS! EAT THE EARTH!

EAT! EAT! EAT! EAT THE DIRT OFF THEIR TOES!!

IT'S THAT TIME OF THE YEAR WHEN THEY HAVE TO GO TO THE HILLS

AND HOWL! HOWL! HOWL! HOWL! UNTIL THE ADAM'S APPLE CRACK

FOR JUST A LITTLE IS ENOUGH MOST OF THE TIME BUT PEOPLE ARE SOMEHOW

GREEDY SO THEY WILL SHOOT FOR THE MORE UNLIKELY THAN THE NORM

AND FALL INTO THE TRAP OF THE NIGHTINGALE WHO CAN REALLY SING THE SONG

SO WELL AND WO WEAL THE CHILDREN AND PUPPIES AND KITTENS

SHALL ALWAYS BE DREAMING FIRST FOR YOU CAN SEE THE SMILES

AND THERE'S NO TIME TO PRETEND

OTHERWISE

FOR THE END IS JUST BEHIND THE DOOR

AND THERE'S NO RESPITE BECAUSE RESPITE IS FOR COWARDS AND COWARDS

WE ARE NOT FOR AS LONG AS WE USE FORCE FOR ANYTHING YEAH MY FRIENDS

WE BECOME COWARDS AND WHETHER WE ARE FEMALE OR MALE OR ANYTHING ELSE

THE LAST THING IN THE WORLD WE WANT TO BE KNOWN IN MELBOURNE

OR DENMARK OR KAZAKASTAN GIRLS BEING REALLY HOT AND CHUMMY

AND YOU WANT TO SNIFF THE BELLY BUTTON THEN YOU DARE TO WRITE

THAT LETTER NOT SENT BY INTERNET OR COURIER EXPRESS BUT BY THE SLOWEST

SNAIL SNAIL MAIL SO HE HAS TO WAIT THREE MOONS FOR IT TO ARRIVE

AND HE'S ALREADY MARRIED HIS SWEETHEART'S COUSIN, IT'S CRAZY

IN THOSE DAYS FOR THE SPELL WAS STILL STRONG

YOU CAN GO TO MADAME CRYSTAL PALACE OR MASTER OF PITTSBURG

WHEN YOU ARE ALREADY OLD WITH SILVER ALL OVER

YOU CAN BREATHE THE SCENT OF HER PURE VIRGIN SKIN SO MUSKY

WHEN WET N STEAMY N GLOWING IN BLOOMS OF INNOCENCE IN LOUD CLOUD

JUST SO IT RHYMES OR THYMES OR SHYMES OR GHYMES OR BHYMES OR LHYMES

OR PHYMES OR MHYMES OR QHYMES OR XHYMES OR AHYMES OR EVEN WHYMES

AND THE MESSAGE IS ALWAYS….

YES! YES! YES!!! YES!! YES!!!! YES!!!!!!!!!!!

AND HE'S SO PROUD HE FINALLY LEARNED TO REASON

AFTER SUCH A LONG TIME THAT HE HAD GIVEN UP HOPE AND WHATEVER

YOU CALL THAT POETRY???? I VOMIT AT YOUR TREE!!!!

YES! YES! YES!!! YES!! YES!!!!!! YESSS!!!!!!!!!!!!!!!!!!!!

CAN YOU SAY IT IN TAMIL??? IT OPENS THE DOOR!!!

GO! GO! GO AHEAD! NEVER TURN BACK!!!! IT'S DANGEROUS!!!!

GO! GOOOOO!!!! GOOOOOOOOOOO!!!!!!!!!!!

GGGGGGGGGGOOOOOOOO!!!!!!!!!

IT'S NO USE... DOCTOR FRANKENSTEIN!!! STOP!!!!!!!

YOU ARE ONLY MAKING IT WORSE!!!! YOU ARE USELESSSS!!!!!!!

HISSSSSS!!!!!!!!!!!! HIIIIISSS!!!!!!!!!!!!!!!

HHHHHHIIIIIIIIIISSSSSSSSSS!!!!!!!!!!!!!

IT'S NO USE! IT'S NO USE! HIT THE SWITCH NOW!!!! DON'T WAASTE TIME!!!!

LET' S DO IT!!! LET'S BLAST THE WHOLE UNIVERSE!!!!

FOR SO MANY CANNOT MAKE IT TO MARS COSTING SO MANY HOUSES AND HOUSES

IN MONOPOLY COSTING LESS THAN HOTELS AND WEE OFFTEEENN WONDEERRRR

WHHHHTYYYY ALLLLL THEEEE HHHH EEEEE LLLLLLLLL WOWWWOOOORRRRDDDSSSSS

AALL IIINNNCCCAAPPPPIIITTAAALLLLSSS!!!!!

LAST CALL!! LAST CALLLL!!!!!

"SORRY, MADAME, WE ARE CLOSING IN THREE HOURS! ANYTHING ELSE YOU NEED???"

"IS THE MOON BLUE YET?"

"WHAT'S YOUR NAME???? WHY ARE YO

"I'M GOING TO

"WANNA COME?"

"YOU MAY NEVER COME BACK

"IF IT HAPPENS, IT WILL BE GREAT TO KNOW THAT I LEAVE WITH NOTHING! NOT EVEN A HAIR!"

"BRUSH YOUR NOSE INTO THE SOIL! RUB MUD ON YOUR FACE!!!"

"STOP IT! YOU ARE SCARING THE DEER! SHE

"I LOVE YOU! I LOVE YOU!"

"PLEASE! PLEASE! WE CAN'T LEAVE YOU HERE TO DIE! WE WILL RESCUE YOU!!"

"OK!"

BYE!!! BYEE!!

SEE YA! BYE! BYE!

BLACKBIRD!! BLACKBIRD!!!

SKIP TIPPIT'S RAVEN!!!

THE TRAIN TO NOWHERE

Departing from the Holy Holy Temple of the Trinity, Jeremiah hurried to One Tree Hill where he would be taking the train to The Beach to deliver the message to Ruby Fish, his fifth sister. To be honest about the whole thing, he wasn't so sure if he would be able to find her at all. Is it so easy to look for a person you have never met with just a black and white photograph which was taken before you were born?

Walking against the wind which was unusually strong during that time of the year, he thought about the day his Father called him into His Study to educate him on the matter of the family members. It was the first time that he had been inside His Study and he was quietly proud to see that his Father was such a well-read man for there were thousands upon thousands, maybe even ten thousands upon ten thousands or so volumes of thick, heavy books neatly arranged in those vintage looking bookshelves of oak or mahogany so shiny so dark so he dared not look too long at the books for it was impolite to be spying on the belongings of others even if He's his own Father and all, he didn't really know Him all that well so he kept his gaze on the Turkish carpet which covered the entire floor and he wondered how they made such a big piece since His Study was slightly bigger than a professional sized Bullring but oval in shape. Then, he heard his Father speak to him, directly, for the first time, and he thought, He sounded like He was talking through a microphone or something for His voice was incredibly clear, authoritative, and audible even though He was some distance away.

"JEREMIAH!"

"Yes, Father. I'm here..."

"YES... DO YOU KNOW WHY I HAVE SUMMONED YOU HERE??"

"No, Father... I... Have..."

"YOU ARE MY ONLY SON SO I'M ENTRUSTING YOU WITH THE TASK OF KEEPING TRACK OF ALL YOUR SISTERS FOR THE TIME IS COMING THAT YOU WILL BE DELIVERING A MESSAGE OF UTMOST IMPORTANCE AND YOU ARE THE ONLY ONE WHO CAN DO IT, ACCORDING TO THE TRADITIONS AND CULTURE OF OUR TRIBE."

"Yes. I will..."

"HERE IS THE BOOK AND YOU ARE TO MEMORIZE ALL THE IMPORTANT INFORMATION ABOUT EACH AND EVERY ONE OF YOUR SISTERS. IN LIGHT OF YOUR TENDER AGE AND THE GREAT NUMBER OF CHILDREN BORN TO OUR FAMILY, YOU SHALL ONLY REMEMBER THEIR ORIGINAL NAME, CURRENT LOCATION, AND APPEARANCE FROM THE PICTURES. DO YOU HAVE ANY QUESTIONS??"

"What happens..."

"ALRIGHT. THAT'S ENOUGH. I HAVE AN APPOINTMENT WITH THE KING'S TAILOR SO I HAVE TO LEAVE IMMEDIATELY. AFTER YOU HAVE DONE THE WORK, REMEMBER TO DROP THE BOOK INTO THE MINI FURNACE SO IT MAY BE DESTROYED. DON'T TELL ANYONE ABOUT ANY OF YOUR SISTERS, INCLUDING YOUR MOTHER. UNDERSTAND?"

It didn't really take him all that long to memorize all the information about his sisters and after only one reading of their data and one glance of their photographs, Jeremiah had successfully photocopied pages upon pages of the weirdest names and strangest appearances mentally and stored them most securely in the safest safe of his mind. According to his Father's instructions, he dropped the book into the mini furnace and watched it get licked and devoured by the greenest of fires and at the end of it, he found it quite fascinating that such a big book could be turned into ash flying up in the air at the completion of the process which took around thirty seconds or less, extinguished and blown away by the sudden gush of bright breeze blowing in oval fashion around the book shelves and it was such an intoxicating aroma that Jeremiah experienced the wild sensation of rolling under the carpet to weep for the first time in his life but he succumbed not to the Temptation for he considered himself to be a strong fellow so he would rather shed blood than tears.

From his fragile position, Jeremiah could see that the station was not so far away, surely, not more than a hundred paces or so and he would arrive at One Tree Hill where he would board the train. Yet, he couldn't be quite so sure that he would arrive before the next train was scheduled to depart which was more than seven hours away and considering the fact that he's hardly moved an inch since two in the afternoon, he could hardly be blamed for any short confidence or logic. Rather the opposite from a fellow of exaggeration, Jeremiah was a person of science, strictly adhering to all the conventions, measurements, and formulas of the discipline so when he said that the wind was blowing at the speed of three hundred and eighteen miles per hour, you shouldn't doubt that he was telling the truth if he had the means to measure the speed of the wind at such and such a time but on that day, he hadn't the instruments so it's quite impossible for him to take such measurements and when you were struggling against the wind with all your might just to maintain your position without being blown further back, it's quite futile to think about how fast the wind was blowing, isn't it? According to Jeremiah, and it was the best that he could describe the strange circumstances on that day as he was walking towards One Tree Hill, he was forced to face a wind so powerful that it stopped him in his tracks, his footsteps frozen, suctioned to the ground, his yarmulke flying off to some unknown destination, his Arabian trousers flapping frantically like the fin of a fish swimming against the strongest of currents to escape a legion of predators snapping furiously inches behind while a little further up, his oversize silk top was blown in such a manner as you are blowing up a balloon so he appeared to be hunching or otherwise the velocity of the wind was so fierce and piercing to the marrow, it blew his eyelids shut, his chin pressed tight against his rib cage, yeah, he thought, amusingly, he must have looked like a tortoise at a certain angle and at another, even a snail. For how long the wind blew, Jeremiah had no such notion but he knew that it blew at a constant speed almost throughout the entire ordeal if you could call it that, and the direction was also quite constant in that it blew from the front, going all the way, way way behind though he had no idea at all about where it's headed or where's the place where it finally stopped but he knew that Da-jo-ji would be too stubborn to concede the stalemate for it lasted for half a day or more but he didn't yield even a fragment of a millimeter.

There was no storm and not the slightest of drizzles. The atmosphere was still a little damp and the sky was still pregnant with the grayest gloomiest clouds on the verge of dripping sulphur and Gomorrah kind of dense dramatic tension so breaking at the seams so he could easily pull off the shelves to show off his glistening muscular biceps so blinding so you should shut your eyes just for a second or three to shield the sun which was burning hotter than ever and ever so much so that Jeremiah was perspiring and you would be foolish to think otherwise but isn't it sensible at all that he would be combusting like a star that had gone beyond the threshold of the highest temperature imaginable after all the work which was done though he hadn't moved even a tiny tiny bit as opposed to the cold of his sweat surging out of his skin and if it had not been absorbed by his clothes, you would have witnessed a river of human hard labor, flowing into the land, moistened and softened with a virgin's piss so pure so golden so he sank up to his waist, laying the foundation for his battle with the cruelest, most devastating Hand of Nature, stopping him on his journey to The Beach, he was so drained of energy that he couldn't even breathe for a second or less, he was wondering how he was going to get out of this ordeal and he was questioning within himself that surely, it's not going to end there and then, surely, he should be strong enough to breathe a few seconds later, and a few seconds later, he discovered that he was thinking in an infinite loop, replaying the same thought or the memory or shadow of the thought in slow motion echo of disbelief that it's happening to him at last, the moment he understood his whimsical, fragile existence but he's shaking his head in grand denial in his mind, losing the energy to even think, clearly or not, brighter or dimmer, he couldn't sense anymore the heat of the moon on his hair, the fragrance of the rainbow disappearing as soon as it appeared right in front of his closed eyelids, the colors of gemstone music fading in the tunnel of his ears, just another moment, just another fifteen shades of a moment, vitally, he thought, it's not happening to him, no, not at this time, not at his young age, not at this godforsaken place where he was only passing, passing away, slowly and surely, black is turning white or red, he's not so sure anymore, he remembered the little silk purse his Mother had given to him before he embarked on this fateful trip, and then, in the most crucial and dangerous junction of his life, he thought, O how good if he could take out that precious treasure from the secret pocket of his trousers and open it with his nimble fingers to take out the mysterious object, and Voila! he would be whisked away from any type of peril, instantly.

Climbing out of the hole, he's feeling extremely hungry as he came to the realization that he hadn't had a full meal for more than a few days but he's not quite certain whether it's three or four and in the whole grand scheme of things, he remembered, it didn't really matter and he imagined how if he ever told his

Father about such a thing, he would simply brush it off and relate all about how he was able to hide in his cave for more than a few months without anything necessary to sustain life, yeah, even without any sunshine or water. Sure, Jeremiah was angry about how the long strong wind had disrupted his mission but at the same time, he was grateful that it also blew some fresh leaves straight to his mouth as well as some fruits small enough to be blown straight into his stomach such as persimmons, lemons, dragon fruits and so on so he could stay alive in the gentle shade of the Hand of Providence, so assuring and so he thought about a lot of things which were not in the domain of a boy of his age.

By the time he arrived at One Tree Hill, it was already morning and the station was so crowded, he couldn't even find a vacant seat and he found himself standing in the seventh row which meant that he had to wait for the seventh train and though he spied lots of tempting foods in the vending machines, he didn't make it a point to purchase anything, no, not because he couldn't afford to pay for it but it's more accurate to reveal that he's absolutely driven by the task that he thought it's more important to get his Father's message to all his sisters in the least time possible and he estimated that it would take another day or so to get on the next train for the rows were gaining very quickly so when he turned around, he saw their sweaty and desperate faces, all than the Most Royal Mattresses to Protect You from Magnanimous Backaches and Fraudulent Heartaches when You Hear of yet Another Tale of Heart Break and How Many More Heart Breaks can a Person Take Before He or She Turns Purple and We All Know How Painful It was to Bury Miki after He was put in the Earth with His Jaw Torn Off by the Monster to Terrorized His Wife and it was such a Sad Scene that Some People can Laugh but to Each His or Her Own but Miki was the Dachshund of All Dachshunds because He's the Most Intelligent of them all and One Day as Soon as He was Old Enough, He Hunted Down Ten Hideous Rats in Just a Few Hours and Placed them Side by Side in a Straight Line so the Corpses are Laid on the Side and He's Smart Enough to Turn them of their Left Side so they all appear to be Facing the Sunset as usual when they are Entering Nederland and in His Prime, He Even Hunted Down a Pigeon and How Happy She Patted Him on His Head and Murmured What a Super Animal He was Just, Able, and Full of Surprises and You can Imagine how He Pretended to be Asleep so the Dove thought it Would be Safe to Pick all Morsel of Corn Near His Nose and he Did Such a Fantastic Job of Closing His Eyes so Tightly Enough so he could Still Spy on Her and O Sleeping Buddha She's a Safe and Patient One even by Your Standards but It was a Super Hot Day so You will need at least five glasses of water to quench your thirst after walking for more than a few miles only and even then you cannot eat the excellent prepared Venice Dumplings with the Richest Pesto Sauce Definitely being the Wrong Choice but Who Cares anyway You Just Sat down for the Liquids Waterfalling into Your Dry Cracked Throat like those Dry Earth around Boulder or Lafayette or maybe even Upstate Michigan where some Psycho is Lurking in those Faraway Motels with Creepy Vibes being the Favorite Haunt of Horror Writers who Delights in Scaring the Bear Shit Out of the Reader and it's so Rude to Honest Some Times She Will be Looking Up at the Sun and Wonder if It will get any Hotter for She Thinks She will Surely Faint if the Temperature Rises by Just a Few Degrees More for We are Created in Such a Way that We Should Know these Simple Things if We are to Survive the Holocaust and Day of Reckoning to be Observed Every Seventh of July for at least Seven Thousand Seven Hundred and Seventy Seven Years of Prosperity as There's Not Even a Cloud in the Sky, It's Crazy How He even Faked the Deep Snore to Trick Her into Thinking that He's Dreaming of Running in the Meadows with All the Wild Flowers Brushing His Nostrils Steaming with Passion and Debonair Air of Gentleman Clark, He Wrestled Her Hear Away from Tupac, Her Mix Champion Line Rottweiler Brother, and whenever Snoop's in Heat, He will be Standing Guard like the Fiercest Most Loyal Warrior King Scorpion for It's How He Managed to Subdue Tupac who was Ridiculed but It's True, he thought He was Truly Mean and Savage so he became an Absolute Celibate while Miki was Screwing Snoop more than a Dozen Times a Day and even when He's Near Old Age, He's still a Loving Husband and Great Soul Mate to Her so It's a Love of the Ages until They Brought the Maniac Spastic Killer to Change Things around and Sure Enough, *Bitter Harvest* is a Great Album with Zero Dislikes Now so Now the Haters can Come and Talk about How Strong their Army How Vibrant their Economy How Cultured their Race How Rich their History How Glorious their Olympics How Quick their Lightning How Great Thou Art How Great Thou Art How Great Thou Art Following Bird Calls enticing You to Go Deeper into the

Forest where You may Find Some Food Right in Front of the Cave and You Think It's Easy Meat, Retreat, and Leave with No Trace as Quietly as Possible to Tip Toe in Reverse, Do It… Do It… as I'm telling You Now to Close Your Eyes for Just a Couple of Seconds to Take In the Great Spirit and Feel Her Going into Your Bowel and If You May Do It For the Final Time… Do It… Do It… but she wasn't so Lucky that Day for Miki Sprang Into Life Imbued with all the Ferocity, Speed, Agility, Thirst for Blood, Predator Instincts and Wisdom of Neith, He Crashed into her Breast Cage, Knocking her Unconscious for it was Execute at such a level of Stealth that she didn't even Know Anything when He Ripped Out her head to ensure that she's passing over as Peacefully as ever and Hestia didn't hesitate to pick up the Dead Wood to make Fire to cook a most Sumptuous Soup of Turtle, Snake, Dove and Ancient Herbs and Strange Plants Known as The Heart of Woman which gains Animation or Auto-motion after a thousand years or more only so she's a Distant Kin of the Gingerbread Man who is more well-known in the West but She's Quite well-known in the East for The Primitive Indigenous Dwindling Tribes in the Mountains Still Believe that Triple Boiled Extract of The Heart of Woman, the Result of a Secret Tryst Involving Hegemone and Yan Wanli, it was so Secretive She Didn't tell Anyone that She was with Child and it's such a Miracle for there's no Sign of Pregnancy so there's no Stomach or all Symptoms of Pregnancy throughout the Seven Moons for the Birth was Natural but the Child was so Wise beyond her years so she didn't Cry at all for in those Days, It's Against all the Laws and Regulations to Fornicate with Polar Opposites and the Punishment for Gods and Goddesses who Breaks such a Doctrine is Exile, the Worst Thing to ever Happen to

Anybody for it Means that There's One Place where It's Forbidden to Visit and It's more Atrocious because some how they found out about it so they were going to take the Child away and Train her to become a Forest Fairy so it's Imperative that she starts to learn about plants and herbs and all that and at that tender age of one or two when she's not supposed to be remembering things like her past lives, she's able to tell about the time when Mrs. Robinson lost her Senorita Coonskin Cap when she was still seventeen only and she was able to tell how the cap was returned by the Boy who Lived Down the Lane who lived with his Widow Mother who was always telling him that the Larder is Empty and it's Time to Harvest the Pumpkins but he's always Busy running here and there, returning things for he's not too keen about Black Sheep or Anything Black for that Matter and Cactus of Knowledge is Good too if You have No Worries in Life and How Nice will It Be to Be Free from All Worries of Life for No Matter How Cool You Think Suave James appeared when he's wrestling with Medusa and the Snakes on her Head is Spitting Poison into his eyes and he's still absolutely under icy cold control while they are biting his face so he's bleeding so profusely that you will think he will surely die this time and you are reaching for the tissues but winds keep blowing off the cigar for that's how Wild it was in the Wild Wild West and it's not Disastrous to imply that the Scent has waned or ceased to exist so it's just pure common to Question the Timing of it All when the hammer came down so loudly that the Gypsy Lady Sleeping on the Final Row She's Dreaming Yeah She's Dreaming of Lying Her Head on that Pillow of Log and Lying Down on the Coyote Shit and She's Quite a Bundle of Jazz Orgasm Away from the Climax and Many an Intelligent Human has Pondered on this Mystery for so many

Ages, it's quite a shame that it's still a Big Unknown, this Thing called Love and Life and it's not use to watch those blue films about Spanish Fly Landing and how they used it to get Her so Glowing with Electricity and without a Warning, the Snakes were All Asleep and then She Planted that Kiss of Life on His Lips, Spurting the Antidote into His Limp Tongue and His Face had Certainly turned Purple and His Peacock Too for that's what She has Her Eyes on His Jewels and They have Shrunken into Macadamia Walnuts or Tiberius Walnuts of Stone and Her Most Sublime Weighted and Burning Fingers of Breezy Brilliance Emitting Florescent Green Light for that's how She was Instructed to bring Him Back to Life for at the Moment He Shut His Eyes Forever, She Felt such a Darkness in Her Soul that She Decided She Cannot Go On Without Him so She Broke Her Own Ribs to Keep His Mouth from Shutting Too but the more She Wished and Harder She Tried, She Saw that He was Fading and Fading until all Life is Drained and Exhumed His Final Breath and She's Weeping and Weeping and Weeping and when She Thought She's Over It, She's Weeping Again so She Remembered What Her Mother Told Her on the Day of Her Wedding…

GO TO THE BIG APPLE!!!

GO TO COLORFUL COLORADO!!!!

GO AND SIN NO MORE!!!!!

GO TO KATHY KATHMANDU!!!

GO TO BALI MANALI!

GO YE… AND SI…

GO! GO! GO!!!!

BYE! SEE YA!

PSSSSSSSSSSSSSSSSSSSSSSTTTTTTSSSSSS SSSSS…

In Inaudible Whisper, the Goddess Dayang Masalanta who only Whispers to those who have Ears the Song of Song She tells You it's not Simply blank pages or white spaces or a waste of Mother Earth's Resources for those are Talisman for the Warding Off of Evil so wherever You Come into Contact with Danger or Catastrophe of Any Kind at Any Time at Any Place, Calmly, Tear Off A Little Piece of the Page or Two and Crumple it into a Ball like those You Normally Destroy the Idols and It's the Truth, they will Laugh and Sneer and Crucify You for Tearing the Other Pages but if You Cannot See, the Alternative is Any Page is Possible so It Should be

Known Earlier You Should Plant a Drop or Drip of Your very Own Saliva into the Center Part so if You Cannot Imagine It, Picture Two Line from One Corner to the Opposite One and Where the Line Intersects, There's the Center so Without Further Ado, You Should Invoke the Name of Bastet and then Light it Up, sending Most Ancient Smoke Signal to the Great Spirit and She will Come to Your Rescue and You will be Healed of All Ailments if You Mix the Ash with Pre-Prohibition Style Whiskey and Drink it Straight Down in One Gulp with No Chaser and It's Concocted in Such a Way that it will Lighten the Boulder a Little or Color the Mind a Little or Blowing Softly at Your Face…

Breathe… Breathe… Breathe… Ma Muse M'amuse… Maltese Bacon Farm… Fraise Et Crème Fraiche… Got to Go… Business as Usual… America… America… Thou Art… America…

"How's the Weather There? Are There Storms and Earthquakes?"

"It's Six O Clock in the Morning! Can We get Some Water?"

"I Just Want to Say…"

"What's the Opposite of Reproduction?"

"Some African Drums will be Good!!!"

"Are You Going to the Pulling Out the Weed Contest?"

"No… I Just Wanna Chill Out in the Deck…"

"Ladies and Gentlemen… the Sultan's Picnic…"

"IT'S TIME! IT'S TIME!!"

"How Long More Are You Gonna

"Bring Him to Yama… Only He Holds the Key!"

"Pleaaaaaaasssssssssssseeeeeeeeeeeeeee STOP IT!"

"Am I in Paradise???"

"No, Madam, You are in the Picnic. Don't Look Left! Look at the TV! It's Rainbow!"

"How Heavy the

"I Don't Want to Go to Heaven! It's

"Do You want to Go to the Gardens of the Gods?"

"NO! I Want to Burn Forests! I Want to Chop Trees!"

"Excuse Me Sir I Need to Go to the Mesa Table Loop…"

"Wait for a Minute! Be Patient!"

"Look at the Constellation! Aren't They Lovely?"

"Her Boyfriend's Little Bird…"

"THIS IS THE LIFE!!!"

"My Daughter's in New York City… My Son's in…"

"My Daughter's in Seattle. Can You

"Last Monday, We Celebrated His Second Birthday! It was a Blast!"

"Greater Harmonics, please…"

"Gentler, Gentler, Go Ye Into the Cave of Light
It's the Easiest Path to Salvation and It's Free of Charge

Seventy Four Likes to Zero Dislike
What Can You Say
To The Mousai Blowing the Fire of Music
In Your Shadow

Pray Mary Magdalene as well as Mary St. Louis
In Time, Old Santa will Deliver the Presents and Parcels
All Your Wishes Fulfilled Without a Single Qualm of Parasites
Sucking the Marrow of the Tree Camel Motif Evaporating

Slowly into the Clouds like a Wisp of Silent Seductive Smoke
Floating and Disappearing at the Same Time

There's No Kind Fox Paw Marks

Please...
Cry a River for the Harp Player
For Her Fingernails are Cheese
Please...

Line the Lips with Beewax and Peruvian Wines
Get Ready for the Flowering Opera Queen of Piano
For Her Juices Taste More Sublime with The Sound
Fit for Ears of Gods and Goddesses in Forbidden Capital
Where You Lick the Sweat on Slope of Mound of Venus

Nor Downside of Mt. Vesuvius

In the Valley... Mixed in Blossoms and Ants and Millions of Illuminant Insects

You Can't See Because It's in the Day and at Such a Time
There's the DO NOT DISTURB SIGN on the Door Knob

It Makes Perfect Sense to Practice Abstinence

It Awakes You… It Waters You… It Dreams You….

It's There where the Cradle of Creation is Swinging
Yesterday, the Thief Loved Your Egyptian Massage Music
In the Valley where You find the Hidden River
Soon Flowing with Isis Tears and Humanities
Warm not Cold or not Hot

THE COLOR PURPLE!

Drink It! Sleep It! It will Make You Feel Much Better!

What's Your Name?

What's Your Address?
What's Your Social Security Number?

IT'S TIME! IT'S TIME!! IT'S TIME!!!!
Is He Still Sleeping? It's Already Fall!!!

Warm is the Right Pitch
If It's Too Hot… It Burns Your Tongue
If It's Too Cold… It Freezes Your Soul

Rocky Mountain High…

Have You Met the Happy Sheik? He's Blue!

Wait Here! I Will Search for Your Husband!
She's Here! She's Here!

Is She Coming? I Want to See Her Pearls!
Would You Like Some Snake Soup? All You Can Eat!
How about Some Paprika, Provence Herbs and Squirrel Droppings?
Does It Make a Difference?

Let's Add Some Bird Droppings and Some Butterfly Wings

No… He's not Alive when They Crucified Him

Do You Have the Time to Spare, Ma'am, Sire?

Jeremiah? He's Going to the Beach…
For a Sun Tan? For a Peach? For a Sun Set?

Coconut Trees Swaying and Dropping Coconuts
On Heads of Lovers who were about to Lock In
Getting Down to Business in Wild Bushes of Moonshine

Casting Topaz Shadows on the Tropicana Hula Hoop Dancer

The Special One, She's Winking at You in Secret

As Soon as It's Eight Twenty-Six in the Night
And the Sun is Still Going Down the Eternal Horizon

A Few Hours Later Emerging from the One Man Cave

They Would Need a Real Sharp Antique Rare Katana
To Separate Mr. and Mrs. Casting Nets of Terpsichore
Who's Surely More Wondrous than Thaleia
In Her Catting Talents and Skills
For She's the Original

The One All the Gods in the Universe Lusted After

Of Course, They were Afraid to Offend the Powerful Sadducees
Who Were All Very Sad when They Found Out the Truth
Yeah, They were less Intelligent than a Six Year Old Lion Boy

So Whether You Elect the Apollonides or the Titanides

Just Go! If You have the Opportunity… Go with Your Heart!

Better to Speak than to be Silent when You Are Not Dumb!!

GO!! GO!!! GO!!!!

BREATHE! BREATHE! BREATHE! THE ELIXIR OF THE GODS!!!!

TODAY! TODAY IS THE DAY! SHE'S GONNA COME!!!

I love Erato more than all the Others.

What's a Revolution?
If It Boils Not Your Blood?
If Not Even One Vehicle is Burned
Or Overturned??
If the Earth is Still Cracked???
If the Wicked and the Corrupted are Still Laughing
At YOU???

Do You like to Eat Fish of Mercury???

It's 1996… That's When I Got It All Figured Out!

Have You Met Sir Charles Duke? He's the Cup Bearer of the Queen. One day, he heard some seriously inner inside information about the State of the Union and he recognized how he can Profit by investing in Petrol Stocks now that they are at Historic Lows so it made sense that he sold more than ninety percent of his lands at discount prices just so he can put all his eggs in one basket and though it's still at the Edge of the Table where the Giant is Sleeping Again and It's Poised in such an angle that it may topple over any time sooner or later than he expected, it's been more than sixty moons and the Price is still Stagnant so he would have lost almost his entire fortune just because he believed in it so much, he declared bankruptcy and soon after, he entered the Other Realm.

No! He's Not Interesting! I want Captain Caveman!!!

IT'S TIME!!! IT'S TIME!!! IT'S TIME!!!!

THOU SHALL

NOT

THOU

ART

AMERICA

Ticking Away, Just the Skeleton, I Ventured a Deeply Personal Private road trip which is So Sacred, I Humbly ask You to Retreat and Put the Damn thing Down or Off It for that Matter but if You will take Another Breath to Go Another Step, Hide Out My Shadow, Casting a Glance in the Direction of Some Mysterious Dame Working the Night Shift and What Does She Dreams about the Unseekable and Wholesome Longsome I have since Wondered Why I Write or Unwrite or Pray for Your Safety and Peace and Nothing more to Add Except maybe a Toast to The Bard for Bringing Some of Us Home so Many Years Ago when the Land was Still Fertile and Her Gaze was that of a Woman Looking at the Mirror for the Longest Time up to the Point where She's Supposed to Say "More Firewood" for the House is getting Colder kind of Illogical No Point Reckless Bastard Bum Whacking the Monkey until Dawn just to See the Sun Rise One More Time Kind of Wasted Kind of Vision to Seek the Impossible or so to say to Seal the Deal because it has been such an Impressionistic Jungian Trip, it's Surreal, Everywhere I went, I was Welcomed and Embraced so I would say without any Spices or Rotten Tomatoes and

Hungarian Flour Espionages to the Wild for the Exploration of Humankind and Beyond, the Wide Open Mouth of The Unnamed and Unsensed and Uncleansed and Unholy and Unheroic Dolphin Riding Cowboys Acting Civilized and All that Good Old American Hospitality whether it's the Corn Mother, the Sad Eyed Lady of the Cottage with Swing, the Momo Loving House Cleanser, the Pack of Young Cats in the Mountains, The Chief who has Hopped Off the Train with his Blessed Family, Tis-See-woo-na-tis, Nahiosis or Mona, they Contributed Hair and Nail for the Completion of this Short Term Memory Loss Memoir or Travelogue or Novel, I Don't Know but I Know, I have Accomplished the Impossible if You are Even Here, I Shall Congratulate You for You are Officially Crazy and You Don't Need any Shrink who Shrinks Your Self Confidence The More You Consume those Pills and in the End, You will be a Vegetable but I Suggest, Even in that Position, and Frozen, At Least Request that They Put this Book in Your Hands as the Camera Rolls as You must have Known, It Never Stopped Rolling, the scene is such that You are Reading but In Reality, You are Only Staring at the Same Two Pages for the Whole Day and I Shall Ask You How Long is Twenty Four Hours for My Time can be Counted as Incomplete just because Dusk is Coming and the Road is not even as Dangerous as Some of those Coffin Roads in China or the Death Mile in Nepal or Hindustan I Forgot, Who Cares, We know they are true, and that's enough and at this point, I will like to Confess I went on the road fully expecting to be abducted again or spy on shape shifters or something out of the ordinary to bring You the Miracle I Know It's out There but Why Should We Expect Anything Less so on that day when I set out on that Dim Road, I was fully prepared to just Disappear off the Surface of the Earth for I had been Touched by the Hand of the Great Spirit Everyday Since I Ate of the Soil and Drank of Her Waters, yeah, It would have been the Greatest Escape, and I was Thinking about *Amerika, The Man who Disappeared*, and I thought how Appropriate that I Should Just be Invisible and Nobody will Know about How I Appear in Your Dream and Somehow, You will Know, It's… Shakyamuni… Shakyamuni… Shakyamuni… it's unfinished and sure, it wasn't meant to be published as are most of his work and it confounds me to Ponder why People think it's even Work at all when it's even extra dangerous to drive in the night so at least It's a Little more Challenging, and by the time I stepped on the pedal, I had already Known that It was Unpublishable for the Small Presses just because of the Law Suits and Big Machine Flattening Small and Indistinct Literary Voices so We can All Sound Alike and Look Alike Someday, really, but The Chief was Frank and Generous, I Thought, It's No Big Deal, I was Going to be Zapped so There's No Difference when It's Christmas, Everybody is Happy, and fact I can be in Queens Right NOW Typing Away in the Middle of the Night when the entire City is Sleeping is Virtual Proof that I didn't Disappear at all or in the case that this work is not published, it…

Driving out from Denver, You Have to Shoot for Grand Junction, taking 70 West, some three hundred miles away and it's a beautiful drive, especially with the Rain coming down and You are a little pissed because then You Are not able to wind down the windows so You can breathe in the Rocky Mountain High Air, and it's quite frustrating because it rained not for more than a few days but just when You are heading out on the Most Important Journey of Your Life, it had to rain and it rained for quite some way so even though the Mountains are so Majestic and the Landscape so Inspiring as You pass by the smaller towns like Silverthorne, Vail, Newcastle, Parachute, Breckenridge, Copper Mountain, Arapaho National Forest, White River National Forest, Grand Mesa National Forest, and so on, there are the most serene lakes and awesome ski resorts but even if it's towards the end of Summer and Winter is not due for another few moons, it's no problem, the further You get from Denver, the Rain is Subsiding somewhat so You are Driving just as Saint Dean and Drunkard Sal used to do so many years ago when they were zooming across The New World for it was still New in those days when they could travel so cheaply on the highways and God Knows how many trips they made, criss-crossing the land with such mad energy and broken Jazz records playing in the winds blowing at their hair as they smoke a joint or cigarette, talking incessantly all the time, somehow, the hair tonic in those days were more genuine so their hair stayed in place all the time, not like Yours, tossed and blown from all directions for all the four windows were open fully to air the car, somehow, You can almost Hear It, the Great White Noise of the Great Continent, Similar to the Sound of Traveling whether You are taking a Bus or Walking or Driving or Training or Flying, It's Always There, Like a Vacuum Cleaner Sucking All Memory Away, it's Urging You On, Hurry, Hurry, the Sun is Setting and so You drive even faster, aiming to arrive at Grand Junction before FOUR PM so You may hit Highway 50 just as the Sun is Setting as it would be the most perfect postcard Vision imaginable, the deepest blues and the most florescent greens and the most sour amber, there's No Time to Waste, there's No Time to Waste, and Sure, You arrived at Grand Junction quite quickly and You may be tempted to go Wine Tasting in Fruita for many people go there for this purpose, leave it for another day, there's No Rest until Highway 50, Remember, Sometimes, it's also known as The Road to Nowhere for they say there are these long meditative stretches of the road where You will Feel so Relaxed, You may Fall Asleep so It's Recommended that You Smoke to Stay Awake but If You Prefer Gum, Go Ahead, Rub on the Stone, Hear Angels Blowing their Bugles in Your Ears and... to that Guy who wrote about how he was able to hear the rub of rubber on tar, I Couldn't Really Hear that Type of Music for It's True It's Impossible Since the Sound of the Winds Blowing In Equalizes Everything Else so We are in Equilibrium for it's more Accurate to say You will hear the Swish Swash Swish Swash or Wish Wash Wish Wash Continuously but Right Now, You are not There yet, You still have to go a small distance into Utah before You reach the Bridge to Paradise and it's here that You have to be Careful because It's Highly Logical to Fill Your Tanks at Fruita before Entering the Beehive State and it's quite Believable You shall find a lot of beehives there for we all know how the Mormons love their Honey but You will be Entering a Zone where there are No Services of Any Kind for Quite a Long Stretch but Otherwise, the Views are Spell-binding in the Real Sense of the Word and it's quite Interesting how the Landscape changes quite Distinctly from One State to Another so when You cross over to Utah, You just Know You are in Utah as You can already feel the Constrictive Air which is certainly not as Free as that of Colorado but You will still find some great Photo Opportunities at Some Great Viewing spots where You can take some robotic panorama shots of the landscapes framed by dramatic clouds with poignant rays of the sun bursting through, bringing winds of promise of what is to come for it's the different hues of blues combined to create a palette worthy of the brush of Monet and if he was traveling in that car that day, he will surely smile as he admires my pictures, at the same time, it got me thinking how he must have a photographic memory of colors for when I look at his works, I'm most intrigued by the kaleidoscope of the spectrum of a single color so it's like he has a few hundred variations of each color and even when he uses black which is technically not a color, there are so many different emotions, You feel like You are not looking at the same thing and for me, that's the magic of Chagall and some big shot critic is going to come and say how my POV is wrong but I say a Giant Gilded Fuck You to You for the World has enough problems already so let's try to make it Brighter for Everybody and Yeah I Accept I may be Wrong in Forming Own Cheap Skate Conclusions about Art and Letters but even if I'm Wrong, Nobody has the Right to tell me Anything for I'm in the Driver Seat, You Scum, One Hand on the Steering Wheel and One Hand on My Camera, Click, Clicking, Clicking, Click, Clicking, Capturing the most Romantic Colors of America, yeah, the likes of which is Transient enough to make You Believe in Love again and if You can see how the Pink of the Sun flows into the Orange, Kissed by the Violets of the Heavens and so many fucking beautiful colors to make You Explode in Dumbfounded Belief in the Creation of the Gods, flying at more than 120 miles or more an hour, leaving the Black Dragon behind in the Dust of Tomorrow not Coming or Going, Trickling Down and Evaporating like the Vapors of Hope, not found, not touched, not far, not near, it's just You and the Road and the Occasional Car You pass on the Right, the Day creeping away and You know You are not going to see it again, the Fields of Gold, the Mountains of Night, My Friend, take a

Second to Kiss the Air, Yeah, Kiss it for me, Kiss it for Your Love, Kiss it Forever, somehow, On that Day, the Dusk is especially long, especially magical, especially forlorn, and there's a Sense It will never Disappear though the Light is Fading, the Colors of Paradise Eclipsed by Chorus of Insects Chiming the Song of Forgotten Longing and in that Final Breath, the Sun Sinks beneath the Horizon, so softly, so longingly to rise again in another Day but it's another Day You will not see any more as You Press On, Stabbing More Deeply into the Heart of Hesperides, turning into water, shooting for the vast desert of Nevada, still going West, still Clicking away, the Road turning White, Postcard Scenes of Wild America Overtaken by Ratri, and it's especially Dark for Chandra is especially busy with Jeremiah's sisters, all Twenty Seven of them, it's such a Peaceful and Calm Night with Nobody to Chase, Nobody Behind, THERE, You don't feel the need to run away from Nobody as You are Wont to do when the Car behind is Flashing at You, it's so Unpleasant so it's an Incredible Blessing to have the Road all to Yourself, Yeah, Yours and Yours Alone, and You can go as Fast as You Desire or as Slow as You Desire with Nobody to Honk at You or Give You the Middle Finger or Challenging You to a Race, You can even STOP in the Middle of Road… Hypnotized by the Designs of the Stars, Surely, You are Tempted to Step Out and Take in the Incredible Music of the Night but I Tell You, Forget It, Forget It because True Gauchos never STOP, They Go On and On, even when the Road Ends, They Still Go On and On, and Further More, It's Dangerous to STOP in the Middle of Nowhere, Potentially Endangering the Lives of Other Drivers and No Matter what You do, You must Never put the Life of Another Person in Danger, No Matter What You Do with Yours, it's Immaterial, the Slow Swirls of Neon

Road Signs Warning of Sharp Turns or Antelope Crossing at Specific Favorite Spots for You Think HMMMMMM why do they choose to cross at those places and not others but then You realize, You are not an Antelope or What's the Point or Wondering Why They Think like this or like that as Modern People like to Waste their Time reading about This person Wearing this Outfit or Changing Hair Style and all that Nonsense which doesn't add ONE BIT to Your Development as a Person but Why Should I Waste my Time Thinking about You when I'm Still Burning Rubber so Fast and Furious, randomly passing Signs with Highway Number and the Word WEST on a Separate Plate a Little Beneath It to Confirm You are on the Right Track for without It, It's True, You May be Driving on any Road in the World, maybe even in Mozambique or Slovenia or Afghanistan or Brazil Priming to Host the Summer Olympics but also for the Unique Colors of the Air and the Perfume of the Land Asleep, it's also in these Moments You become more Anxious to reach the Next Town for Lonesome is the Night and in Absolute Wasteland, You Develop a Fragile Need to Reach Out, and Soon, You Come to Old Nevada so named because You forgot its Name but You Know there's a Hotel Nevada there with Strange Mural of Cartoon Horse in Full Cowboy Uniform with Big Hat and Gun and Gloves and Boots and he's Cooking Some Beans over Wood Fire with the Words WESTERN HOSPITALITY right in front of his face and You may think how why promote outdoor living when You are trying to Get More Customers in Your Hotel kinda Ill Logic not Worthy of Your Time but You Quickly Know the Town is very, very, very, very, very, very Small with Population of about Fifty on Lucky Days but it's so Bright though there's not even a Ghost around, without Stopping, You Continue,

Checking to see You have enough Gas to get to the next Town, it's most Important and if You are Quite Forgetful, You may End Up Stranded in the Middle of Nowhere and in that Situation, Good Luck, Just Push the Car to the Side, Open the Boot and Take Out the Triangular Warning Sign and Put it Out to Warn the Driver Coming from Behind and there's no Telling What May Happen, Good Samaritan or Serial Killer for it's a Perfect Setting for such things, Don't You Think, Doesn't It has all the Essential Ingredients of a Fantastic C Grade Horror Movie? HA HA But This Time, Let's not be Distracted or Detour as in Previous Times, Let's Press On and Finish It, YEEEEE HAAWWW, Arriving at the Charismatic Ghost Town of Eureka, You are Thinking about how Euripides or Archimedes jumped out of the bath tub in such excitement, exclaiming EUREKA! EUREKA!! EUREKA!!!, running around Naked but Nobody understood his Euphoria or Took him Seriously but if He was also Available, Coming Along for the Ride, He may Frown and Wonder why Somebody will use his famous Word as the Name of a Town in the Middle of Nowhere, Any Royalty?, Frowning on the JACKSON HOUSE HOTEL SALOON & CAFE which was Proudly Established around One Hundred and Fifty Years Ago, No Less, No More, Frowning on the Court House with Big Proud Stars and Stripes, and It's there You took The Photograph of Your Life, On Behalf of the Estate of Euripides or Archimedes, I Charge You, The Town of EUREKA, I Charge a Fee of Only Five Thousand Dislikes a Year, and in that EUREKA Moment, Everything Comes Together as AMERICA AMERICA THOU ART AMERICA Comes to Fruition in Your Soul, You could have stripped off all Your clothes and ran around the whole town without Worrying about Anything, Quietly Wondering What's Playing at The Famous EUREKA OPERA HOUSE and what Zero Self-Esteem Troupe will ever come to Town to perform to such a small audience of less than three paying patrons per show unless they are desperate amateurs or rich passionate actors and singers because Opera requires You to Sing as well as Act, there's a Post Office as well as a Chevron Station to Save Your Life with ATM Machine which is located inside the Store but it's closed so if You have No Credit or Debit Card, You are in Some Trouble, Fortunately, Everything Worked Out, and You are Amused by the OWL CLUB BAR & STEAKHOUSE for it also has a Mascot in Full Cowboy Gear, just like the Horse earlier but this time, of course, it's an OWL! and it would have been so Great if You can go Inside and Order a Big Cowboy Steak and Big Glass of Icy Cold Cowboy Beer but it was already CLOSED so it's Time to Hit the Road Again, Zipping Past Countless Miles, Coming Upon the Patch where Rabbits are Jumping Across the Road for No Apparent Reason and It's Such a Pity So Many of Them Perished, Flattened to a Pulp to be Eaten by Crows in the Morning, Yeah, I Tried to Dodge Them as Much as Possible, Zooming Over One so Its Ears were Grazed by the Underside of the Car but I Think It Survived but the Next One was not so Lucky for it's very difficult Steer the Ship at such high speeds and dangerous too but I found out it's no use to slow down too for they were still Crossing the Road as if their Lives depended on it so I thought, it's best to Warn them by Honking so I Honked… and Honked… and Honked… at Intervals and It seemed to Work, I was Pleased, Fatigued, and Sleepy, Flying for Austin, I Remembered, How Great Thou Art, How Great Thou Art, How Great will It be if It All Ended in that One Glorious Moment… the Crystal Cold Desert Winds Drying my Face… Hair Flying in All Direction… Softly Illuminated by Glow of My Pipe… Blessed Smoke Drifting Out of My

Mouth… the Radio Buzzing with no Channel to be Picked Up… the Camera Fully Pregnant… the Wheels Screeching in Harmony… as One… as Usual… as Hope of America Still Burning Valiantly… Land of the Brave… Home of the Free… I Salute You… I Bless You… I Love You… O Sweet Lady Liberty… Tonight… We Sail to the Amber Moon… Tonight… We Go Up to Ruby Mountains… Tonight… We Picnic Beneath the Tree of Shoes… Tonight… We Turn the Road to Gold… Tonight… We Dream of Old America… Tonight… We Run the Eternal Mile… Tonight… Tonight… Tonight…

www.ingramcontent.com/pod-product-compliance
Lightning Source LLC
LaVergne TN
LVHW041105080826
845145LV00007B/1689

* 9 7 8 0 9 9 8 5 4 8 8 6 9 *